DESERT BORN | BOOK TWO

Desert Bold

GIN COLEMAN

Black Rose Writing | Texas

ISBN: 978-1-68513-644-4
LIBRARY OF CONGRESS CONTROL NUMBER: 2025933456
PUBLISHED BY BLACK ROSE WRITING
www.blackrosewriting.com

Printed in the United States of America
Suggested Retail Price (SRP) $25.95

Desert Bold is printed in Minion Pro

*As a planet-friendly publisher, Black Rose Writing does its best to eliminate unnecessary waste to reduce paper usage and energy costs, while never compromising the reading experience. As a result, the final word count vs. page count may not meet common expectations.

I dedicate this book to my husband and soulmate,
Lawrence Michael Coleman.
He stands behind me and beside me,
and in front, when necessary.
Thank you, Larry.

"I am my beloved's, and my beloved is mine..."
- Song of Solomon 6:3

Desert Bold

CHAPTER 1

The rumbling noise grew louder, and the wind screamed over the fuselage. Kira's arms ached from holding the duffle bag tightly to her chest. "Oh, God, oh God," she prayed, eyes clenched shut as she braced for impact. When the engines exploded, her eyes flew open, and she saw her world turned upside down. Crates and bags floated around her head, and her nostrils filled with the smell of burning fuel. She screamed in terror when her father's bloody face filled her vision, and she clawed her way to the exit, threw open the door, and stepped into nothingness.

Falling, falling, surrounded by darkness, her screams were cut short when she landed in water. She sighed as she floated weightless in cool, blue-green water. The plane had vanished, and her world was silent. Relieved, she inhaled, but her mouth filled with water. Choking! choking! She kicked and flailed, desperate for air. Suddenly, the water disappeared, and she was stretched out on sand, enveloped by the heat of the desert sun. Turning her head from the blinding light above, she cried out with joy. She could see her valley again—her secret valley— the one her horse, Amber, had led her to after the plane crash. Her heart soared at the sight of crumbling ruins, the herd of mythical horses, and the silver-blue river that ran through the rolling hills. Finally, she was safe! Or was she?

Confused, she rose and stared at the blue-green expanse of a lake, its surface like a blanket of diamonds in the brilliant sunlight. How could she be back in the valley? She didn't know how to get back there. While she pondered that mystery, she felt a strange tingling in her hand and opened her fingers to reveal a great golden medallion. Her father's medallion—the one he had bought in the marketplace when they first arrived in Cairo! But no, wait…it couldn't be her father's. Sheik Qadir had stolen it from her when he kidnapped her. No, this was the other one, the ancient one she had unearthed in the valley and buried there before she left.

As she stared at it, a loud buzzing filled her ears and the gold disk began glowing, its yellow gems flashing like stars, and its blue stones rippling like water. When it abruptly rose into the air and flew toward the far cliffs, it called to her, and compelled, she followed. But as she did, it vanished, and the valley faded. "No!" she cried out in anguish. Then her world went dark, and her ears filled with the distant sound of pounding. The pounding grew louder, pulling her from the inky abyss, and she suddenly awoke to find herself tangled in her sheets, her silk sleeping tunic damp with sweat.

Disoriented, she heard more pounding, this time accompanied by a familiar voice. "Kira! Kira! Are you all right?"

Kira stumbled into her main chamber and paused, breathing deeply. Her heart was still racing. When she opened the door, she saw her friend, Fatima, twisting her hands with worry.

"Kira, I heard you screaming! Was it that dream again?" Fatima said with concern.

Kira knew Fatima was referring to the nightmare that plagued Kira since their rescue from Qadir, the evil sheik who kidnapped her out of revenge. "No, it was the plane crash," she said without elaborating.

Fatima shook her head. "I am so sorry. I wish I could ease your pain."

"Oh, Fatima, you saved my life! I wouldn't be standing here today if you hadn't found me passed out in Qadir's bed and dragged me to safety. Besides, this one wasn't as bad as the last one," she lied, hoping to erase the look of worry from Fatima's face.

"Maybe you are getting better? I hope you will forget it in time. It is what I pray for," Fatima said earnestly. "Is there anything I can do for you? Do you wish to talk about it?"

Kira flinched inwardly. She couldn't talk about it because she had vowed to the keep the valley a secret. "You are so kind, Fatima, but I think I'll be okay. I'll feel much better after my morning ride."

"You and that horse," Fatima said with knit brow. "I do not understand this attraction to horses. You are just like my Amal. Is Amal's brother, Saad, the same way?"

"No, but Saad's son, Jabari, is. When I traveled with Saad's family on the trade route, they were always checking out the horses in the kingdoms we visited. I guess I was meant to be found by them because I, too, am obsessed with horses. But I don't know why. Maybe God made me that way for a reason," Kira said.

"Well, that is another thing we can agree on. I also believe we have a purpose in this life," Fatima said with a nod. "If you are sure you are okay, then I will go. I am meeting Amal for the morning meal."

Kira smiled at the blush spreading across Fatima's face. "Ah, yes, Amal," she said with a knowing wink. "You don't want to keep him waiting."

Fatima laughed lightly. "No, I don't."

"Well, thank you for checking on me. I'll see you at the evening meal," Kira said. Fatima nodded and headed down the corridor.

Still reeling from her dream, Kira closed the door and moved to sit at her table to marshal her thoughts. Pouring a glass of water, she sipped slowly and tried to clear her mind of the last vestiges of the nightmare. She could still see lingering images of her beloved valley—the valley she had discovered before being attacked by the lion and being found by her adoptive family. And she could still feel the pull of the ancient medallion. What did it mean? Why did it call to her? She sighed in frustration. Her father's medallion was lost forever, and the other one— the one she found in the secret valley—she had left behind, burying it there before she had left. She knew she would never see them or the valley again, and though she'd tried to convince herself she didn't care, she missed them more than she could say.

But as disturbing as the nightmare was, it was infinitely preferable to the one she often had of her night with Qadir. It was filled with visions of his leering face, the agony of his whip, and the humiliation of his touch. She thanked God she had no memory of Qadir's last act. His mother, First Wife, had drugged her and Kira had passed out.

Shivering and feeling a rush of emotions, Kira bowed her head. So much had happened to her in the past year. Why did she have to endure such loss and pain? What had she done to deserve being kidnapped and assaulted by Qadir? Why couldn't she find her way home? Tears of anger and anguish threatened, but she refused to succumb. *I will not cry!* It was over and done with, and it was time to put the past behind her. She couldn't blame God for what had happened.

As she refilled her glass, she tried to look on the bright side. She had much to be grateful for. After all, who walks away from a plane crash and survives being attacked by a lion? She should be grateful for being alive. And she should thank God she'd never have to worry about Qadir. Someone had murdered him that fateful night, and she might have suffered the same fate, had it not been for Fatima, the harem girl who had helped her escape.

And she also had a new home, if she wanted, with Sheik Ehsaan's tribe. Weeks ago, when her adoptive family moved to Jalil's kingdom without her, Ehsaan had invited her to stay and offered to help her find a way back to her grandmother in Arizona. Kira enjoyed living at Ehsaan's. She loved his wife, Sheikha Issa, and his daughter, Adara. And God had given her Amber, the golden horse who had saved her life. Really, she had so much to be grateful for, until she thought of Jalil.

Sheik Jalil was the only man who had ever made her feel like a woman, and she couldn't help wishing Issa could have healed her worst injury. Then maybe Kira could have had a future with Jalil. But as soon as she had that thought, she chastised herself for even thinking that Jalil would consider her as his Sheikha. She was a nobody in his world, and thanks to Qadir, she could be no one's wife, much less the wife of a sheik.

Feeling sorry for herself and eager to dispel the awful memories of her downfall at the hands of Qadir, she concentrated on getting ready for her morning ride. After splashing water on her face and donning boy's trousers, she grabbed a robe and hid her glorious silver-gold hair in a head wrap. Issa wasn't comfortable with her running around outside dressed like a boy and had asked Kira to keep herself covered. Kira preferred riding in trousers, but was happy to comply, at least until she was out of sight of the compound. She hurried to the back pasture where she found Amber already waiting for her, as usual. Scrambling onto Amber's back, Kira galloped into the hills, but not before leaving the robe and head wrap hanging from a bush not far from the pasture gate.

Racing across the low hills, bent close to Amber's silky golden neck with the wind whipping through her long locks, her troubles faded. She became one with her horse, and for a time, she felt as if they were standing still, and it was the earth that moved past them. But sadly, it didn't last, and reality returned.

When they neared the stream that meandered through Sheik Ehsaan's kingdom, she stopped to admire his herd. His horses were beautiful, but none were as fine as Sheik Jalil's golden mares, at least according to Jabari, her adoptive brother. If Jalil's mares were anything like her horse, Amber, they had to be magnificent.

Kira had never seen Jalil's herd, although she'd tried once. After her adoptive family found her, she joined them on their travels. They had stopped to trade with Jalil's tribe, but being both a foreigner and a woman was dangerous in a land where the former was likely to be killed and the latter enslaved. So, her adoptive father, Saad, made her dye her skin dark, cover herself completely with a robe and veil, and remain hidden in her tent during the day.

But Kira couldn't help herself and snuck out early one morning, dressed as a boy, hoping to see Jalil's golden mares. When Jalil saw her petting his prize stallion, Mirage, she narrowly avoided being caught.

Jabari distracted Jalil with a fake injury and told him she was his boy cousin Bassam, so Jalil was none the wiser, but Jabari's mother, Samira, found out. Luckily, she forgave Kira, and the fictional Bassam became something of a family joke.

As she idly twirled a bit of Amber's golden mane, Kira watched the play of sunlight on the silken strands, ever amazed at their iridescence and texture. So soft, so rare. Lulled by the warmth of the desert sun and the murmur of the nearby stream, she closed her eyes and allowed her mind to drift. But Jalil's green-gold eyes and flashing smile suddenly popped into her head, making her heart race and disrupting her mood. *Why can't I stop thinking about him?*

Amber must have sensed her mood and snorted loudly, pawing at the ground. Startled, Kira pressed a hand to her chest and her fingers closed over her father's ring suspended from her mother's chain. She took great comfort in wearing them. They were all she had left of her parents except for one of her father's shirts, his money belt, and his compass. She still missed his medallion, the one she used to wear. It often glowed and warmed her skin, reminding her of the valley—her secret valley—the place where she'd been happy and safe.

Although she tried to fight it, an intense feeling of longing rose within her when she thought of the valley. She wished she could return, and her heart filled with hope, but her wish was like a desert mirage, visible but for a second then gone just as quickly. She didn't know how to get there. Only Amber knew, and Amber wasn't talking. The peace she normally found during her morning rides had shattered, and sighing deeply, she slowly made her way back to the compound.

Later that afternoon, she worked on her latest basket weaving project. Making baskets was a skill she had perfected as a young girl under her grandmother's tutelage and had rediscovered during her time in the valley. She was almost finished when someone knocked on her door. It was Sheikha Issa.

"Hello, Kira. May I speak with you?"

"Certainly, Sheikha. Please, come in," Kira said formally, gesturing toward the table.

"Thank you," Issa said, settling into a chair. "We missed you at morning meal."

"I wasn't hungry, and well, you know how much I love to ride in the early morning," Kira said.

Issa chuckled. "Oh, yes, I noticed that about you. You remind me of my daughter. It is likely she will do the same someday."

Kira smiled. "Yes, Adara loves horses as much as I do. And I am afraid there is no cure for that."

"I expect you are right. She is very like her father. Which is probably a good thing since he is insistent she will be the next sheik," Nasira said.

Kira nodded. She had learned a great deal about the culture of the people during the past year. Traditionally, a sheik's heir was male, but since Ehsaan and Issa had only the one child, Adara, Ehsaan had named her his heir. Highly controversial, but after getting to know Adara, Kira figured she could pull it off. "I have heard a great deal about that from the future sheik." She laughed and was glad to see Issa took no offense.

"Yes, well, we shall see. The future is a long way from here, is it not? But speaking of Adara, that is why I came to see you. I am planning her thirteenth birth-year celebration, and it is not far off."

"How exciting! I hope I am here to see it."

"Oh, you will be. We still have not heard of a caravan headed to the coast, but Ehsaan continues to send your messages with anyone who passes through, so there is always hope. But I had another reason I wanted to speak with you. I am inviting Jalil and his family, along with Saad's family. Is that a problem for you?" Issa's brow furrowed.

Kira couldn't fathom why Issa looked nervous. "No, I think it's wonderful. But why would you be worried about me?"

"I thought maybe you might not want to see Jalil. I mean he saw what happened to you at Qadir's ..." Issa's voice trailed off, and she looked embarrassed.

"Do not worry. Seeing Sheik Jalil is not a problem for me," Kira said as convincingly as possible. "But thank you for considering my feelings."

"Oh, I am so glad. I have already sent the invitations, and they will be here in a week's time," Issa said with obvious relief.

"A week?" Kira said with barely concealed alarm. She had thought she would be long gone and never see Jalil again.

Luckily, Issa didn't notice. "Yes, and I have much to do. Besides the food, I need to organize the decorations and the gifts. And I don't know how I'm going to keep Adara out of everything."

Kira was still thinking about Jalil, but when she saw Issa looking worried, she offered her help. "I think I could keep Adara distracted, if that would help."

"Indeed, it would. Thank you, Kira." Issa rose to depart then paused with a look of concern.

"Was there something else, Sheikha?" Kira said.

"Well, I know you were not well a few days ago, and I wanted to be sure you were feeling better," Issa said with eyes downcast.

Kira knew what Issa wanted to know. It had been over a month since her kidnapping and she had been on pins and needles, worried about her monthly cycle. But it had finally returned, ridding her of her greatest fear. She believed the trauma of her night with Qadir had delayed it. Knowing how much Issa cared about her, her question did not offend her. "Yes, all is well," she said with a smile.

Issa looked relieved. "I am happy to hear that. But if you need anything, anything at all, please let me know."

"I will. And thank you, Sheikha." Kira bowed.

"You're welcome. Now, I must leave but I will see you at evening meal," she said and departed.

Kira closed the door and leaned back against it to think about what she had heard. Apparently, she didn't have a lot of time before she would once again see the man who consumed her thoughts during the day and haunted her dreams at night. How was she going to avoid him? Then she remembered all his actions indicated he didn't want to be with her, and she relaxed and returned to her basket project. *It will be easy,* she thought, but when a little niggle of doubt crept into her mind, she closed her eyes and prayed silently. *God, help me.*

CHAPTER 2

Jalil chuckled at Jabari's youthful exuberance as he watched the young boy perform intricate patterns on his horse in the corral. An excellent rider, Jabari sat straight in the saddle with his hands steady on the reins and his chin held high, his silver eyes flashing. When the sun reflected from the highlights in Jabari's hair, something tugged at Jalil's memory, but before he could give it further thought, his mother, Nasira, distracted him.

"Hello, Jalil," Nasira said as she joined him at the rail.

"Hello, Mother," Jalil said then gestured toward Jabari. "Well, what do you think of our young student?"

"He is very good. In fact, he reminds me of another young boy I once watched in this same corral," Nasira said.

Jalil glanced at her and smiled. "This one does not argue as much, though," he said with a wink.

Nasira laughed. "Perhaps, but he is still young. Give him time."

"No doubt you are right," he said with a laugh then turned serious. One of Ehsaan's men had arrived earlier with four messages. One was for Jalil from Ehsaan and dealt with their joint operation monitoring the nefarious Hashem, the upstart who had taken over Qadir's kingdom after Qadir's murder. Another was a formal invitation to Adara's birth-year celebration. A third was for Saad, and the last one was for Nasira.

It was Nasira's letter Jalil was curious about. "Tell me, what did Issa have to share?" he said nonchalantly.

"Oh, the usual. She is fine. Adara is fine," Nasira said, her eyes on the boy in the corral.

"Is that all?" Jalil was thinking about Kira but dared not say her name, aware his mother would pick up on his interest in the woman. His mother dreamed of grandchildren.

"Well, Issa is excited to report Saad's brother, Amal, has proposed to Fatima," Nasira said, her eyes flickering toward Jalil.

Jalil noticed and proceeded with care. "That is indeed good to hear. She will be an excellent addition to Ehsaan's tribe," he said, but he wasn't thinking of Fatima. "So, has Kira left for America yet?" He tried to keep from sounding anxious.

"No," Nasira said. "She has received no replies to the messages she sent to her family in America, but I understand she is seeking passage with a caravan soon."

Jalil hid his displeasure and tried to sound sincere. "I am sorry to hear that. I know she longs to return home."

"Yes, but I also hear she hates the idea of leaving Amber behind, and according to Issa, Kira is happy living with their tribe. Issa also says she spends a great deal of time with their herdmaster, Baqir." Nasira turned to look at him with an innocent expression. But Jalil knew better.

"Issa certainly has a lot to say," Jalil muttered under his breath. He was happy to hear Kira had yet to find a way to leave the country, though he had no reason to be. It was clear she had no interest in him. But his mother's last words ate at him—he couldn't stand to think of Kira with another man, even one as honorable as Baqir. He believed she would not be interested in any man, not after what Qadir had done to her. He shuddered inwardly at the thought she might yet be with child. How would Kira be able to handle that? But as soon as he had the thought, he felt shame. Kira was as brave as any man, and he knew in his heart she would manage somehow.

Nasira interrupted his gloomy thoughts with more news. "Maybe she will find a young man and decide to stay. And from what Issa said, that could very well happen now that Kira has returned to normal. Thank Allah she was spared a child by Qadir."

Jalil's heart stuttered, and he struggled to hide his relief. "That is good news…for Kira," he said hastily then cleared his throat. "It will make her return trip to her country easier." He noticed Nasira staring at him with an odd expression, but he kept his eyes on Jabari.

When he failed to elaborate, Nasira sighed. "Well, I need to speak with Samira about new garments for the celebration. I will see you at evening meal." She patted him on the arm and took another long look at Jabari before heading back to the house. It was obvious to Jalil that she was as fascinated by the boy as he was.

Jalil didn't understand why he felt the way he did about Jabari. After all, Jabari was just the son of a simple trader, and yet Jalil wanted to teach the boy all the things that he had learned from his own father, Akeem. So he was teaching him swordplay and herd management and even let him sit in on his meetings with Fahad, his trusted advisor, when they discussed tribal issues. Jalil found Jabari to be a quick learner.

Growing closer to Jabari, Jalil often wondered what it would be like to have children of his own. Unfortunately, such thoughts made him think of Kira, which was often painful and frustrating. It took a great deal of effort to not think about her, and he had almost convinced himself he no longer cared about her, until he had received Ehsaan's invitation. All his hard work to forget her vanished like a mirage. He couldn't wait to see her again.

When he joined his family for the evening meal, he listened to his sisters and mother discussing what gifts they could give Adara on her special day. Tuning out their chatter, he was thinking of his choice of gifts when he felt a burning sensation on his chest. Startled, he laid his hand on the medallion hidden beneath his robes then remembered he hadn't revealed it to his mother yet. She would be interested to learn how he found her murdered husband's stolen medallion in Qadir's bedchamber when he rescued Kira. He should have told her the day he returned home, but the combination of winning the Tri-Annual race, being shot during the race, and the rescue mission on the way home had left him exhausted.

It had been a traumatic time for everyone, and he had meant to tell Nasira, but never seemed to find the right time. It wouldn't be wise to keep it from his mother any longer, especially since he planned to confront Kira next time he saw her. Kira's old traveling companion, Cassie, had told him the medallion belonged to Kira's father, and Jalil wanted to know how he got it. His sisters disrupted his deep thoughts by begging Nasira to help them select the clothes they would wear while at Ehsaan's.

"Mother, I want to wear the yellow silk tunic, but Akilah says I can't. You know I look better in yellow," Lina said, her eyes flashing and her hands on her hips, looking just like a miniature of Nasira.

Jalil hid his smile and said nothing as he watched his mother masterfully settle the issue.

"Girls, girls, calm down. We can talk about this in your chambers," Nasira said calmly, but firmly. Akilah and Lina scowled at each other, eliciting more chastisement from their mother. "All right. That is enough. I see I am going to have to make some decisions for you both," Nasira said as she pushed her chair back.

Jalil realized his window of opportunity was dwindling and laid a hand on her arm. "Mother, could you stay a moment? I need to speak with you."

Nasira glanced at him and must have realized it was a serious matter. She dismissed the girls, assuring them things would go better if they would go to their room and take a few minutes to reflect on their choices before she came to talk to them. They nodded sullenly and marched from the room. Once they had disappeared, Nasira sat back down and faced Jalil.

Hesitating, then taking a deep breath, Jalil withdrew the medallion from beneath his tunic, slipped it over his head, and held it out to her. Unsuspecting, she reached out, and he placed it in her hand. She stared down at it, uncomprehending at first, then realization dawned upon her face. Her eyes widened, all color drained from her face, and she fainted.

Alarmed, Jalil sprang to catch her and lowered her gently to the floor. Grabbing a cloth from the table, he dipped it in his water glass and held it to her forehead. She woke, gasping and coughing, and when she opened her eyes, Jalil sighed with relief. Helping her back into her chair, he handed her a glass of tea, insisting she take a sip. "Are you feeling better? Shall I call Maryam? Maybe she can give you something…"

"Oh, no, that is not necessary. Maryam would only fret and make me drink something unpleasant. I will be fine. It was just a shock." She smiled a little sadly.

"Yes, I am sure it was." Jalil was thankful she seemed to have recovered. He had never seen his mother faint, even when his baby brother was stolen years ago and his father, Akeem, had been murdered. She had always been strong, and seeing her vulnerability was very disturbing.

As the color returned to her face, she fingered the medallion, the medallion that had been Jalil's father's prized possession, still clutched in her hand and looked at her son with tear-filled eyes. No one had seen it since Akeem was found murdered in the north pass. "Where did you find this?"

While Jalil told her the story of everything that had happened after the race, he held her free hand and watched her closely, seeing a multitude of emotions cross her face—joy, sadness, shock, and anger. When he finished, ending with finding Qadir dead and the medallion with him, he sat back with a sigh. "I only wish I had the original chain," he said, shaking his head ruefully.

Nasira's fingers curled around the medallion, and Jalil could see her knuckles were white from holding it so tightly. She bowed her head and closed her eyes, and when he saw a tear rolling down her cheek, he knew she was remembering Akeem. He waited silently, wondering if he should give her a moment of privacy, but she suddenly raised her head and opened her eyes to gaze at him.

"The chain is nothing. It is the medallion that matters," she said fiercely.

"Why? Why is it so important?"

"I wish I could tell you, Jalil. But I know little about it. I only know it passed to Akeem when his own father died. Akeem said it was tradition, but he always insisted it was his greatest treasure. He said it was worth more than his life, but he never explained why," she said, rubbing her fingers over the rough turquoise. "He said one day he would tell you why and that upon his death, it would pass to you." She sniffed as a single tear formed in her eye.

Jalil didn't know what to say. She stared at him intently for another moment then kissed the medallion and handed it back to him. "Jalil, you are the sheik of this tribe, and you are the rightful bearer of the medallion. Protect it with your life," she said solemnly, unknowingly repeating the same words Akeem's father had said to Akeem.

Jalil closed his hand around the medallion, but when he felt a tingling in his palm, his eyes widened as he glanced down at it. *Did it just glow?* Dismissing what had to be a product of his imagination brought on by the seriousness of his mother's voice, he slipped it over his head. It settled inside his tunic to rest against his heart. For a second, it felt strangely hot again then cooled just as quickly. Disconcerted, he took a swallow of tea. The medallion was becoming more of a mystery, but he would have his answers soon.

Later, as he slipped into his bed, his last thought was of Kira. He couldn't wait to see her, convinced she could help him solve the mystery of the medallion and his father's untimely death. He drifted to sleep thinking of her golden hair and blue-green eyes. *Soon,* he thought, *soon.*

CHAPTER 3

Jabari had managed not to think about Kira over the past few weeks but for an entirely different reason—he was so engrossed in learning everything he could from Jalil, he didn't have time. His daily routine kept him so busy he barely had time to eat. It was frustrating because Jabari loved to eat. The day the messenger came, he had finished his morning riding lessons and was enjoying a midday meal with his mother when his father, Saad, rushed into the house.

"Oh, Samira, great news," Saad said excitedly. "Sheik Ehsaan is planning a feast for Adara's birth-year celebration and has invited Jalil and his family. And even better—Amal sends word that he is to be joined with Fatima during the same celebration, so we are invited too. Is that not wonderful?"

Samira looked stunned. "When is this to happen?"

"Within a week's time," Saad said as he took a seat at the table and filled a plate with Samira's spicy stew.

"A week?" Samira's voice rose. "That means we have very little time to prepare!"

"You are right, my flower. And I will get right on that…just as soon as I finish eating," he said, before taking a heaping spoonful of the savory mixture.

Jabari remained quiet and picked at his food, distressed by the news he had less than a week to come up with a gift for Adara. She was his dearest friend, and they had bonded over their shared love of horses. Saad, on the other hand, ate quickly and, after thanking Samira for the meal, he rushed off, saying he needed to prepare for the upcoming trip.

Samira must have noticed Jabari's continued silence and said, "Jabari, what is wrong? I thought you would be excited to see Adara, as well as Kira."

Jabari waffled for a moment before answering her. "I am! But that is not the problem. It is Adara's birth-year celebration, and I must give her a gift. But what can I give someone like Adara? She is the daughter of a sheik." He would not insult his mother by saying that as a poor son of a trader, he had little to offer. "All I have is Sarii, my horse, but Adara would not want Sarii—she has Shar," he said, referring to the huge black stallion Jalil had taken from Qadir as part of his winning the Tri-Annual race, as was his right. Qadir had ruthlessly whipped Shar at the finish line, blaming the poor stallion for losing to Jalil. Kira had attempted to stop the beating thus incurring Qadir's wrath which led to his kidnapping her in revenge. Thank Allah, Jalil had rescued Shar from Qadir and gifted him to Ehsaan.

Jabari stared down at his half-eaten meal, his appetite eclipsed by his dilemma, and his mother was quick to notice and tried to help.

"Oh, Jabari, do not be that way. I am sure we can think of something. Why not ask your father? Maybe he can come up with a gift like a new bridle for Shar or maybe a blanket. I could help you with that." She smiled encouragingly.

Jabari looked up at his mother's loving expression and felt a little better. "Maybe you are right," he said.

"I usually am," she said with a chuckle.

His good mood restored, but still wanting to find something special for Adara, he went in search of his father. But as the day of departure neared, he felt more and more sorry for himself. He was no closer to finding a gift. Everyone noticed and tried to help him by making suggestions. It only made him more frustrated.

The day before they were to leave, Jabari met Jalil in the corral to practice his sword work, but was having trouble focusing, and not just because of his constant worry over Adara's gift. He was also feeling guilty for having forgotten about Kira. Jabari loved working with Jalil and thanked Allah every day that his family was now part of Jalil's tribe. Thanks to Jalil, Jabari had a job and a horse, and his family had a permanent home. Some days he had to pinch himself. It all seemed like a dream. But he knew in his heart he had Kira to thank for it. She had brought them together and saved his life, and he had never thanked her. He resolved to rectify that the next time he saw her.

Being distracted was his downfall, and he felt the sting of Jalil's sword on his left thigh. "Ouch!" Jabari cried out, rubbing his leg. Jalil never cut him but would catch him with the flat of the blade as he taught Jabari some of the trickier moves.

Jalil smirked. "It doesn't pay to daydream when someone is attacking you with a sword," he warned.

"I know, I know. I am sorry, my sheik. I will do better," Jabari said, assuming a defensive stance.

"Jabari, you have been a mess all week. I thought you would be excited to take Sarii on the road. What is bothering you?" Jalil danced around him, waving his blade.

"Oh, I am excited, but I haven't been able to find a present for Adara yet," Jabari said as he twisted and turned, trying to keep his blade up.

"I see," Jalil said and smacked him again.

"Ouch!" Jabari flinched and paused to rub his other leg then eyed Jalil with a rueful expression. "This is not a fair fight. Your sword is longer, and mine is not much bigger than my dagger."

Jalil stopped to give him a rest. "Our swords are the same length, Jabari, but someday you may have to fight someone who has a longer sword. And you will need to fight with whatever you have, even if it is just a dagger," he said.

Jabari laid his sword down and reached into his pocket to pull out his dagger—the gold dagger given to him by his adoptive father years ago. "Even a dagger as small as this?" he asked. The sun flashed from the gems embedded in its gold handle.

Jalil stepped forward. "May I see that, please?" When Jabari handed it over, Jalil studied the beautiful piece and tested the blade. Then he said, "May I see the sheath, too?"

Jabari passed him the sheath and watched as Jalil turned it back and forth, scrutinizing the jewels and engravings.

"Jabari, where did you get this?" Jalil said with a stern expression.

"My father gave it to me." Jabari didn't elaborate about his strange origin, having always been afraid if anyone found out he was not the real son of Saad and Samira, he might not be allowed to stay with them.

"Hmm. It is quite valuable, and you should be very careful where you keep it. I would not show it to anyone." Jalil studied it a moment longer then slipped the dagger into the sheath and handed it back.

Jabari looked closely at the dagger he had examined many times since his parents had given it to him, marveling at its beauty and workmanship. It was a mystery he had given up trying to solve, but something Jalil said stuck in his mind. *It is very valuable.* Suddenly, Jabari knew what he would do with it. It would make a wonderful gift for the daughter of a sheik. It was small and easily handled, and he was sure Adara would be able to master its uses. It might even save her life someday. The thought that he could in some way protect her in the future made him feel ten feet tall.

Putting it back in his pocket, Jabari found he could focus clearly again. "My sheik, it appears I have regained my strength and am ready to teach you a lesson."

Jalil laughed loudly. "Then, my friend, prepare yourself!"

Jabari grinned, and he forgot all thoughts of Adara.

CHAPTER 4

It was late in the day when Kira heard the gunshots from the main pass announcing visitors, and she rushed outside to join Ehsaan and Issa on the front steps. Adara followed closely, bouncing up and down, clapping her hands with excitement.

Kira struggled to hide her own emotions when she saw Sheik Jalil riding toward them on his silver stallion, Mirage. Behind him were Nasira and her daughters, Akilah and Lina, escorted by a dozen of Jalil's finest warriors. And riding alongside Jalil's sisters were Jabari and his parents, Saad and Samira.

Ehsaan's tribesmen greeted the visitors with enthusiasm, and with good reason—they were all invited to the celebration feast. It promised to be a night of elaborate food and drink, and rumors circulated that a famous magician would entertain them. The household was still in an uproar with the preparations for the feast to be held in a few days. As Ehsaan's sole heir, Adara's birth-year celebration was always a momentous occasion, but it was even more important this year because the tribe would also celebrate the joining of their newest members, Amal and Fatima.

Kira felt thrilled to see her adoptive family, but seeing Jalil again made her heart pound. While he dismounted and strode forward to greet Ehsaan, she tried not to stare but couldn't help herself. Her eyes traveled lovingly over his tall form, but when she looked up at his handsome face and saw him staring at her with an inscrutable look, she blushed and dropped her gaze.

After Jalil and Ehsaan exchanged formal greetings, Jabari ran forward and greeted Ehsaan and Issa first before declaring he would dedicate the rest of the afternoon to Adara's happiness. Adara begged her father to let her take Jabari straight to the stables, insisting that Shar was waiting to see him. Ehsaan laughingly agreed, and the two dashed off.

While Ehsaan's men helped Jalil's men set up their camp, Kira helped Issa get the women and girls settled in the guest rooms that had been prepared for them. She was looking forward to having Samira nearby as she had much to discuss with her adoptive mother. But Samira was tired from the journey, so they agreed to meet the next day for the midday meal.

Hearing Jalil would stay in the chamber two doors down from hers made Kira nervous. She longed to talk to him but feared running into him in the corridor, alone. *What if he can tell how I feel about him?* Unsure if she could hide her feelings, she sent a message to Nasira, excusing herself from dinner. Then she remained in her room, enjoying a light meal and working on the baskets she was making for Adara.

When she heard boots in the corridor, she held her breath when they stopped outside her door. But after a moment, she heard them walking away and sighed with relief. It had to have been Jalil, she thought, and she couldn't help feeling a little excited that he was thinking of her too. Later, as she slipped into bed, she felt a new sense of calm and found herself looking forward to the next few days.

Kira awoke early the next morning, eager for the day ahead. Too excited to eat, she downed a glass of lemonade, grabbed some fruit, and went to check on Amber. On the way to visit her friend in the pasture, she saw Amal working with Shar in the corral and stopped to watch. When Amal stopped and gave Shar a break, he saw Kira by the fence and walked the big stallion over so she could pet him.

"Good morning, Kira."

"Good morning, Amal. Shar is looking so much better. You have done an amazing job with him."

Amal beamed. "Thank you. It has been hard for him, but he is doing very well. Unfortunately, he will still not allow anyone on his back, but maybe in time…" Amal looked hopeful.

Kira stroked Shar's glossy neck and smiled. "Amal, I have witnessed many miracles since coming to your land. I will pray for Shar."

In the short time she'd been at Ehsaan's, Kira managed to make friends with Shar. They had both been whipped by the same man— Qadir, and they both had the scars to prove it. She was relieved to see that most of his had faded. Her fingers traced the thin ones she found on his neck and shoulder, and she shivered as she thought about her own. Nickering softly, Shar nudged her arm, pulling her away from the terrible memories. Maybe he sensed she was still recovering too, she thought as she gave him a pat then stepped back to let Amal continue his training.

Focused on Shar, Kira was unaware that Jalil had joined her at the fence until she felt a presence and turned to see him watching the stallion. When he glanced her way and smiled, she couldn't help herself and smiled back. Seeing his smile grow, she blushed and ducked her head, returning her attention to Shar. Amal led Shar back over to the fence so Jalil could pet him, and Kira listened closely as Jalil shared his training tips with Amal. Seeing the rapt expression on Amal's face, it was obvious to Kira that Amal admired and respected Jalil.

Not wanting to draw Jalil's attention, Kira slipped away and headed to the back pasture where Amber was already waiting. Kira, who wore her boy's clothes under her robe, climbed on Amber's bare back, and the two galloped off. Once they were over the first rise, she threw off her robe and headwrap, dropping them on a clump of bushes. With a new sense of freedom and optimism, she rode with delight, enjoying the warmth of the sun and the wind in her hair. Kira was so focused on her ride that she failed to notice Amber's ears swivel and was startled to discover Jalil and Mirage drawing alongside them.

Kira looked over at Jalil and saw him studying her intently, as if waiting for her permission to join them. Smiling, she urged Amber into a fast gallop. Caught unawares, Mirage faltered then leapt to the challenge. Glancing over her shoulder, Kira saw Jalil laughing as he raced to catch up. On flat ground, Mirage was faster, and soon Kira and Jalil were racing side by side, both caught up in the joy of riding.

Before long, both horses slowed of their own accord, and when Amber circled back toward the house, Mirage kept pace with her. Finally, they eased into a walk, giving their riders a chance to catch their breath. Hearing Jalil chuckling, she glanced over to see him patting Mirage on the neck. *Is he laughing at me?* "What is so funny, my sheik?"

Jalil looked up. "Kira, please call me Jalil. I was laughing at Mirage. It appears he is not as fast as he thought, and he is not used to competition. I believe he is upset that Amber can keep up with him. She is fast for a filly. Or is she a mare? Has she ever been bred? How old is she?"

They were simple questions, but the look on his face made her think he was looking for more than simple answers. *Is he trying to figure out where she comes from?* Her mind in a whirl, and not wanting to tell him about the valley, Amber's birthplace, she tried to think of some way to change the subject.

Jalil must have noticed her discomfort for when she failed to answer right away, he spoke quickly, "Are you all right, Kira? I did not mean to ride so fast. I am sorry if I have caused you any pain."

Relieved that he had provided her a reason to avoid the subject of Amber, but seeing the honest concern on his face, she wondered if he was remembering what had happened the last time they rode together. She had still been recovering from her ordeal with Qadir, and that day she had ridden too hard and had almost collapsed. Jalil had taken her in his arms to prevent her from falling, and she had reacted poorly, mistaking his embrace in her clouded mind with Qadir's violent restraint. She had been frightened, and Jalil had obviously been confused and hurt by her reaction.

Shaking her head to clear the memory, she finally spoke, wishing to dispel his worry. "I am fine, Jalil. Perhaps I should not have ridden so hard."

"Oh, Kira, I am sorry. Maybe you should not be riding. I could carry you back to the house?" He edged closer.

Alarmed at the thought of being in his arms again, Kira blushed furiously. "No, no, really. I can manage. I'll be all right in a minute. Maybe you should go on without me." She was having difficulty breathing but not because of their impromptu race.

"Oh, all right," Jalil said, fumbling over his words. "If you are sure, then I will leave you for now. I hope you feel better, and when you do, I hope you will allow me to join you on another ride, but perhaps we will not go as fast." He bowed his head. "Please let me know if I can do anything for you," he said earnestly and departed.

Watching him ride away, she was relieved to have successfully diverted his attention away from any details about Amber, but then her worries shifted to something else entirely. Plagued by continued thoughts of Jalil, she knew of only one explanation, and though she didn't want to admit it, she knew she was falling in love with him. Despite her earlier assumptions about him, she could sense his attraction towards her. The thought was startling and should have brought her joy, but she felt only regret. She knew she could never be part of his life.

Jalil was the sheik of his tribe, and she was a foreigner, a nobody in his world, with nothing to offer him. And even if he could look past that, there was the fact that custom demanded the sheik's wife be a virgin. *Wife? What am I thinking?* She was not worthy of being his wife. Overwhelmed with sadness, she suddenly felt like crying. But in that moment, Amber huffed at her, as if she knew Kira's thoughts, and Kira's dark mood disappeared. She drew strength from Amber and felt filled with a new resolve. She was tired of crying, tired of feeling sorry for herself, and tired of feeling unwanted. Just because she was not a suitable candidate for a sheik's wife didn't mean she couldn't still live her life and find someone who could love her as she was.

Returning to the compound, picking up her robe and headwrap along the way, she left Amber in the pasture and stalked inside the house. Sadness took a back seat to determination as she decided it was time to take charge of her life. She would sit down with Sheikha Issa after the celebration and talk about her future. Feeling better, having made at least one positive decision, she grabbed a clean tunic and slippers and headed to the bathing pool.

After a long soak and an application of soothing oils, her good mood was restored. She joined Samira, as promised, for a midday meal and had a lovely visit. They talked for hours until Kira finally excused herself, claiming she needed time to prepare. Having accepted her situation and feeling confident she could handle Jalil, she had decided she would join the families that night for the evening meal.

***

While Kira dressed for dinner, convincing herself she was in control of her emotions, Jalil was doing the same. Except he couldn't stop thinking about Kira and how she looked racing through the pasture. When he saw her riding ahead of him on Amber with her golden hair streaming in the wind, he encouraged Mirage to catch up with her. One look at her lovely face with her flushed cheeks and shining eyes, and he wanted to pull her from the saddle into his lap. Unfortunately, he had forced Kira to ride too fast, just as he had weeks before in the process of her rescue. He would have been at fault if she'd gotten hurt. *I should not have pushed her so soon.* But once again, he felt frustrated she would not allow him to help her.

Jalil was surprised and pleased when Kira appeared at the evening meal. She looked relaxed and happy, and he realized he had never seen this side of her. When he glanced at her across the table, he caught her staring at him, but then she turned her attention to Jabari, who was attempting to fool Adara with one of his magic tricks. Jalil studied her profile, watching her laugh at the children, and he felt the earth move.

When Nasira turned to ask him something, he was so focused on Kira that Nasira had to nudge his arm to get his attention. "Jalil, do you want to leave the morning after the celebration, or do you want to stay one more day?"

"What? What did you say, Mother? I was thinking about something." He pretended to study the selection of fruits on a nearby platter.

"I said, do you still want to go home the morning after the celebration?"

"Oh, yes. There are things that need doing that I have been putting off," he said vaguely as he chose a cluster of grapes and began eating them, one by one. He cut his eyes over to Kira then back quickly, hoping his mother hadn't noticed.

She smiled at him knowingly. It appeared she had. "All right then. I will make sure we are ready. Do you still have Adara's 'present' well hidden?"

"All is taken care of," he assured her, finishing his grapes and reaching for his tea.

"I am so glad you are doing this for her and Ehsaan. Your father would have approved. It is something he always talked about doing."

"I am glad too. Ehsaan and his tribe have been good friends and powerful allies. I will make sure we honor them and keep our relationship strong in the future."

Loud laughter interrupted their conversation as the others watched Jabari execute one of his better tricks, causing Adara to clap with glee. "Jabari, I do not know how you do it, but one day I will figure out all your tricks, or I will make you show me how they are done." She glared at him in mock anger. "For now, you are pardoned, but I expect a truly amazing show at the feast."

"Yes, Adara, daughter of Sheik Ehsaan, Jabari the Magnificent is yours to command," Jabari said, bowing low. Everyone laughed again, and Jabari winked at Jalil then sat down to finish his meal.

Jalil watched Ehsaan with Issa. They treated each other with such respect and love. Envious, Jalil sighed and felt a sense of inexplicable loss that he didn't have his own sheikha—until he heard Kira's soft laughter, and his heart filled with new hope. Perhaps he might have found his sheikha after all.

CHAPTER 5

The sun was barely a golden glow over the eastern mountain tops when Issa rose to begin what for her would be a very busy day. Ehsaan had already departed to take care of the items she had assigned him. As usual, he had tried to be quiet when he left, but she remembered a soft caress on her cheek and his gentle kiss on her forehead. Seeing the hot tea on their dining table, along with a platter of fresh fruit and warm bread, she smiled at his thoughtfulness.

After a light meal, she donned a serviceable outfit and went to awaken Adara. Her daughter was still abed with Gigi, her domesticated sand cat, laying curled up by her side, and Issa paused to memorize the sight. *She is changing so fast. Before long, she will be a woman.* Her heart ached at the thought that someday she would have to say goodbye to her little girl. Looking down at her angelic face, Issa sighed and lightly caressed Adara's cheek, smiling when Adara opened her liquid brown eyes.

"Mother," Adara murmured with a grin.

"Good morning, special girl," Issa said, leaning down to kiss her cheek. "Time to wake up. We have a great deal to do today, and you cannot be lying about like a camel in the sand." She knew the minute Adara remembered what the day was and laughed.

Adara's eyes popped open, and she abruptly sat up, sending Gigi scrambling to safety with a petulant meow. "Mother, why did you let me sleep so long!" Adara leapt from the bed and rushed to her cabinet, intent on finding something to wear.

"Slow down, daughter. You have plenty of time, but you are not going anywhere until you have something to eat and drink," Issa said, pulling her over to the small table where a platter was waiting.

"Oh, Mother, do I have to? I am not really that hungry," Adara whined but dutifully sat down with a thump.

"Adara, this won't take long. Just try to eat a little, and then you can go," Issa said as she laid out a sturdy tunic and robe for Adara's use. She knew Adara would be into everything that day and was notoriously hard on her clothes, what with her lessons in riding, swordplay, and herd management. Issa knew Kira wore boy's clothes under her robe when riding, and though scandalized at first, she was thinking maybe it wasn't such a bad idea after all. Now that Adara was turning thirteen, it wouldn't be long before men began to notice her. She was already a beautiful girl and promised to be even more beautiful with time.

Adara finished her meal in record time and was about to dash from her room when Issa stopped her with a few words of caution. "Adara, please try to stay out of the way today, and be sure to give yourself time later for a bath and to get dressed. And don't forget, this is also Fatima's joining day."

"Yes, Mother, I know, and I'll be back in plenty of time to get ready. But I'm so excited. Today is the day! And it's going to be wonderful," she exclaimed as she ran from the room.

Shaking her head in exasperation, Issa hurried off to find Nasira, who she planned to enlist in overseeing the food preparations. Samira had already agreed to help Fatima prepare for her joining. By midday, after being informed by several concerned servants that Adara was driving everyone crazy, Issa asked Jabari to help. He had been working in the courtyard and was more than happy to take Adara away on the pretext of solving a problem he was having with Sarii's training.

Amid the hubbub of preparations, a messenger arrived with a missive for Ehsaan. She heard Ehsaan call for Jalil and watched the two of them disappear behind closed doors. Apparently, it was news of some importance, but Issa knew her husband would share anything he learned. He kept her as informed as his advisors. She loved that he treated her with such respect and as an equal.

She enjoyed seeing Jalil again. He was a wonderful son and had grown into such a good man. Wise and kind, he was also loved, admired, and respected by his tribe, and Nasira was lucky to have him. But seeing Jalil with Jabari reminded Issa of Nasira's tragedy—her kidnapped baby, Talib. He would be about Jabari's age now, but they never found him. It was a mystery still, one Nasira wouldn't talk about. It took Nasira a long time to get over it, and frankly, Issa thought she never did. Issa's heart hurt for her best friend. No one, man or woman, who loses a child ever gets over it. All one can do is live with it, as Issa well knew.

Issa had lost a boy baby long ago too, but he had been stillborn. Even Adara didn't know about that, and maybe one day Issa would share that story with her daughter. A woman should know what can happen, what can go wrong, and that she can survive such a tragedy. Standing in the blazing sun, staring at the far hills, Issa mentally slapped herself to lose the morbid thoughts. It was Adara's big day, and it would be Fatima's, too. A day when a young girl stepped closer to womanhood, and a young woman became a wife. It was a time to celebrate, and shaking off her sadness, Issa vowed to be happy for her daughter and her new friend, Fatima, and returned to her preparations.

***

Jalil spent the morning with Ehsaan, and they discussed the latest news from Qadir's kingdom. Kira's rescue had left Qadir's tribe in a state of confusion, and rumors were flying as everyone tried to figure out who killed Qadir and who had poisoned his mother, First Wife. Some said Jalil had done the deeds, while others said that Kira killed them. Another rumor was that a crimson-haired foreigner had something to do with it. Jalil knew they were talking about Cassie—the redheaded woman who had survived the plane crash with Kira. Jalil remembered her. She had shown up in Qadir's chamber the night he discovered Qadir's body. But no one said anything about Fatima. Apparently, as a mere harem girl, she had never drawn attention, and many didn't even know who she was.

Then Jalil had a stray thought about Qadir's captain, Hashem. No one remembered seeing him during the raid. Hashem was shifty, ruthless, and disrespectful, and he reminded Jalil of Qadir. *Maybe Hashem killed them?*

But when Ehsaan interrupted his thoughts, Jalil put Hashem from his mind. He and Ehsaan had other business to discuss—trade routes, the increasing number of foreigners arriving in the ports, as well as other important topics. Jalil was already aware of some of these issues through his own network of informants. Overall, the region was quiet, except for some trouble with Sheik Amit, Qadir's biggest ally. Some thought Amit might try to take over Qadir's kingdom since it was common knowledge Qadir had no heir. Jalil wasn't sure Amit could legally do that because Fatima had mentioned Cassie claimed to be pregnant by Qadir. But so far, no one could verify if that was true.

After several hours of discussion, trying to separate fact from fiction, the two men decided they needed to clear their minds and enjoy the rest of the day. Jalil saddled Mirage, and Ehsaan saddled his stallion, Mukhtar, and together they toured Ehsaan's pastures, examining his water supply and the youngest additions to his herd. They both came back in a much better frame of mind, relaxed and ready for the celebration.

As the hour approached, Jalil returned to his room to find his ceremonial clothes laid out in readiness. After a refreshing dip in the bathing pool, he dressed in his finest, and when he finished tying the cord on his head wrap, he stepped back to look in the long mirror. His tunic bore little embellishment—the gold and blue bands were enough for him. Staring at the gold medallion in his hand, he studied the new gold link chain he'd had made for it. He wished he had the original one, but when he found the medallion at Qadir's, the original chain was missing.

He was fortunate to have found the medallion in Qadir's bed chamber the night he rescued Kira. But in his brief encounter with Cassie, who was also in Qadir's chamber that night, she said the medallion had belonged to Kira's father, who bought it in Cairo. *How did the medallion get to Cairo? What does Kira know about it? Will I ever find my father's murderer?* It still infuriated him that he couldn't solve the mystery, and he knew he would always search for the answer, but not that night. That night was about little Adara and Amal and Fatima. That night was about joy, family, and celebration. Placing the medallion around his neck, he tucked it inside his tunic. He wasn't ready to reveal his tribal symbol that night.

Slipping into his gold and white robe, he hurried to the courtyard to join the men, eager to see Kira in her finery. He didn't have to wait long. He was standing by the head table listening to Ehsaan when suddenly the older man stopped in mid-sentence and looked over Jalil's shoulder. Ehsaan's eyes widened, and a grin spread across his face. Jalil turned to see what Ehsaan was smiling at and noticed everyone looking towards the courtyard entrance. His own eyes filled with admiration when he saw the women filing in.

Issa came first, and Jalil watched Ehsaan's face fill with love. She smiled as she approached and walked to his side, looking up at him with love and joy. Adara marched in behind her, looking more like a young woman in her elegant robe, and smiled and waved at her tribal members. Ehsaan gestured regally to direct Adara to her seat of honor, and she bowed her head then took her place amid the indulgent smiles of her tribesmen gazing upon her with obvious pride.

Watching his mother walk in with a firm step, Jalil's heart went out to her. Nasira smiled proudly at him as he escorted her to her seat, but he could see a bit of sadness in her eyes. He knew she missed Akeem, who should have been there to sit next to her. Next came Akilah and Lina, side-by-side. They had decided, as sisters often do, that they would enter together, but when they moved to sit next to Jalil, he motioned to them to leave the seat next to him open. They looked at him oddly until Nasira glanced around him and nodded. Some secret language, Jalil figured, because they both smiled and moved down a seat.

When Kira entered, the crowd looked stunned, and Jalil watched, entranced, as she walked toward him. Her golden robe shimmered in the torchlight and waved gently with the motion of her walk. Unbound, her hair flowed down her back in a golden waterfall from beneath diaphanous silk. She clasped her hands at her waist, but as she neared, he could see them trembling.

The courtyard faded until all he could see was Kira, and Jalil felt a sudden need to take her in his arms and banish her fear. It was like he was seeing her for the first time, and when she looked at him, he felt the earth move. Inhaling sharply, he resisted the urge to run to her, and he waited.

CHAPTER 6

Kira felt like she was in a dream. Earlier she had joined Nasira and Issa, along with Akilah and Lina, in the bathing chamber to help each other get dressed. Nasira had made each of them a new tunic decorated by Issa and Fatima with lavish embroidery and embellishments. She also provided exquisite outer robes of delicate silk that crossed at the waist, highlighting the ornate necks of the tunics worn underneath. Issa gave everyone a new pair of gilded slippers and diaphanous silk scarves that doubled as veils.

Nasira and Issa had coordinated their work to produce lovely garments in subtle colors. Nasira wore turquoise, gold, and white, the colors of her tribe. Her daughters wore matching pale turquoise and white. Issa wore her tribe's colors, emerald, silver, and white, and Adara's outfit was pale green with silver highlights.

Kira was delighted to wear her own fine ensemble. The bodice of her pale gold tunic was sprinkled with tiny clear crystals, and her robe was white with narrow gold bands. Simple and elegant, it was a lovely outfit that complimented her golden hair and skin, but she had a fleeting wish that she too could have worn tribal colors, especially turquoise.

Fatima cried when Issa presented her with a gorgeous robe and tunic of pristine white silk adorned with pearl embellishments. Seeing Fatima in her wedding finery, Kira had mixed feelings. She was happy

Fatima escaped Qadir's notice, but sad she herself couldn't say the same.

Thankfully, Nasira had distracted her from those thoughts, and Kira was glad for the reprieve. Outlining Kira's eyes in a dramatic black with gold and silver bands, Nasira then dyed Kira's lips a pale pink and dusted her face with a light powder of shimmery gold. Akilah, Adara, and Lina were only allowed to dye their lips and wear light eyeliner, but that was enough to thrill them. They couldn't stop admiring their outfits and were breathless with excitement, only calming down when a servant appeared to let them know the men were waiting for them in the courtyard. Kira was just as excited as the girls, but also nervous, and her heart raced as she followed behind the sheikhas and the children. She was about to see Jalil, and she couldn't wait.

But when she entered the courtyard, Kira's nervousness escalated. Everyone was staring at her, and she almost turned and fled until she made eye contact with Jalil. He stood behind his chair, and his warm smile beckoned her onward. She walked toward the end of the table, away from Jalil, thinking she wasn't supposed to sit with his family, but he surprised her when he gestured toward the empty chair by his side. She looked at the chair then at his sisters. They nodded and smiled, as did Nasira.

Kira sat down and focused on the courtyard, trying not to think about the man standing inches away. She couldn't believe she was sitting next to the most handsome man at the party. Almost against her will, she risked a glance at him, and her eyes widened. From the expression on Jalil's face, she felt like the most beautiful woman in the world. She inhaled sharply, and for a second the earth stood still, and the world fell silent until a sudden blare of a horn broke the spell. Ehsaan captured her attention when he walked around to the front of the table and raised his arms.

"Honored guests, tonight we celebrate the thirteenth birth-year of our own Adara and witness the joining of two new members of our tribe. We also welcome our ally and friend, Sheik Jalil, his family, and the members of their tribe. Let us give thanks to Allah for providing this opportunity to share these great moments in our lives." This was received with much yelling and table thumping but, thankfully, no gunshots, and when the crowd quieted, he continued, "We will begin the feast after the joining of Amal and Fatima. Then we will witness an astounding performance by a famous magician, and after being properly mystified, we will pay a special tribute to Adara. So, Amal, please come to the front of the table."

Amal, dressed in a white tunic and robe, moved to stand in front of Ehsaan. Ehsaan signaled the musicians, who began playing a haunting tune with flutes, and Amal turned to face the entrance. When Fatima entered the courtyard, smiling, and walked toward Amal, Kira saw the look of amazement on his face. He was clearly smitten. She knew Fatima had never considered herself a beauty, but that night, Fatima was beautiful, as every woman is, when encircled by love and respect.

As Ehsaan performed the ceremony, Kira listened teary eyed while the couple exchanged vows of love, followed by the exchange of rings. Amal and Fatima never looked at anyone but each other, and Kira could feel the love that emanated from them. After proclaiming them joined for life, Ehsaan had to clear his throat to get the newlyweds' attention. They looked around as if they'd just awakened, and everyone laughed. Once they took their seats, Ehsaan and others presented the newly joined couple with gifts ranging from clothing to household items.

When Baqir delivered Ehsaan's gift to Amal—a young blood-red horse—Amal looked stunned. Issa presented Fatima with a special loom for her use in making silk veils. And Jabari received a hearty laugh from Amal and a blush from Fatima when he offered to give her free riding lessons. Kira chuckled, remembering Fatima's infamous ride during Kira's rescue. When Fatima helped her escape from Qadir's house, they ran into Jabari outside. He had appropriated a loose horse, which he later named Sarii, from one of Qadir's men. Kira was able to ride Amber, but Fatima had to ride double with Jabari. Having been in Qadir's harem from early childhood, Fatima had little experience with both horses and men. Her ride to freedom had been a real trial, both physically and mentally.

After the last gift, Ehsaan waved at the musicians, who played a lively beat, and the feast began. Kira tried to keep up with all the stories and conversations and pretended to listen to everyone, but in fact, she barely heard anything. As she watched the people surrounding her, they reminded her of her grandmother's tribe, where everyone took care of each other and worked together as a community. Filled with equal parts jealousy and sadness, she longed to be part of a family again, and she pressed her hand to her chest where her father's ring hung on her mother's chain beneath her tunic. It was a shame her parents would never know these people because she knew her mother and father would have loved them. Lost in thought, she jumped when Jalil lightly touched her arm.

"Is everything all right, Kira?"

"What? Oh, yes, my sheik. I was just remembering my parents," she said sadly.

He squeezed her arm lightly. "Kira, I miss my father every day. I know how you feel."

She had been acutely aware of his presence during the ceremony, and seeing the understanding in his eyes, she felt a sudden warmth and pleasure at his concern. "Thank you, Sheik Jalil. I will try not to think of it tonight." She removed her hand from her chest, and he let go of her arm. Seeking to divert his attention that was making her increasingly warmer, she smiled. "Isn't it about time for our famous magician to appear?"

"Why, yes, I believe you are right. Let us check with Ehsaan and see if he knows when he will appear." But before he could speak to Ehsaan, the musician's horn rang out.

Kira saw Saad enter, carrying a bag and a small table, placing them in the center of the courtyard before returning to his seat at the table. Then Ehsaan stood and made an announcement. "Honored guests, I would now like to present the very famous and world-renowned mystic and magician, Jabari the Magnificent!"

Kira gasped in delight as Jabari rode in on Sarii, with no reins or saddle, his arms outstretched, holding the edges of his magician's robes, allowing them to billow around him like wings. The courtyard filled with laughter and sounds of disbelief as everyone recognized Jabari. Unfazed, Jabari began his show, and soon the guests were not only laughing but also applauding his skills.

Jabari performed as he had at the Tri-Annual pre-race feast months ago, and his audience was just as amazed as he once again played tricks on the guests, making objects disappear and appear with ease. When he ended his show by producing a live bird out of thin air, it was a white dove that he presented to Adara. She was thrilled and promptly declared him to be the greatest magician in the world. After bowing deeply, he whistled for Sarii, who trotted in. He jumped onto her back, rose to his feet, and waved at the crowd as she cantered out of the courtyard amid thunderous applause.

Once Jabari returned to his seat, Ehsaan stood and again called for attention. "My honored guests, my daughter, Adara, would like to say something before we begin the presentation of her gifts."

Adara stood and smiled. "I want to thank everyone for helping celebrate my birth-year. I especially want to thank Sheik Jalil and his family for coming." The guests clapped politely, and Adara nodded then raised her hands for silence. Kira noticed Issa shaking her head at her daughter's regal showmanship, but Ehsaan was staring at his daughter like she'd hung the moon. They reminded her of her own mother and father. Such parents were a treasure.

When Adara sat back down, Kira watched as Jalil rose and bowed to Adara then to Issa and Ehsaan. "Adara, I would like to present a gift from my tribe to you, in honor of your birth-year," he said formally then smiled at Adara and gestured toward the courtyard entrance where one of his men entered leading a tiny golden filly, one of the fabled golden horses belonging to Jalil's tribe alone. She wore a green halter decorated with silver bells that chimed as she pranced behind her handler. Whinnying, she seemed perfectly at home amongst all the people. The courtyard fell silent, and Adara stared, her eyes wide, and for once, she was speechless. Kira was just as impressed.

Issa nudged Adara and whispered, "Adara, say something."

Adara looked at Jalil with a confused expression. "Where did she come from? I did not see her with you when you arrived."

"Maybe it was magic." Jalil winked.

Adara glanced once more at the filly then back at Jalil. "Is she really mine?" she asked, disbelief written all over her face.

"Yes, Adara, she is yours to raise and train as you command," Jalil said, bowing to her.

Ehsaan rose and laid a hand on Jalil's arm. "Jalil, are you sure?"

"Yes, my old friend. It is as my father would have wished. Akeem would have wanted me to honor the very best of our allies." Jalil bowed.

Issa's eyes shone with joy, but Nasira's shone with pride. By giving the filly to Adara as a gift, Ehsaan couldn't refuse. It was a brilliant move on Jalil's part, Kira thought.

Ehsaan took Adara by the hand, and together they walked out to meet her new filly. The horse was a delight, and Adara promptly kissed her on the nose. Ehsaan walked around the filly, trailing his hand on her shining coat, admiring her excellent conformation. Speechless, he turned and bowed to Jalil, who grinned back at him. Applause filled the courtyard. Ehsaan's tribe obviously knew what this would mean for their herd, and Kira knew they would never forget it.

Stunned by Jalil's generosity, Kira stared at him in wonder. When he glanced down at her, his grin grew even bigger. Thrilled by the expression of joy in his eyes, and slightly star-struck, she blushed and turned her attention back to Adara. Seeing the young girl's excitement reminded Kira of her own feelings when she found Amber, and she knew Adara would never forget this moment, either.

Ehsaan turned to Adara and asked if she would allow Baqir to take her filly and prepare a stall for her. Adara agreed but held her hand up one more time. "I have already decided on her name. She shall be known as Hiba, for she is a true 'gift.' Thank you, Sheik Jalil. I shall honor her, and she will become a member of my family and my tribe,"

Adara said solemnly, sounding much older than her thirteen years. After kissing the pretty horse once more on her nose and giving her a hug too, Adara returned to her seat and watched proudly as Baqir led Hiba away. Taking a long sip of her tea, she struggled to regain her composure as she surreptitiously wiped away a tear.

Kira enjoyed watching Adara open her other gifts. It was obvious Adara loved the tunic from Nasira, and she exclaimed over Akilah and Lina's gift of perfume. She thanked Kira for the two baskets Kira had made for her, agreeing that one was perfect for Gigi's toys but laughing at the suggestion that Gigi could use the other one for a bed. "Kira, you know she prefers sleeping in a real bed," Adara said, but then she must have realized she might have hurt Kira's feeling and quickly added, "But it would be perfect for Gigi's kittens!" Kira struggled not to laugh at the look of worry on Issa's face.

After Issa presented Adara with a delicate jade necklace with matching earrings, her father gave her a diminutive sword with an intricately carved blade and bejeweled scabbard. As Kira watched and listened to people around her, she allowed herself to absorb the joy and happiness that filled the courtyard. It was a heady feeling, and she joined in the applause when Adara proclaimed it was the most wonderful celebration ever.

***

Watching Adara receive her presents, Jabari waited impatiently for the perfect opportunity to give her his gift. After she had opened her last gift, he sprang up from his seat and dashed towards hers. Ehsaan's eyebrows rose when he rushed up, but Nasira and Issa both smiled mysteriously.

"Sheik Ehsaan, Sheikha Issa." Jabari bowed. "I have a gift for Adara, if it is permitted," he said then waited, his silver eyes shining.

Ehsaan was the first to answer. "I have no objection, Jabari. I am honored for you to give my daughter a gift."

"As am I," Issa chimed in.

Adara was looking at Jabari expectantly with a big smile. "Jabari, I am honored to receive your gift," she said.

Jabari glanced around the table to be sure everyone was paying attention. His parents smiled but looked faintly curious. Jalil stared at him with narrowed eyes, but Kira smiled encouragingly.

Jabari swallowed nervously. He had prepared for this moment, eager to prove that even the simple son of a trader knew how to honor the daughter of a sheik. Once all eyes were on him, he reached into his pocket and pulled out the gold dagger. But when he handed it to Adara, several things happened at once.

Adara held it up to the light and exclaimed, "Oh, Jabari, it is beautiful!"

Samira cried out softly, "Oh, Jabari, no!"

Only Jalil was quick enough to catch Nasira when she fainted. He tried to rouse her, but she remained unconscious, and he picked her up in his arms and hurried away. Issa followed behind him, her face filled with alarm. Kira remained seated, looking uneasy.

Adara was still holding the dagger with a worried expression on her face when Ehsaan suggested she invite Jalil's sisters back to her room to play with Gigi. Adara smiled at Jabari and thanked him again before reluctantly departing with Akilah and Lina.

Jabari was crestfallen. His joy at Adara's excited reaction to his gift turned to bewilderment. Ehsaan was staring at him with disbelief, and Samira reflected great sorrow. When Ehsaan suggested he and his parents return to their rooms, he was happy to leave the courtyard. Confused, he hoped his parents would explain, but they remained silent until they reached their room. Once there, his mother asked, "How could you give away your legacy?"

Jabari had no idea what a legacy was. "I don't understand? It's just a dagger."

She shook her head dejectedly. "Never mind, Jabari, it is late. Go to bed, and we can talk about it in the morning."

But Jabari had no desire to go to bed. He waited until they closed the door and hurried to the stable to check on Sarii. His horse was the only one he could talk to. He knew she wouldn't care if he gave the dagger away. Grumbling under his breath, he hastened outside.

CHAPTER 7

Jalil paced back and forth as he waited for his mother to awaken. It wasn't often he felt true fear, but his heart had stopped when she had fallen at the feast. Thank Allah, he'd caught her before she hit the ground, he thought. Glancing through the doorway to where she lay upon the bed, he thought she was sleeping peacefully, but he had to be sure. He started toward her until he heard Issa clear her throat. Glancing back, he saw her gesturing toward the table where she sat.

When he hesitated, she whispered loudly, "Jalil, please stop. Come and sit. She will wake when she is ready."

With a last look at his mother, he joined Issa but sat where he could see Nasira.

"Jalil, you know how strong your mother is. She will be fine," Issa said in a low voice.

"I expect you are right, Sheikha, but until I hear her speak, I cannot rest." Jalil said and continued to watch his mother. Issa's words didn't offer him any comfort. He had seen a hint of worry in her eyes.

It seemed like forever but was probably only another hour when he noticed Nasira moving slightly. Jumping up, he ran to her side, relieved to see her eyes opening. Leaning down, he took her hand in his and called softly, "Mother? It's Jalil. Can you hear me?"

Nasira seemed to come to her senses and turned her head to look at him. "Jalil?" she croaked, her eyes uncertain.

"Yes, it is I." He laid his hand gently on her cheek. "Thank Allah you have come back to me," he said fervently.

When she tried to speak again, Jalil could see she needed water. Carefully slipping a cushion behind her back, he handed her a cup. But as she reached for it, her hands started shaking, so he held it to her lips. She took a sip then sighed and smiled up at him, her eyes clear. Relieved, he wanted to speak, but Issa jostled him when she pushed between them to feel Nasira's forehead. He almost laughed when he saw his mother swatting ineffectually at Issa's hand.

"I am all right, Issa. I am not sick," Nasira grumbled.

Issa was not easily put off. "Nasira, tell me the truth. Are you really feeling better?" Her voice carried concern.

"Yes, Issa," Nasira said, but she struggled to sit up, and Issa was quick to prop more cushions behind her back.

Jalil grabbed a chair to place by the bed for Issa, then glanced at Nasira. "Mother, if you are truly fine, then I will tell the others. But when I return, I would like to talk with you about what happened."

"Thank you, Jalil. But I…," Nasira tried to speak, but Issa interjected.

"Jalil, your mother needs to rest. Perhaps your conversation can wait until tomorrow?"

Jalil hesitated because his mother did look troubled. "Issa, perhaps you are right. Tonight is not the time for questions."

Nasira seemed relieved. "Thank you, Jalil. And you too, Issa. But really, I am feeling much better." She smiled.

But Jalil wasn't entirely convinced. "Mother, I was planning for us to leave in the morning, but if for any reason you do not feel up to traveling, we can certainly stay another day."

"Nonsense. I will be ready," she said without hesitation.

Knowing it would do no good to argue, Jalil nodded in defeat and went in search of Ehsaan. He found him waiting in the courtyard.

Ehsaan was genuinely distressed. "How is Nasira?"

"She seems recovered and wants to go home in the morning."

"That is good to hear. But Jalil, I cannot imagine what could have happened. I have known your mother since the day she joined with Akeem. She is one of the strongest women I have ever met, and it was shocking to see her like that. One minute she was watching Adara accepting Jabari's dagger, and the next, she fainted away."

"Yes, it is strange, but the past few years have been hard on her. Maybe it was just the excitement. This has been the first time she has traveled beyond our borders since my father's death."

"I pray that is all it is," Ehsaan said with relief. "Well, I will say good night then. I know you want to check on your men and make sure all is ready for tomorrow. But I want to thank you again for the golden filly. You bestowed a great honor on Adara and my tribe." Ehsaan bowed low.

"The honor is mine, Ehsaan," Jalil said, bowing in return. Ehsaan smiled and Jalil departed to check on his men.

Finding all in readiness for the trip home, Jalil realized he hadn't checked on Kira. Feeling guilty knowing she would be worried about Nasira, he hurried to her room. Knocking on her door, he waited, and when she opened it, he knew he was correct. She was still in her elaborate robes, her lovely face tight with concern.

"Jalil! How is Nasira? Tell me she is all right!" Kira laid her hand on his forearm, likely without even thinking.

Aroused by her touch, he was even more excited to hear her call him Jalil. "She is fine, Kira. She merely fainted."

"Oh, I am glad. I was so worried. Thank God you caught her. She could have been hurt. But tell me, is there anything I can do to help?" she said with an earnest expression.

"I believe Issa has everything under control but thank you for offering."

"Um, you're welcome. But do you know why she fainted?"

"We do not have a clue, and if she knows, she's not saying. In fact, she is making light of the whole incident, but I think there is more to it. I can only hope if something is troubling her, she will let me know."

"So, I guess you are still planning to leave tomorrow?" she asked, then dropped her eyes for a second, but her tone was wistful.

"Yes. My mother wants to go home, as do I," he said, but he was having difficulty marshalling his thoughts. Kira was still holding on to his arm, and he laid his hand atop hers, pleased she allowed it.

"Oh," Kira said with obvious disappointment.

Not wanting to leave her yet, Jalil massaged her hand lightly with his thumb as he searched for something else to say and came up empty.

"Yes, um, uh, I guess I should let you go. You must finish packing for the trip." Kira blushed and abruptly withdrew her hand and averted her eyes.

Disappointed, Jalil was suddenly at a loss. The thought of leaving Kira was painful—it was a new feeling for him. But what could he do? Racking his brain, he had a sudden inspiration. "Kira, I am worried about my mother. It is a two-day ride to my kingdom, and she has had a shock. I expect Samira will try to look after her while we travel, but Samira is still recovering herself. Her head wound from being shot at during your kidnapping has healed well, but it was a close thing. I don't suppose…," his voice trailed off.

Kira's head snapped up, and her eyes widened. "Yes, Jalil?" she asked a little breathlessly.

"Would you consider coming home with us tomorrow? It would be a big help. Unless, of course, you have already made plans to travel to the coast. And of course, if you yourself are feeling up to it."

"Oh, I'm fine and have no other plans. I would love to go. I could ride by her side and keep an eye on her. But I need to let Sheik Ehsaan and Sheikha Issa know. I will go find them right now," she said with a smile, her eyes dancing with excitement.

Mesmerized, caught in her spell, Jalil unconsciously leaned forward, only catching himself at the last minute. He had to look away to break the spell.

"Well, Ehsaan is in the courtyard. You might catch him if you hurry." He glanced down the corridor. "Issa is probably in my mother's room."

Kira nodded, but a touch of worry returned to her face. "Jalil, do you think it will be all right with your mother?"

"Oh, I am sure she will not mind. She will be excited for you to join us. I will go speak with her now." Jalil's grin spread across his face. He was thinking it was he who would be more excited. But when he gazed into her shining eyes, and she blushed, he couldn't look away.

When he failed to move, Kira asked, "Is there anything else, Jalil?"

Startled, he stepped backward into the corridor. "No, um, I guess I need to speak with Nasira," he said somewhat lamely then paused. "Do you need any help packing?"

"No, thank you, Jalil. I do not have much. All I need is my pack and Amber. I will see you in the morning. Good night, my sheik." She smiled sweetly as she brushed past him and headed down the corridor.

Sighing, he watched her walk away, still savoring her parting smile, until she disappeared from sight. Turning, he strode toward his mother's room, but when he reached her door, he heard voices and decided he would speak with her in the morning. He knew she wouldn't have a problem having Kira join them. And maybe once they were safe in his kingdom, his mother would tell him exactly what made her faint, and he might also get to question Kira about the medallion. Feeling better than he had in weeks, Jalil went to finish his own packing, looking forward to the journey home.

***

After Jalil left the room, Nasira sighed, relieved that Issa had put a stop to Jalil's questions. She wasn't ready to talk to him just yet, not until she could confirm her suspicions. And she didn't want to wait until the morning to do so. Aware Issa was watching her intently but knowing her friend had noticed her reluctance to discuss what had happened, she waited for Issa to speak.

"Nasira, we have been friends for a long time, and you cannot fool me." Issa scooted her chair closer to the bed. "What is on your mind?"

"You were always so perceptive, Issa. Yes, there is something, and I need your help."

"What can I do?" Issa said.

"Could I speak with Adara before she goes to bed? Could you bring her to my room and have her bring Jabari's present?"

"Certainly. I will fetch her at once," Issa said.

"And I also need to speak with Samira and Saad. Could you send them to see me after Adara?" Nasira could tell Issa wanted to ask her why, but thankfully her friend merely nodded and went to fetch Adara.

Feeling nervous, she worked to calm her nerves. She had to find out if what she had seen was real. Her mind told her it couldn't be, but her heart said otherwise. Tired of lying in the bed, she rose and changed into a simple robe then sat at the table while she waited for Issa and Adara. When they arrived, Nasira's heart warmed when the young girl ran forward and hugged her.

"Are you doing better, Sheikha? I was so worried." Adara was obviously upset.

"I am much better, thank you, but I want to apologize for ruining your celebration."

"Indeed, you did not! Do not even think such a thing. It was the best celebration ever. And did you see all the wonderful gifts I received? But Sheik Jalil's was the best! I cannot wait to train my Hiba. She will be the greatest horse in my kingdom."

"Better than Shar?" Nasira teased.

"Well, at least as good, I think. And perhaps Father will let me breed her to Shar someday. Oh, would not that be wonderful?" Adara's eyes shone with excitement at the thought.

"Yes, it certainly would. And the sheik and I are so happy you like your gift, but you received another special, one from Jabari."

"Oh, yes, my beautiful dagger. Mother said you wanted to see it."

"If you do not mind?"

"Of course I do not mind, Sheikha," Adara said and pulled the dagger from the hidden pocket in her robe and held it out.

Nasira took it hesitantly, almost afraid to touch it, and her vision narrowed to exclude everything but the jeweled object in her hand. Running a finger over the familiar embossed gold and turquoise stones, she watched the light dance and sparkle on the embedded yellow gems, the same as those found on Akeem's medallion. Her heart raced, and she took a deep breath then pulled the blade from its sheath, turning it toward the light to scrutinize its gleaming surface.

Inscribed on the blade just below the hilt was the telltale mark, one Akeem had put there just for her—a tiny, running horse. She opened her mouth to say something but found she couldn't speak. A single tear fell from her eye, and she slowly slipped the blade back into its sheath and dropped her head.

When she looked up, Nasira saw Adara staring at her with alarm. "What is wrong? Do you not like it?"

"Oh, Adara, nothing is wrong, nothing at all. Thank you for showing me Jabari's gift. It is truly magnificent. It's just that I had one like it once, and I treasured it. I received mine as a gift, too."

"What happened to yours?"

"I lost it a long time ago. So, Adara, be very careful with your dagger. Keep it close to you, and when you are not wearing it, keep it in a safe place. But Adara, I would like to ask you a favor. Do you mind if I borrow this for a little longer tonight? I promise to give it back to your mother before I go to bed."

"Certainly, Sheikha Nasira, and I hope you feel better. Maybe we can come visit you next time."

"I will look forward to that. Now your mother said you need to get to bed if you are going to get up early to see us off. I will see you in the morning."

"Thank you, Sheikha Nasira. Come, Mother." Adara waved and smiled as she took Issa by the hand and tugged her toward the door.

"Nasira, I will let Saad and Samira know you are ready to talk to them," Issa called back over her shoulder.

"Thank you, Issa," Nasira said with a low chuckle. Adara was truly a force of nature.

When Saad and Samira arrived at her door, looking decidedly uncomfortable, Nasira waved them in and gestured to the chairs across from her. She hastened to put them at ease. "Thank you for coming. Though we will be on the road together tomorrow, I needed to talk with you both in private."

They looked slightly alarmed at her words and even more so when Nasira laid the dagger on the table.

"Jabari's dagger!" Samira exclaimed.

"Yes. I asked Adara if I could borrow it. Can you tell me how Jabari came to have it?"

Saad exchanged a worried look with Samira, then blurted out, "He did not steal it, Sheikha!"

"No, Saad, I would not think that of Jabari," Nasira said with assurance, but when he failed to continue, she waited, curious why they kept looking at each other, as if unsure what to say.

Finally Saad spoke. "We found it."

"I see. Do you remember where?" Nasira leaned forward in anticipation.

"I think it was at an oasis on our northern route," Saad said, fidgeting in his seat. "We do not travel that road anymore." He cast a warning glance at Samira, who nodded but remained silent.

Nasira sensed she was making the other woman uncomfortable, but she had to know more. "Exactly how long ago did you find it?"

"Oh, a long time, maybe eleven or twelve years, at least," Saad said, looking at Samira again as if for confirmation.

Samira finally spoke. "Yes, my husband, I think that is right," she said, still keeping her eyes averted.

"Hmm. Eleven or twelve years, you say? That is a long time indeed," Nasira said and watched them carefully. They nodded and seemed to relax until she shocked them with her next words. "Well, I know who this dagger belongs to."

Eyes wide, the couple leaned forward, gripping the arms of their chairs, and asked in unison, "Who?"

"Me," Nasira answered, relaxing back in her chair.

"What?" they exclaimed at the same time.

"Yes. That is why I fainted. I recognized it, but I have not seen it for thirteen years. Until tonight, I thought it lost forever."

"But how can you tell?" Saad sat back with a skeptical expression.

Nasira calmly picked up the dagger, pulled the blade from its sheath, and held it to the flickering light, pointing to the running horse engraved just beneath the handle. "Because this is the mark my husband, Sheik Akeem, placed on it before he gave it to me on the birth of our son Talib. But someone stole the dagger many years ago. So, you see, that is why I wanted to know how it ended up with Jabari." She watched them closely now.

Samira took the dagger and studied the blade, running her finger over the engraving. "I never noticed this. I wonder how I missed it," she said, but her hands shook slightly as she carefully laid it back on the table. She took a deep breath and glanced at Saad. When he nodded, she continued. "We found the dagger wrapped in an old robe beside the oasis. When our son, Jabari, was old enough, we gave it to him because it was easy to carry and just the right size for him to use for protection." Samira kept her eyes on the dagger and wouldn't look at Nasira.

Saad chimed in, "Sheikha, if what you said is true, then you are its rightful owner, and Adara must give it back."

Nasira had listened to their explanation and sensed something about their story was off but decided it was too late to solve the mystery that night. "I appreciate your saying that, Saad. This dagger is most precious to me, and I have missed it all these many years. Not for its gold and jewels, but as a link to my beloved husband, Akeem. I believe it is kismet. This dagger ended up with someone who needed it and deserved it, if only to be given to another who may need it and certainly deserves it. I can honestly say I am proud that Jabari bore it for many years and even happier it will now be part of Adara's life. It will be a new link between your family and mine. I will share this story with Issa and will leave it to you to share with Jabari. Thank you both for your honesty, but now I must say good night, or I fear I will never be able to stay on my camel tomorrow," she said, laughing lightly, hoping to ease the obvious tension she saw on their faces.

After they departed, she decided she'd wait and share the details with Issa in the morning but would wait until she got home to tell Jalil and her daughters. Exhausted, she returned to the comfort of her bed. She hoped her daughters had gone to bed but knew somehow they were undoubtedly still awake in Adara's chambers, playing with Gigi. Nasira sighed, knowing that one day there would likely be a little sand cat running around in her house, too.

***

As Nasira drifted off to sleep, Samira and Saad finished their packing in silence, each wrapped in their own thoughts, remembering that fateful night long ago. Saad remembered the slain bodies all dressed in black, and Samira remembered the feeble cries of the baby left to die. Samira's hands began shaking, and when she felt Saad's powerful arms surround her, she sobbed. Each knew what the other was thinking—they hadn't told Nasira about the baby.

CHAPTER 8

As the travelers assembled at sunrise, Nasira watched Kira say goodbye to Issa, Adara, and Fatima. The women shared a few tears while they hugged, and she saw how close Kira had grown to Ehsaan's family. As Jalil led the group toward the pass, Nasira glanced back to see her friends waving goodbye from the steps. Wiping her own tears, she forced herself to look away, knowing she was leaving her treasured dagger behind with Adara. It was a hard decision, but in her heart, she felt it was the right thing to do. She had shared the details of the dagger's origin with Issa, who had also insisted it be returned to her. But Nasira shared her belief as to its destiny and convinced Issa to accept it. Once they cleared the pass and headed east toward home, Nasira relaxed and settled in to enjoy the journey.

Glancing over at Kira, she saw her riding Amber, looking comfortable, and she shared a smile with her. Jalil had approached her before sunrise to make sure she didn't object to Kira coming home with them, and Nasira assured him Kira was more than welcome. She knew Jalil thought she needed to be watched after her fainting incident and found it amusing he had asked Kira to accompany them, supposedly for just that reason. But since Samira was more than capable of helping her, Nasira was excited to think Jalil had other motives for inviting Kira. And when she noticed Jalil glancing back often at Kira, she thought there might be hope for Jalil after all.

While Jalil rode up front in the lead, she watched Jabari dashing about on Sarii, much to the amusement of the men. Nasira laughed at his antics. He never stayed in one place long enough before he would laugh and dash away. He was a joy. But when he spoke to her, and she saw his shining silver eyes, she felt a strange sense of familiarity and couldn't fathom why. Jabari was a mystery she hoped one day to solve.

All in all, it was a pleasant journey, and they proceeded at a leisurely pace, spending only one night under the stars. Nasira had forgotten how much she enjoyed traveling and vowed she wouldn't wait so long to visit her dear friend, Issa, again.

The sun was low in the sky when she heard the gunshots in their pass, announcing their arrival. Tired and dusty, she urged her camel forward, pleased to see Fahad and Sakhr waiting for them on the steps.

Fahad ran forward to greet her. "Welcome home, my sheikha." He bowed then stepped closer.

"Thank you, Fahad. It is good to be back," she said, smiling and placing her hands on his sturdy shoulders as he helped her dismount.

"How was the journey?" he asked as he untied her bags and motioned for a man to take the camel.

"All went well. Adara's feast was most enjoyable," she said but chose not to mention either her fainting spell or the cause of it. She knew Fahad would be most interested in learning the fate of her stolen dagger, but that could wait for a more private setting. "Was everything all right here?"

"Yes," he said, but his voice seemed to falter.

She looked at him and saw his eyes flicker. Nasira had known Fahad for over thirty years and had learned to read him. He could often communicate his thoughts to her with just a glance. "Do you have something to discuss?" she said.

"I have a few things to go over with you and the sheik, but it is not urgent. Perhaps we can get together tomorrow," he said, his voice low as he carried her bags to the steps.

"I will look forward to that. I also have some things to discuss."

"Thank you, my sheikha," he said formally and turned away then paused, looking uncertain.

"Fahad, is there something else?" She was curious.

"Um, no, not really…I am just glad you are home, safe and sound," he said in a husky voice. He was staring at her intently, and Nasira's eyes widened. But before she could respond, a servant appeared and took her bags, and Fahad bowed low and joined the men assembled by Jalil.

"Thank you, Fahad," she whispered as he walked away. Both amused and flattered, she was making her way indoors when she spotted Kira hugging Amber's neck. As she watched, they touched foreheads, and Nasira could see her talking to the horse but couldn't make out the words. Kira looked tired and forlorn, and a little lost. In the general chaos of the homecoming, she had forgotten about Kira. Instantly concerned, Nasira walked over to speak with her. "Kira, I would like for you to stay in the guest wing. Would that be all right with you?"

Kira smiled. "Yes, Sheikha, I would be honored to be your guest, but first, I need to take care of Amber."

Nasira, seeing an opportunity, called out to Jalil, who was speaking with Sakhr. As Sakhr led Mirage toward the stables, Jalil walked over but kept his distance from Amber. "Yes, Sheikha?" Jalil said, his eyes flickering toward Kira.

"Jalil, Kira may need help with her horse. What do you suggest?"

"Kira, I will be glad to help you with Amber," he said eagerly.

Nasira watched Kira closely, pleased to see Kira blushing.

"Thank you, Sheik Jalil, but I don't think Amber will let you," Kira said softly.

Jalil stepped closer but kept a wary eye on Amber, who appeared to be watching him. "I think she will understand that I only want to help."

Kira was biting her lip and looked torn. Nasira held her breath but sighed with relief when Kira said, "I... I guess you could try."

Nodding, Jalil turned to face Amber and held out his hand. Amber sniffed his palm and raised her nose to his face, blowing gently, then allowed him to run his hand over her cheek and down her arched neck. When he slid his hand under her mane, Nasira saw him pause. Lifting the silvery golden hair, Jalil scowled when he saw the ragged scar. He shot a questioning glance at Kira, but she remained silent. Moving to Amber's side, he deftly released the small saddle, a parting gift from Ehsaan to Kira, and pulled it from Amber's back. The golden horse shook all over, obviously happy to have it gone.

Nasira had paid little attention to Amber during their journey home. But seeing how Jalil stared at the horse, Nasira knew she must be special. She continued to watch Jalil examine her, and her eyes widened when she saw the scars on Amber's hip. Jalil's smile vanished. His eyes cut to Kira again, as if seeking an explanation, but Kira merely shrugged and said nothing.

His brow furrowed, Jalil traced the four deep grooves lightly with his fingertips, but when Amber flinched slightly, he immediately withdrew his hand. Then he inhaled sharply, and Nasira figured he must have suddenly figured it out. She already had. Only one thing could have made those marks. *Lion!* There could be no doubt, and she looked at Amber with new respect.

Seeing Kira's shoulders drooping, Nasira called to Jalil, "Jalil, I think Kira is tired, and I expect Amber is as well."

He nodded and stroked Amber's face once more, whispering words that only Amber could hear, and Amber nodded her head as if in agreement. Then he turned to the assembled men and made a formal announcement. "This horse is known as Amber, and she belongs to the woman known as Kira." He gestured toward Kira. "She may run free in my lands, and no one shall touch her." Then Jalil stepped back, and Amber whinnied and galloped toward the pasture, passing Kira without stopping. A tribesman ran to open the gate, but Amber ignored him and sailed effortlessly over the fence. When Kira turned, Nasira saw her trying to hide her tears.

Jalil must have also seen her tears because he approached Kira, but Nasira stepped in front of him. "Not now," she mouthed silently. Seeing the puzzlement on her son's face, Nasira could only shake her head. *Sometimes men are so dense. How can they be so smart and yet not?* He looked as if he was going to say something then sighed, picked up Kira's saddle, and carried it to the stable.

Nasira wasn't entirely sure, but she had an idea why Kira was upset. Until now, Jabari was the only person besides Kira that Amber would tolerate. Why Amber had suddenly changed her mind was a mystery, but Nasira could see it had upset Kira. She wanted to help but knew it could wait until Kira was ready to talk about it. And they would have plenty of time. Nasira would make sure of that.

After showing Kira to her room and making sure she was comfortable, Nasira stopped by to check on Akilah and Lina. Satisfied they were getting ready for bed, she left and went back outside to check on Samira. As she crossed the compound, she glanced up, captivated by the sky above. It had deepened to a dark blue, and thousands of stars emerged in chaotic swirls. The moon had yet to rise, but large torches cast dancing fingers of light, illuminating the low walls surrounding her house. Beyond, she could see tiny flickers from the many firepits that warmed their warriors' tents. She paused and listened to the comforting sounds of home carried upon the breeze—distant neighing, muted conversation, and laughter. But the rising wind nipped at her hem, and the temperature was dropping, so she picked up her pace.

"Come in, Sheikha," Samira said when she opened the door.

"Thank you," Nasira said, stepping into the cozy room. A fire already burned in the small fireplace, but Samira was still in the middle of unpacking. "Oh, I see you haven't had time to settle in. I could come back tomorrow…"

"No, please, stay. I was about to fix a cup of tea. Will you join me?" Samira cleared one end of her table and gestured toward a chair.

Nasira nodded and waited for Samira to join her before speaking. "I wanted to see how you were doing. Are you having any headaches or difficulty seeing?" Nasira was concerned. Head wounds were dangerous, and Samira had suffered a bad one the day of Kira's kidnapping.

"No, Sheikha." Samira said with assurance.

Nasira was vastly relieved. "Well, I am glad to hear it. But you should rest for a few days, just to be sure."

"I will take it easy, but I am ready to get back to work." Samira was referring to the weaving projects she did as her contribution to the tribe.

"Samira, I am so glad you and Saad chose to stay with us. Saad has been a great help to Jalil, and your work is beautiful. Thank you for joining our tribe."

"Oh, Sheikha, it is us that should thank you. Living here is a dream come true. We will work hard to deserve your kindness," Samira said, her eyes brimming.

"It is our pleasure, Samira. Your family is a great addition to our tribe. Even Jabari contributes," Nasira said.

"I am glad Jalil has put him to work. Jabari is an energetic boy and needs something besides that horse to occupy his mind," Samira said with a chuckle.

"Indeed, he does." Nasira grinned then changed the subject. "Samira, I am worried about Kira. Has she said anything to you about what happened to her at Qadir's?"

"No, Sheikha, she has not spoken a word," Samira said, her face reflecting her concern. "I wanted to question her, but Sheikha Issa suggested we wait and give Kira more time. If Kira was drugged, like Fatima said, it may be some time before she remembers. But I am afraid of what she will do when she does." Samira was visibly upset.

Nasira laid a comforting hand on Samira's arm. "I must agree with Sheikha Issa, but I also think this is something Kira needs to face, sooner rather than later."

Samira nodded in agreement, and the two women continued to share their thoughts, enjoying each other's company and the warmth of the fire. But when Nasira saw Samira growing tired, she thanked her for the tea and returned to the house.

***

While Nasira was visiting with Samira, Kira sat on her bed feeling overwhelmed. Seeing Amber allowing Jalil to handle her had filled her with dismay and a little jealousy. She wondered what Jalil has said to her. When Amber ran past her without stopping, Kira felt betrayed. *Perhaps Amber doesn't need me anymore?* It was a depressing thought, even though she knew she should be happy for Amber. Kira would have to leave her behind when she returned to America.

Too tired to give it further thought, Kira cleared her mind. All she wanted to do was get under the covers and forget her troubles for the night. Sighing, she opened her old travel bag and pulled out her meager supply of clothes along with her father's money belt and laid them on the bed. When she saw her father's tattered shirt wadded up in the bottom, she pulled it out, thinking to check on her medallion. When she unrolled the fabric, the gold chain that came with the medallion her father bought in Cairo spilled onto the bed. She had taken to wearing the medallion on a leather cord so as not to draw attention. But there was no sign of the medallion, and she panicked. *Where is it?* Not thinking clearly, she felt her neck frantically, but then she remembered Qadir holding the medallion up to her and asking where she got it. *Qadir took it from me! How did I forget that?* As she stared at the meager reminders of her former life, all the tears she hadn't cried since the night at Qadir's came pouring out. She was so distraught that she didn't hear Nasira come into the room.

"Kira? Kira, what is wrong?" Nasira's voice penetrated her deep grief, but Kira didn't lift her head until she felt someone sit down beside her and lay a soft hand on her shoulder.

When she looked up, Nasira opened her arms, and Kira fell into her hug and cried out, "Oh, Sheikha, what has happened to me? Why did he do that to me?" Nasira remained silent and rocked her gently as Kira continued to cry.

Finally, her sobs dwindled, and sniffling and ashamed, Kira raised her red, puffy face. "Sheikha, I am sorry. I couldn't help myself."

"Kira, you do not have to apologize. After all you have been through, you needed to let it out. Now, come, let's get you into bed. You need your rest." Nasira fetched Kira a cool damp towel to wipe her tear-stained face, then found a soft, silk tunic for her to sleep in. When Kira allowed Nasira to help her undress, she heard Nasira gasp and realized she must have seen the scars. Embarrassed by the evidence of her downfall, Kira quickly donned the tunic and slid into bed.

Nasira said nothing as she covered Kira with a blanket and tucked her in. But when she turned to leave, Kira grabbed her hand.

"What is it, Kira?"

Kira looked up at her and hesitated. She didn't want her to go but didn't know what to say. She only knew she needed to talk to someone. "Sheikha, I...I..."

Nasira's face softened with understanding. She sat back down on the bed, and Kira moved over to give her room. Squeezing her hand, Nasira spoke gently, "Kira, dear, I truly believe you need to talk about what happened."

That was exactly what Kira wanted to do, but she was afraid. Nasira must have seen her fear and ran a soothing hand down the side of Kira's face then cradled her cheek in her hand like a mother comforting her child. It had been forever since Kira felt a mother's touch, but she shivered, unable to forget Qadir's touch.

"I don't know if I can," Kira said, struggling not to start crying again

"Kira, you need to try. It will only get worse if you hold it in. What can you remember?"

Seeing the compassion in Nasira's eyes and hearing the truth in her voice, Kira swallowed hard and steeled herself for what she had to do. With a quick prayer, she tried to piece together what had happened the night of her kidnapping. "Well, I remember being locked in a small room. Then Qadir came in and made threats. He tore my clothes then hit me." Kira shuddered, remembering the look in his eyes when he tore her father's medallion from her neck. But she couldn't bring herself to reveal the medallion to Nasira and continued, "Then he left, and that's when an old woman came and took me to the harem bathing chamber. They took my clothes, bathed me, and tried to remove the dye from my skin." Kira's heart raced as the memories became clearer. "I tried to fight. I really did! But there were too many of them." She clutched Nasira's hand in desperation.

"You did nothing wrong, Kira. This was not your fault," Nasira said soothingly, and Kira relaxed her grip. Nasira gave her a moment before saying, "What happened next?"

Kira inhaled sharply, and she felt a surge of anger at the memory of seeing her father's mistress in Qadir's harem bath. "I saw Cassie!"

"Cassie?"

Kira had forgotten that Nasira had little knowledge of how she had come to their country and the events that followed the plane crash. "Yes, Cassie, uh, Cassandra Miller. She was on the plane with me when it crashed. But she left me in the desert, and I thought she had died there. I don't know how she came to be at Qadir's." Kira was worried about having to explain more about Cassie, but luckily Nasira didn't seem to be interested in her.

"So, what happened after you saw her?"

"They dressed me up, and that's when I met Fatima. She was so kind. She explained enough so I knew what was going to happen. And then the guards took me back to the small room, and the old woman told me I had to do whatever Qadir said, and she gave me something to drink. She said it would help."

"Do you know what it was?" Nasira said with narrowed eyes.

"No, no. It tasted like wine, but it was a little bitter and very sweet." Kira grimaced at the memory.

"Hmm, that sounds familiar. Kira, I am a healer, and what you described sounds like a potion, a powerful one, one that is dangerous if not used correctly."

Uncomfortable with what she still had to reveal, Kira coughed lightly, sending Nasira to fetch her a drink of water. Kira drank slowly in order to delay what was coming, but she knew she needed to tell it all. It was time.

Nasira must have sensed her thoughts. "What happened with Qadir?" Nasira said gently.

"They took me to his chambers and he... he..." Kira's face twisted as painful memories flooded her mind, and embarrassed, she looked away. When Nasira once again took her hand, Kira felt something shift deep inside, and the words rushed from her mouth like water through a broken dam. "He tied me up! And he beat me! He beat me and beat me, and I couldn't stop him! And he laughed and laughed. And he flaunted himself... he was naked." She clenched her eyes tightly and began shaking. "He was furious about the medallion, and he kept asking me about it." In her haste to tell the distasteful tale, Kira forgot that she'd wanted to keep the medallion a secret.

Luckily for Kira, Nasira didn't seem to notice and asked softly, "Did he touch you, Kira?"

Kira fell silent for a moment. Then the truth spilled out. "Oh, yes, Sheikha. It was horrible! He touched me all over then he touched me..." Kira's eyes flickered downward as she was filled with shame.

Nasira closed her eyes and seemed to collect herself. Then she asked the question Kira had been dreading. "Kira, can you tell me if he took you—as a man takes a woman?"

"Yes!" Kira said. The memory of that night festered in her mind, but talking to Nasira somehow lessened its hold on her, encouraging

Kira to tell the whole sordid truth. "He ruined me, and I couldn't stop him. Fatima saw the evidence, and she showed it to me. The stains..." Kira rolled over, away from Nasira, unable to stop the tears.

Nasira gently rubbed Kira's shoulders. "I imagined that was the case. I am so sorry." Her voice hardened when she spoke again. "Qadir was evil, and he deserved what happened to him!"

Kira's crying stopped abruptly at Nasira's tone and words. She rolled back over to look at her. "Did anyone ever figure out who killed him?"

"The rumor is that you did," Nasira said matter-of-factly.

"No, Sheikha! No, I didn't...I couldn't, I wouldn't. You know that don't you?" Kira was stunned. She had certainly wished him dead that night, but she was certain she didn't kill him. Except she had no memory of what happened between passing out in Qadir's bed and waking up in his harem pool. Could she have done the deed? But Nasira's next words put her at ease.

"Don't worry, I believe you, and anyone who knows you, will believe you. And Fatima explained how she had to untie you from his bed. You could not have done it."

"Thank you for believing in me," Kira said and closed her eyes, exhausted from having to relive the experience but relieved to have confirmation she had not done the deed.

Nasira must have sensed how tired she was. "Kira, we will not speak of this again unless you wish it. But I want you to know that you are safe here, and we will protect you. Now rest and let me know if you have any pain or need anything. There is a guard posted by the entrance to your corridor. Ask him to call me if you need me," she said with a gentle smile.

"Thank you, Sheikha. Thank you for everything," Kira said gratefully.

Nasira nodded, and after refilling Kira's cup, she left the room.

Kira lay quietly, thinking over their conversation. Knowing Nasira believed in her went a long way to restoring her self-confidence, as well as ease some of her shame. The more she thought about, the more she agreed with Nasira. She had done her best. Unfortunately, it hadn't been enough to save her. At least not then. Sighing, she closed her eyes, said a quick prayer, and allowed her mind to rest. She drifted off to sleep, lulled by the whisper of the night wind through her shutters, carrying the ever present scent of sand.

CHAPTER 9

Jalil had been looking for his mother in the guest wing when he heard crying coming from one room. Alarmed, he peeked inside but froze at the sight of his mother and Kira on the bed. Neither seemed to notice him. Nasira held Kira while Kira sobbed harshly. Aware he was witnessing a very private moment, he'd silently backed out of the room, closing the door quietly. Not wanting to interrupt but desperate to find out what was wrong, he stopped to listen outside the doorway with his back pressed against the wall.

Kira's heart rending sobs reminded him of his mother's, the day he brought his father's body home—he could still hear her crying, her heart broken. He frowned as he listened to Kira's cries of anguish and tried not to think of the implications of what Qadir had done.

After what seemed like an eternity, Kira's sobbing faded until all he heard was his mother's soft voice as she soothed the distraught girl. Realizing he shouldn't be eavesdropping and knowing it was not the time to ask questions about the medallion, he slipped away. After a long soak in his pool, he sat down to consume a light supper before retiring to his bed. But when he could finally fall asleep, he was still worried about Kira.

The next morning, he woke strangely refreshed. He still felt the exhilaration of having won the Tri-Annual Race that year and the relief that his greatest enemy was destroyed. But he'd also been plagued by drama until now. He was finally free to concentrate on the things that mattered most—his family, his herd, and his tribe. Eager to get back to his normal routine, he donned a simple tunic and sandals and went to check on Mirage.

Finding all was well in the stables, he returned to the house to join his mother and sisters for the morning meal. While his sisters prattled on, sharing their favorite memories of Adara's celebration, he exchanged a look with his mother, signaling he wanted to talk with her privately. When they finished their meal, Akilah and Lina begged to visit Kira, and Nasira relented but warned them not to distress her or stay too long. The girls surprised Jalil when they both hugged him fiercely before dashing from the room.

Nasira must have noticed his expression. "They were very upset when you got shot during the race. I don't think they are over it yet. You know they love you very much."

"I know. And I love them," he said seriously then hesitated, unsure how to ask the questions that were on his mind.

Nasira seemed to sense his consternation and waited a moment before speaking. "What is troubling you?"

"You know me too well, Mother. The fact is, I need to confess something." Jalil pushed his plate aside.

Nasira set her cup down and waited for him to speak.

Taking a deep breath, Jalil took the plunge. "I was looking for you last night. I did not mean to eavesdrop, but I heard Kira crying, and I saw you with her. Can you tell me why she was so upset?"

"Jalil, after what she has been through, you have to ask?!" A protective fire burned in her eyes.

Jalil hung his head. "I am sorry. But I do not want to make assumptions. Can you tell me, are her wounds healing?"

Nasira seemed appeased. In a softer tone, she said, "Yes, from what I can tell, but it is the wounds we cannot see that I am worried about."

Jalil shifted uncomfortably in his chair. "Mother, I have not told you everything I saw that night at Qadir's because I dislike thinking about it. It was obvious he restrained her and…." Jalil had to stop for a second when he felt a surge of fury remembering the bloody whips and the cords on the bed. "I do not understand men like him. I do not know all of what he did to her, but I do know he deserved to die."

Nasira agreed wholeheartedly. "Yes, Jalil. I have seen the evidence of her physical torment, and there is no doubt Qadir deserved to die."

"Well, at least she will not have to suffer his child," he said, surprised at how good it made him feel.

"Yes, thank Allah," Nasira agreed.

"Do you think she will ever be able to put it behind her?"

"I hope so, but until then, all we can do is treat her with kindness and give her time to decide what she wants to do. She is also feeling the loss of her new family now that Saad and Samira are setting up a permanent home here. I believe Kira feels like everyone has abandoned her."

"I think I understand, but I have questions about the medallion that only she can answer."

"Yes, I've been thinking about it. Do you believe what that woman, Cassie, said?"

"She sounded very certain, but I do not know if I can believe her. From all accounts, she is a deceitful creature," Jalil said.

"But if what she said is true, and Kira's father bought it in Cairo, how did it get there?" Nasira said, looking perplexed.

"I do not know, and I have not asked Kira about it yet. Mother, I must find out…I have to know."

"Yes, my son, I understand. I too wish to know. Perhaps if we give Kira a few days, she might be open to talking with us. But I think it would be best if you do not talk to her by yourself. She might be more comfortable if we all sat down together."

"Is she not comfortable with me alone? Is that why she acted so strangely when we arrived last night?" Jalil felt taken aback. He prided himself on his ability to read people and hated to admit he hadn't understood Kira's reaction to him.

Nasira put a hand on his arm. "Jalil, you must understand how her life has changed. She lost her father, and, maybe now, her adoptive family. She got lost in the desert and mauled by a lion. She was kidnapped and beaten, and worse, by a horrible man. And she has no way to get home. Amber is all she has left that she can call her own. I think seeing you with Amber and how Amber responded to you may have been the last straw. I believe Kira fears she may have also lost Amber now, and I am afraid she might never fully recover. And Jalil, it is up to us to make sure she does."

Jalil felt a rush of many emotions. "I am sorry about Amber, but I meant no harm. She is an amazing horse, and I wanted her to trust me. I will do as you say and use all in my power to help Kira. And I promise to give her time. Will you let me know when you think she is strong enough?"

"I will, my son, but how long will she be staying with us?"

"Um, well, I do not know. I just asked her to travel with us…to look after you." Jalil smiled awkwardly.

"Jalil, what were you thinking? I will find a time to talk to her after she has a chance to settle in. But I think she should stay with us for as long as she likes," Nasira said with a knowing smile.

"That is a great idea," Jalil said, returning her smile. "Thank you. Now, I need to check on the herd. I will see you at the evening meal." He leaned over and kissed her on the forehead and strode from the room, praying he could talk to Kira soon.

CHAPTER 10

A few days later, Kira awoke in the middle of the night with mild cramps. Her monthly cycle was right on time, her second since that horrible night with Qadir. Rising, she found a few items she had brought with her from Ehsaan's, and seeing it was still dark out, she snuck back into bed to wait for the sun. But when she fell back to sleep, she had a dream, one she hadn't had since coming to Arabia. The tribal outpost back home in America was just as she remembered it. Packed with every imaginable item, from blankets to farm implements, it served as a trading post, mail drop, and general meeting place. The counter was lined with colorful pottery bowls, and baskets and hats hung from the rafters overhead. Her mother stood behind a mammoth cash register perched like a bronzed gargoyle on one end of the counter, and Kira could even hear her humming wordlessly. As Kira was arranging a stack of tribal blankets on a nearby table, a young woman entered the store, her baby wrapped and supported in a sling to her side.

While the woman spoke with her mother, Kira studied the baby, marveling at the perfection of his skin and the length of his eye lashes. A tuft of glossy black hair had escaped from beneath his swaddling, and as she stared at him, his eyes suddenly popped open. She caught her breath, captured by his shiny black eyes, alive with curiosity. And when his little bow mouth spread into a huge grin, she felt the strangest urge to take him in her arms. It was much like how she felt with newborn puppies and horses, but so much stronger.

The sudden loud clunk and ringing of the old cash register startled her and the baby. His smile vanished, and his eyes narrowed. Kira almost reached out to soothe him, but his mother quickly reached down and caressed his plump cheek. He instantly settled, and he looked up at her expectantly. The mother smiled and whispered Zuni words of love. The baby's smile returned, and Kira also felt warm and happy. So strange. At that moment, Kira looked up and saw her mother watching her with a secret smile. Embarrassed, and not knowing why, Kira turned to resume folding and staking her blankets.

When she woke again, she glanced up and watched the play of light on the ceiling from the sun shining through her window. It had been a short dream, but it left her with mixed emotions and longing for a mother's touch. Remembering the baby, she wondered what she would have done if she had gotten pregnant by Qadir. Waiting for her cycle at Ehsaan's had been frightening, and her relief had almost been palpable. Yet, when it happened, she had also been depressed because she knew in her heart she still wanted children. And she also knew she would have wanted that child too, even though it would have been Qadir's. It was confusing and depressing, made worse because she was alone.

Ever since the plane crash, she had been on the move, constantly searching for a way home. But now that she thought about it, she had really been searching for a family of her own. And not just since the wreck, but since she lost her mother when she was ten. In a way, she had lost her father at the same time, long before the plane wreck. *Why God? What am I doing here? What is your plan for me?* When she heard no answer, she sighed. Apparently, she would have to wait for her answers. Feeling depressed remembering her mother and in need of a mother's counsel, as well as more supplies for her cycle, she went in search of Samira, the only mother she had now. Throwing on some clothes, she hurried across the compound to Samira's house. When she knocked on the door, Samira quickly appeared.

"Kira, what a pleasant surprise. Please, come in."

"Thank you," Kira said as she entered the small front room.

"Come, sit. Let me fix you something to drink," Samira said, gesturing to her small table. Kira nodded and settled at the table but was hesitant to voice her worries and searched for something to talk about. "I love your house," she said, studying the soft yellow stucco walls. Several small woven pieces hung on one wall, adding to the overall feeling of home. Kira ran her hand lightly over the carved table and admired the four sturdy chairs accompanying it.

"Oh, Kira, I do too! Sheik Jalil gave us the furniture and Nasira gave us sheets and towels and even a rug," Samira said, proudly pointing to the floor.

Kira admired everything about the house. It was much simpler than the guest room she was in, but it was far better. It was a home. Thinking of home, she remembered Samira's dreams and had to ask, "So, you and Saad are comfortable here?"

"Oh yes! Saad loves working with the sheik, and Jabari has his own tent by the stables. He is working with Sakhr. Yes, it is everything I wished for. Except for one other thing. And we are working on that." Samira chuckled and winked.

Kira's heart swelled with joy for her, but at the same time, she felt a stab of jealousy. A home and a husband…and maybe a child. Her face fell, and Samira must have noticed because she looked suddenly worried.

"Kira, I do not wish to invade your privacy, but I must ask. Have you had your cycle yet?"

Startled, Kira looked up, but seeing no censure in Samira's face, she nodded. "Yes, I had one at Ehsaan's and am having my second one now."

"Thank Allah," Samira said fervently.

Hearing the relief in Samira's voice, Kira understood her response. No one but Issa knew that she'd had a monthly while at Ehsaan's. Samira must have assumed she might be pregnant. Kira hurried to explain. "I'm sorry I didn't let you know. But I had no way to tell you."

"Oh, do not worry. We will talk no more about it."

"I was hoping you had some extra supplies?"

"Of course. Wait here," she said and disappeared into another room. In a few minutes, she returned with a cloth bag and placed it on the table.

"Thank you," Kira said.

"Now, tell me. How are you feeling?"

"Well, actually, I feel very good."

"Have you told Nasira yet?"

"No."

"Kira, do me a favor and tell her as soon as possible. I know she will want to know because she cares about you too."

"All right, Samira, I will," Kira said, taking a deep breath. But now she was worried how in the world she could approach Nasira. Samira must have noticed her worry as she immediately changed the subject.

"Kira, do you like the wall hangings? I made them," she said with obvious pride.

Diverted, Kira gazed at the hangings, admiring the way the sunlight through the window set the bright colors ablaze. "Really? They're beautiful, but I always knew you were talented."

"Thank you. Nasira has invited me to join her in weaving the cloth for the garments she sells. Look." Samira pointed to the far corner.

Kira had noticed the small loom by the window. "Oh, that is wonderful," she said wistfully.

Samira saw Kira's pensive stare. "Kira, do you know how long you will stay?"

"No, Samira. Actually, Sheik Jalil only asked me to come because he wanted me to watch over Nasira during the journey. So, I really don't know. But frankly, I could use something to do," she said.

"You must speak to the sheikha. I am sure she can find something for you to do."

"Well, I didn't want to bother her."

"Oh, Kira, it would not be a bother. I know she would want to help you. She admires you. I think you should go see her at once. You have so many talents. You make beautiful baskets, you sew well, and you would be an excellent teacher. Jabari is much better at English after working with you. Maybe you could teach English?"

Kira's face brightened at the thought. She could teach other subjects too—like math and science. And even engineering. Suddenly energized, she rose to her feet. "You are right, Samira. I never thought about that. I will talk to the sheikha."

Samara also stood with a laugh. "I am glad I could be of help. But could you maybe sit just for another minute and visit? We have not been together for a long time. I would like to talk some more."

Kira sat back down and took Samira's hand. "Yes, I can take time. I have missed you so much. Tell me more about your weaving."

Samira's face lit up, and she launched into all the details of what her family had been doing since the fateful kidnapping. After an enjoyable hour, Kira finally bid her farewell and went in search of Nasira.

She found her in the main hall, talking with Fahad. Seeing that she was busy with her adviser, she hesitated but stopped when Nasira called to her.

"Kira, wait. I was looking for you. Do you have a moment to speak with me?"

Kira nodded but waited and watched as Nasira passed a scroll to Fahad. Fahad bowed to Nasira and nodded to Kira as he passed on his way from the room with a serious look on his face.

"Come, Kira. Please, sit." Nasira gestured to a seat next to her.

Kira bowed before taking a seat, feeling self-conscious. But seeing the kind smile on Nasira's face, she felt better and relaxed.

"I was going to send someone to find you. I was not sure if you might be out riding Amber," Nasira said, reaching for a pitcher of water to refill her glass. "Would you like something to drink?"

"No, thank you. I just left Samira's."

"Well, then, do you have everything you need? Is your room to your liking?"

"Oh, I am fine, sheikha. Although I wanted to talk to you too…about several things." Kira hesitated now, uncomfortable with what she needed to tell her. But seeing the patient look on Nasira's face, she took a deep breath. "I woke up this morning and have started my cycle." She blushed and waited for her response.

Nasira looked oddly guilty. "Kira, I must confess. Issa told me you had a cycle while staying with her. I did not want to ask, but personally, I am glad."

"I guess it would have been a terrible disgrace," Kira said averting her eyes, feeling ashamed in the sheikha's presence. Startled, Kira felt her hand being taken by Nasira, who then cupped her chin with the other hand, forcing her to look up.

"Kira, listen to me. I cannot stress this enough. What happened is not your fault. We do not choose for bad things to happen. But you can choose how you deal with them. Know this. It is done. It is in the past, and all that truly matters is the here and now. I do not judge you, and neither does anyone I know." Her voice was firm, but she was smiling.

Hearing the truth in her words, Kira sat up straighter. "Thank you, sheikha."

"You are welcome. But from now on, please call me Nasira in private."

"All right…Nasira." Kira grinned with new confidence, but when she remembered why she had sought to speak with her, she hesitated, and Nasira misunderstood.

"I expect you will need some supplies?"

"Oh, no Nasira. Samira had what I needed for now."

"Excellent, but just let me or a servant know anytime you need something," Nasira said.

"Thank you, I will."

"Was there something else you wanted to talk to me about?" Nasira looked curious.

"Well, I wasn't sure how long I would be here. Sheik Jalil didn't say." Kira held her breath, praying she wouldn't have to go back to Ehsaan's yet.

"Oh, I was hoping you could stay for a while. I've been wanting to speak to you about that, to make it clear you were welcome to stay as long as you wanted. And I am sure if Sheik Ehsaan finds a caravan or receives a message from your family, he will let us know. Would you like to stay longer?"

Kira was relieved and happy to hear the invitation. "Yes, I would love to stay. I mean, Amber is comfortable here, and I love seeing Jabari and Samira again. But I will have a lot of free time and would like to contribute to your tribe while I wait for word from Ehsaan," Kira said.

"I am so glad you brought it up. I was going to talk to you about that very thing. There are many things you can do to help. I expect you have greater skills besides weaving, though. Please tell me, what do you like to do?" Nasira sat back and folded her hands in her lap.

"Well, let's see. I can clean and cook. I make baskets, and I sew fairly well. At least Samira thinks so." Kira's brow furrowed as she thought about it.

"Kira, I have plenty of help with cleaning, cooking, and sewing." Nasira laughed. "And I am sure your baskets would come in handy, but I expect you have other talents, am I right?"

"Oh, well, then, um…" Kira paused, then the words just spilled out. "I spent many years in school in my country, and I know a great deal about English, math, and science. Maybe I could teach your people?"

Nasira sat up with a look of interest. "Now, that is an excellent idea. We have heard that more foreigners are coming into our country. In fact, I was just sending a message to Issa about selling garments in the port cities. But we do not have people who can properly negotiate with the foreigners. Saad could do it, but we dare not send him. We need him here. That being said, I am sure you could help by teaching our people English and the customs of the foreigners. And Jalil wants to educate the children as well. Would you consider teaching them, too?"

"Absolutely. I would enjoy that." Excited at the prospect, Kira could actually envision having classes with the adults and the children, and her mind spun with the possibilities.

But when Nasira mentioned teaching the children, she wore a troubled look.

"Nasira, is something bothering you?"

"What? Oh, no, Kira. I was just thinking about Jabari. I would like you to teach him all you can. He has great promise and needs to be able to navigate in this new complicated world," she said cryptically.

Kira wondered why Nasira was so focused on Jabari and could see the hint of worry remaining in her eyes. "Are you sure there's nothing else"

"Hmm? No, do not worry about me. I have to speak with Jalil about something and, well, it's nothing." She waved her hand dismissively then pelted Kira with questions about teaching, and soon they were immersed in Nasira's plan to educate her tribe. Kira was amazed at Nasira's determination to educate her people about the bigger world around them and secure their place in it. Kira felt nothing but pride knowing she could help Nasira realize her dreams. *Maybe I will realize mine too someday.* She smiled inwardly, dreaming of a brighter future for herself too.

CHAPTER 11

When Jalil passed by the main hall on his way to the stables, he saw Kira talking with his mother. They spoke in low tones, and he couldn't make out what they were saying, but based on their expressions, it was serious. But as much as he wanted to ask Kira more about the medallion he had recovered from Qadir, Jalil knew better than to interrupt. And his mother had promised to tell him when she thought it was appropriate, so he would just have to wait.

He had been watching Kira carefully since her arrival. He rarely spoke to her because whenever she was close, he became distracted. She was becoming more beautiful to him, and he couldn't help staring at her whenever she made her way around the compound.

Sometimes he secretly followed her, just so he could watch her riding with her hair loose and streaming behind her. At those times, he felt a tightening in his body and a yearning to touch and hold her. Frustrated, his rides back were uncomfortable, and made more so by Mirage. His stallion seemed to sense his discomfort and usually treated him to a very rough trot. But Amber had yet to let Mirage come close too, so Jalil couldn't help take some satisfaction knowing Mirage was probably just as uncomfortable.

Unknown to Kira, Jalil also lingered near the stable where he could watch her tending to Amber. Feeling vaguely guilty for eavesdropping, he would listen to her talk to her horse, gaining more insight into her thoughts. It saddened him to hear how lonely she was, and he vowed to speak to his mother about it. It must be hard to not have a family or a home. He couldn't imagine that at all. Surely there was something they could do to lift her spirits while she waited for word from America. He knew Ehsaan had sent several messages, and Jalil planned to do the same, although the idea of her leaving was becoming painful to think about.

Besides watching Kira, Jalil also watched Amber. She was a pleasure to see in motion, and he considered asking Kira about the possibility of breeding Amber to Mirage someday. But then he thought better of it. Until Kira decided what she wanted to do, he was sure she wouldn't entertain the idea. Whenever he saw Kira wrap her arms around Amber's neck, he felt a wave of tenderness toward her.

Discouraged, but resigned, Jalil met Sakhr in the stable and was discussing the breeding schedule when Hasher, one of his tribesmen, appeared with a message.

"My sheik, the sheikha would like you to join her in her chambers for midday meal," Hasher said and bowed.

"Thank you, Hasher. Please tell the sheikha I will be there," Jalil said.

"My sheik," Hasher replied and left the building.

Jalil turned his attention back to Sakhr. "I think we have a good schedule for now." He was about to say more when a flash of gold in the back pasture drew both men's attention. Jalil watched Amber moving with grace and speed.

"It is too bad we cannot breed that one to Mirage," Sakhr was bold to say.

"Yes. Now that would be a match made by Allah. But unfortunately, she will have nothing to do with Mirage, and she belongs to Kira," Jalil said with a rueful shake of his head. They continued discussing their breeding plans for the mares Jalil had won from the losers of the recent race until the sun was high overhead. Then Jalil headed to the house to join his mother.

His mother opened the door, but he was concerned to see her frown. She invited him to sit at her table and after she poured him a glass of lemonade, he said, "What did you want to see me about?"

"I need to talk to you about what happened at Ehsaan's, but first, why don't we just enjoy our meal. It has been a long time since you and I have shared a meal alone," she said quietly.

Concerned, Jalil studied his mother's face, and though she looked more peaceful than he had seen in quite some time, something was bothering her, so he readily agreed. "I would enjoy that too," he said as he helped himself to a serving of kabsa, a traditional dish of savory chicken and rice.

After an enjoyable half hour of delicious food and light conversation, Jalil finally pushed his plate aside and poured a fresh glass of tea. Glancing at Nasira, he noticed she once again looked serious. When she turned to face him with her hands clasped in her lap, he waited for her to speak.

"Jalil, the reason I fainted at Adara's party was simple. The dagger Jabari has been carrying around most of his life was mine."

Jalil's mouth dropped. "What?" He struggled to understand what she had just said. He had forgotten about the incident in the excitement of returning home with Kira.

"I know. I should have told you sooner, but bear with me, and I will try to explain." She swallowed and drew a deep breath. "You will not remember this, but when my baby boy, Talib—your little brother—was born, your father gave me a gift. It was a small gold dagger, designed to be hidden and worn as part of my ceremonial robes. I treasured it and kept it in a carved box on the table in Talib's chamber."

Jalil wanted to ask more questions, but seeing the play of emotions on her face, he knew this was a hard story for her to tell and held his tongue.

"I did not notice it was missing until long after Talib was kidnapped," she said, dropping her gaze and slumping in her chair as if exhausted.

Jalil's head was spinning as he remembered that night so long ago. *Had it really been thirteen years?* The kidnapping happened just before that year's Tri-Annual Race. His father had decided not to race because his primary stallion was too old to compete, and Rayham was too young. As the previous winner, Akeem normally would have hosted the required pre-race meeting, but since he wasn't racing, the honor fell to the second place winner, Qadir's father. But Qadir's father had died, and his son Qadir was to be the host. Not having an entry, Akeem was not required to attend the meeting, but Qadir insisted all the sheiks in the region attend, including those not racing. He was proposing changes to the rules, ones that would affect future races, and all sheiks must come to vote. Akeem and Jalil, along with a contingent of their men, made the four-day journey to Qadir's kingdom. It was while they were at Qadir's that tragedy struck back home.

Those left behind reported a disturbance in the main pass and strangers near the stables, and someone spooked the herd. They sent men to investigate the pass and more to search for the horses, leaving the compound with fewer guards. Nasira had left Talib in his chamber with a servant while she bathed. When she heard what was going on outside, she ran to check on her baby, horrified to discover the servant lying on the floor, her throat cut, and little Talib missing.

Nasira immediately sent a messenger to Akeem and Jalil, but it took three days of hard riding to get the news to them, and another three days for them to get home. They returned to a house of grief and chaos. Akeem sent for Issa, and she stayed with Nasira night and day during the next two weeks while Akeem spent every waking moment looking for his lost son. Jalil, only sixteen years old, had to manage the day-to-day business of the tribe and the herd. Patrols scoured the region, but they never found a trace of the missing baby. Weeks went by, then months, until eventually, they gave up the search.

Nasira was so wrapped up in her grief she didn't notice the dagger was missing until months later. When she could finally bring herself to clear out the nursery, she opened the box and found the dagger gone. No one connected it with the kidnapping, and a few thought a servant might have stolen it. Jalil remembered the scandal but had never seen the dagger.

The memory still pained him, and Jalil felt fresh shame for his failure so long ago. "Mother, I am so sorry I did not save little Talib. I feel like I failed you."

"Oh, my son! You could have done nothing to prevent what happened. You were not there. Do not carry that weight on your shoulders. You have always been a wonderful son."

He raised his eyes to look into hers and saw her love and felt some peace. "If we had only not gone to that cursed meeting at Qadir's." His voice took on a hard tone.

"You could not have avoided it. It was mandatory," she said and reached for his hand.

Jalil felt her warm hand and shook off his anger. "You are right, but I shall never be able to truly feel that I did all I could to find him." He felt her squeeze his hand then release it. Still in shock to discover that Saad's family—the same family that showed up every year to trade— had the dagger and that Jabari had been carrying it around in his pocket all this time was almost unbelievable. Jalil was astounded. "Kismet."

"What was that?" Nasira looked up, her brow furrowed.

"Kismet, Mother. All this time, Jabari had it. But what I want to know is how he got it."

"Saad and Samira said they found it at one of the northern oases over twelve years ago."

His eyes widened, and he abruptly sat up. "I remember Akeem searching all the oases we were familiar with. Maybe we missed that one. I will have to talk to Saad." He tried to rise, but his mother tugged on his hand. He looked down to see her shake her head.

"What?" he asked.

"Jalil, it has been too long. I have learned to let this go. You need to as well. We will never know what happened to Talib. I am just thankful some part of him was returned to us."

"So you have the dagger?" he asked.

"No, Adara received it as a gift, and I will not take it from her. I believe Allah had a hand in this. The dagger is where it is supposed to be now. Be glad of that." She released his hand and stood. "And now, I am tired, and I think I will take a nap."

Jalil stood and nodded, but feeling nostalgic and sad, he pulled her into an impromptu hug. She stiffened for a second then melted into his arms. After a long moment, he released her and stepped back, pleased to see her smiling again. But when he opened the door to depart, she stopped him one more time. "Jalil, have I ever thanked you for all the times you helped me while your father searched for Talib?"

"Yes, and you know, Mother, I will always do my best to take care of my family and my tribe…and especially you." Seeing his mother's eyes fill with tears, he stepped back to kiss her on the forehead and quickly left, afraid she might see his damp eyes.

CHAPTER 12

The next day, Jalil had just returned from his morning ride when his mother knocked on the door. He opened it and was taken aback at her expression. Her brow was furrowed, and her hands were clasped tightly in front of her. She looked so serious, he was somewhat alarmed. "Yes, Mother, what is it?"

"I wanted to talk to you about Kira. She has agreed to meet with me in the dining chamber for the midday meal. I would like for you to join us, but first, I need to speak to you privately," she said.

"I can certainly join you, and I also wanted to speak to you. Give me a minute and I will meet you in your chambers."

"Thank you, Jalil." She nodded and walked down the hall.

Closing his door, he hurried to change his clothes. Running a comb through his hair and adjusting his clean tunic, he put on soft sandals instead of riding boots. Striding down the hall, he ordered his thoughts. He wasn't sure what his mother wanted to talk about, but he was glad she had set up the meeting, hoping she would tell him he could finally ask Kira about the medallion. However, he wanted to talk about something else entirely.

A few minutes later, he sat in her chambers, waiting for her to speak first.

"Jalil, I spoke with Kira and invited her to stay as long as she likes. But the more time I spend with her, the more I am impressed by her.

Jalil, I would like for us to invite Kira to join our tribe. What do you think?" Nasira said with a hopeful expression.

Stunned, Jalil stared at her for a second. "Mother, that is exactly what I was going to talk to you about. I have been thinking about it, and I have watched her working with our people. She is amazing, and everyone loves her. It is like she is already part of the family," he said earnestly.

His mother's relief was obvious. "Oh, thank Allah. I too love her. She is so kind—and smart. Did you know she studied engineering and geology?"

Jalil's eyes widened. "Really? I did not know that, but then, she has not spoken to me much. But I have seen how resourceful she is, and there is no doubt she has the courage of a man." He leaned forward. "Do you think she would accept?" He was eager to hear his mother's opinion. She obviously knew Kira better than he did.

Nasira's eyes narrowed as she looked back at him. "I think she will consider it. And I think we should ask her today. That is why I set up the meeting," she said, nodding sagely.

Jalil felt a surge of excitement he couldn't explain and wrestled with new feelings, feelings he wasn't ready to reveal to his mother. He wanted to rush right out and ask Kira, but he needed to ask his mother one more question. "Do you think she would be open to talking about the medallion?" He held his breath.

"I think it would be all right to ask. But if she becomes uncomfortable, you must let it go for now."

"I understand. I do not want to pressure her, but I really must find out what she knows," he said as he stood. "Come, it is almost time. Shall we?" He held out his arm, and his mother smiled up at him and allowed him to escort her down the hall.

As he walked, his mind was spinning as he tried to decide the best way to ask Kira about the medallion. He had neglected that conversation long enough. Or was he wrong? Perhaps he should wait until after he offered her membership in the tribe to bring it up. Then maybe she would be more open to talking about her past with him.

Smiling and feeling clever, he walked into the dining chamber and saw Kira seated at the low table which was already set for their meal. When she looked up with obvious surprise, he hesitated. *Uh oh. Nasira didn't tell her I was coming.* He felt his mother squeezing his arm, and he kept silent when she looked at Kira with an apologetic smile.

"Kira, I asked Jalil to join us, too. He has some important things to discuss, and I wanted to be here to help. I hope that is all right with you," Nasira said as she sat down across from Kira.

Kira looked confused and wary. "I am sure that will be fine, Sheikha."

Jalil offered his warmest smile and sat down next to his mother. "Thank you, Kira. And let me begin by saying that you look very well today." Nasira bowed her head and coughed lightly, and Jalil thought he saw her hiding a smile. Kira blushed lightly and thanked him.

Feeling encouraged, Jalil soldiered on. "So, Kira, the sheikha and I have been talking, and we have something we would like to say to you. Since we have met you, you have impressed us with your courage, honesty, and resourcefulness. Everyone who has met you agrees with me. You have proved to be of great help to our tribe, and we are all benefiting from your knowledge. Thank you for sharing it with us."

When he noticed her blush had disappeared and she was looking decidedly pale, he hurried to finish. "Today, I would like to invite you to become a member of our tribe and consider our kingdom your home. Of course, that includes Amber, too." Pleased with himself, Jalil sat back, waiting for her to smile and accept.

He did not expect the reaction he got. Kira was not smiling. In fact, she had a frown on her face, and Nasira was quick to apologize. "Kira, I am sorry for not letting you know Jalil was joining us today. I was so excited to do this that I forgot to tell you."

Jalil was relieved to see Kira's frown disappear, but she still looked serious. He felt better at her next response.

"It is all right, Sheikha. And I am very honored by your invitation, Sheik Jalil," Kira said, looking at Nasira and Jalil. "I must confess, I have thought about this many times and wished for this very moment. I love your tribe. Your people are warm and generous, as are their ruling family." Both Jalil and Nasira smiled, encouraging her to continue. "Everyone has treated Amber and me with respect and affection. I could not ask for a better home, but I haven't been able to contact my family, though there is only one person left, my grandmother. She is quite elderly, and I have no idea if she is still living." Pausing, Kira took a drink. "Before I decide, I would like a little time. Would that be acceptable?"

Jalil nodded at once. "Kira, we do not wish to pressure you. Just know that we would like you to stay." Nasira nodded in agreement.

"Well then, I will say this. Finding myself halfway around the world, with people whose language and customs are so different from my own, has been a life-changing experience for me. But I have learned that we are not so different after all," she said with a smile. "If I decide to stay, I would be honored to become a member of your tribe."

Nasira beamed, and Jalil wanted to shout his happiness at the world. His smile was huge, and once again Kira blushed. "This is wonderful news, Kira. You have made me very happy… I mean… us… you have made us very happy," he stuttered a bit.

Nasira hid another smile behind her hand, but Jalil's grin faded when he saw Kira's sudden frown.

"I think you said you had something else to discuss? You said 'things.'" Kira's voice shook, though she clearly tried to hide it, and her hand trembled when she reached for her tea.

"Well, yes." Jalil was feeling decidedly uncomfortable but needed to find answers. He pulled the medallion over his head and handed it to her. Kira took it with raised eyebrows, obviously curious, but as she stared down at it, her face lost all expression. Jalil couldn't tell what she was thinking, but when he saw her eyes rolling up and her body falling, he scrambled over the table in his haste to catch her.

Holding her in his lap, he stared down at her pale face, his eyes tracing the tiny freckles on her soft cheeks and the long golden-brown lashes hiding her blue-green eyes. He sighed. She had become precious in his sight, and at that moment, he knew for the first time in his life he was in love.

Unaware that his feelings were showing on his face, he missed the look of joy on his mother's face. But he caught sight of her tears and misunderstood, thinking she was concerned for Kira. He took the damp napkin she passed him and gently patted Kira's face with it then pressed it to her forehead.

Kira came to almost at once and when she opened her eyes to stare up into his, everything around him faded as Jalil focused his entire being on her. Nasira remained quiet for a moment then cleared her throat. Jalil shook his head as if coming out of a daze and lifted Kira into her chair before returning to his own.

As Nasira cleared spilled cups and scattered dishes, she gestured to Jalil, staring pointedly at his chest. Confused, Jalil looked down to discover the remains of their meal sticking to the front of his tunic. Embarrassed, he blushed and grabbed a cloth to brush it off.

Nasira hid her smile and turned to Kira, taking her by the hand. "Kira, are you all right?"

Kira shook her head gently and held her hand to her face. "Yes…I think so." She took the goblet Nasira gave her and gulped the sweet beverage. Closing her eyes for a moment, she appeared to steady herself, and Jalil watched anxiously, ready to assist again if needed. When she set her goblet down and met his gaze, he could see she was feeling better. He wanted to speak, but she raised her hand. "Please wait. I must first apologize." She blushed furiously.

"Nonsense, Kira. I am the one at fault. I startled you, though I did not mean to," he said, regretting he had caused her violent reaction. "We just wanted to talk to you about the medallion, but if you do not feel up to it, we can wait." It took a lot for him to say that, and he noticed his mother smiling at him with pride.

"It wasn't your fault, Sheik. You must understand. I recognized the medallion—it belonged to my father. But the last time I saw it, Qadir was holding it. It was right before he, well… anyway, it was a shock." She shuddered delicately.

Jalil hated hearing those words, and he was surprised to realize he cared more about Kira than the answers he had sought for so long. He silently vowed to give her more time if she needed it.

But evidently Kira felt up to the task. "First, how did you come by it? I'm certain I know, but to be sure…"

"I found it in Qadir's bedchamber the night you were rescued."

She nodded. "Then you must have wanted to talk to me for a while now, so why don't we just get this done?" She took a deep breath and looked down at the medallion still clutched in her hand and placed it gently on the table.

Before Jalil could speak, his mother gave him a look, so he allowed her to talk first. She told Kira the tale of the medallion and how her husband, Akeem, valued it and always kept it close, but then it disappeared the day he was murdered.

Kira listened, wide-eyed, glancing down at the disk then back at Nasira. When Nasira finished explaining how they found Akeem murdered without his beloved medallion, Kira looked at Jalil with her eyes full of understanding before turning back to Nasira. "I am so sorry for your loss, Sheikha. And yours, Sheik. Though I do not know what it feels like to lose a husband," she paused and looked back at Jalil, "I know what it is like to lose a father."

Jalil almost reached out to touch her arm when he saw the sadness in her eyes. "Thank you, Kira."

"Perhaps this is a good time to tell you my tale." Sniffing and clearing her throat, she launched into her story, telling them everything about her life growing up in the American southwest. Then she described the events leading up to and past the plane crash, including how she found Amber in the desert. She surprised Jalil when she shared everything she remembered of her kidnapping and subsequent beating.

It was obvious she was leaving out details, but Jalil couldn't blame her. And even though she had averted her eyes, he could see her blushing and hear the tremor in her voice. While she told her story, his emotions ran wild as he tried to comprehend all she had endured. He wished he could have been there to save her from the suffering in the desert, the pain of the lion attack, and the horror of Qadir. Kira had survived what most couldn't have, and he knew deep down that he would never let her suffer again if she stayed in his world. He only interrupted her to ask a few questions about the man and the marketplace in Cairo.

When she was done, no one spoke. The sound of distant hoofbeats drifted through the shuttered window, and the muted voices of the servants echoed down the hall. They continued to sit quietly, looking at the medallion, each wrapped in their own thoughts.

When Kira abruptly stood, almost knocking her goblet over, she startled Jalil. His mother stared at her, and Jalil gave Kira a questioning look.

"I need to get something from my chamber. I will be right back." She didn't wait for a reply and dashed from the room. Bewildered, Jalil looked at his mother and she shook her head, just as puzzled.

When Kira returning to the dining chamber, she sat down to face Jalil and placed a thick gold chain next to Akeem's medallion. "I think this belongs to you."

Jalil gasped, and Nasira reached over to touch the chain, a look of shock on her face. She looked at Kira and impulsively grabbed her hand. "Thank you, thank you," she whispered.

Barely aware of them, Jalil stared down at the chain and medallion which seemed to glow for a second. Puzzled, he looked at his mother and Kira, but they didn't seem to notice. *Am I the only one who saw that?* Picking up the chain, he gripped it tightly in his large hand, feeling the smooth, heavy links. He had recognized it at once. *My father's chain!* He smiled grimly when he considered what he would do to whomever had taken the medallion and chain from his father, along with his father's life.

He felt a stab of regret that his father never explained the significance of the medallion because he knew deep down in his very soul it was critically important. Akeem had called it his greatest treasure and promised to tell him when he was ready to retire. Unfortunately, he never got that chance. *If only Akeem had told Nasira*, he thought, but he never had.

Suddenly aware of the silence in the room, he looked up to see his mother watching him closely. But Kira was frowning, and he hastened to assure her she had done the right thing. "Thank you, Kira, for restoring my father's legacy." When she nodded and smiled, he was relieved.

Removing the newer chain from the medallion, Jalil replaced it with the original, and slipped it around his neck. Closing his eyes, he laid his hand on the medallion resting against his heart. For just a second, he saw his father's smiling face. Opening his eyes, he gazed at Kira again, and seeing her smile tinged with sadness, he knew she shared his pain. His father wasn't the only one who had worn the medallion. They had more in common than he had originally thought. Perhaps, in time, it would be enough.

CHAPTER 13

Early the next morning, Kira was returning from her daily ride when she saw Jalil and Jabari sparring in a corral. He was teaching the young man how to fight with different weapons, and she stopped at a discreet distance to watch. Her eyes followed Jalil, watching the muscles bunch in his strong thighs as he strode around the corral, always one step ahead of the boy, and she admired his flashing white teeth in his handsome face when he smiled and laughed. It appeared he thoroughly enjoying working with Jabari, and Jabari looked like he was enjoying it too, with his silver eyes flashing and his caramel hair flying as he twisted and turned to avoid the slaps of Jalil's sword.

Struck anew by their resemblance, Kira cocked her head. Maybe it was all the time they spent together, she thought. *That must be it.* When they appeared to be stopping for the day, she dismounted and led Amber inside a stable. She was still unsettled after sharing the details of her ordeal at Qadir's and did not wish to speak to Jalil.

After giving Amber a good rubdown and turning her loose for the rest of the day, Kira went to her chambers, planning to freshen up before beginning her daily activities. Walking briskly, as she often did when deep in thought, she turned the corner into the guest hall and ran right into Jalil. He reached to catch her, and when his long arms wrapped around her body and his large warm hands slid down to rest on the small of her back, her hands came up to rest against his broad chest. It took them both a minute to recover, but when they did, neither of them pulled away.

Raising her head, Kira saw his face just inches away. He was gazing into her eyes, as if searching for something, and they were so close she could see flecks of green shimmer in his eyes. Before she could ask what he was doing in the guest wing, she was distracted by the growing thunder of his heartbeat under her hands and her own heart raced to catch up. Feeling hot and flushed, she dropped her eyes to stare at his lips. Unaware of her actions, she raised her hand, wanting to brush an errant lock of hair from his forehead, but when she felt his heartbeat increase, she looked up and saw his eyes darken, and she couldn't look away. When he lowered his head, she unconsciously lifted her face, and her lips parted slightly. His lips parted in response, and he gently pulled her to his chest. All she could think about was getting closer, and sighing, she melted in his embrace.

Suddenly, their lips almost brushing, the sound of running footsteps jolted them from their spell. Kira gasped and stepped back. Jalil was still leaning toward her, his eyes half closed, and he barely caught himself from falling into her. His face mirrored her surprise, but before either of them could speak, a fast-moving bundle of energy named Jabari ran around the corner and ploughed right into both of them. They all yelled in surprise, but Jalil caught the other two before all three of them ended up on the floor. They were holding on to one another when Nasira came upon them.

"What is going on? Is this a new game of which I am unaware?" She smiled mischievously and laughed at their red faces and embarrassed expressions.

"It is all my fault, Sheikha. I was in a hurry to talk to my father and wasn't looking where I was going. I apologize, Sheik Jalil, Kira." Jabari's face flushed with embarrassment.

"Apology accepted, Jabari, but you must be more careful in the future, especially inside the house. This is not the stable." Jalil smiled gently. "Kira, are you all right?"

"Yes, my sheik, I will survive," Kira said, relieved that Jabari had interrupted them when he did. Things had almost gotten out of hand. Seeing the downcast expression on Jabari's face, she was quick to add. "I'm looking forward to riding with you, Jabari, and seeing how well you have trained Sarii."

Jabari's face flooded with relief. "Oh, Kira, you will be amazed when you see what she has learned. And, again, I am sorry, but I must find my father." With that pronouncement, he turned and dashed off then seemed to think better of it and slowed to a fast walk.

Nasira chuckled and turned to Jalil. "I believe Fahad is looking for you," she said, with an arched eyebrow.

With a quick glance at Kira, Jalil nodded and departed, walking almost as fast as Jabari. Nasira chuckled again. "Kira, will you join me for the midday meal? I would like to talk about a new class for the children."

Kira was still thinking about Jalil and wondering anew what he was doing in the guest wing. Had he been looking for her? It was a tantalizing thought, but seeing Nasira waiting patiently for her reply, she put Jalil from her mind. "I would be delighted, Nasira. Thank you."

Nasira smiled and walked away, leaving Kira standing in the corridor, still slightly dazed. Kira retired to her chambers, not only needed to freshen up as originally planned, but needing to collect her wits as well. The incident in the hall had shaken her to the core. She was becoming more aware of Jalil every day, seeing him in a whole new light. Knowing she would have to leave someday, she feared her growing attraction to him, and it was increasingly difficult to remain detached from him and his family.

Haunted by the prospect of leaving, she also thought more and more about her grandmother. She missed her desperately, but it seemed impossible to get word to her. Worried about her, Kira often prayed late at night, hoping her grandmother would somehow hear her and know she was all right. When she thought of her, Kira remembered how her grandmother used to tell her life was a journey filled with crossroads, and that Kira would have to make choices to continue forward or turn along the way. She said there would be unforeseen obstacles placed in her path—obstacles that would force her down a different path, one she might not have otherwise chosen. How she handled them would be very important, but she must always keep going and never give up. Kira found her advice to be cryptic and a little beyond her understanding, but many other lessons she taught had served her well.

Later that evening, as Kira lay in bed, she thought about how she ended up in a remote mountain kingdom in a country far from her home. And she wondered, for the first time, if the bad things that had happened—the plane crash, the death of her father, the lion, and Qadir—were just obstacles that had led her to this new path. Maybe she needed to follow it to see what was at the end. Sighing, she settled deeper into her blanket and prayed for a night without dreams, and her prayers came true except for the haunting visions of green-gold eyes.

CHAPTER 14

Samira sat with a slight smile on her face, sliding her shuttle back and forth, lost in a daydream. Nasira had given her a portable loom, one she could use inside the house or outside if she wanted. It was easy to handle and perfect for making smaller decorative sections of material for garments. Samira enjoyed the work. When she was weaving, she had time to think, without Saad calling for something or Jabari pestering her with questions.

Her family had settled into their new house and routine with a minimum of fuss. Sometimes she missed the freedom and excitement of trading along the routes, but she enjoyed the safety of four walls and a roof and having a place to store her things without having to keep them in a bag. Having privacy was a bonus, something they never had during their travels. On the road, she and Saad had their own tent, but Amal and Jabari were always close by.

Hearing someone approach, she paused in her work, wondering who it might be. When Jabari leaned in the doorway, she gazed at him with love, amazed at how he was changing, becoming more handsome every day. He didn't dash about as much as he used to and was growing up, learning to slow his steps and walk more like a man.

"Mother, may I have a few dates for Sarii?"

"Yes, Jabari. You know where I keep them. But first, tell me, how is your day going?"

"I have been learning more about stallion and mare selection. Sakhr is an excellent teacher."

"Indeed, he is. And are you still practicing swordplay with the sheik?"

"Of course! He says I am doing very well, and soon I will learn to spar with more than one opponent."

"Well, be careful. Seeing you with a sword is scary to me." Samira was still not used to seeing him dance around as Jalil slashed and stabbed at him. As a mother, it was hard to watch.

"I am always careful. And besides, I am good," he said with a wink.

"One of these days, Jabari, you are going to meet someone who is better. So, pay attention," she admonished and reached for a spool of yarn, but when she leaned over, she felt a small cramp and winced.

"Mother, are you all right?"

Samira smiled. "I am fine. Now get your treats. I need to get back to work."

"Thank you, Mother," he said, leaning down to give her a quick kiss on the cheek then filled a pouch with sticky sweets for Sarii and departed.

Samira continued to work, but with a bigger smile on her face. *Yes, I am indeed all right.* She wasn't ready to tell Jabari yet, not until she could tell her husband first. Her miracle had finally happened, and she could barely contain her excitement. *A baby, finally, after all these years.* When she first missed her monthly, she hadn't thought about being pregnant. Her cycles were never regular, but when time stretched longer than usual, she realized the miracle had happened. Adjusting the cushion she sat upon, she sought a more comfortable position. She wasn't far along, but already she could imagine her baby growing inside, and she even thought she could feel it move.

Laying her hand on her stomach, she sighed happily. *A baby!* She still couldn't believe it. *But why now?* she thought. *After all this time?* Perhaps it had to do with their new lifestyle. Having a house and the privacy it afforded had certainly led to more intimacy with Saad, and settling down removed the stress from her life. A trader's life was hard.

So many things could go wrong, and it was dangerous too. Maybe that's why she hadn't been able to have children.

But thinking about the many dangers reminded her of that fateful day, over thirteen years ago, when they were trading along the old northern route. She sat up a little straighter as she had a random thought. That day, they had been travelling northwest of Jalil's kingdom and had stopped to make camp. While Samira prepared a meal, Saad and Amal unloaded the camels. When possible, they tied the camels to a handy tree or bush or hobbled them by tying their front legs together with leather straps. In the place they camped that afternoon, there was nothing to tie them to, and Amal had to use the straps. After erecting the tents, they discovered one camel had wandered off.

Normally, Saad would have left Samira to guard the camp, but with the threat of predators like the desert lions and hyenas known to inhabit the northern route, he felt it was safer if they stayed together. Samira was following them when several black spots high in the sky drew her attention. The desert born knew the sign of vultures. Frowning, she watched them circle and noticed the men increase their speed when they saw them too. She hurried to catch up, feeling a strange sense of foreboding.

Pulled from her memories when she heard voices outside her house, she resumed feeding her shuttle back and forth again, re-establishing the rhythm needed to continue her weaving. As she allowed her thoughts to drift back to the rocky path they had traversed that day, a word popped into her mind, something Nasira had said. *Kismet.* That gave her pause. *How had Amal been able to find that camel?* The ground was stony, and it was impossible to see any tracks, but they had found the camel drinking from a pool in a small hidden oasis. They were excited to discover an unknown source of water, knowing it would prove helpful in their future travels.

And that should have been the end—until they found the bodies. A strong smell of decay rose from behind a nearby pile of rocks. Even now, she grimaced, remembering the gruesome scene. Four men clothed in black robes thrown carelessly in a heap, their throats slashed, and the sand stained with their blood. Saad waved at her to stay back, and she was ready to comply until she heard a sound. "Saad, what is that noise?"

Saad was standing closer to the bodies. "What noise, Samira? I hear nothing," Saad said. He glanced at Amal, who merely shook his head.

But when she heard a feeble cry, she didn't hesitate. "The baby, I have to save the baby," she cried and rushed forward. Both men tried to hold her back, but she pulled free and scrambled into the pile.

She rose holding a bloody bundle, and Saad and Amal stared in astonishment when a tiny hand emerged from the rags. Running to the pool, she sank to her knees, laying the bundle on the sand. Carefully removing the blood-stained folds of cloth, she uncovered a baby boy, his face covered in dried blood. His tiny eyes were crusted shut, and his lips were dry and cracked. She took the bottom of her robe, dipped it in water, and used it to wash the grime from his face. He was in poor shape and had fallen silent.

Samira's concern grew to alarm until finally, as the late afternoon sun gilded the oasis in golden light, the baby opened his eyes. They glowed with a silvery sheen, and she had never seen such a beautiful sight. As she lifted him to hold him tightly to her chest, she saw the dagger, Nasira's dagger she now knew, tangled in the rags.

As the images faded from her mind, Samira stopped weaving, letting the shuttle fall from her hand. In that instant, she felt again the overwhelming love of a mother for her child and now understood Nasira's grief. Bowing her head, she began crying. The dagger wasn't the only thing that belonged to Nasira.

＊

When Saad came by for his midday meal, he found Samira slumped over her loom, sobbing piteously. "Samira, Samira, my flower!" Alarmed, seeing the look of misery and despair on her beautiful face, he rushed to kneel by her side.

"Saad, oh Saad! We must tell Nasira about the baby!" Her voice was full of anguish.

Saad's world came to an abrupt stop. He wanted to yell, "No!" and cry and stomp and tear out his hair. But he knew Samira was right. He had made the connection the night Nasira had shared her story about the dagger, but he couldn't admit it to himself. Jabari was the brightest star in their sky, and the thought that he belonged to someone else, that he was some other man's son, ripped his heart in two. Bowing his head in defeat, his tears joined those of Samira's. She fell into his arms, and Saad rocked her gently while they shared their greatest sorrow.

Saad was unsure how much time passed. They had missed their meal, but neither of them had an appetite anymore. He stood and helped his wife to her feet, and they sat at the table, holding hands, and tried to figure out what they should do. Samira wanted to tell Jabari, but Saad said they should talk to Nasira first. He was clinging to the hope that perhaps Jabari wasn't the kidnapped baby. How could anyone prove such a thing? It had been so long ago, but when he remembered the dagger, he knew he was grasping at straws.

Samira finally agreed it would be better to talk to Nasira first. "She will be overjoyed, Saad. But what if she blames us for what happened? Will she believe our story? What if she sends us away…or worse?"

Saad squeezed her hand gently. "My flower, I am sure she will listen to our story. The sheikha is known for being reasonable," he said reassuringly.

Samira nodded numbly, then voiced Saad's greatest fear. "But how will Jabari take it? Will he resent us for keeping him in our lives as the son of a trader instead of letting him live as the son of a sheik? Oh, Saad, I cannot bear the thought of my son…I mean Jabari…hating us." She dissolved into tears.

Saad took her in his arms and held her until her cries slowed and finally stopped. When she lifted her reddened eyes to his, he leaned down and kissed her lightly. "I will find Nasira and ask her if she can meet with us tomorrow."

"All right, Saad." Samira dropped her head with a sigh of resignation.

"And Samira, I think we should make sure Jalil is with us when we meet."

"That would probably be wise." Samira rose, wiping away the rest of her tears. "Saad, would you mind if I did not make supper tonight? I am not feeling well."

"Do not give it a second thought. I have no appetite either. Why don't you go lie down for a while, and I will speak with Nasira, and when I return, we will go to bed early. We will need all our strength tomorrow."

"Thank you, my husband." She turned toward the bedchamber then looked back. "I love you, Saad."

"Oh, Samira, you are and always will be the only woman I love."

With a tired smile, she turned away. Saad sighed, squared his shoulders, straightened his tunic, and left to find Nasira. As luck would have it, he saw Jalil walking toward the house from the stables and called out to him.

Jalil stopped and waited for him to catch up. "Saad, my friend. What can I do for you?" He stood with his hands on his hips.

"My sheik." Saad nodded formally. "I find myself in a very awkward position, and I need to speak with you and the sheikha, if you can spare the time."

"Well, I was on my way to cleanup for evening meal. Is this a matter that we need to discuss now?"

"Oh, no, my sheik. It is late, and Samira will also need to be in our meeting. She is not feeling well, but I am sure she will be fine tomorrow."

"Now you have me worried, Saad. I hope you are not planning to leave us." Jalil looked concerned.

"No, no. Would you and the sheikha be able to meet with us in the morning?" Saad struggled to speak calmly.

"I am sure I can arrange that. I will speak with her tonight, and if there is a problem, I will send word. Otherwise, let us meet in the main hall after the morning meal."

"My sheik, the matter we wish to discuss is of a very personal nature. Would it be possible to meet somewhere more private?" Saad twisted his hands nervously, feeling awkward making such a request of his sheik.

Jalil raised his eyebrows but said nothing of Saad's nervous behavior. "Certainly. Why don't we meet in my chambers?"

"That would be most acceptable. Thank you for granting us this audience." Saad bowed low.

"You are welcome, Saad. I will see you tomorrow." Jalil nodded and continued to the house.

Saad stood for a long minute, watching the man he admired and respected, the man whose tribe he had sworn allegiance to. *After tomorrow, will Jalil still want us as members of the tribe? Will he want to punish us for what we did?* Disturbed by such thoughts, Saad returned home to find his wife sound asleep in their bed. But unable to sleep, he sat down at their table to ponder their predicament. The moon had dipped below the horizon before he finally laid his head down on his arms and fell asleep, dreaming of black-robed men, golden daggers, and silver eyes.

CHAPTER 15

"Jalil…wait!" Nasira called to him, but Jalil dashed from her chambers as if chased by a desert lion. After their meeting with Saad and Samira in his chambers, Jalil had escorted his mother back to her room in silence. Her face was pale, and she kept her hands clenched at her waist. He could see she was struggling to understand and realized he needed to give her time to absorb the news. He was also still reeling from what he had learned that morning and needed to escape to think.

He made his way to the stables and was soon astride his horse. Jalil pushed Mirage faster and concentrated on riding. It was the one thing that would always take Jalil out of his world, allowing him to clear his mind until nothing else remained except the feel of his horse beneath him, the thunder of hoofbeats, and the rush of the wind in his hair. Everything else disappeared. Unfortunately, it couldn't last forever, and eventually Mirage slowed. Jalil felt him breathing hard, and coming to his senses, Jalil eased off the reins and sat back in the saddle.

He pulled Mirage to a halt atop a lone hill where he could see his kingdom spreading around him. *His kingdom.* The kingdom that had been his father's, his grandfather's, and all their fathers back through time. This was where he had been born and raised. He grew up learning everything he could to help his father rule, sharing as much of the burden as his father would allow him, knowing someday he would become sheik. When his brother Talib was born, Jalil was happy knowing he would have someone to share in the responsibility, someone who could help him until he could have his own son.

Then tragedy struck, and overcome with grief, his father spent every waking hour trying to find his missing son. And all the responsibility fell upon Jalil's shoulders, and he took charge because his parents couldn't deal with anything else for a while. It took his father years to accept his loss, but just when he took the reins of control again, he was murdered. Jalil then became the sheik in every sense and had never faltered in his duties. But he would have liked to have had help, and a brother would have been that help.

When he thought back to that time, he remembered his own grief. It was not as deep as his parents because Talib was a baby, too young to forge a connection with Jalil. Now, as he sat feeling the midday sun burning though his robe, Jalil felt angrier than he had when it had happened—angry at the men who had robbed his father of a son, his mother of her child, and him of the brother he never had the chance to know. He bowed his head and struggled to control his emotions. As if sensing Jalil's mood, Mirage stood still, waiting patiently for his next command.

Hearing horses nearby, Jalil slowly raised his head to gaze across the pastures. Mares with their foals grazed along the banks of the creek, and sunlight danced on their shiny coats, highlighting all the colors of the earth. Brown, chestnut, black, white, and gray. And gold. Seeing the glory of his herd, the proof of Allah's blessings, Jalil felt his anger dissipate like smoke in the wind, and he felt a new peace in his heart. His horses were magnificent, he was alive, and he was sheik. The world was in his grasp, and he had just discovered he had a brother again—Jabari, the boy with the shining, silver eyes. Jabari, with his irrepressible curiosity and outrageous sense of humor. Jabari the Magnificent. Suddenly, Jalil's heart filled with joy. He picked up the reins and signaled Mirage to canter back to the house. Full of questions, he needed to talk to his mother.

When he knocked on her door, he could barely hear her response.

"Come in," Nasira said quietly.

Jalil opened the door to find his mother seated at her table, staring down at the ring of gold on her finger, the ring that matched his father's. She was twisting it gently round and round, and her face was still pale. It was obvious she was still in shock, and he felt guilty for having left her so suddenly. He sat next to her and laid a comforting hand on her shoulder. "Mother, I am sorry," he said.

Nasira remained silent for another moment then slowly shook her head and looked over at him. "For what, my son?"

"I should not have run off. I just…." He tried to explain, but she waved a hand in the air.

"Nonsense. It was just as hard for you to hear the story as me," she said with a sad smile.

Dumbfounded, Jalil said, "But why did they wait so long to tell us?"

"Oh, Jalil. Could you not see? Samira could hardly speak. Can you really blame her? She had wanted a baby so badly, and Allah gave her one. She did not know it was mine. It was kismet, Jalil. I understand because I probably would have done the same thing. It is what a mother does."

"So you are not mad at her?" Jalil studied his mother, watching the play of emotions parade across her face.

"Oh, no. I do not blame her. It is too late for that. They did not steal him. They found and rescued him. And they didn't care who he was and brought him up with love and care. But now she will suffer as much as I did then because she is about to lose her only child. And I cannot describe to you what it feels like to have your child taken from you. It could destroy her, and I hate to be the one to break her heart. But Jabari must be told. He is the son of a sheik, and he deserves the life he was destined for."

Jalil sat back in his chair as the image of the dagger kept flashing in his mind. What were the chances a kidnapper would steal the one thing that would identify the baby as Akeem's? And then for everyone to be killed at the oasis, except the baby? And again, the dagger being left behind? It was beyond his comprehension. How did this happen? And why? Maybe his mother was right…again. *Kismet.* The answers would probably remain a mystery forever, but Jalil found he didn't care anymore. All he could do was think about Jabari, but when his mother chuckled, he stared at her in confusion. "What is so funny?"

"Now I understand why he seemed so familiar. His face is like yours, his laughter like Akeem's, and his silver eyes are like his grandfather's," she said.

"I wish I had known my grandfather," Jalil said wistfully.

"You would have liked him," she said. He died not long after Akeem and I came here. I really did not know him very well, but I remember his eyes—pale gray—Jabari's eyes."

He watched his mother bow her head and waited a moment before taking both her hands in his. "It may surprise you, but I have always felt like I knew Jabari, too. He just seemed so familiar, and now I know why," Jalil said. Filled with a new joy, he squeezed her hand gently. "Mother, I have a brother, and I cannot stop thinking about it. I have to tell you—I am happy, so happy, and I cannot wait for him to join our family."

She looked up suddenly. "Jalil, I do not know what to say. Of course, I am beyond happy too, but this will not be easy for Jabari…I mean Talib. And that is part of the problem too. What is he to be called? And what if he doesn't want to be a part of our family? What if he wants to stay with Saad and Samira? I do not know if I can let him go again." Her face filled with dread.

Jalil tried to assuage her fears. "Oh, surely, he will want to be part of our family. He is the son of a sheik, and he could be so much more than the son of a trader."

Nasira's dread seemed to a have vanished, and her voice held a warning when she spoke. "Maybe he enjoys being the son of a trader. You need to be careful, Jalil. It sounds like you think there is no honor in being a trader."

"Of course I don't think that. But he can be anything he wants, and I can help him do that," Jalil replied enthusiastically, squeezing her hands tightly.

"Jalil, I know how you must feel. You have a brother now, and that must be exciting, especially one such as Jabari. He is an exceptional young man already, but you would do well to remember that he has become who he is from being the son of a trader."

Jalil stopped short when he realized what she was saying. "I am sorry. You are right. I am ashamed of suggesting that being a trader is not as worthy as being a sheik. But I am still excited. When do you think they will tell him?"

"You heard them. They promised they would talk to him today. They know how important this is for Jabari, and us, too."

"So, when will we know that they have?" Jalil was eager to speak with Jabari as soon as he could.

"I expect they will send word. Then we can decide what comes next, or perhaps Jabari will make that decision for us."

"Well, we can only wait and see, but I need to take my mind off it," Jalil said.

"Why don't you talk to Kira? I think you can share this news with her. I trust her to be discreet," Nasira said.

"Yes, I would like to do that." He stroked his chin thoughtfully. "I will go find her now," he said. Kissing his mother's forehead, he rushed from the room, leaving her shaking her head as she mused out loud, "Just like Jabari… how did I not see that before?"

CHAPTER 16

Kira was grooming Amber inside the stable when she heard a noise behind her. She turned and saw Jalil standing in the doorway, gilded by the sun, and was struck speechless. Surely Apollo himself was not so handsome, she thought silently, then kicked herself mentally. Remembering to breathe, she smiled tentatively, and he grinned and strode forward.

"Kira, would you join me for a few minutes after you finish with Amber?"

The glow of happiness on his face was hard to miss, and she wondered what had put him in such a mood. Nervous but excited to see him, Kira said, "Yes, I am almost done. Can we meet by the corral?"

He nodded and walked outside. Kira finished brushing Amber in record time and placed a bowl of grains on the floor for her to eat. Trying to still her pounding heart, she left the building to find Jalil sitting on a bench in the shade. *Oh, my. He is so handsome.* When she approached, he moved to the far end of the bench, allowing for a suitable distance between them. She sat down and turned to hear what he had to say, keeping her hands in her lap to hide their trembling.

Without hesitation, Jalil launched into the tale of the dagger and the kidnapped baby. When he finished, Kira sat with her mouth open, stunned. He seemed surprised by her reaction. "Kira, you have been traveling with Saad's family for a long time. Didn't you ever wonder about Jabari or the dagger?"

"Why would I question them, Sheik? They introduced Jabari as their son. And as for the dagger, I only saw it once or twice, and I understood it was a gift from Saad. I had no reason to think they were lying. They saved my life. And now I find out that my friend is the son of a sheik…and your brother. It is all so fantastical. I don't know what to say."

"I guess I can understand, but it is hard to accept that we lost thirteen years of his life when, all along, he was always near."

"I am sure it was a shock to you and the sheikha. How is she taking it?"

"Shocked is an understatement, but she will be fine. It is all up to Jabari now," Jalil said, but he looked concerned.

"So, has he been told?"

"Saad said they would tell him today, but I do not know when."

"Well, I'm sure everything will be all right. He loves his parents and just needs time to sort it all out. You need to be patient and give him that time. He might surprise us all."

Jalil appeared to be listening intently to her words, but his eyes glowed with new emotion, mesmerizing her. Startled by Amber's loud neigh, reminding her the horse was waiting for her in the stable, Kira suddenly stood. "Well, I must check on Amber and take her back to the pasture. Perhaps you can let me know later how this all works out."

Jalil jumped up and took a step forward. "Thank you for listening, Kira. And could you please keep this information to yourself for now?" She nodded in agreement, but before she could leave, he asked, "Do you think we could do something together sometime, like take a ride?" He leaned toward her and smiled hopefully.

Kira froze, fascinated by the tiny golden flecks dancing in the deep green of his eyes.

"Kira?" His smiling inquiry broke the spell.

"Uh... wha... um... oh, yes. Yes, Jalil... maybe tomorrow. I will let you know. I need to go now." She turned and hurried back inside the stable, leaving Jalil smiling in her wake.

Kira was leaving the back pasture when she saw Jabari galloping at a breakneck speed toward the far hills, and she knew at once he had been told the truth. She considered riding after him but decided he needed to process what must be overwhelming news. Sighing, she headed to the house, her thoughts turning to Jalil's family. No doubt Nasira was thrilled, but Kira knew she must also be feeling the pain of missing Jabari's youth. No doubt Akilah and Lina would be ecstatic. They loved Jabari and were probably jumping up and down to learn they had a brother. And Jalil—joy was written all over his face. She remembered what it was like to be part of a loving family and wished deep down that she could be a part of theirs.

She had almost reached her room before she remembered another family. A family that must be feeling something entirely different. *Samira! I forgot about Samira!* Kira wanted to run to her and comfort her, and her heart filled with pain for the only family she had now. *She has to be devastated! Surely her heart is breaking. And Saad. His only son!* Her eyes filled with tears at the thought of their grief. But now, they would have to wait to see what Jabari would do. And Kira would wait as well.

Seeking anything to take her mind off the unfolding drama, she picked up an unfinished basket and began adding the finishing touches. Working with the reeds helped free her mind to think about everything that had happened in the last few months. Hearing Jabari's story made her think about her own family and the letters she had written to her grandmother. Between Ehsaan and Jalil, she had sent many messages and had yet to receive any reply. Reminding herself that it was a long way to America and an even longer way to the desert of her people, Kira had continued to pray she might hear something, but lately half-hoped she wouldn't.

And as much as she couldn't bear the thought of leaving Amber, she realized she would miss Jalil even more and had to admit to herself she was falling in love with him. But though he seemed to like her, she wasn't sure about the depth of his affections. Maybe she had read too much into the looks he gave her now and then, and she was worried that it might just be a physical thing for him. And there was the fact she was a foreigner.

After a few minutes, she set her work aside and flexed her stiff fingers before reaching for her tea. As she sipped it slowly, she faced the reality of her situation. After what happened at Qadir's, she knew she could have nothing permanent with Jalil. It was just wishful thinking on her part. She could be part of his tribe, but she could never be part of his life. As she set her cup on the table, she had a horrible thought. *What if Jalil takes a wife? Can I live here, seeing someone else by his side?* Kira felt a sharp stab of pain in her heart. No, she couldn't bear it.

Blinking rapidly against the threatening tears, she sighed and picked up her basket. She tried to clear her mind, but the thought of him with another woman had her feeling sick, and she tugged angrily at a stray reed, forcing it back into shape. *I am a fool! Jalil is a sheik, and he needs an heir. He will find a proper wife and have a family.* Kira knew she would have to live with that, or she would have to find a new home. She knew of only one place she could go. The valley. In the valley she had been free with no one to judge her and no decisions to make. *Perhaps I can go back there? If only I knew the way.*

Restless and unable to finish the basket, she set it aside and stood to stretch her cramped muscles. Tired of wrestling with her troubles and worrying about the future, she splashed her face with water, donned an appropriate robe, and went in search of Nasira. Perhaps she would be up to some company.

CHAPTER 17

Jabari's meeting with his parents didn't go quite as well as the one between Jalil and Kira. He had joined them for the midday meal and was telling them about his progress with Sarii when Saad interrupted him, saying they needed to talk about something very important. They held hands while they told him the familiar tale of finding him at the oasis, but this time they added the part about the dagger. Jabari was completely stunned by the news and unsure of what to say.

"Jabari," Samira said softly, "Jabari, speak to us, please." She looked distressed and was on the verge of tears. Saad looked sad and nervous.

Jabari was still processing the startling news of his real origins and had yet to wrap his mind around it. *Nasira is my mother? Jalil is my brother? How is this possible?* He had always known part of the story, that he was a foundling. His adoptive parents had never hidden that from him, but he had never thought he would find out who his actual parents were. Not in a million years. It was a part of his life that he had buried, an unsolvable mystery. Now he had just learned he was the son of a sheik, and not just any sheik, but the great Sheik Akeem, and that Jalil, his most favorite person in the world, next to Kira, was his brother. It was all too much, and he didn't know whether to laugh or cry.

Taking a deep breath, he looked at Saad and Samira with a sad smile. "You know how much I love you both. You have been my parents, and I will never forget that, but I need some time to think about this. Please, forgive me." Running out the door, he didn't stop until he reached Sarii's corral. Tying a rope to her halter, he led her through the gate into the pasture and jumped on her back. In a flash, they were off, galloping toward the hills. Just like Jalil, Jabari needed to clear his mind and block all thoughts for a time.

When Sarii showed signs of tiring, he signaled her to slow, and soon they were walking along, both catching their breath. Stroking her neck, he marveled again at his good fortune. Sarii was strong and responsive, fast and agile. He loved her and imagined she loved him, too. She was a gift from Allah, and he believed he was meant to find her that day at Qadir's. And he had thought she was the only horse he might ever be able to call his own. But as they moved through the pasture, he watched the horses that meandered by and was overwhelmed. *Jalil's herd. My herd?* He struggled to comprehend it all, his mind filled with conflicting emotions.

It was difficult to get excited when he was still angry, but not at his adoptive parents for having kept anything from him, or because he had to grow up on the routes as the son of a trader. He was angry because he missed those years with Jalil's family, and he would never know his real father. Though he had never met Akeem, he had a vague memory of seeing him win the Tri-Annual Race three years ago, looking so regal riding the mighty Rayham. Even then, Jabari saw how men respected Akeem and how Akeem respected others. And Nasira—he wondered what it would have been like to know her love. Then he thought of Jalil. How Jabari had envied Jalil and his golden horses.

Now as he sat looking at those very horses, having just found out he was part of the family and tribe that owned them, he knew he should be excited, but he couldn't help thinking of Saad and Samira. How sad for them. They considered him their son and had always treated him as if he were. It was Saad he had to thank for teaching him the important lessons about trading and traveling the routes, how to take care of himself, and how to survive in any conditions. Samira, always the loving mother, had taught him to respect women and all life. Even Uncle Amal had always treated him like a beloved nephew. They had rescued him and raised him with love. Without them, he would be nothing—he wouldn't even be alive. Jabari could find no fault with his adoptive family. His life had been good, even as the son of a simple trader. Could he leave all that behind?

Gazing at the land that stretched out as far as he could see, Jabari felt a sudden longing to see what lay beyond and thought about the opportunities he had yet to take advantage of and the mysteries he had yet to solve. Maybe he would have the chance to do that now. Filled with hope, he realized his heart was big enough to embrace both of his families. When the westering sun eased toward the horizon, reminding him of the late hour, he turned his mare toward the stables. It was time to meet his new family, but first he needed to see his old one.

When he stopped by before the evening meal to make sure they knew how he felt about them and to thank them for all they had done for him, he saw Samira's face fall. "Mother, what is wrong?"

"Oh, Jabari, I knew in my heart you would choose to be with your real family."

"Of course I want to be with them, but I also want to be with you. I was hoping we could still share meals, and I could come to you for advice," he said, glancing at Saad.

"Son, I will always be here for you… always," Saad said with a heartfelt expression.

"Jabari, we love you, and our home will always be your home too," Samira said, wiping the tears of relief from her eyes.

Jabari grinned. He loved them so—that would never change. But when Samira chose that moment to share her news, he almost fell out of his chair.

Saad was just as stunned and stared at her in confusion. "I am having a baby?"

Chuckling, Samira reminded him that, no, he was not having the baby. She was. Whereupon Saad jumped up and started running around trying to figure out how to make her more comfortable, asking if she needed anything, and what did she want him to be doing. Jabari laughed and laughed until Saad finally came to his senses and sat down, and then he too laughed.

Samira gave Jabari permission to tell his new family about her baby, and he couldn't wait to share the news. When he left them, they were still talking about the baby and seemed to have forgotten all about him for the moment.

Rushing to his tent, he dug through his pack and assembled a clean outfit to wear to the evening meal. He fussed with his clothes, trying to ignore the feelings of inadequacy because of the condition of his simple garments. Brushing out the wrinkles, he hesitated, wondering how in the world he would fit in with the sheik's family until he realized he shouldn't feel that way at all. Being kidnapped wasn't his fault. He belonged with them now. Squaring his shoulders and taking a deep breath, he headed to the main house, determined to embrace his place as the son of a sheik.

CHAPTER 18

As soon as Nasira received word Jabari was in Saad's house, she went directly to see her daughters. When she explained about finding their missing brother, they sat in total silence, looking shocked and confused. But when she finished, Akilah and Lina could barely contain their excitement and jumped up with shouts of, "Who doesn't like Jabari?" and "Wait until Adara hears about this!" They wanted to rush right out, find him, and welcome him home. Their enthusiasm was contagious, and Nasira laughed at their reaction.

"Girls, girls. Wait! Jabari just learned about this himself, and he needs time to decide what he will do. He might want to stay with Saad and Samira."

Akilah was the first to respond. "What? Of course, he will want to move in with us. But even if he doesn't, he is still our brother, and he will live in the compound. Oh, I cannot wait to talk to him. I want to hear more about the trade routes and the port cities. I bet he has seen so many places." Ever the inquisitive one, Akilah always wanted to know what lay beyond the horizon, fascinated by stories of the foreigners seen in the region.

"Mother, can I ask Jabari to teach me to ride?" Lina asked, her face shining with happiness. Unlike her sister, Akilah, she was more interested in her four-legged friends.

"We will have to wait and see what Jabari wants to do. But you must both promise me you will leave him alone until he has reached a decision," Nasira said, giving them a stern look. She was speaking more to herself than her daughters, though. Waiting for Jabari was tying her stomach in knots. When both girls nodded in agreement, she smiled. Whatever the result, it would be better than what had been.

Nasira hadn't expected to see Jabari at the evening meal, even though she sent him an invitation, and felt thrilled when he joined them. She could tell Jalil must have thought the same thing because when he showed up, he stopped at the doorway, and his jaw dropped when he saw Jabari already seated next to his sisters, laughing merrily. Everyone in the room, including Kira, saw Jalil standing with his mouth half open, and the room erupted with laughter.

Closing his mouth with a snap, Jalil tried to look angry, but he laughed too. "All right, all right, enough with the laughter. I am here to dine with my family. Is there any left for me?" He looked hard at Jabari with a twinkle in his eye. Jabari was famous for his hearty appetite.

"Well, brother, you need to be on time in the future, or I cannot be responsible." Jabari boldly winked back at him.

Once again everyone laughed, and Nasira's heart filled with love hearing Jabari call Jalil "brother."

The evening turned into a joyous event, and she was pleased to see everyone working together to make Jabari feel welcomed. But when she noticed Kira's wistful expression as she watched the family talking and laughing, she surmised Kira was missing her own. Saddened to think that Kira was all alone in the world, she felt sorry that Kira had yet to receive word from her grandmother. Seeing Jalil watching Kira with the same wistful expression, Nasira vowed to make her feel more like part of their family. Perhaps she could convince her to stay with them forever.

A burst of merriment across the table startled Nasira from her thoughts. Jabari had just made his napkin disappear to the amusement of his new sisters, and she laughed along with Jalil, putting her worries for Kira aside for a time. That night was all about Jabari. Her son.

The next morning, Nasira sent Samira a selection of her finest materials to make clothes for her baby, and she asked Jalil to give Saad what else they might need. When Jabari had delivered the good news the previous night, it had delighted Nasira because she was feeling guilty for having stolen Samira's only child. She prayed the new baby would lessen the blow. It was a miracle and what could have been a time of sorrow for Samira had turned into one of tremendous joy.

Nasira had enjoyed her morning meal with Jalil and Jabari. Jalil gave Jabari a room of his own in the main house, and Nasira laughed when Jabari declared he would also keep his tent, explaining that Sarii might miss him. When Nasira and Jalil informed Jabari about their decision to have a celebration feast to welcome him to the tribe, he insisted they have Jabari the Magnificent perform. They both found it amusing he still wanted to keep practicing his magic, but they readily agreed.

It was Nasira who suggested that since they had missed the previous thirteen years of Jabari's life, they should use the feast to honor his birth-year too. Jabari was thrilled and ran off to share the news with Samira and Saad. When Jalil asked her if they should invite Ehsaan's family, Nasira said she wanted this first celebration to be just their family and tribe. But she sent a message to Ehsaan and Issa, sharing the news about Jabari, and Issa's response was full of happiness. Nasira knew Issa would understand, more than anyone, how wonderful it was to have found her missing child.

When they announced the celebration to the tribe, it seemed everyone wanted to give Jabari a gift, and the entire kingdom helped with the preparations. Nasira threw herself into the activity, wanting to make sure Jabari's fourteenth birth-year feast would be memorable.

Soon everything was in order, and the day of the celebration arrived. Holding the feast in the courtyard allowed the entire tribe to take part. After the speeches were made and the food was eaten, Jabari performed with his usual flair. Afterwards, he was presented with his gifts, and Nasira watched as he opened each one with his eyes wide and his face full of excitement. He loved the new robes sporting his tribal colors his sisters gave him, confessing he had always known he would ride in splendor someday. Slipping on the armband Nasira gave him, he admired the flashing yellow diamonds sprinkled among the blue stones. Saad gave him a new saddle, and Samira had woven a beautiful saddle blanket with turquoise and gold stripes to go with it. Jabari wanted to take them to show Sarii right away, but Jalil suggested he wait until after the celebration.

Kira's gift was a sturdy basket for his magic gear, and she laughed when he took it and ran over to his old magic bag and dumped everything into the new basket. Fahad gave him a finely worked short sword with a gilded scabbard. It was a very grown-up gift, and Jabari accepted it gravely. He already seemed to understand the importance of his new position as the brother of the ruling sheik. His mood lightened when Sakhr presented him with a pair of leather riding boots like Jalil's. He immediately put them on and strode around, mimicking his brother, much to the amusement of all.

After Jabari opened all his gifts, Jalil took him by the arm and led him to stand in front of the center table. Nasira held her breath. This was the moment she had been waiting for. Jalil cleared his throat and addressed the tribe. "Today is a very special day. I know that most of you have heard the good news that my brother, Talib, who was stolen from us so long ago, has been returned to us. Praise Allah! There can be no doubt who he is, and today we welcome him home to his family and his tribe. Please honor him as you honor me."

The guests cheered and thumped the tables. Akilah and Lina cried openly, and Nasira saw Kira wiping her eyes, too. She was pleased to see that even though tears coursed down Samira's face, she also smiled, and her eyes shone with pride. Then Jalil waved his arms to call for silence. When the crowd settled, he turned to speak to Jabari.

"Jabari, you were born Talib, but you became Jabari. It will be up to you which name you use in the future, but we welcome you to our family and tribe under any name. You are my brother, the son of Sheik Akeem and Sheikha Nasira. As such, you have all the powers granted to our family. To honor you, I would like to give you a gift from our tribe… and Mirage." Grinning, he gestured toward the entrance of the courtyard.

Nasira chuckled to see Jabari speechless as Sakhr entered, leading a colt with a dark red coat and black stockings. He shimmered in the torchlight—it was obvious he was a son of Mirage. The colt made it all the way to the table before Jabari regained his senses. She knew Jabari remembered how young horses spooked easily because he talked soothingly while walking slowly toward the colt. The colt responded by turning to focus on him.

Jabari reached out his hand, palm up, and the colt sniffed loudly. When he nibbled at Jabari's hand and Jabari leaned over and touched noses with him, the colt tossed his head and let out a squeal and a snort. Laughing softly, Jabari stepped forward and the colt stood still while the boy petted and talked to him, and Nasira felt her tears begin anew seeing the them already becoming friends.

Jabari turned to face the table, his smile brighter than the torches, and bowed to Jalil, who bowed in return. Then he raised his arms to get the attention of the crowd. "I would like to thank my sheik and my tribe for the generous gift of this colt. I will treasure him always. He will be a valuable member of my family, and I will protect him with my life. He will be known as Rizu because he will be 'mighty' indeed. I also want to thank everyone here for accepting me and for making my other family a part of your tribe. It is a great honor, and I will serve you all until my death."

Again, everyone clapped and cheered, but he waved his hands once more. "And now I must tell you that even though I was born Talib, I choose to be known as Jabari, son of Akeem." He smiled at Jalil and Nasira but looked long and lovingly at Samira and Saad. They both nodded, and Nasira could see how proud they were, too.

Before Sakhr led Rizu away, Jabari gave his colt one last hug then he rejoined his family at the main table. By midnight, the last of the crowd dispersed, and Nasira rose to retire with the rest of her family but stopped when Jabari ran up.

"Yes, my son?" Nasira's heart swelled with happiness. It was the first time she had called him such.

"Sheikha, is it all right if I visit the stables for just a minute? I need to say goodnight to Rizu, and I must tell Sarii she is not being replaced by my new colt." He waited politely for her response.

"Of course you may visit the stables. Jabari, this is your home now and you may do as you wish but thank you for asking."

Jabari bowed with a smile and dashed from the courtyard. As Nasira watched him disappear into the darkness, she was filled with a new determination and made a silent vow. No one would ever take her child from her again.

CHAPTER 19

Strangely restless and unable to sleep after the excitement of the celebration, Kira lay on her bed, trying to clear her head. When the night breeze sighed through the shutters in her room, bringing the sharp scent of warm sand and the cool crisp smell of the mountains, it reminded her of the valley. Filled with a sudden longing, she couldn't resist. She threw off her sleeping tunic, quickly donned her boy's clothes, and twisted her hair into a loose braid. Grabbing a dark robe and a pair of soft slippers, she hurried to the window to make her escape.

When Kira first moved into the room, she had discovered a loose shutter panel on her lower window, and rather than have it fixed, she reset it so she could remove it easily. Though she could come and go as she pleased, Kira knew Nasira wouldn't want her riding around in the middle of the night, and the guards posted by the front door might stop her. Setting the panel aside, she dropped lightly to the sand where she remained crouched, waiting to be sure no one had seen her. Once she determined the way was clear, she crept toward the back pasture. A full moon was rising, and it was bright enough for her to find the gate, and as always, Amber was waiting for her.

She pulled herself up on Amber's back and urged her into a gallop. Freeing her hair, Kira let it fall to catch the wind, and closing her eyes, she felt transported to her beloved valley. She could see Ndee, the golden stallion, and hear him galloping beside her.

Amber slowed as they neared the cliffs where the water pooled next to the rocks. It was the spring, the source of Jalil's water and one of Kira's favorite places. She had often wished she could swim like she used to in the valley but dared not take the risk during the day. As Amber stopped to take a drink, Kira studied the pool, entranced by the water glowing in the brilliant moonlight and swirling gently in the breeze. Sliding off Amber, she walked to the water's edge and was suddenly filled with the need to feel the freedom of floating on the water under the desert moon. Reckless with excitement, she removed her clothes and laid them on a nearby boulder. She shivered in the chilly night air but was determined to take the plunge.

As she waded forward, she felt the bottom dropping away and eased in until the water reached her chin. Moving further into the water, she held her breath and sank until her feet touched the smooth pebbles on the bottom. When she looked up, she saw the shimmering white disk of the moon, and infused with the magic of the water, she raised her arms and pushed off the bottom. She shot up into the air and fell back with a splash, to float with her hair swirling and undulating in the current. Kira felt nothing now, but the water, still warm from the heat of the desert sun. Closing her eyes, she drifted lazily and could finally clear her mind.

It was but a moment when a sudden sound disturbed the quiet. Alarmed, she raised her head, and her body submerged as she looked around wildly. Seeing Amber undisturbed and standing quietly on the bank, Kira relaxed. But her peaceful mood was gone, and aware of the growing cold, she swam toward the bank.

When she rose from the water and saw someone standing by the rocks, her hand flew to her mouth, and she stifled a scream. The moon had passed behind a cloud, but as it sailed into the clear, she recognized the intruder. *Jalil!* Dropping her arm to cover her breasts, she tried to cover the top of her thighs with her other hand. But before she could draw another breath, he was beside her, wrapping his warm arms around her shivering wet body, pulling her closer until her thighs molded to his and her breasts pushed against the soft fabric of his tunic.

Shocked by how fast he had moved, Kira looked up to see the flash of his eyes and his mouth set in a tight smile and was unafraid but unsettled. "What are you doing here?"

"I couldn't sleep. I thought if I took a ride it would help." His voice wavered and he looked as if he wanted to ask her something.

"What do you want, Jalil?" Kira whispered, feeling breathless.

"You," he whispered as he lowered his face and pressed his lips to hers.

Consumed by feelings she had never known, Kira gasped at the suddenness of his kiss, and he slipped his tongue inside to tangle with hers. Swept away by the desires he roused in her body, she wrapped her arms around his neck. He growled against her lips and lifted her, his hands cupping her bottom, holding her tightly against his hard body.

She moaned and tried to get even closer. The kiss seemed to last forever, and she was rapidly losing control and finding it harder to breathe. Holding her head with one large warm hand, he released her lips, leaned her back, and began feathering kisses down her jaw and further down her neck and further still as he sought the soft fullness of her breasts. She didn't know what she wanted. She only knew she wanted whatever he was doing to never stop.

When she felt his fingers trace a trail over her shoulder and down her chest, lightly caressing her breast, she moaned and whimpered. Warm feelings curled up from deep within and ignited into flames. He leaned back to look into her eyes, and she saw the fire in his too. Reaching behind his neck, he removed his tunic and pulled her hard against his bare chest. She could feel the heat from his medallion pressing against her breasts and she slid her hands down his smooth muscled back until they found his lean hips. He stared into the pools of her eyes and stroked her breasts before leaning down to kiss and nibble, driving her passion like fanning a fire.

At some level, Kira was aware something important was happening between them, but then he was kissing her again and all rational thought fled from her mind as she rose higher and higher. She was dimly aware his hand was sliding down beneath her breasts and over her belly, but when he reached even lower, she stiffened in shock at his touch. Panicking, she looked up and saw the face from her worst nightmare. *Qadir!* Her ears roared, and her heart raced with fear when she found herself back in Qadir's arms, and it was Qadir's hand between her legs and his face leering down at her. Engulfed with terror, she began to fight, squirming against Jalil's muscular arms, but he seemed unaware of her fear.

It might have gone further had Mirage not chosen that moment to make his desires known. A bugle and a sharp whinny startled Jalil, and Kira broke free of his embrace. Overcome with shame, she stumbled back, breathing like she had run a race. Amber was stomping as Mirage came down the trail, prancing like he was finally going to get her full attention.

Jalil's gaze remained fixed on Kira's body, but when he suddenly looked up and made eye contact with her, his brow knitted in confusion, and he swore softly. He turned and yelled at Mirage, but his stallion ignored him and tried to sidle closer to Amber. Only she was having nothing to do with the big stallion.

Kira, stuck in her flashback, saw Qadir standing before her, scrambled to grab her clothes, and ran to Amber's side. Naked, she pulled herself up onto Amber, who immediately wheeled and took off.

Kira leaned low on Amber's neck, breathing harshly, urging her horse to go faster. The cold night wind bit into her arms and legs, and she shivered violently. Suddenly aware of her nakedness and praying she had lost her pursuer for the moment, she stopped to pull on her trousers and tunic. She climbed back on top of Amber, and they galloped back to the stables. Not wishing to attract attention from any of Qadir's men who she imagined were lying in wait for her, she hid Amber in an empty stall, telling her to stay put until she got back.

Terrified that Qadir was chasing after her, she threw caution to the wind and ran to her window, jumped up to catch the bottom rail, and pulled herself up and over into the room. Frantic, she rushed to fill her old travel bag with everything she thought she might need.

The bag still contained her father's money belt, along with other items she found useful when she travelled with the family. After adding some extra clothes, another pair of slippers, and a blanket, she filled her old waterskin with water. Seeing the tray of bread and fruit on the table, she rolled some in a towel and threw that in as well.

She had to hurry now. Qadir would be back any moment, and she couldn't bear for him to touch her again. Crying softly, she donned a dark robe and headwrap and hurried back to the window. Placing the waterskin around her neck, she dropped her bag outside, lowered herself to the ground, and ran to Amber's stall.

Kira placed her saddle on Amber's back and tied her bag to it before leading her out of the building. Climbing into the saddle, she urged Amber into a full gallop, leaning down close to Amber's neck and directing her toward the main pass. All she could think about was getting away from Qadir.

Belatedly remembering the guards at the pass, Kira started hyperventilating, thinking they would catch her and take her back to Qadir. But when Amber slowed to a soft, silent walk, Kira felt a sense of calm from her four-legged friend and allowed her horse to take control. Moving as quietly as only the desert born can, Amber became just another shadow in the rocks. Kira leaned close to her neck and prayed silently, but no one saw them. Once they were clear of the pass, Amber turned westward, and Kira sighed with relief. They had escaped, and her troubles were behind her now. At last, she was going home.

CHAPTER 20

Jalil cursed Mirage for having picked the worst time to court Amber. Feeling the sting of Kira's rejection, he remained for a while by the pool, knowing that Kira wouldn't want him to chase after her, especially since she was obviously afraid of him. Seeing her jump naked on her horse and gallop across the pasture completely bare was enough to renew his raging desire, but he restrained himself. She had made it clear she didn't want him.

The image of her naked body floating in luminescent water—surrounded by her silvery hair, her arms outstretched, and her legs slightly spread—filled his mind. When he'd seen her moon-kissed breasts and feminine curls, he wanted to kiss her, touch her, and give her the pleasure he knew he could, if she'd only let him. Filled with an uncontrollable urge, he struggled not to leap over the rocks and swim to her side. And he almost succeeded until she rose from the water, and he lost all control and ran to her side with only one thing in mind.

But Jalil didn't think he would ever forget the sight of her beautiful face full of fear and disgust nor his disgust at himself for his obvious failure to control his own urges. The magic of the night was gone, lost to him. Full of regret for having forced himself on her, he headed back to the stables but took a longer route. He needed time to cool off and think about what he was going to do. Luckily, Kira was nowhere in sight by the time he got back to the house.

Jalil spent the remainder of the night tossing and turning, reliving his amorous attack on Kira. It was late in the morning when he finally rose, still full of anger at himself and pent-up desire for her. *How am I going to fix this?* For a few minutes, he lost control and was in the middle of taking out his frustration on anything he could get his hands on when he heard an insistent knocking at his door.

"What?" he yelled as he threw open the door.

His mother took a step back, looking wary. "Who are you and what have you done with my son?" she said.

When he glimpsed himself in the nearby mirror, he understood her reaction. His hair flew in every direction, and dark circles hung under his bloodshot eyes. "What do you want, Mother?" he said brusquely.

"Well, I was going to wish my son, the sheik, a good morning and see if he had a few minutes to spare his old mother," she said, peeking around his shoulder. He glanced back and it looked like a sandstorm had blown through. The room was littered with overturned chairs and clothes, and something was dripping down the wall. "Perhaps I should have sent someone to request an audience?" she asked tightly, looking at him with those "I am your mother...you had better behave yourself" eyes.

Feeling ashamed, he softened his tone. "I apologize, Mother."

"Jalil, I have never seen you like this. What is going on?"

Leaning against the door frame, he sighed, dropped his head, and rubbed his forehead. When he looked up, his eyes mirroring his mood, she reached out to feel his forehead. "Are you ill?"

He gently grasped her hand and pushed it away. "No, I am not ill. Please, come in. I need to talk to someone." He sat down at the table and leaned over, holding his head in his hands.

Nasira sat next to him and waited patiently for him to speak.

Finally, he raised his head. "Have you seen Kira this morning?"

Her eyes registered her surprise. "Well, no. After morning meal, I went to the stables to look for you. When Sakhr said he had not seen you yet, I assumed you were still in your room, and I came straight here. Why?"

Embarrassed, Jalil blushed and looked away as he spoke. "I think Kira might be mad at me."

Nasira looked curious. "Why would you say that? Did you two have a fight?"

"Um, not exactly." He looked down as if suddenly fascinated by the inlaid blue stones and yellow gems of the massive gold ring upon his finger—the ring every sheik of his tribe had worn since time unknown.

"Jalil?" She paused until he looked up at her. "You need to tell me why Kira, someone who admires you and someone you care about, would be mad at you."

Jalil sighed, leaned back in his chair, and blurted out, "Because I attacked her."

"What? You attacked her? What are you talking about? Did you hurt her?" His mother leaned forward, her eyes wide with alarm.

"Of course I did not hurt her, Mother." He couldn't help feeling offended. "I did not really attack her. I mean, well, I, uh, I took a liberty last night... after the celebration."

His mother surprised him with her next words. "So, you kissed her." She had an uncanny knack for knowing things before he said them.

"I did not just kiss her." He looked away when he saw her alarm return.

"Can you tell me exactly what you did to her?" Nasira said hesitantly.

Jalil squirmed. "Um, well, um, we were at the pool by the cliffs, and there was some kissing, and…and she seemed to like it." As soon as he said it, he suddenly had another thought. "I might have touched her…" he was going to say more, but Nasira cut him off.

"Stop! Stop this minute! I do not need to hear anymore. Just tell me this, Jalil. Did you have her permission?" His mother's tone was sharp and a little desperate. Evidently, what she wanted to know was very important.

"I did... well, at least I thought I did. Up to a certain point, she seemed to return my affection, but then it was like she went crazy. I have never seen her look like that. She was terrified. That is when I knew I had gone too far. She also looked disgusted." Jalil hung his head, awash with feelings of shame.

"Oh," she said, then fell quiet.

Fully expecting her to chastise him for his poor behavior, Jalil tried to justify his actions. "Mother, I… I really like Kira, and I respect her too. I never intended to approach her like I did, but, well…" His voice trailed off. He was finding it more difficult than he thought to explain his feelings for her. How could he tell his mother that Kira roused him more than any other woman ever had?

She saved him from further explanation. "Jalil, let me ask you something."

"Yes, Mother?"

"Do you know what Qadir did to Kira?"

His clenched his fists with renewed anger. "He beat her, and he whipped her."

"Yes, he did. But do you know what else he did to her?"

"He used her as a man uses a woman!" Jalil said, his anger spiking. "I saw the evidence that night."

"Yes, Jalil, and what should have been an act of love was a nightmare of pain and shame for Kira. It is likely you scared her, but not the way you might think. She has not dealt with what happened to her yet. I also expect she thinks you might not respect her anymore and likely does not respect herself. None of what happened at Qadir's was her fault, but often, we mistakenly hold ourselves accountable for things beyond our control."

Jalil was stunned. "I did not even think! I am worse than Qadir because I knew she had been abused, and yet I could not help myself. She must hate me!" Suddenly overwhelmed with the need to ask Kira's forgiveness, he jumped up. "I must find her at once and apologize!"

His mother stood and grabbed his hand before he could dash from the room. "Jalil, wait. Slow down. You will just scare her more. You must give her time to think about it. She will come to understand you are not anything like Qadir."

He stopped and closed his eyes. "I pray you are right, Mother."

"Well, I hope I am right, but we shall see. Now, why don't you clean up in here and make yourself more presentable, and I will check on Kira. She might need a woman to talk to."

When she reached up and pulled his head down to place a kiss on his forehead, he pulled her into a quick hug then quickly released her, and she departed.

Jalil straightened his room and took a quick dip in his pool before heading to the stables. His anger had dissolved into concern for Kira, but he needed to find something to take his mind off her. On his way, he was flagged by one of the guards. Evidently, a sentry had heard something strange in the main pass the previous night, but no one had seen anything. Jalil thanked him and resolved to speak to Fahad about it later. Right now, he needed to take that ride. He saddled Mirage and rode off to check on the herd. When he returned, he couldn't wait any longer and went to find his mother to see if she had spoken to Kira yet. On his way, he heard a gunshot from the direction of the main pass. On alert, he stopped to listen. One shot meant foe. Two shots meant friend. Relieved to hear the second shot, he climbed the steps at the front of his house to wait for whoever had sought entry to his kingdom. Two of his house guards flanked him.

A few minutes later, two men rode up, escorted by one of Jalil's guards from the pass. They stopped in front of the house, as was customary, to wait for the sheik's invitation to dismount. Jalil noted their tribal colors and knew they were Ehsaan's men.

One man addressed him at once. "Sheik Jalil, we bring a message from Sheik Ehsaan," he said, handing Jalil a green leather bag.

"Thank you. I may need to send a reply. Can you wait for it?"

They agreed, and Jalil sent men to see to their comfort and provide food and water for their horses. He retired to his chambers and opened the bag to find a scroll bearing the emerald seal of Sheik Ehsaan. Ehsaan asked if he could bring Issa and Adara for a visit. His daughter wished to see her dear friend Jabari. Jalil found it interesting that Ehsaan also mentioned hearing of tribal unrest, as if an afterthought, and mentioned Jabari as a friend and not as Jalil's brother. Perhaps it was a clue as to the seriousness of the visit, and he figured he'd better talk to Fahad and Nasira before he sent a reply.

He found his mother in her chambers sorting yarn samples Saad had brought from a tribe that specialized in raising sheep for wool. Her door was open, but he stopped and knocked first.

When she saw him, she smiled and beckoned him to have a seat. "Is this about Kira?" She poured herself some tea and offered him a cup.

He waved it away. "No, but have you talked to her?" he asked hopefully.

"I was going to stop by her room before my meal, but I thought she might need a little more time."

"You are probably right, as usual," he said ruefully, resigned to having to wait.

Nasira chuckled softly. "Well, if this is not about Kira, what is on your mind?"

"I just received this message from Ehsaan," he said, handing her the scroll. Most men wouldn't seek advice from a woman, but Jalil learned a long time ago that a woman, and even more so a mother, often had a special sense about things. Many times, Nasira had seen something or thought of something that he might not have, and he gladly sought her counsel. He idly peeled a tangerine while she read the note.

When she finished, she looked up at him. "So, there is a problem in the tribes, and Ehsaan doesn't want to risk a detailed message. He also omits any mention of your new brother, nor does he mention the name Talib, but he obviously wants to talk about Jabari." She amazed him by how easily she read between the lines.

"My thoughts exactly. Shall we invite them for a visit? I was going to send a reply but wanted to make sure you were up for having visitors." He popped a slice of tangerine into his mouth.

"I appreciate your asking, Jalil. I will always welcome Ehsaan and his family, and I have something I want to talk to Issa about, anyway. But would you ask Ehsaan to bring Amal and Fatima as well? I know Saad would like to see his brother, and I expect Kira would like to see Fatima."

"Certainly. I will take care of that in a minute." He reached for a cloth to wipe his hands before asking in a more serious tone, "Will you try to talk to Kira today?"

"Yes, Jalil, I promise. Now, go prepare your reply. I will send word to the servants to ready the guest rooms and check on the provisions."

He touched her hand lightly. "Thank you, and if you need me, I am meeting Fahad later in the main hall. One of the guards reported hearing something strange in the main pass last night. And now that Talib, I mean Jabari, has been returned to us, I want to talk to Fahad about future security issues."

She nodded. "Fahad has proved his worth so many times. You are blessed to have such a trusted adviser and captain," she said.

"Yes, indeed. I better hurry, but I will see you at evening meal," Jalil said.

Jalil returned to his chamber to inscribe a reply to Ehsaan on a fresh scroll. Once it was dry, he rolled it up and sealed it with his signature turquoise wax stamped with his ring. Placing his message in Ehsaan's pouch, he sent a guard to fetch Ehsaan's men. They came without delay, and after thanking him for their meals, they departed. Ehsaan wouldn't get his reply until late the next day, but knowing Ehsaan, he was already prepared to travel. Jalil figured they would be here in less than four days, and he needed to be ready. With that on his mind, he went to find Saad and Jabari to let them know that Amal and his bride were coming for a visit.

Not surprisingly, when Jalil informed Saad and Samira of the pending visit, they were excited. Jabari was thrilled. He said he couldn't wait to show Adara everything he'd taught Sarii and immediately ran off to practice the special tricks he was teaching his little mare. Smiling to see him in such a state, Jalil understood Jabari's enthusiasm to share everything with Adara. He felt the same way about Kira.

Consumed with thoughts of Kira, Jalil could hardly concentrate during his meeting with Fahad. As soon as they were done, he couldn't wait any longer to check on her to see if she was all right and if she'd forgiven him for his impulsive behavior the previous night. He hurried to the guest wing, but when he knocked on her door, there was no response. He knocked again, impatiently tapping his foot.

A passing servant stopped to speak with him. "My sheik, she is not there."

"Do you know where she has gone? Did she go for a ride?" he asked.

"I do not know, my sheik. I checked on her early this morning, but she did not answer, and I have not seen her all day."

Jalil thanked the servant, but puzzled, he called out and knocked again. When there was still no answer, he tried the door and found it locked. Sensing something wasn't right, he forced it open only to find another room that looked like it had been hit by a sandstorm. A chair was knocked over, clothes were tossed everywhere, and the bed was in disarray. Stunned, Jalil stared at the mess, and the hair stood up on the back of his neck. With a feeling of foreboding and growing alarm, he cursed and ran out and down the hall. Flagging a servant on the way, he sent him in search of Fahad and Nasira.

Breathing fast and knowing he needed to calm down, he steadied himself and stopped to think. *Where could she be? Of course! She's gone for a ride!* He strode out the front door, maintaining a steady pace. It wouldn't be wise for the sheik to be seen running through the compound. He bumped into Sakhr on the front steps.

"Good morning, my sheik," Sakhr said, bowing his head.

"Sakhr, have you seen Kira this morning?"

"No, my sheik, I have not. Fahad informed me of Sheik Ehsaan's visit, and I was searching for Saad. I need to speak with him about provisions for the horses. Have you seen him?"

"No, I do not know where he is. But are you sure you have not seen Kira? What about Amber? Have you seen her?" Jalil roughly ran a hand through his hair, feeling his panic return.

"No." Sakhr must have noticed, and his voice tightened. "What is wrong, Sheik?"

"Nothing... nothing. Where is Jabari?" He looked around the compound.

"He is with Rizu in the foaling stable," Sakhr said. "Shall I get him for you?"

"No, I will find him," he said then turned but stopped when Sakhr spoke again.

"Sheik, I remember one of my men mentioned seeing Amber standing in her stable, but I do not know when that was."

Well, that was unusual, Jalil thought. Amber rarely spent any time in the compound, seeming to prefer the open pastures. "Thank you, Sakhr, but if you see Kira or Amber, please let me know at once."

"Yes, Sheik, I will." He bowed and headed inside.

As Jalil started toward the stables, he heard his mother calling his name from inside the house. He turned and hastened to her side.

"Jalil, I went to check on Kira, but she is not in her room, and someone forced the door," Nasira said, her faced filled with panic.

"Oh, I am sorry. That was my fault. I broke in, but she wasn't there. Has anyone seen her?" he asked desperately, his eyes aflame with all his hopes and desires.

"I am sorry, Jalil. She has taken her things. I fear she is gone."

CHAPTER 21

The first thing Kira noticed was light. Faint at first, ebbing and flowing in shades of pink and gold across her eyelids. Movement. *How strange.* As her senses returned, one by one, she heard discordant notes overhead then heard another sound, like a sigh but more regular. *Breathing?* In and out. In and out. *Is that me?* No, it was something else. *Or someone else?* She tried to open her eyes but to no avail. *Why can't I open my eyes?*

She touched them. They felt sticky and gritty, and she rubbed them lightly to break the seal. When she was able to open them, she saw splashes of color—broad strokes of pale blue streaked with dark green and lemon yellow—and struggled to focus. *Palms?* The colors sharpened into shapes, and she watched the palm fronds above her head moving ever so gently, casting slivers of shadow across her face. Little birds fluttered here and there, and again, she heard their high-pitched notes.

Lying motionless, she waited for her mind to catch up. *Where am I?* Hearing the breathing again, this time closer, she turned her head to see a horse's nose right by her shoulder. The nostrils flared gently, inhaling, exhaling, and she began matching the rhythm. The horse's lips nibbled at her robe, pulling and playing with the material, and when Kira raised her eyes, she saw a familiar golden face and heard a soft nicker.

"Amber!" Kira cried aloud, and her horse whinnied with relief, it seemed. *But where am I?* Sitting up and bracing her hands behind her, memories came rushing back, flooding her mind. *Qadir! No, wait? Jalil!* Confused, her eyes darted left and right, taking in the nearby pool of clear water surrounded by palms and low scrub, and she inhaled sharply. *Could it be?* Taking a deep breath, she focused, calming when she recognized the clearing and the birds. *The oasis!* It was the same oasis Amber had led her to after the plane crash. It seemed so long ago, a lifetime. *But where is Qadir?*

Just as she had calmed down, violent images and thoughts assailed her mind, and she began shaking and trembling. Dropping her head, she wrapped her arms around her body and rocked back and forth, trying to make sense of it all. Her mind was screaming at her to run. He was attacking her and hurting her, and she heard his sneering voice, cruel laugher, and the crack of his whip. Then he touched her!

Qadir's evil face grew until it was all she could see, and she crab-walked backward in a rush, only to end up falling into the pool. Floundering and splashing, she breathed in water and emerged choking and spitting. When she stopped coughing, she sat in the shallow water, scrunching her eyes and praying. When she finally opened them, she saw she was alone. No one else was there except Amber and the tiny birds. Qadir was gone.

Filled with relief, but unsure what had just happened, she only knew she wanted to be clean. Pulling and tugging at her water-soaked clothes, she threw them on the bank and lay back down in the water. Her hair was a tangled mess, but she ignored it and leaned her head back until her ears filled with water, blocking all sounds. Keeping her eyes closed, she floated peacefully, and as she relaxed, her mind filled with images again, but this time, she saw a different face and heard a different voice. Green-gold eyes and a bright smile. Deep chuckles and strong, gentle hands and warm, firm skin. *Jalil.*

Seeing his handsome face, she jerked upright and ended up floundering, half submerged, and, again, gulping water and choking. Scrambling toward the bank, she pulled herself out to sit on her sodden robe. *Jalil!* With her hand held to her mouth, she began sobbing when she realized what she had done. She had let him take liberties. She had responded like a wanton woman. And then she had run away, like a madwoman! *Oh my God! What must he think of me?* When Amber eased forward to nudge her shoulder, Kira stood and flung her arms around Amber's neck to cry out her sorrows. Amber stood patiently, as always, until Kira's sobs became sniffles and Kira regained control of her emotions.

Sighing deeply and wiping her nose with the back of her hand, Kira noticed she'd forgotten to remove her saddle and travel bag from Amber's back. Feeling guilty for not having taken care of her horse, she quickly untied the bag and pulled off the saddle. Amber whinnied as if to say thank you, shook all over, then started pawing the ground. Kira knew what was coming, and a small smile worked its way onto her face. Amber lowered herself and rolled around on her back, kicking her legs in obvious enjoyment. She made funny noises, and Kira stifled her laughter. It wouldn't do to laugh at Amber. A horse on the ground has little dignity and doesn't like to be reminded of that. When Amber stood and shook off the sand, Kira marveled at Amber's unique coat. Besides its rare iridescence, nothing seemed to stick to it.

Aware she was naked, but knowing she was alone, she stepped out of the shade to absorb the powerful heat of the sun, letting its warmth fill her and dry her. Refreshed but emotionally drained, she donned dry clothes then gathered her wet garments and hung them over nearby bushes to dry. Hearing the birds set her stomach to rumbling, and she remembered the dates to be found in the nearby clearing. Filling a head wrap with the sweet morsels, she settled on her blanket by the pool and ate, enjoying the solitude.

She tried not to think about anything, but she couldn't banish Jalil from her mind. He had tried to seduce her at the pool by the cliffs, but she could hardly blame him. After what she had done with Qadir, he probably thought she would be open to his affections. But she knew there could be nothing serious between them now.

In her twisted thinking, she considered herself unworthy and felt she would never be free of what had happened to her. Her reaction during her encounter with Jalil cemented that thought. And even if she was capable of allowing someone that close to her, Jalil deserved more than a used harem girl. He needed a woman who was unspoiled, as his tradition required, to be the mother of his children and the sheikha of his tribe. Kira could never be that now. *Should I go back anyway?* Trying to convince herself she would be happy just being a member of the tribe, living in the community along with Jabari, Samira, and Saad, she realized she was only fooling herself. After what she had felt with Jalil, she could never stand to see him with another. She had experienced physical longings new to her, and even now her body reacted to the memory of his kisses and caresses. No, it was better if she never went back. *But where can I go?*

As Kira pondered her predicament, she watched Amber nosing around, finding treats of her own, when she had a sudden thought. She stopped chewing and stared harder at her horse. The last time they had been at this oasis, Amber had led her to the secret valley. *The valley!* It must be close—it had taken less than a day to get there from the oasis. Thinking hard, she tried to remember what direction they had taken. *North, maybe?* Gazing at the sun, she knew it was still early and figured if they left now, they could find it before sunset. But would Amber take her there again?

Energized, Kira dug around in her bag for her comb and braided her hair, tying it off with a piece of leather cord. Using a dry cloth, she lightly cleaned Amber's back before hoisting the saddle up and cinching it tight. Her clothes were almost dry, and she rolled them up in her blanket and tied them to the back of the saddle along with her bag. After filling her waterskin, she led Amber to the north side of the clearing and climbed up in the saddle.

Amber stood as if waiting for a command, and Kira stroked her neck and leaned forward to whisper in her ear, "Amber, please take me to the valley. We need to find Ndee." She sat back and waited to see what the golden horse would do. Amber raised her head and huffed, testing the air, then began walking northward at a steady pace. Kira recognized the heading she took, and smiling in triumph, she relaxed to enjoy the ride.

Later in the day, as the sun approached the western horizon and indigo shadows gathered around enormous sandstone boulders, she recognized familiar rock formations rearing their ruddy stone faces from an abundance of dry scree. When the way became steep and treacherous, just like she remembered, Kira dismounted to follow Amber on foot. *This is the path!* Her heart pounded, and her spirits rose. She knew she was right when, at the top of the trail, Amber lowered her head and squeezed behind the large boulder that marked the opening to the hidden tunnel.

Kira fought the urge to run, remembering they had to be careful in the long dark of the twisting tunnel. She followed Amber slowly, but when she saw the growing light at the end, she walked faster, and Amber too quickened her pace. By the time they burst into the light, they were both running. The valley spread out before them, drenched in the deep golden rays of the setting sun. Seeing the deep green of the palms surrounding her old camp, the pale green of the reed beds, and the silver blue stream curling and winding through the groves, Kira shouted with joy. Amber neighed loudly, and Kira heard a sound from her dreams, the bugle of a wild stallion. Ndee was on his way. She was finally home.

CHAPTER 22

While Kira and Amber were running down the hill from the tunnel into the valley, Jalil was running out of his house to the stables. "Sakhr, Sakhr!" he shouted. Sakhr was coming around the building, and Jalil ran to meet him. Sliding to a stop, he grabbed him by the arms. "Sakhr! She's gone! She's disappeared!" he yelled, drawing the attention of other men in the compound.

"My sheik. What are you talking about? Who is gone? Who has disappeared?" Sakhr tried to calm him.

"Kira! And Amber! Have you still not seen them today? Has anyone seen them?" Jalil said frantically and turned to the other men who came running. They looked at each other with apprehension then back at him, shaking their heads. No one remembered seeing the girl or her horse, except for one guard who stepped forward. "My sheik, I think I saw Amber before sunrise this morning."

Jalil let go of Sakhr and grabbed the man. "Where? Where did you see her?"

The guard's eyes widened, and he looked a little frightened. "I... I... I think I saw her standing in the doorway of the stable," he stuttered.

"Yes, yes, Sakhr mentioned that earlier. But what was she doing?" Jalil shook him.

"Just standing there, my sheik. It was still dark, and I did not pay that much attention. She is a wild thing and goes where she pleases, as you commanded. Did I do something wrong?"

The man's fearful expression finally registered with Jalil, and he calmed himself, releasing the man. "No, my friend, you have done nothing wrong. It is I that did something wrong."

Jalil collected himself and started issuing commands. "Sakhr, ready ten of our fastest horses." He turned and strode back to the house. "And someone find Fahad. Ask him to join me in the main hall."

Nasira met him at the front door. "Jalil, what are you going to do?"

"Mother, you are welcome to join me in the main hall. I am getting ready to send out search parties for Kira. She could be somewhere out in the pastures and hurt." He kept walking.

"No, my son. I do not think she is anywhere close."

"What makes you say that? What do you know?" He whirled back around.

"I searched her room, and she has taken all her traveling things. I think she has run away."

"But where would she go? To Ehsaan's? She knows of no other place. She has no other home." Filled with frustration, he was unwilling to believe she would have left without a word.

"I do not know, but my heart tells me she is going somewhere only she and Amber know about. Maybe we should talk to Saad and Samira. They might have some idea. And for that matter, Jabari might know something too. He is very close to her."

"Yes, yes! Can you send someone to bring them to the house now?"

"Yes, I will do that immediately and then join you."

"Thank you."

Nasira nodded and hurried away, leaving Jalil standing in the hall.

Jalil was still in shock. He couldn't comprehend that Kira had left his kingdom. It would take days of travel for her to go anywhere from there, days of danger. Alone, she would be unprotected from predators, both man and animal. What would be so horrible to make her risk her life? *Is the memory of Qadir that raw? Or does she fear me?* Those thoughts tore his heart in two, and he held his hand to his chest and grasped the medallion as if it could stop the pain somehow, but it gave him no comfort. He needed to find her—there was no other option. Determined, he headed to the main hall.

Unfortunately, Saad and Samira could shed no light on Kira's whereabouts. "My sheik, Kira said she travelled southeast from the plane wreck until the lion attacked her in the foothills."

"That's right," Jabari chimed in. "She never spoke of having gone anywhere else."

Jalil noticed Samira frowning. "What is it, Samira?"

Startled, she looked at him. "I am sorry, my sheik. I was just thinking about Amber and Kira. When we found them, they were so tightly bonded, as if they had spent a long time together. Longer than a few days in the desert."

"Well, she *did* save Amber's life," Jabari said.

"Yes, saving someone's life can create an unbreakable bond," Jalil said. He knew firsthand from having saved Mirage who he found injured in the mountains of the north pass after Akeem's death.

"Perhaps…perhaps," Samira said, but her frown remained.

Nasira had been quiet up to that point but suddenly spoke. "What about the westward trail?"

Jalil shook his head. "Surely, she would not go that way. According to Saad, she's never been in that direction."

Saad agreed. "That is correct. Your kingdom was the farthest point on our route."

Nasira didn't look appeased, and Jalil saw her exchange a look with Samira. It worried him greatly. He knew about a mother's intuition and prayed she was wrong. The west trail led nowhere but into desolate mountains.

After Saad gave directions to the location where they first found Kira, Fahad sent one search party to follow Saad's route to the southeast, and Jalil sent another group eastward, praying she might have headed to Ehsaan. He sent a few others to scour the pastures and search the north pass, one little used but well-guarded. Knowing how dangerous it would be for Kira if anyone knew a fair-haired foreign woman on a rare golden horse was traveling by herself, Jalil cautioned his men to be discreet. They were only to ask anyone they met if they had seen anyone or anything unusual.

Of course, Jalil wanted to go too, until Fahad reminded him of Ehsaan's visit. With all the drama of Kira's disappearance, Jalil had forgotten. Fahad was right. He couldn't leave, but he hated staying behind.

Distracted, Jalil lost his appetite and couldn't sleep. Obsessed with finding Kira, he drove everyone crazy until his mother reminded him he was neglecting his duties and responsibilities as sheik. So by the time Ehsaan and his family arrived two days later, Jalil had regained some sense of control. But it was a very fine veneer covering his remorse and anxiety at Kira's continued absence. Ehsaan already knew about Kira, having met one of the search parties on the way to Jalil's. Nasira immediately took Issa off to her quarters, and Akilah and Lina took Adara to the stables to watch Jabari performing ticks with Sarii while Amal and Fatima left to spend time with Saad and Samira.

Grateful to be left to themselves, Jalil took Ehsaan to his quarters where they could meet in private. Ehsaan must have sensed his inner turmoil. "Jalil, you know of Kira's resourcefulness and her desert training from having traveled with Saad's family. On top of that, she has Amber, who is also desert born, to protect her."

Hearing the truth and wisdom in his words, Jalil felt better. "You are right, my friend. So, what of the news you bring?" It was time to focus on the purpose of Ehsaan's visit.

"I have learned that someone has assumed rule over Qadir's kingdom, and that someone is none other than the crafty Hashem."

"What?! How can Hashem take control? What gives him the right?"

Ehsaan sipped his tea before telling the most interesting part. "Well, apparently, he claims he is Qadir's half-brother and that the old sheik was his father. Qadir's mother was a harem girl who became First Wife and sheikha, but Hashem's mother was only a servant. The old sheik died when Qadir was very young. Murdered, some said, but no one could ever prove it. So Qadir's mother ruled until Qadir was old enough to take charge." Ehsaan paused and took a bite of his bread. "I met her once. She was a cold person, and Issa always suspected she had something to do with her husband's death."

Jalil quietly digested this new information. He knew little of Qadir's story, but Akeem would have known about it, and perhaps Nasira would know something as well. "Well, now it seems one snake has been replaced with another, and it is not like we do not know how to deal with snakes. I agree this is not good news, but you could have sent this news by messenger." Perplexed, Jalil looked at Ehsaan.

"Yes, but there is more," Ehsaan said in a voice laden with concern. "Hashem has contacted Qadir's old allies, and I have been told they are holding meetings."

"So? I would expect him to do something like that." Jalil still didn't see the importance.

"Normally, I would agree, but he has also been spreading the rumor Kira belonged to Qadir and you stole her."

"But Hashem is the one who kidnapped Kira in the first place, under Qadir's orders. I would gladly kill Hashem for shooting Samira. He almost killed her, in fact he meant to. Thank Allah, his aim was off. And he tried to kill Jabari. He might have succeeded if Kira had not intervened. Hashem is as evil as Qadir!"

"I agree, Jalil. But he also says you murdered Qadir and the old sheikha the night you raided his compound."

Enraged by the accusation, Jalil slammed his hands flat on the table. "But I did not kill Qadir, and I did not even know who the old sheikha was!"

"Calm yourself, my friend. I know you did not do it. You would never kill a man in that way, and you certainly would not kill a woman. But Hashem says he has a witness that saw you do the deeds."

"WHAT?!" Jalil jumped up in alarm.

"I know, I know. It is preposterous." Ehsaan shook his head and raised his palms in a calming gesture. "And there's more. I have heard a rumor that Hashem is demanding 'blood money'."

Shocked, Jalil flopped back down in his chair, unable to speak. "Blood money" was an ancient form of punishment, but an acceptable one. The accused could choose three ruling sheiks to serve as judges to hear the charges. If found guilty, payment could comprise several things—the accuser could demand the life of the accused or one of his family members or require horses from his herd. If the accused failed to comply, his tribe could not take part in future Tri-Annual races. They wouldn't know exactly what Hashem expected until he presented formal charges, along with the evidence. The whole thing was contemptable, and Jalil's shock turned to rage.

When he gained control of himself, he looked at Ehsaan. "I do not know what to do about this. What do you advise?"

"Well, I suggest we send word to our allies and tell the true story. Then we should send word to Hashem's allies and let them know they are being lied to. I expect most of them already know that, but it needs to be said all the same. At least we have Fatima for a witness, but we must keep that a secret, or her life would be in danger. And we need to find Kira and find out what really happened that night."

"Well, that might be a problem, Ehsaan. Even if we can find her, she may not want to come back."

"But I thought she liked it here? Some have suggested that she might even like you." Ehsaan looked truly puzzled, but he must have noticed Jalil's face redden. When Jalil did not speak, he continued. "May I ask exactly what happened to make her run away?"

Jalil took a deep breath. He was embarrassed, yet he needed to talk to someone who might understand, someone he could trust. A man, like his father. So he described the events at the pool, and though he glossed over the more intimate details, he had the distinct impression Ehsaan read between the lines. "So, you see, you can believe me when I say she has reasons now for staying away. But I have had time to think about it, and I am worried this has something to do with what Qadir did to her."

"Jalil, you are a man, and you have found someone who you like but also admire and respect. What happened was inevitable, and what is important is how you handle it when you find her." Ehsaan's face was full of sympathy and honest concern.

"Thank you, Ehsaan. I hope I can convince her to come back. I have discovered I want her in all the ways a man can want a woman. She is worthy of being my sheikha."

Ehsaan sat back with a look of surprise. "Jalil, do you know what you are saying?"

"Yes, I do."

"Even with what must have happened with Qadir?"

Jalil looked at him and replied with absolute sincerity, "Yes. That does not matter in the least."

Ehsaan smiled. "Then I will do everything in my power to help you prove your innocence and find your sheikha," he declared and raised his cup in salute.

Jalil acknowledged his salute with one of his own. Then he remembered something he meant to ask Ehsaan earlier. "By the way, Ehsaan, just who is the witness that said I killed Qadir and his mother?"

"I do not know."

"Well, it does not matter. I am innocent. Come, let us finish our plans for the messages we need to send out. We have much to do," Jalil said, putting his worry for Kira aside for the moment. He knew what Hashem was up to now and wouldn't let him get away with it.

After Ehsaan and his family left, Jalil ordered more patrols, but they all came back empty-handed. Apparently, Kira and Amber seemed to have disappeared completely. Jalil's optimism faded to be replaced with guilt and depression, and while he continued to perform his duties, he didn't seem to care as much anymore. Everyone was aware of his distress and tried to pull him out of his dejected state but to no avail.

His mother finally took him aside. "Jalil, I am worried about you. I know what it is like to lose someone you care about. I do not know what will happen with Kira, but I do not want you to sink into despair like I did."

"I know, Mother. Thank you for your concern." But despite his words, his mood didn't lighten, and his mother left him, looking dejected herself.

Meanwhile, rumors of growing tribal unrest continued to surface, and at first, Jalil was concerned, until he began receiving responses to the messages he and Ehsaan had sent out. Many sheiks reaffirmed their desire to be Jalil's ally, and quite a few remained neutral. Unfortunately, a few said they still wanted Jalil to pay for his crimes. His future was cloudy, but he prayed and continued to hope they could find Kira. Heeding his mother's advice, he threw himself into his tribal duties, hoping to bury his concerns, but he knew he would not rest until he found out what had happened to Kira.

CHAPTER 23

"Ouch! Stop pulling my hair!" Cassie screeched at the servant who was trying to help her get ready.

"I apologize, Sheikha. I did not mean to hurt you," the young girl said, her hands trembling as she tried to arrange Cassie's crimson locks.

"Oh, just forget it. Here, give me that!" Cassie jerked the comb from the girl's hand. She was on edge because that night was the feast Hashem had organized for Qadir's former allies. Planning to shower them with food, drink, and gifts, he was going to make sure they heard the story of Sheik Jalil's treachery. Before the evening was over, he hoped to secure their support in his plan to make Jalil pay for the crimes. Cassie was all for seeing Jalil punished, especially after he abandoned her the night of the murders.

Seeing the servant girl twisting her hands nervously and waiting for her next order, Cassie waved her off. "You're dismissed. I will send for you if I need you." Frowning, Cassie watched her scurry away. *Stupid girl. Why can't I find anyone in this god-forsaken country that can do hair properly?* Checking her face in the mirror, she was pleased to see significant improvement. Being pampered and avoiding the sun for the last few months enabled her to keep her hair and skin in the best possible condition, but she wished she could say the same about her weight.

The hardest thing to do was watch her figure. Without a means to exercise and limited to in-house activities, she was feeling decidedly plump. It was hard giving up her usual treats, but dieting was the only way she could keep her body going from lush to plush. Thankfully, Hashem didn't seem to care about her weight. His fascination with her continued, and only a night or two had passed when he didn't send for her.

She had continued her farce of being pregnant in order to make her selection as Hashem's sheikha believable, but she had a continual fear of becoming pregnant for real. Luckily, she learned of a potion from a servant that would prevent it, but the woman warned it would only work if consumed the morning following intimacy. After the woman showed her how to make it, Cassie made her drink it first. After that, Cassie only drank the potion she made herself. She remembered the sight of First Wife lying dead on the floor, the empty goblet by her side. Cassie feared being poisoned as the harem continued to shun her. And Qadir's old favorite, Zahra, gave her the evil eye whenever their paths crossed. She didn't trust anyone, not even Hashem.

She still wondered what happened to Fatima. It had been a few days after the night Qadir and First Wife were murdered Cassie had noticed she was missing. She had decided it had been Fatima she had seen escaping through the secret door that night. *But why did Fatima run away? Did she have something to do with the deaths?*

She could understand Fatima wanting to get rid of First Wife—the old woman was a terror and universally hated. But why would Fatima kill Qadir? Rumor was that she was still untouched, having never slept with the sheik. *Probably because she wasn't very attractive,* Cassie thought to herself. Still, it was a puzzle. *But who was the other woman who escaped with Fatima?* When Cassie discovered that none of the harem girls had disappeared, including Zahra, she surmised the other woman must have been Kira. Now she was a more likely suspect. In her mind, Kira must have killed Qadir because she was the last person with him that night, and she certainly had a reason. But in the end, it didn't matter to Cassie who actually did it. As long as they punished Jalil for the deeds, she would be happy.

When Hashem was gone from the house, she could order the servants to do anything she commanded, almost. Although the harem girls continued to avoid her, she didn't care anymore because they had to do what she said now, all except Zahra. Cassie wished Zahra had been the one to disappear. The former favorite hated her, but now that Qadir was dead, Zahra was almost friendly, which Cassie found highly suspicious. And though Hashem never mentioned her, Cassie had a sneaking suspicion he was sleeping with her, but Cassie hadn't figured out how to catch them in the act yet.

Aware the time was passing, she finished applying her makeup, and after dusting her face with a golden powder, she headed to her chambers. As she walked, she thought more about Hashem and Zahra and decided she didn't really care if Hashem was sleeping with her. There might have been a time when she would have been jealous, but not anymore. She was tired of being stuck in this house and this country, and Hashem was just another way to get out. *But what if Zahra becomes pregnant?* She stopped in the middle of the hall when she suddenly realized that might be Zahra's plan. If Zahra became pregnant, she could produce an heir and claim the title of sheikha. If that happened, Zahra would make her life miserable. *Oh, that just won't do at all.* She prayed Hashem had inherited the same problem as his half-brother Qadir, but Cassie would still take the morning potion, just to be sure.

Knowing she had little time to devote to her schemes at the moment, she picked up her pace. As the current sheikha, Cassie had power and enjoyed certain freedoms, and she had appropriated First Wife's chambers. She had gone to great lengths to erase any sign of the old sheikha. Gone were the creepy jars and hanging herbs. Cassie had replaced the furniture and added a colorful mix of hanging silk panels and comfortable cushions.

As yet, Hashem showed no interest in visiting her chambers—she was called to his chambers when he wanted his pleasure. And he always wanted his pleasure. Cassie had never been with a man who was just as sexually needy as she was. He never seemed to tire of her, and she always found her pleasure, even without his help. How that was possible with the disgusting Hashem was a mystery that she had ceased to worry about, though. Hashem was just a means to an end, and he would serve until she could find another, preferably a long way from here.

Sending for a servant to help her dress, she chose her robes carefully. The ivory silk tunic was perfect for her coloring, and she admired the flash of the lights on the intricate pattern of rubies and onyx stones interspersed with creamy pearls adorning the bodice. A crimson robe completed the outfit. *Perfect.* Ordering the servant to wait in the hall, Cassie locked her door and went to the only piece of furniture of First Wife's she had kept, a large carved cabinet. Removing the bottom drawer, she reached inside and pulled up gently on the back panel. Tucked in the hidden space behind was a plain wooden box. Setting it on the table, she opened it and sighed at the sight of the glittering jewels.

Finding the box had been purely accidental. As she was clearing out First Wife's clothes from the cabinet, the bottom drawer had been stuck, and impatient, Cassie jerked on it hard enough to pull it completely out. She noticed the drawer was not as deep as the drawer above it. It seemed odd, and upon further investigation, she soon discovered why. Ecstatic to find the gems First Wife had been hiding behind the back of the drawer, Cassie knew she would never reveal their hiding place to Hashem. She would need them when she escaped.

Smiling, she poured over the contents of the box, riffling through the bejeweled hairpins, necklaces, bracelets, and rings. Unable to resist, she chose a few small pieces—a simple ruby drop necklace, a choker of black onyx, hair pins adorned with pearls, and several thin gold bracelets. If Hashem asked about them, she would say they were gifts from Qadir. Closing the box tightly, she returned it to its hiding place.

The final piece of her outfit was a gossamer-thin scarf she draped over the top of her head, secured with hairpins, and crossed loosely over one shoulder. *Yes. This will do nicely.* Stepping into golden slippers, she made her way to the feast hall, pausing outside the doors to clear her thoughts. She was the sheikha, and she wouldn't be dancing that night. Hearing soft music and men talking, she prepared to enter.

When the musicians finished their piece, the guards opened the doors, and she strolled in, swaying her hips to the haunting notes of a single flute. Keeping her face forward, she surreptitiously cut her eyes left and right, looking out from under her half-closed eyelids outlined in bold, black kohl and highlighted with ruby red and gold. Her long crimson hair curled around her ample breasts, and the men fell silent. She could see them watching her with lust and jealousy as she slowly made her way to stand in front of Hashem.

Hashem was wearing Qadir's finest garments with every embellishment, including an outrageous ceremonial turban. Leaning back in his chair with his booted legs thrust under the table, he rested his clasped hands in front of his chest so that his sheik ring was in plain view. Seeing his predatory smile, she bowed her head and waited. He made her wait longer than she thought was necessary, but knowing how much he enjoyed taunting her, she held her temper, gritted her teeth, and remained silent.

Finally, he raised his arms and announced to the room, "My fellow sheiks and guests, I present to you my sheikha."

Raising her eyes, she smiled seductively, but he merely gestured to the cushions in front of the table at his feet. Hesitating, she fought hard to control her emotions, but she had to play the part for now, so she sank gracefully onto a large cushion, pretending to await his pleasure. The men resumed their conversations, and the feast went on. No one offered her food or drink, and she sullenly accepted that to Hashem, she was nothing but a glorified harem girl.

After what seemed like hours, Cassie was close to losing control. Hungry, and tired of sitting on the pillow without moving, she fidgeted until Hashem finally seemed to notice her discomfort. When she saw him looking at her and smiling, she returned his smile, thinking he was finally going to let her join him at the table. But when the guards stepped forward, lifted her to her feet, and gently, but firmly, escorted her toward the door, she could barely hide her anger.

Aware that he was showing the other sheiks that she was not his equal, she held her head high and allowed the guards to lead her from the room. But just before she walked through the doorway, she glanced back over her shoulder and smiled at Hashem with all her seductive power, pleased to see him look both annoyed and aroused.

Once she returned to her room, she hid the jewelry before ripping her clothes off and throwing them on the floor. *Damn that man! He's an animal! I have to get away from him.* Covering her nakedness with a thick robe, she grabbed the goblet of tea her servant had left for her earlier, gulped it down, and tore into the sweet bread and soft cheese from a platter on the table. Chewing furiously, she stomped around the room, cursing silently. *Oooooh! Just wait, mister! You'll get yours!*

Frustrated, she stalked to the harem bath and immersed herself in the soothing water, and while she floated, she contemplated all the evil things she would like to do to Hashem. Unable to find the calm she searched for, she returned to her chambers and prepared a mild sleeping potion. She was just about to drink it when one of his guards stopped by to summon her to the sheik's quarters. Her anger returned in full force, and with a curse, she threw the goblet against the wall. Wincing, the man hurried away, and the girl who helped her dress earlier appeared, intending to help her dress for Hashem. When Cassie saw her cowering at the door, she impatiently waved her in. *Might as well get this over with.*

Hours later, she lay beside Hashem, and while he rattled on about his plans, she barely listened. Still furious at the way he publicly embarrassed her, she had fought him this time, but he seemed to enjoy it and had taken her with more passion than usual and, as usual, brought her to completion. *How does he do that? Why do I let him?* Now she would have to remember to take her special potion in the morning.

Hashem interrupted her chain of thought with is insistent voice. "Cassie? Are you listening to me?" He rolled over to look at her, his dark eyes flashing in anger.

Cassie knew he hated it when she ignored him. "What? What did you say?" Lying naked, flat on her back with her hands on her belly, she refused to look at him.

"I said, I told everyone tonight about Jalil and how he killed Qadir and the old woman. Most of them agreed to help me. There are a few who are afraid of Jalil and his allies, but I am not concerned. I have enough men without them." When she did not immediately respond, he reached over and pinched the tip of her breast.

She flinched at his cruel touch and looked at him askance. "And just what do you plan to do, my sheik?" she asked with an insolent smile.

"When I am ready for you to know, I will tell you. For now, I need you to talk to your old friend Kira," he said, watching her closely.

"Kira? And just how will I be able to do that? Because unless you have a crystal ball, you won't be able to find her," she snapped, rolling over to face him. "Besides, even if I could, what good would that do? She hates me. I don't think she'll talk to me again."

"Oh, I don't need a crystal ball. I know where she is. She's with Jalil. And it seems Jalil is very protective of her, so I am thinking he is going to want to keep her around."

"What? That little half-breed! He won't keep her. He knows Qadir had his way with her. I made sure he saw the evidence," she shot back.

"What else did you tell Jalil?" he hissed menacingly.

Cassie knew she needed to be careful about what she said next. She had never shared the details of her conversation with Jalil that night. And Hashem had a habit of pushing her buttons, and she often said more than she meant to when she was emotional. "I didn't tell him anything except what I already told you," she said defensively but felt a fission of worry seeing the doubt in Hashem's eyes.

"Cassie, who else did you see that night?"

Closing her eyes, she struggled to control her emotions, not wanting to reveal too much, but knew he wouldn't let it go, so she threw him a bone. "I told you already. I didn't see anyone except some guards and a few harem girls running around," she said, then pretended to have a sudden thought. "Oh, I forgot. I *did* see Zahra. She didn't seem upset by everything that was going on that night. And I think I saw Fatima and Kira sneaking out through the storeroom," she answered peevishly. "Look, Hashem, we have been over this so many times, and I'm really getting tired of you asking me…"

Before she could finish, Hashem suddenly reached over and pulled her on top of him. "It's 'my sheik' to you, Cassie. Remember your place," he said harshly, sliding his hands downward and gripping her bottom tightly. She gasped, instantly aware of his returning passion. Struggling, she tried to rise, but he rolled over and pinned her beneath him. When he slammed his lips down on hers, she ceased struggling and wrapped her legs around his hips. All thoughts of Qadir and Jalil flew from her head as she succumbed once more. As they coupled in wild abandon, they were unaware that someone watched from a secret place—someone who was thinking their time would come, but they would never know until it was too late.

CHAPTER 24

Time had no meaning in the valley, and Kira should have been able to relax, and she did, to a certain point. The first days she concentrated on making a new home under the palms with a decent fire pit and a better shelter. She collected food, made baskets, and tried not to think about Jalil.

Compelled for reasons she couldn't fathom, she dug up the ancient medallion and chain that she had buried by her campsite the last time she had been in the valley. She studied the familiar pattern of turquoise stones and yellow gems. The fact Jalil wore its twin comforted her, and she often wondered why there were two so alike. And why one was here, forgotten in time, and the other worn by the sheiks of Jalil's kingdom. But the answer eluded her, and in time, the medallions didn't seem as important, and she stored hers in her pack, along with her father's ring and her mother's necklace.

As the days passed, Kira's connection with Ndee grew stronger. He allowed her to approach him and stroke his neck occasionally. He tried to get closer to Amber, but she wouldn't let him near, not as a stallion anyway. Having seen Jalil's golden mares, Kira pondered the mystery of their existence. Why was Jalil the only one outside of the valley who had them? And why were there no golden stallions except Ndee? Would Ehsaan be able to produce the golden horses from the golden filly Jalil had given Adara? The puzzle of their breeding was fascinating, and she speculated on what pairing could produce another golden stallion.

One day, as she was watching the foals who were born while she had been away, she was curious to see one filly in particular. Her coat was dark, like polished pewter, but when the sun was just right, she seemed to shimmer with silver. Kira almost felt like she imagined it then figured she was just missing Mirage.

Ever curious, Kira eventually grew bored with her daily routine and one morning decided she wanted to survey the valley in greater detail, hoping to discover more about the people who once lived there. Grabbing her father's worn compass, she started at the main entrance and followed the western cliffs, spending two days mapping the boundaries. She discovered a few ruins and earmarked them for future exploration, but one piqued her interest, not because of the typical eroded walls or even the mysterious shallow pits surrounded by fire-blackened stones. It was the mounds of broken rock and stone close by. They reminded her of tailings—piles of debris generated by mining operations.

Dismounting, she took a handful of the rocks from one mound and relying on her extensive knowledge of geology, sorted them by texture and color. When she saw small, dark chunks tinged with red, magnesium ferric immediately came to mind—a mineral often found near gold deposits. Curious, she dug further into the mound, and her eyes widened when she saw pieces of material that sparkled in the sun. *Pyrite!* She recognized it at once. Her father had brought her a new mineral every time he returned from his expeditions. He wouldn't tell her what they were, and she had to research and figure it out. She chuckled, remembering how he smiled when he gave her a rock like these. Convinced they were going to be rich, she was furious when she learned it was just pyrite and immediately understood why it was called fool's gold. Like magnesium ferric, it also formed naturally around gold veins.

Realizing the significance at once, she hurried past the mounds, searching the base of the cliffs until she found the source of the tailings—a rough tunnel carved into the rocks. She knew she had discovered something of great importance and itched to explore, but her common sense kept her from entering. Mines were always dangerous and even more so when abandoned. *What had they been looking for? What did they find?* Frustrated, her mind spinning with possibilities, she sighed, and with a last look of regret, climbed back up on Amber. It would have to wait until she was better prepared.

She rode further along the cliffs until she came to an extensive landslide. She thought it was probably from an earthquake having seen evidence of the same geological upheavals while traveling with Saad's family. When Saad mentioned he had felt the earth shaking once, she tried to explain the science behind it. He seemed amazed by her education—his people had little knowledge of such things—but he grasped the concepts with ease

After they skirted the larger boulders and general debris, the ground became more sandy than usual, and Amber slowed to a cautious walk. Kira was wondering why until she caught a whiff of something strange. *What is that?* Her nose wrinkled at the bitter smell. It was coming from a dark depression in the sand just ahead. Signaling Amber to stop, Kira slid to the ground to investigate.

Wary, she moved forward cautiously, testing the sand and holding her breath at the increasing stench. It reminded her of the spilled fuel from the plane wreck, and when she got close enough, she was astonished to see something she had only read about in her college studies. *Oil sand!* A source of raw bitumen, oil sand was a black, oily, viscous substance associated with oil deposits deep in the earth. Throughout the ages, civilizations had used it for many purposes, from caulking boats to sealing coffins. It was waterproof and flammable. And dangerous, she thought as she slowly backed away. She was glad Amber was aware of it because just like the Le Brea tar pits she had read about, it was a death sentence for any animal unlucky enough to fall in. Still, it might prove useful, she thought. Giving the area a wide berth, she was relieved when they were beyond the danger and relaxed, thinking she couldn't possibly find anything more interesting that day. But she was wrong.

They had returned to following the cliffs and were approaching the pool that fed the lake when Amber suddenly came to a halt. Puzzled, Kira looked ahead in time to see Ndee walking along the base of the cliffs. He appeared to be searching for something about a hundred yards from the spring when he disappeared behind a massive boulder. Kira waited to see what he was up to, but when he didn't immediately return, she grew curious.

Dismounting and leaving Amber at a safe distance, Kira eased around the big rock where Ndee disappeared. In front of her was a dark opening, just big enough for a single horse to pass through. *What? Another tunnel?* Excited and unable to resist, she stepped inside the opening and stopped to listen. Unable to detect a sound, she took a few tentative steps forward but had to stop and allow her eyes to adjust to the Stygian darkness.

Though she still couldn't see well, she continued forward. Intrigued, she kept one hand on the wall and one hand above her head, slowly moving forward and testing the ground with each step. The going was easy. The tunnel floor rose steadily, but the walls were damp, which differed from the tunnel she had followed into the valley. She breathed deeply and smelled the cool, cave scent of moist earth and felt a slight breeze. The air was fresh, encouraging Kira to keep walking.

Finally, as the darkness began fading slightly, her ears detected a roaring sound, and she felt the wall beside her curve away and the ceiling rise beyond her reach. She took a few more steps and abruptly halted, aware she had entered a cavernous space. The roaring sound grew louder, and she peered into the gloom, searching for its source. It was coming from the floor in front of her and she approached carefully until she could make out several holes. Testing the ground by the closest one, finding it to be solid, she crouched down. Leaning over the hole, Kira tried to see what was causing the sound and gasped when she felt droplets of moisture and saw an alluring glint. *Water! Rushing water! Not a spring, but a hidden river under the mountains!* Just as her father theorized. It was what he had been searching for. Using her geological and engineering knowledge to make sense of what she was seeing, she could only surmise that the buried river ran east to west, and it was, without a doubt, the source of the lake. *But where was the light coming from?*

Looking up, she saw slivers of light from a few natural fissures in the high ceiling, but they did little to penetrate the gloom. Rising carefully, she scanned the cavern in all directions but still couldn't see much until she noticed a darker section on the wall to her right. Wary of the holes in the floor, she kept close to the wall and walked around until she stood in front of an opening, roughly the same size as the one she had just come through. It was too dark to see any detail, but Kira recognized it for what it was. Having taken trips to mines back home as part of her studies, she knew this was a man-made tunnel. Based on the stones and pebbles in front of the opening, though, it had not been in use for some time.

As she ran her hand around the entrance, she discovered what felt like an engraving about chest high. It was uniformly circular and had three evenly spaced raised bars. But before she could give it further thought, she heard a noise from across the cavern. Alarmed, Kira momentarily froze then bolted back to the tunnel that led to the valley. She made it outside without injury and stumbled to hide behind a nearby boulder. Holding her breath, she trembled with fear as the noise grew louder then exhaled with relief when she recognized the sharp clatter of hoofbeats. Peering around the stone, she watched Ndee emerge from the rocks, walking fast. Slumping down, she tried to catch her breath, but when she looked up again, he had disappeared.

She stood and stared hard at the entrance to the cavern. *Where had he been? What was he up to?* Suddenly, it was clear. *There must be another tunnel!* Excited, she needed to find out more about the cavern. Remembering how dark it was, she paced back and forth, trying to think of a way she could see. *Fire!* She needed fire. What could she do? Then it came to her. *Bitumen.* Energized, she ran to Amber and vaulted onto her back, urging her into a gallop.

Riding straight to her campsite, Kira grabbed two baskets, a small clay pot she had excavated from the ruins, a set of sticks she used to make her fires, and some dried reeds. Something made her retrieve the old medallion from her pack, and she placed it around her neck, almost without thinking. Backtracking to the western ruins she had discovered earlier that morning, she filled the pot with oil sand and headed to the cavern.

Once she had a fire going, she took a stick from her fire and held it over the pot of bitumen. It immediately ignited, and she set the small pot into a larger basket so she could carry it without burning her hands. Mentally crossing her fingers, she entered the tunnel.

With her makeshift lamp, she could go much faster, but when she reached the cavern, she almost fell to her knees when she saw the surrounding walls. Horses of every color, including gold, appeared to gallop around the chamber walls. They looked as fresh as if painted that day, and when she stepped closer and held up the pot, their coats sparkled just like Amber's.

But more stunning than the horses were the bands of painted turquoise and white encircling the walls, above and below the horses. At the very top was a wide band of gold. It was too high to reach, but Kira had the strangest feeling it wasn't paint. When she placed her little firepot in the middle of the cavern, the gold band reflected the light, illuminating the entire cavern as if by design. She stood silent, gazing around her in awe, until she noticed the other tunnel openings.

Counting the one that led to the valley, there were four in all. Beside each entrance was a carving, and she hurried forward to get a better look. When she did, her medallion suddenly felt warm, and glancing down to where it lay against her chest, she thought she detected a faint glow. *Must be the firelight,* she mused and returned to studying the carving. It was comprised of three raised bars that matched the bands encircling the cavern—turquoise, white, and gold—reminding her of Jalil's tribal colors.

When she moved to the next tunnel, the one she suspected Ndee must have used, she found a slightly different story. Two of the bars were painted white and gold, but the third was a deep ruby red. The color combination was not familiar. Then, glancing to her left, she saw the last tunnel, but upon closer inspection she found the carving had been obliterated. By the look of the deep gouges and scrapes, she thought it was likely done on purpose. And unlike the other tunnels, rocky debris littered the entrance. Curious, she ventured a few steps inside, only to find her way completely blocked by piles of rubble and packed stone. Her first thought was it must have been a cave-in until she remembered the destroyed carving. Another mystery but one that would have to wait.

She wasn't sure how long she'd been in the cavern and knew she should return to the valley soon. Night was coming and it wouldn't be wise to be caught this far from the safety of her fire. But something drew her back to the far tunnel. She saw Ndee's recent tracks on the well-worn stone floor leading into it. If he used it, it was probably safe. Unable to resist the urge to explore, she picked up her little pot of light, took a deep breath, and entered. It rose fairly straight into the mountain, and after only one turn, she found her lamp to be unnecessary as the surrounding light grew brighter. Soon she saw an opening not far ahead. When she reached it, she paused just inside the mouth of the exit and waited for her eyes to adjust. At first, all she saw was a tall, stony cliff a few feet away, but when she stepped out, she glanced left and saw a skinny trail meandering through a narrow trench cut into the cliffs. It disappeared around a bend not far away.

Leaving her pot inside the opening, she followed the path until she reached a large boulder. Edging past it, she stepped out into an open area surround by cliffs. It reminded her of a box canyon back home. But unlike a true box canyon, other paths led away into the stony outcroppings. Looking behind her, she eyed the boulder she had just walked around. It effectively hid the tunnel, like the one guarding the main tunnel to the valley. *But why did Ndee come here?* She wanted to explore, but it was growing late, and she had no supplies. With unanswered questions, Kira reluctantly made her way through the cavern and returned to the valley.

As she rode back to her camp, Kira couldn't stop thinking about the mystery of the cavern with its tunnels and carvings. What did it all mean? Where did the other tunnels lead? Why did they exist in the first place? What was their purpose? Plagued by questions throughout the rest of the day and into the evening, it took her a long time to fall asleep that night.

CHAPTER 25

The next morning, Kira woke feeling refreshed and alive. As she sat by her fire pit, she gazed out over the valley, listening to the birds in the reeds by the marsh. The horses were visible in the distance, and she heard Ndee calling to his mares. In the solitude of the early morning, she had time to think, but instead of the cavern and tunnels, her thoughts were of Jalil. The memory of his eyes and his touch caused her heart to race and her body to feel warm. Normally, she would seek distraction by taking a fast ride on Amber. When she was racing through the hills, everything faded away but the heat of the sun, the sound of hoofbeats, and the scent of sand. But lately, she enjoyed the memories.

Unfortunately, more troubling memories, ones not easily dismissed, pushed all else from her mind. When she first returned to the valley, she had spent many sleepless nights thinking about her night with Qadir. Initially, she was glad she had passed out before he had taken her, but now she struggled to remember more. If she concentrated, she could see his eyes inches from hers, dark and dilated, and even smell his breath, sickly sweet. She heard him say something, his voice distorted. Then he was falling toward her, and…. She drew a blank. There the memory ended. Something bothered her, skittering just beyond her recall, something about his breath. Suddenly, she sat straight up. *Was he drugged, like me?* That was a startling thought.

Another immediately followed it. *Maybe he didn't take me completely? Foolish girl,* she thought sadly when she remembered the pain of his intimate touch and the ruined tunic.

Depressed and feeling the need to clear her head, she rode to the pool by the cliffs to take a swim. Spending time there helped her remember her last night with Jalil, a memory she no longer feared. She regretted running away from him, knowing now that what happened was simply a flashback of her night with Qadir and had nothing to do with Jalil.

Floating in the cool waters she wondered if she was truly over the trauma and could be with Jalil again. *But what if I have the same flashback? What if I cannot get past it?* As much as she longed to see Jalil, it would be a disaster if it happened again. It wouldn't be fair to him, and what would be the point. Even if she could get past the trauma, she was not fit to be his sheikha. *Oh, but it would be wonderful to see Saad's family again and Ehsaan's family too.*

Kira smiled, thinking of Adara and Gigi, and wondered what was happening with Shar. *Was he able to get over what Qadir had done to him?* If he had, perhaps she could too. It might take a long time, but if she went back to Jalil's, she would have people to talk to and friends who would support her. She considered leaving the valley but couldn't bring herself to do it—not yet.

After her swim, she stopped by the old ruins to sit on a crumbling wall and watch the herd playing by the lake. Laughing at the antics of the young ones splashing in the shallows, she idly rubbed the old medallion resting on her chest. Wearing it along with her father's ring brought her a sense of peace. It seemed warmer than usual, but she assumed it was just absorbing her body heat. It reminded her of the cavern and its mysterious tunnels, and her thoughts strayed to the people who once lived here. *Why did they leave?* They had two of the most valuable things in the desert—water and horses. And from her discovery of the old mine, she knew they also had another source of wealth. Gold. *What happened to them, and where did they go?* That was the greatest mystery, and it filled her with a powerful urge to find out, but without written records, she would probably never know.

Later, Kira set off in search of something for her dinner. It was the time of day when the hills, the stones, and even the ground glowed as if lit from within, as if the sun had filled them with light before beginning to slide toward the horizon. The sky blossomed pink and pale lavender, and all was still and quiet. She was walking along the stream, thinking about catching some fish, when a movement at the water's edge startled her from her musings.

Astonished, she stopped abruptly at the sight of an old woman with long, braided hair wearing a simple leather dress, standing barefoot on the bank. When the woman turned to face her, Kira fell to her knees. "Hotda? Grandmother?" She unconsciously spoke in her native tongue.

The old woman smiled and nodded. "Yes, Kira. It is I."

"But...how...where...?" Kira couldn't speak coherently, and her mind filled with questions. *Am I imaging this? Is this real?*

"How can I be real? Is that what you are thinking?"

"Yes, Grandmother. How can you be real? You're in America, and I'm here."

"Did you forget all I taught you? If you have faith, all things are possible. But you are right. I am not here, but I am no longer there either."

"I don't understand," Kira cried, tears beginning to fall. "I have missed you so much, and I wrote to you, but I never heard back."

"I got your letters, Kira, and I know about the crash. Do not worry. Your father is with your mother now, and all is going to be fine."

"But, Grandmother, how do you know this?"

"Because I have seen them, and now I am going to be with them, too. Kira, I am no longer a part of your world," she said mysteriously.

"What?! Grandmother, I wanted to see you again. I need to talk to you! So much has happened to me. I need your advice. And now..."

"And now I can give it to you. Kira, you are torn between two countries and two ways of life, and you must make this decision for yourself. But have great courage and great faith, and I know you will be all right. You also have a great love to share, and I think you have found someone to share it with."

In her heart, Kira knew she was speaking of Jalil. "But, Grandmother, I can't be with him. Something happened to me, something horrible," Kira said, hanging her head in shame, unable to say the words aloud.

"Kira?" her grandmother whispered.

Kira looked up, her eyes red and her body trembling, alarmed to see her grandmother beginning to fade.

"Kira, you are not to blame for what happened. You are still untouched, in all the ways that matter, and when you give your heart, you will know that. Do you understand?"

"I don't know, but I'll try to understand... and remember what you said." Kira grew desperate when she saw her grandmother fading even more. "Grandmother! Don't leave me!" she cried out, kneeling with her arms outstretched.

"I must go now, Kira, but do not worry. I will always be with you…always. Go, Kira, and follow your path. Be brave and strong, and you will find your answers." With those final, cryptic words, the image of her grandmother turned to pale gray mist, floating up and wafting away in the breeze.

For a brief second, Kira thought she heard a soft laugh and felt a gentle kiss on her forehead. Sobbing bitterly, she slumped to the ground, unaware the sun had disappeared until she looked up later and saw thousands of stars in the deep purple-blue sky. One blinked brighter than the rest. "Goodbye, Grandmother," she whispered. "I love you."

She returned to her camp and settled by her firepit, idly stirring the embers with a stick. The fire popped, sending bits of embers flying, and she watched them dance skyward. Mesmerized, she closed her eyes and was transported back to the desert of her birth. The fire was the same, and the wind was the same, as was the sound of horses in the hills. When she opened her eyes, a flash of light in the sky drew her attention. A star fell earthward, blazing in dying glory. *Not dying*, she thought, remembering her grandmother's words from long ago. Her tribe believed when a warrior died in battle, his spirit would ascend to the heavens to become a star, providing light and direction for his earthbound brothers below. He would serve there until he was needed once again, and then he would descend in a blaze of glory to be reborn. *A warrior,* she thought. *Maybe he will be the one who will help me.*

Feeling numb from the events of the day, she crawled into her shelter, wrapped herself in her old blanket, and lay where she could look up into the night sky. As she studied the Milky Way flowing like a glowing river of stars, the image of the river inside the cavern haunted her. Whoever had lived here had known about that river and had made those tunnels.

Reaching into her robe, she drew out the ancient medallion and held it up. It felt warm to the touch, something she had noticed more and more, and it shone in the starlight. Rubbing the worn turquoise stones, she remembered her grandmother's words, and something clicked deep insider her. It *was* time to get back on her path. It was time for her to go.

Someday, she would get the chance to solve the mystery of the cavern, but for now, all she could think about was how much she wanted to share the discovery of the valley with someone. And maybe she could do just that, for she had decided her path led back to Jalil's kingdom. Whether it ended there or continued on remained to be seen. But she would be brave and strong, like her grandmother said, and Kira would face her future and discover what God had planned for her.

CHAPTER 26

Cassie's morning started out well enough. After a rousing session with Hashem in bed, she was relaxing at his table, and, picking at a selection of fruit and watching him eat when they were interrupted by one of his men.

"My sheik. I have some information to report." The tribesman looked nervous and would not look at Cassie.

Hashem nodded and Cassie turned away, pretending not to listen as the two men talked. She could care less about the news that someone had been stealing food from the kitchen again. And that a strange man had been seen in the compound several times since Hashem's takeover. But Hashem looked worried, and she was curious why. As soon as the man departed, she turned back to Hashem. "What is so alarming about someone stealing food?"

"I could care less about a hungry thief. It's the stranger. I thought I saw him the other day. And for a second, I thought it was…" Hashem cocked his head looking puzzled.

"Who? Who did you think it was?"

"Nadim."

Nadim? Who is that?

"Someone who should be dead." He said then shook his head. "No, it couldn't be him. I killed him." He returned to his meal.

Cassie stared at him for minute. His puzzled look was replaced with a familiar emotion…anger, and she wondered what else was bothering him about the message. Was it the part about Jalil finding his long-lost brother? Evidently, Jalil had found a boy he believed was his brother, the one kidnapped as a baby. It sounded like an unbelievable story to her. Maybe it was the news about Kira? According to one of his spies, the girl had ended up at Jalil's just as Hashem had suspected but had since run away. Cassie inwardly fumed to hear of Kira's good luck until she also learned Kira had stolen one of Jalil's golden horses and run away. *Stupid little half-breed.* To leave Jalil for the desert was beyond ignorant. She smiled, relishing the thought Kira was probably dead.

Her curiosity as to what was troubling Hashem was soon satisfied when he suddenly slammed his goblet down with a curse.

"Now I'm going to have to kill him all over again?!" He rose and began pacing back and forth.

Cassie flinched but kept her expression neutral as she watched him. "Kill who?" she cautiously asked.

"That stupid magician," Hashem snarled.

"What magician?" Cassie had no idea who Hashem was talking about.

"Jabari the Magnificent," Hashem said sarcastically. "The boy Saad claimed was his son. The boy Jalil now claims is his missing brother. Ridiculous!" Hashem spat then suddenly stared at her, his eyes unblinking. "Why are you smiling?" His voice took on a deadly tone.

Cassie tensed. She had tuned out his tirade while she ruminated over Kira's plight and had forgotten about his recent mood swings. It took very little to set him off. "Um, well, I was thinking about Kira running away. I bet Jalil's devastated. And for her to steal one of his prized golden mares? That's rich. I wish I could have been there to see his face. But, Hashem, what is so important about the boy?" She prayed silently, hoping to turn his attention back to the message. She remembered him telling her about the boy who he kidnapped with Kira but had managed to escape.

Diverted, Hashem dropped into a chair across from her. "If the rumors are true, Jabari is Talib, Jalil's brother and heir. But he is not supposed to be alive!"

Cassie's ears perked up now. Hashem often revealed important information when he was having one of his fits, and information was power. She needed to know more, but she had to be careful. He was in a full rage. "So, Jabari is Jalil's heir. I still don't see how that's a problem."

Hashem looked at her like she was crazy. "Idiot! If I get rid of Jalil, I have to get rid of the boy, too. I thought I already had. I left him to die at the oasis years ago, but evidently that fat trader found him. Now I have to find a way to get rid of him…again." He slumped forward, staring down at the maps spread before him.

Cassie was intrigued. He had just revealed he was the one who had kidnapped Jalil's baby brother and left him to die in the desert. That was a valuable piece of information, and she was considering how it might benefit her until she noticed Hashem staring at her with a speculative gleam in his eyes.

"Yes…it might work…" He rubbed his chin thoughtfully.

"What might work?" Cassie said carefully, feeling a sense of foreboding.

"It is like you said. Jalil is devastated. He has been sending out search parties day and night. I am sure he is missing having a woman in his bed, and he has no harem to turn to," Hashem said. His anger was fading, and she grew alarmed to see his calculating smile emerge. "I saw how he watched you at the pre-race feast, Cassie. I bet he would be very glad to see you again."

"Are you planning to invite him for a visit?" she asked, barely hiding her sarcasm.

"No, I am quite sure Jalil would not want to come and see me," he said, seemingly oblivious to her attitude. "No, I will send you to Jalil. You will find a way to make him and his family trust you. Then you will kill the boy."

"What?!" Cassie sat straight up. "I'm willing to do a lot of things, but killing is not one of them."

"Liar! I saw what you did to First Wife."

"I didn't kill that crazy old woman," Cassie blustered. "I thought you did."

"I wish, but no, I did not have that pleasure. If you didn't do it, do you know who I can thank for getting rid of her?" he said, eyeing her closely.

"How would I know? After I spoke to Jalil in Qadir's chambers and he left, I went straight back to my room. People were running everywhere and…" Cassie paused as a memory flashed in her mind. After Jalil left her in Qadir's chambers, she had hurried back to her room, intent on escaping. When she passed by First Wife's chambers, the door was standing open, and she had seen the old woman lying dead on the floor with an empty goblet by her side. But in a hurry, she didn't stop to investigate but kept running. The house was in chaos and people were dashing about, all except Zahra. Qadir's old favorite. Zahra was sitting calmly in the harem bathing chamber, sipping wine and laughing as everyone ran about in chaos. It was well known there was no love lost between Zahra and First Wife. And Zahra had the means, the motive, and the opportunity. Cassie's money was on Zahra.

"And what?" Hashem said with narrowed eyes.

"And nothing. I don't know who killed her." Cassie wasn't going to share her last thought yet with Hashem. It was a piece of information she might be able to use to control Zahra in the future. It there was one thing Cassie had learned since coming to Qadir's, it was the power of secrets.

"Well, you're going to kill that boy for me."

"I told you. I'm not going to kill anyone," she said fiercely.

"Oh, you will kill him…or you will never see your country again." Hashem leaned forward with a cruel smile.

"But what if Kira comes back? What if Jalil finds her?"

"Kira is gone. She is either feeding the hyenas or servicing some other man now. Jalil will never see her again." He chuckled mirthlessly.

Cassie struggled to hide her anger. Hashem had been promising her he'd let her go, but she realized she'd been deluding herself. He would never do that. "If I kill the boy, what are you going to do? What are you planning?"

"That is none of your business. Just get rid of the boy." Hashem had returned to studying the maps of the old northern route spread out before him.

"Why do you want his kingdom so much?" Cassie was truly curious.

"I do not want his kingdom. I just want Mirage and his golden mares. I need the money. Qadir's herd is worthless without Shar, and nothing is left of any value here."

His admission surprised her. She assumed every sheik had money of some kind. If he was telling the truth, she'd have to be very careful to keep her gems a secret until she got back from Jalil's. *If I get back.* That brought to mind another question.

"Just how am I going to get to Jalil's? And what makes you think he will take me in? We didn't part on the best of terms the last time I saw him," she said, remembering his actions the night of Qadir's murder. He had left her without a second thought.

"Oh, it will be easy. Even now, his men are searching for a foreign woman. I expect they will find another in need of rescue." He smiled cruelly and returned to the study of the maps.

"But how will I get back here?" she dared to ask.

He didn't look up. "Do not concern yourself with that. Just do what I tell you. Now, go. You will leave today, and I have work to do." He waved his hand dismissively.

Cassie's eyes narrowed as she fought to maintain her temper. *Weasel. I'll show him.* She stalked to her chambers and was laying out several outfits to take with her when two guards showed up. Without so much as a word, they took her by the arms and led her outside. Furious and still smarting from her meeting with Hashem, she railed at them, but they ignored her, and within the hour, she found herself tied to a horse and on her way to Jalil's along with two scruffy men in nondescript robes on rough-looking horses.

She didn't know how far it was to Jalil's, but after four days on horseback, she was certain she'd never walk normally again. It was easy to look the part of a woman who had escaped from slavers. Hashem's men had made sure she looked the part. Her robes were purposefully stained and tattered, and her hair was a snarled mess. She was dirty and covered in grime. Wincing, she ran her hand over her swollen jaw and split lip and cursed Hashem. *Damn them and damn Hashem!* He had ordered one of his men to hit her in order to make her story more believable.

They took her as close to Jalil's as they dared then cut her loose and left her standing alone on the trail, without food or water. She cursed them as they rode off but finally began walking. Luckily, she ran into a search party on their way back to Jalil's, and when she mentioned Kira's name, they rescued her. A man lifted her up to sit astride in front of him, and she groaned when her bottom, riddled with bruises and chafing, encountered the unforgiving leather.

By the time Cassie reached the main pass leading to Jalil's, she was exhausted and half-conscious until she heard the loud reports of two gunshots and the approaching hoofbeats of several horses. Other men joined them, and there was a lot of talking, most of which she couldn't understand, and she shut her eyes and moaned loudly, hoping to speed things up. She was desperate to get off the horse and into a bath. They must have noticed and began moving again.

When they finally stopped, she kept her eyes closed and slumped forward, pretending to be unconscious. Someone pulled her from the saddle and carried her up some steps. Risking a peek, she saw they were moving down a hall and into a room. When she was laid on a soft bed, she moaned in relief, until she heard a woman's voice and fell silent.

"Sheik, please send these men away. I need to check her for injuries."

"Yes, Sheikha. Everyone. Out! Now! And post a guard on this door."

Cassie heard the deep, clear voice and risked another peek. *Oh, my.* Jalil stood tall in the doorway, wearing a short, white tunic, tan trousers, and high black boots. A heavy gold chain encircling his muscled neck, and his head was bare. She had forgotten how handsome he was. Closing her eyes, she listened to him cautioning his mother.

"Mother, I am telling you, I know this woman. She is Cassie, Qadir's former sheikha. And now she is Hashem's. You cannot trust her."

"That may be true, Jalil, but I will not deny her help."

"I do not like this, but I will bow to your wishes for now. Do your healing, but be on the alert. Do not leave her alone, and do not leave her unguarded," he said.

"Fine, Jalil. Now, please, leave me to take care of her. You can question her later."

Cassie heard his grunt of displeasure and waited until his footsteps had receded down the hall as she continued with her subterfuge. It wasn't hard to groan and moan. Her legs and bottom really hurt, not to mention her face, and she was hungry and thirsty, too.

"There, there. Do not rush this." A pair of soft arms helped Cassie to sit up and placed plump cushions behind her back.

Hearing Nasira speaking her language was no surprise to Cassie. Hashem had told her that Jalil and his family could speak English. Opening her eyes slowly and pretending to be dazed and afraid, Cassie tried to get off the bed.

"Easy. Cassie, isn't it? Do not be afraid. You are safe here, and I will help you for now."

Looking at Jalil's mother, Cassie saw a mature woman, still beautiful, with her caramel-colored hair wrapped around her head in an intricate style, dressed in a white tunic lightly embroidered and banded in pale shades of blue. Her only adornments were a necklace with a single turquoise teardrop set in gold and a gold ring inlaid with blue stones and yellow gems. Her expression was one of honest concern, with a touch of wariness.

"Who are you? Where am I?" Cassie asked in faux confusion.

"My name is Nasira, and I am the sheikha of this kingdom. You are in Sheik Jalil's house," she said, holding a glass of warm tea for Cassie to drink.

Acting weak and scared, Cassie let Nasira assist her, but she didn't have to fake her thirst and gulped noisily. When the cup was empty, she held it out. "Please, Sheikha, may I have some more?"

Nasira shook her head. "Not yet. You need to rest first and try to eat something before you drink again," she said, holding a plate of bread and melon slices. "Do you think you could manage this?"

Cassie moved slowly, keeping up the pretense, even though she wanted to stuff all of it in her mouth. Nodding, she ate in small bites, chewing thoroughly and acting as if she had never eaten anything so delicious.

Involved with the food, she began feeling nervous when she caught Nasira staring at her jaw with a calculated look and saw her eyes travel up and down her body. Cassie lightly choked on her melon when Nasira abruptly spoke.

She pointed at Cassie's jaw and said, "I see you are hurt. Are you hurt anywhere else?" Cassie kept her eyes on her plate and shook her head, as if embarrassed. She knew what Nasira was referring to. "Um, uh, no, but I am very sore. I have been riding and walking for days, and I am filthy," she said, looking imploringly at Nasira. "Would it be possible for me to have a bath?"

Nasira stared at her for a moment, but then nodded. Cassie set the plate on the bedside table, held out her hand, and let Nasira help her to her feet. Accompanied by a guard, Nasira took her to a small chamber where an older woman sat quietly sewing on a garment.

"This is Dareen," Nasira said. The elderly woman looked up with a kind smile, but Cassie ignored her. She was too busy looking at a large pool she spied through the nearby archway.

"This is the old harem bath. Jalil does not keep a harem, so it serves our guests instead," Nasira said, guiding her into the larger chamber. "As you can see, there are towels and a clean robe with slippers for your use. You will find oils and lotions on the table and a comb for your hair. Do you need help?"

"Oh, I'd rather do this by myself, if you don't mind. And I would like some privacy. I've had very little of that lately," Cassie said, dropping her head and feigning shame. She saw Nasira from the corner of eye studying her with a passive expression. She might have imagined it, but she thought she saw a hint of pity in the sheikha's eyes.

"Yes, well, I am sure it was not a pleasant experience," Nasira said. "Just take your time, and when you are done, Dareen will escort you back to your room. I will check on you later."

"Thank you, Sheikha." Cassie bowed with false respect. Nasira nodded and left the room.

Once the sheikha was gone, Cassie quickly removed the remnants of her dirty clothes and rinsed the grime from her body before slipping into the pool. Floating languidly, she smiled inwardly at her success so far. Discovering the truth that Jalil didn't have a harem was exciting. That might provide her with a new opportunity.

Already, Cassie was thinking of changing the plan Hashem had come up with. She didn't mind hurting people, but she didn't want to kill anyone. What if she could get Jalil to help her instead? What if she could seduce him? The thought of being with Jalil in bed was stimulating, but she remembered he didn't find her attractive at the pre-race meeting or that night at Qadir's. She would have to find a new way to gain his attention. It would help if she could discover his weaknesses and exploit them, but she might have to employ other methods. If she could get her hands on certain herbs, she could help the situation along.

Without Kira to stand in her way, the only hitch was Nasira. Cassie had to find a way to get around her. Then her thoughts strayed to the boy. Hashem told her to kill Jabari, but he didn't tell her how she was to accomplish the deed. *Typical.* She had no plan, but ever resourceful, she knew she could figure it out if she had to. Cassie was used to getting her way but, so far, hadn't needed to kill anyone. Not that she didn't think she could kill anyone, she just thought it would be messy and take more work. But she wasn't entirely sure she needed to kill the boy—a boy who was almost a man. *Hmm. There's a thought.* He might prove useful and entertaining. *Oh yes. So many opportunities. So much to plan. But not right now.* She set aside any thought of Jabari's demise and focused instead on enjoying the warmth of the pool, as she plotted to seduce the handsome sheik and daydreamed of green-gold eyes and silken sheets.

CHAPTER 27

Cassie was in control again, something she hadn't experienced since she had been with Kira's father. It was a heady feeling, and though Hashem was counting on her to deal with the boy, she had her own plans.

First, she told Nasira the story Hashem had concocted. How he had sold her to slavers and how she had escaped. She felt sure the sheikha believed her story, and Cassie took advantage of Nasira's kindness. The woman provided her with several adequate outfits, along with other items necessary to keep up her beauty regimen. Restoring her beauty, she began the second part of her plan—seducing Jalil.

A master at manipulating men, Cassie fell back on her old tried-and-true tactics. Whenever Jalil was riding Mirage or working with Jabari, she made sure she was nearby. He was taking notice, albeit reluctantly, but she reveled in the thought she was finally getting under his skin.

While she worked on Jalil, she refined her plan. She needed to get pregnant by Jalil or rather lead him to think she was. She often wondered why it hadn't happened with Hashem, especially since she had been with him almost every night since Qadir's death and quite a few times before she started taking her secret potion. Perhaps Hashem had the same problem as Qadir. Whatever the reason, she was profoundly relieved when her monthly cycle started not long after she arrived at Jalil's. She asked Nasira for the items she needed so the woman would be aware she was not pregnant by Hashem. It would make her future subterfuge believable.

When Jalil showed continued signs of resistance, she knew she needed help. Pretending to have cramps from her cycle, she asked one of the serving women with whom she had become friendly for something to ease her monthly pain. It was common knowledge pain often accompanied a woman's monthly cycle, so the servant didn't seek approval from Nasira and supplied Cassie with the herbs she requested. Cassie hid them in her room. It wouldn't do for Nasira to see them. Nasira was the tribal healer and would certainly recognize them.

After making sure she had everything she required, she took the next step. She needed to be alone with Jalil, but it was proving difficult. Guards watched her when she was in the house, and though they didn't dog her footsteps, she knew they were always close by. And Nasira was usually in the house, too. Cassie felt a growing distrust emanating from the older woman and knew Nasira would undoubtedly try to keep her out of Jalil's chambers. So the only way to get to him would be when he was outside, away from Nasira and the guards.

While she continued to follow Jalil around the compound, waiting for an opportunity, she worked her way into Jabari's good graces. It was easy because, after all, he was just a boy and no match for her wiles. She took frequents walks by the stables when he was working with Sarii or his new colt, and she exclaimed over his skill and prowess. Hashem had said he couldn't believe Jabari was the missing baby, but the boy's similarities to Jalil were clear to Cassie. Jabari's eyes were silver, and his hair was lighter, but there could be no doubt.

One morning, she stopped to watch Jabari, admiring his handsome face and athletic abilities, and idly considered what he might be like as a lover. She had given several boys their first taste of a woman, and this boy was almost old enough to appreciate it. She was smiling at that thought when she noticed him staring at her with a dazed look. Realizing he was admiring her, she charmed him. "Jabari... or should I call you Talib?"

"Oh, no, you can call me Jabari," he stuttered.

"Thank you, Jabari. I just want to say you are truly a wonderful horseman. I have never seen anyone as skillful. You must be very smart," she said, giving him a sweet smile.

"Oh, uh, thank you, Cassie. I have worked very hard, but Sarii is smarter than most horses," he said, smiling and blushing at the same time.

"Jabari, I think it is your skill. I wish I could ride like you. Maybe you could teach me?"

Jabari was clearly infatuated. "Certainly, Cassie, I would be more than glad to help you learn to ride. You are nicer than Kira led…" He abruptly stopped with wide eyes. "I mean, umm, when would you like to start?"

Cassie felt a small stab of anger and wondered what Kira had said about her but wisely held her tongue. "Oh, I can't today. I promised to help the sheikha. But maybe tomorrow?" She had nothing planned with Nasira, but the boy didn't need to know that. She just needed to insinuate she was a friend of his mother's.

"Yes, just send word when you are ready. You can always find me near the stables," he said with a huge grin, puffing out his chest.

"Thank you, Jabari. I can't wait." She smiled again and returned to her room. After being invited to eat with the family, she wanted to look her best for Jalil and spent the rest of the day relaxing and preparing.

When she detected a glint of desire in Jalil's eyes during the evening meal, she knew her extra effort had paid off. He didn't smile or say anything, but Cassie could tell. As the meal progressed, she watched him grow more taciturn and smiled inwardly. Based on his deteriorating mood, it was likely he would do what he often did lately, and she planned to take advantage of that. As soon as she finished eating, she retired to her room to get ready.

Applying musky oil to her body in strategic places, she used dye on her lips and breasts. Nasira had provided lightweight tunics for her to sleep in, not knowing that Cassie liked to sleep in the nude. Cassie wasn't about to share that and thanked Nasira for the tunics, intending them for another use. Slipping on one of the more sheer ones, she looked at herself in the mirror, making sure the material was transparent enough before covering herself with a dark robe and tucking her hair in a head wrap.

Checking the hall and seeing no one about, she made her way toward the front door, walking normally so as not to draw attention. She had worked hard to convince everyone she had no desire to rejoin Hashem and was eagerly awaiting a caravan to take her to the coast. When she passed by the guard at the front door, he didn't say a word, nor did he try to stop her. He had grown accustomed to her evening strolls.

Cassie had been watching Jalil and knew he often went riding after the evening meal, and she knew what direction he usually took. Seeing Mirage in his corral and knowing Jalil would be along shortly, she hurried to the pasture gate.

The night was dark, but the moon was rising, and she had familiarized herself with this area during the day, so she moved with confidence. The wind was cooling, and she walked briskly as she listened to the night noises. She was not afraid. Many horses were around, and they would give warning if an intruder was near. When she reached the bank of the creek, she found a place where she could sit and rest.

While she waited, she mulled over her plans, working out different scenarios in her head. Her first option hinged on the success of seducing Jalil. She was confident that once he sampled her charms, she would have him wrapped around her little finger in no time. Then she would share what she knew about Hashem. Jalil was bound to be grateful. And even if he decided not to keep her around, she was confident he would still help her leave the country, if only just to get rid of her. Either way, she won.

Her second option involved Hashem. It was doubtful his plans, whatever they were, would succeed, especially if she shared what she knew about him with Jalil. But if Hashem succeeded, she would have to convince him to let her go. Except after seeing his reaction during their last meeting, she was no longer confident he would. He was spiraling into madness and reminded her more and more of Qadir.

The more she thought, the more she liked her first choice. Resolved, she removed her robe and head wrap and placed them beside her and settled in to wait for Jalil. Watching the water flow past, reflecting the silvery moonlight, she felt her heartbeat increase and licked her lips in anticipation. Jalil would be along soon, and she would make him forget all about Kira.

CHAPTER 28

Jalil hadn't planned to go out after the evening meal but, once again, found himself astride Mirage, riding in the low pastures, seeking relief from the chaos in his mind. Thoughts of Kira—wondering where she was, what she was doing, and if she was all right—drove him to distraction, made worse by the nightly dreams when he knew where she was—in his arms, her bare body pressed against his. Her lips tasting his, his hands caressing her hips and thighs. Many a night, he woke, and unable to sleep, he resorted to a cooling swim or a hard ride.

As time passed, he had thought he would get over her, but if anything, it got worse. He began doubting his feelings for her. Maybe it was just lust. It had been a long time since he had sought the pleasure of a woman's company. The years following his father's death had been too full of turmoil for him to even think about a woman, and now, thanks to Kira, it was all he could think about.

Struggling to control his desires, he thought he was making headway until Cassie had shown up. Cassie's long and tearful explanation of how she had escaped Hashem led Jalil to grudgingly let her stay, but only until a caravan could be found going to the coast.

He avoided her most days, and tried to ignore her, but became suspicious when he noticed her charming his family. She acted like the perfect guest, helpful and generous. And it didn't help that she always seemed to be around when he went to ride Mirage or was working with

Jabari in the corral. Then he would feel her eyes on him and would see her studying him. Though she made no obvious move to tease him or seduce him, he couldn't help noticing her hair, loose and flowing with only the sheerest of silken scarves to cover its crimson glory, and the way her silk tunics clung to her generous curves. Though he wanted to insist that she stay indoors, he couldn't bring himself to say anything. He had to remind himself she wasn't a prisoner, but she was always around when he was outside. It was infuriating.

As Cassie continued to drive him crazy, he took longer rides and spent more time in his pool at night. He knew he needed to do something about Cassie soon. She made him nervous in a new way, and he planned to talk to his mother about her but kept procrastinating, worrying about Kira.

When he suddenly realized Mirage was headed toward the pool by the cliffs, he redirected him toward the creek. The pool was the last place he wanted to go. He put all thoughts of Kira from his mind, but thoughts of Cassie surfaced. Earlier, he had watched her climbing the steps to the front door after her visit with Jabari, his eyes drawn to her swaying hips and shining hair. As much as he didn't like her, or trust her, he couldn't stop looking at her body. Even now, he responded as he had earlier. Cursing silently, he wasn't paying attention to Mirage until his stallion stopped with a snort, his ears swiveling.

Instantly on guard, Jalil looked ahead in the dim light and saw a figure sitting on a boulder near the water's edge. Holding tight to the reins, he called out, "Who is there?"

A sultry voice tickled his ears. "It's me… Cassie. Is that you, Jalil?"

"Cassie? What are you doing out here in the dark? How did you get here?" Jalil rode closer then dismounted and walked toward her.

"I'm sorry, but I couldn't sleep so I took a walk. I didn't mean to come so far. Did I do something wrong?"

"It is not wise for a woman to be alone this far from the house, even in my kingdom. You should have asked a guard to go with you." He stopped a few steps in front of her, almost afraid to move closer. Her robe lay beside her, and her tunic was pulled up past her knees. He could see her pale thighs. She was rubbing her ankle but when she paused and leaned back to look at him, he could almost see her breasts through the transparent silk.

He watched in fascination as she licked her lips and rubbed her ankle again. "Well, I was about to start back to the house when I tripped and twisted my ankle. It really hurts." She bent over, causing her tunic to gape open and expose more of her breasts.

Jalil felt a surge of lust and turned toward Mirage, willing his body to behave. "Then I will have to help you. You ride Mirage, and I will walk." He picked up the reins to lead Mirage closer.

"Oh, I don't know, Jalil. I can't ride very well, and Mirage is so big, I might fall off. You will have to ride with me."

Seeing her lift her arms to him, waiting for his help, he dropped his head and gritted his teeth. Taking a deep breath, he sighed in surrender. "Very well. But you must put on your robe before we head back." He wasn't just thinking about how it would look if anyone saw him with Cassie in her current state of undress. It was becoming more difficult to ignore her lush figure.

She pulled her robe on but tied the belt loosely. When he picked her up, she flung her arms around his neck, pressing her chest against his. "Oh, Jalil. Please don't drop me."

"Cassie, I will not drop you. Now, I am going to place you on Mirage..."

"Oh no, please, I cannot ride astride. Not in this outfit." She leaned back, giving him a clear look at her chest, made easier when the edges of her robe fell open, and Jalil found his problem returning in force.

"All right, I am going to set you down. Hold on to Mirage's mane." She did as he said, and when he had mounted, he reached down and lifted her into his lap. Cassie wiggled around, acting like she was trying to find a comfortable position, and when he felt her pressing her bottom in just the right place, he stifled a groan.

"I think this will work, Jalil. Just don't go too fast. I don't want to fall off." She smiled up at him, leaning back against his arm and pushing her breasts upward.

Looking down, he swallowed hard. He could clearly make out the tips of her breasts through the thin silk. *This is going to be difficult*, he thought. It turned out to be more than difficult and seemed to take forever to get back to the stables. Mirage was choosing the worst path through the pasture as if on purpose, as if he knew what Jalil was going through. By the time they reached the stables, Jalil was close to doing something he swore he would never do. Take a woman for only one reason.

Commanding Mirage to stop, Jalil lowered Cassie down, and she held onto the stirrup until he climbed off. He was anxious to get away from her, but he held out his arm for support. When she suddenly lost her balance, he instinctively caught her in his arms. She snaked her arms around his neck and pressed against his body. Her face was so close he could see her emerald eyes, heavy lidded with desire. Her plump lips were dark red in the moonlight and slightly parted. Losing control, he moaned and leaned down, and his lips found hers, pressing hard and pushing them open so his tongue could delve deep.

He felt her responding, and unlike Kira, she didn't stop. She mewled in pleasure, rubbing herself against him, and as he felt one of her hands sliding down, down, down, over his hips, he knew he was about to do something he hadn't wanted to do with anyone except Kira. Growling when he felt Cassie's hand at the top of his trousers slipping inside, he couldn't help thrusting forward as his body betrayed his mind. He lifted her tunic and grasped her thigh and was pulling her closer when Mirage must have decided he'd had enough. With a snort, Mirage pushed his way between them, knocking them both to the ground.

Cassie scrambled to her feet, pulled her tunic down, and shouted at the horse. "Stupid nag! Get away from me!" Mirage appeared to glare at her, and her eyes widened. "How dare you!" Mirage responded with a long, low nicker that sounded suspiciously like a chuckle.

Breathing hard, Jalil sat on the ground, his trousers sagging, feeling the cold sand underneath him. *She called my horse a nag!* Seeing Cassie stomping around without favoring her ankle, it suddenly dawned on Jalil she had been playing with him. *She had lied!*

Suddenly Cassie must have realized her mistake and covered her mouth as if realizing what she had said. It didn't surprise him to see her anger disappear.

"Jalil, I'm sorry. What just happened?" she asked, acting dazed and favoring her ankle again.

Avoiding eye contact, Jalil picked himself up, straightened his clothes, busying himself and brushing off the dirt. *Thank Allah for Mirage.* "Nothing, Cassie, nothing happened. Put this on, and I will have someone take you to your room," he said, handing her the robe. He was about to go for help when one of his men came running from the foaling stable. "I heard shouting, my sheik. Is anything wrong?"

"No. Our guest was out for a walk and twisted her ankle. Could you help her back to the house?"

"Certainly, my sheik." The man bowed and offered Cassie a helping hand. Cassie stared at the man with a neutral expression and allowed him to assist her.

Jalil quickly turned away and failed to see her look of fury when she glanced back at him. His mind was racing. *What was I thinking?* He knew he couldn't trust her, and not just because of what Kira had told him about her behavior after the crash. Cassie was one of those women his father had warned him about, the ones he swore he would never get involved with. Stroking Mirage and feeling the slow, steady rhythm of Mirage's great heart, Jalil allowed his anger to ebb.

Thank Allah for Mirage, he thought once again. Mirage had saved him from crossing a line. Leaning forward, he rested his forehead on the horse's neck, and it was some time before he made his way to his chambers for the night. Intent on getting inside where he could wash off the scent and memory of Cassie, he failed to see Nasira sitting in the dark on the bench beside the stable.

CHAPTER 29

The next morning, Jalil was watching Mirage pacing in his corral, thinking about Kira and feeling guilty about Cassie, when Nasira appeared.

"We missed you at morning meal," she said.

He thought it was an odd thing for her to say. She knew he often skipped the first meal, usually grabbing a bite of bread or a bit of fruit on his way out the door for his early morning rides. "I was meeting Fahad about the new guard schedules," he said, reaching out to rub Mirage, who had joined them at the fence. "Did you want to talk to me about something?"

"Well, no, not really. But Cassie was also absent, and you both came in late last night, and she was angry, and well, she was not wearing the usual attire. So, I thought maybe you and she…" Her voice trailed off, and she avoided direct eye contact.

Jalil saw she was looking everywhere but at him and knew instantly what she was thinking. He burst out laughing, and she blushed. "So, you thought—well, I can image what you thought," he said. "No, let us just say I was tested and almost failed. You can thank Mirage for averting a disaster."

She glanced at the stallion, who seemed to listen to their conversation. "Mirage?"

"Yes, Mirage. And that is all you need to know," he said with a chuckle. Mirage nodded his head and snorted softly.

Nasira laughed and reached out to pat his soft nose. "Thank you, Mirage, for whatever you did. And I am sorry for doubting you, Jalil, but she is a beautiful woman. I have seen her effect on the other men. But I am worried about her. You were right—we cannot trust her, and I wish we could send her away."

Jalil was about to agree when he suddenly heard two shots from the north. Two men galloped across the back pasture and into the compound. They were part of a patrol he had sent through the north pass in search of Kira. He waved his arms and gave a piercing whistle, and they turned and rode toward him.

Before Jalil could speak, one man leapt from the saddle. "My sheik, we have news!" The man gasped, breathless from his mad ride.

"Steady now," Jalil said.

"It is about the horse," the man said after taking a deep breath.

"What? What are you saying?" Jalil grabbed the man by the shoulders. "You have seen her?"

"No, but we met traders who said they saw a golden horse with a rider near our north pass."

Nasira looked puzzled. "Traders on the northern route? No one has used that route in many years. Who were they?"

"I do not know, my sheikha. They were a scruffy lot and claimed to be from the east."

Jalil was not thinking clearly. All he could focus on were the words "golden horse." *It had to be Amber!* Maybe this was the lead he had been looking for. "When, man? When did they see them?"

"I was told it was little more than a week ago."

Jalil dismissed the men then felt someone tugging on his sleeve. He turned to see Jabari, his young face alive with hope.

"My brother, do you think it was Amber?" Jabari asked.

"I am certain it was, and we must find her, and Kira, but I will need someone who knows the northern route."

"I have never traveled that way, but my father, Saad, used to make that journey a long time ago. It is where he found me. Perhaps he can be of help?"

Jalil was so excited he lifted the boy in a hug then called for his herdmaster, who came running. "Sakhr, I need you. Come with me to the house." He turned back to Jabari. "My brother, find Fahad and Saad and bring them to the main hall." Without waiting for a reply, he raced off, leaving Nasira to follow behind him, her face full of worry.

Dashing into his chambers, Jalil stopped in front of a large cabinet his father had built long ago to store important scrolls. He was busy pulling them out and tossing them to the floor in his haste when Nasira appeared by his side.

"Can I be of assistance, Jalil?" she said, sounding slightly alarmed.

"I am looking for a map. The one father had of the northern route," he said as he continued searching through the rolled parchments.

"Stop, Jalil. I know the one you are looking for," Nasira said in a strange voice and reached up to the highest shelf and slid out the only scroll stored there. Sliding it out, she held it out to him, but when he reached for it, she jerked it back, holding it with trembling hands.

Impatient, he stared at her, puzzled to see her staring at the parchment with a fearful expression. "What is it?"

Nasira shivered then shook her head and reluctantly handed him the scroll. She looked afraid, but Jalil was in a hurry and didn't give her time to explain. He strode from the room and headed to the main hall where he met Fahad and Saad.

Jalil was leaning over the table with the scroll spread out when Nasira caught up with him. Fahad stood to one side and Saad to the other. Sakhr and Jabari sat nearby watching them but not saying a word. Jalil saw his mother's face again filled with fear, but Saad diverted his attention when he answered Jalil's question regarding the northern trade route.

"My sheik, it has been a long time since I made that trip. The last time we traveled that route was when we found Jabari. It is a desolate trail and hard going. We heard rumors of a kingdom far to the north, but we never found it." Saad bent over the map, tracing the faint lines that marked the old trail with one finger. "Low hills border the trail on the north, but mountains line the south side west of your kingdom and all the way east to Qadir's. The mountains are impregnable with no known passes," he said. "We searched for other ways through, hoping to shorten our trade route, but found none."

"There is a pass," Jalil said, "one that leads from my kingdom through the mountains, the same mountains that form the cliffs by our spring. The pass is one of our tribe's best-kept secrets." He paused when Saad and Jabari looked up in surprise. "Now that you are members of our tribe, you can be told of its existence. I only ask that you both keep it a secret." He waited until they acknowledged his request before proceeding.

Fahad was studying the map and suddenly pointed to a series of interconnected marks in a remote section of the mountains west of the pass. One lead as far as the northern route itself. "What are those?"

They all leaned over and tried to decipher their meaning, but no one seemed to know the answer. Jalil was concentrating on the map when Nasira suddenly stepped closer and grabbed him by the arm. "Jalil, you cannot go there!"

Startled, he straightened, taken aback by the look of fear on her face. "What are you talking about? Amber may be on the northern route, and Kira! I must find them, and this is the fastest way."

"Jalil, this is the map your father used. This is where he went that day…the day he was murdered. And just like that day, you received a message about a golden horse. And just like Akeem, you will not listen to reason!"

Taken aback at the ferocity of her expression, Jalil was about to tell her she was being fanciful when Fahad spoke. "The sheikha is right."

Jalil's head whipped around, and he stared hard at his advisor. "You dare to question your sheik?"

Nasira blanched at Jalil's tone, but Fahad didn't flinch. "Yes, my sheik. I took an oath to protect my sheik and my tribe with my life. I do not think this is a wise move." His tone was respectful, but his voice was unyielding. "I was here when someone murdered Akeem. If I had done my job, he might still be here today."

Jalil heard both regret and guilt in Fahad's voice, and he suddenly felt ashamed. He had also been here, and he also had done nothing. He was out riding with Fahad when a messenger arrived with word of a golden horse seen on the northern route. They had ridden up just in time to see Akeem riding off alone on Rayham, but when Jalil started after Akeem, Sakhr stopped him, explaining the sheik had given orders that no one was to follow him.

Jalil was upset, but Fahad was furious. Akeem wouldn't tell anyone where he was going, only that he was heading out the north pass. That was the last time Jalil saw his father alive, and when he looked for the messenger, the man had disappeared. No one could remember seeing him leave, and they never saw him again.

Now, as he looked at Fahad, ever faithful, he had to apologize. "I am sorry, Fahad. I did not mean to snap. And you, of all my people, are not to blame for what Akeem did that day. My father made a choice, and no one could stop him. But today, I will listen to you. I will go to the pass, but I will not go alone." Jalil bowed to Fahad.

Fahad bowed and nodded, his expression fierce. "Tell me what you need, my sheik."

The mood in the room had taken a serious turn until Jabari stepped forward. "Yes, my sheik, I too am ready to help!" He bowed low, and Jalil's heart swelled with pride. His brother was deadly serious, but Jalil would not put him at risk. He was, after all, Jalil's only heir.

"Thank you, my brother, but I will need you to stay here and guard the family and help Sakhr guard the herd. Are you up to the task?" He fixed Jabari with a stern look.

"Oh, yes, my sheik. Just tell me what to do. Sarii and I are ready," Jabari said with a grim smile. No one chuckled at the boy who was fast becoming a man.

"Very well. Fahad will be in charge while I am gone, and he will give everyone their orders. I will take my best warriors and search the trails near our pass." With those last words, Jalil returned to his chambers to gather what he would need then headed to the stables.

His mother was waiting by the front door with a worried expression, and he tried to put her at ease. "Mother, it will be all right. I know this is Amber, and I know Kira is with her."

Nasira grabbed his arm. "How can you be sure, Jalil? It does not seem right somehow. Have you asked yourself how Kira would have gotten to the northern route when she left here through the main pass?"

"We cannot be sure that is how she left—she may have taken the north pass. I do not know why, Mother, but I feel I must go. Please, try not to worry. I am not my father, and I will be careful. I remember what happened too," he said in a soft voice.

She surprised him with a quick hug, but as he rode away, he glanced back once to see her standing on the steps, her arms stiff by her side, and he said a quick prayer. *Allah, please watch over her.* He didn't know, but to her, he looked just like Akeem had that fateful day.

As Jalil galloped into the north pass, he realized he needed to slow down and think. *Am I acting just like my father? Running off without thinking?* A lot of what his mother said was making sense. His father had been so obsessed with finding a golden stallion, he had thrown his customary caution out the door, and someone had used his obsession to kill him. Was he just like his father? Jalil knew there was no such thing as a golden stallion, but he was just as obsessed over Kira.

Having second thoughts, he brought Mirage to a stop. He noticed his men looking at him with confusion, but he motioned for them to wait while he gave himself a few minutes to think. He was sure Kira had used the main pass to the south when she ran away because she couldn't have known about the north pass. This felt wrong, and Jalil was confused. Was he on the wrong track?

Fraught with indecision, he felt his father's medallion warming against his chest and pulled it out. Rubbing it between his fingers, he mulled over the facts. As much as he wanted to find Kira, he had to consider the message was too coincidental. It might be a trap. Feeling a tingle in his hand, he looked down at the medallion and studied the odd shaped turquoise stones and flashing yellow gems. The colors reminded him of the blue-green of Kira's eyes, and he imagined he could see her, floating in the sun, her golden hair spread around her. Suddenly, he had the strangest feeling she was all right, wherever she was, and that somehow he would find her.

Mirage snorted loudly, bringing Jalil back to the present. His horse was undoubtedly wary of this area. It was close to where Jalil found Mirage years ago. Jalil dropped the medallion back inside his tunic. Perhaps his mother was right, but it didn't hurt to take precautions. Seeking the shelter of a projecting ledge, Jalil dismounted and motioned for his men to join him. After he explained what he had in mind, they nodded in agreement and settled in to wait for the sun to set.

If this was a trap, he would know soon enough.

CHAPTER 30

Peering over the edge of the cliff, Hashem watched the trail below. *Where is he?* Jalil should have been there by now. It had been hours since Jalil's scouting party had passed by, moving at a fast pace after being told of the golden horse and its foreign rider. Hashem had seen enough of Kira that day he had kidnapped her and made sure his men were able to describe her. He had been sure Jalil would have rushed out to investigate, but perhaps he had misjudged the man. Maybe he wasn't as confident as Akeem. Or maybe the rumors of Jalil's infatuation with Kira weren't true. Whatever the reason, it seemed Jalil wasn't coming.

Frustrated and tired of lying on the hot stone under the scorching sun, Hashem scooted backwards and slipped into a nearby narrow trench that ran parallel to the cliff edge. It provided some relief from the heat, and he settled into the meager shade, resigned to waiting until the next day to implement his plan.

As time passed, Hashem nursed his anger as he considered the problem of Talib, or rather Jabari. *How had he survived?* Qadir had instructed him to kill the baby and leave no witnesses, and Hashem later told Qadir he had done so. But he had lied. He had killed the men but had purposefully left the baby for the vultures and hyenas, thinking it would be a fitting end for one of Akeem's sons. He still couldn't believe the baby survived. And what were the chances of it being found by traders? Especially since the oasis where he'd left the bodies was well off the beaten path. But even more amazing was Jalil's family's acceptance that Jabari was Talib. It was baffling, and Hashem wished he knew what led them to come to that conclusion.

Feeling a growing thirst, he took a few small sips from his waterskin then carefully sealed it. A dull pain began building in his right temple, and he closed his eyes and tried to will it away. He didn't have time for another troublesome headache and hoped it wouldn't escalate like the others that plagued him recently. Rubbing his temple, he concentrated on another worrisome issue—the deplorable state of Qadir's treasury. When Hashem took control of Qadir's kingdom, he had assumed the coffers were full. Sadly, they were near to depletion, no doubt a result of Qadir's lavish lifestyle over many years and his failure to maintain a viable herd. The final straw had been the loss of the best stallion he had—Shar.

Hashem was not a horseman, nor did he know anything about breeding or herd management, but even he had recognized Shar's potential. Unfortunately, thanks to Qadir's failure to win the Tri-Annual race, he lost the stallion to Jalil. So, until he could find a more lucrative way to increase his treasury, Hashem might have to sell off more horses, unless his plan to steal Jalil's golden mares was successful.

A faint noise from the rocks behind him briefly interrupted his thoughts. He froze, but when it was not repeated, he figured it was a hyrax, a small furry creature that lived in the mountains. It was growing late, and the hyrax was undoubtedly seeking its burrow for the coming night. Hashem relaxed and continued to consider his financial state. His spies reported rumors of another world war, one that might spill over into north Africa and possibly Arabia. It was exciting news. During times of conflict, opportunities to make money were plentiful. Hashem planned to take advantage of that.

When he noticed the lengthening shadows, he glanced up to see the deep gold of the setting sun streaked with bands of orange slowly melting into bloody crimson. It reminded him of Cassie, his red-haired witch. "Jinn" he had called her the day he found her lost in the desert. Whether she was a good or bad spirit, he couldn't say, but the moment he looked into her glittering green eyes, she cast her spell on him. Hashem had never known a woman like her and figured no man could resist her. And yet, if his spies were to be believed, Jalil had yet to fall for her charms. Hashem scowled when he felt a hot twist of jealousy in his gut at the thought of Jalil and Cassie together, but in his heart, he knew she wouldn't fall for Jalil. She had certain tastes that only Hashem could satisfy.

As darkness leached the cream and tan tones from the cliff sides and filled the north pass with thick, murky shadows, Hashem relaxed. Letting his thoughts wander, and he idly played with his sheik's ring, twisting it back and forth. When he had pulled it from Qadir's hand, he felt immense satisfaction and triumph. So many years waiting for Qadir to make a mistake, and then it all happened in one night. *Kismet!* He knew it was his destiny to wear the ring.

Sadly, Hashem found being a sheik was not what he thought it would be. He didn't like being tied to the duties that came with it and needed to find an easier way. He had no interest in the horses, the harem, or the house. With enough money, he could still have all that and not have to deal with running a kingdom, managing a herd, or worrying about an heir.

He thought he heard another noise, this time to the north, and surmised it was one of the two men he'd brought with him on the mission. They were almost worthless but would serve their purpose until he got rid of them—there would be no witnesses. He listened intently, but the night was quiet except for the faint whistling of the night wind blowing through the cracks and crannies of the surrounding cliffs. Shivering, he huddled deeper in his robe, and as he settled lower, he remembered the last time he had been in Jalil's north pass.

Ambushing Akeem had been easy that day. The fool had been so eager to find a golden stallion he had taken off without guards. Hashem had shot Akeem's horse out from under him. Hurt in the fall, Akeem was no match for Hashem. Hashem knocked him out and stole the medallion he found hanging from his neck while his partner, Nadim, stood by, watching, but saying nothing.

When Qadir arrived, he immediately searched Akeem for the medallion while Hashem and Nadim watched. When Akeem refused to reveal it, Qadir lost control, took the man's dagger, and cut his throat. Hashem paid Nadim for his silence then hid the medallion in what he thought was a safe place, but later he discovered it had disappeared. He always suspected Nadim but chose not to confront him for fear the little man would rat him out to Qadir.

In hindsight, Hashem probably should have gotten rid of Nadim that day because Nadim only became greedier, threatening to tell Qadir all of Hashem's secrets and demanding more privileges. Killing Nadim during the botched attack on Jalil during the Tri-Annual Race had been a blessing. Hashem would have needed to get rid of him, eventually.

When stars blossomed overhead with still no sign of Jalil, Hashem had to accept he wasn't coming that night. But what if he didn't come at all? Maybe Jalil wasn't as enamored of Kira as everyone thought. Hashem could almost believe that. Kira was not unattractive, and she would certainly be valuable to slavers, but she was much too skinny for his tastes. He was still mad at how she almost escaped him the day he kidnapped her. But even if Jalil didn't care for Kira, Hashem knew how Jalil felt about the golden horses. Jalil would come.

Convinced Jalil was egotistical and overconfident, Hashem believed he would leave the bulk of his men to guard his compound. Jalil would have only a few men with him, and Hashem had instructed his men to kill everyone. Once Jalil and his men were confirmed dead, they were to regroup in the small canyon not far away where they had left their horses. Hashem's men didn't know Hashem planned to kill them, too. There would be no witnesses this time, and Hashem was not worried about any retaliation from Jalil's tribe. By the time anyone found Jalil's body, Hashem would be safely back in his own kingdom, confident no one would learn of his treachery.

With the death of Jalil and his little brother, Jalil's kingdom would be in shambles. Then Hashem could steal some of the prized golden horses and sell them at market. If all went as planned, he could also disrupt the tribal balance in the region and encourage a return to the days when sheiks were free to battle their way to power. Battles led to wars, and to fight wars, men had to have weapons. Weapons were where the money was in the future, and he intended to be part of that future. But first, he had to kill Jalil. Grinning in anticipation, he pulled his robe tight and lowered his hood, prepared to wait for the dawn. Soon enough, the sun would rise, and Hashem would remove yet another obstacle in his path.

CHAPTER 31

Jalil didn't intend to wait for sunrise. It was a moonless night, and the darkness concealed his movements. He and his men left their horses at the entrance of the pass and moved up the trail on foot, keeping as quiet as possible and sticking close to the side of the cliffs. Everyone froze when one of his men signaled a halt before they had reached the highest point of the pass. Jalil crept his way to the man's side, and the man pointed at his ear then up the side of the west facing cliff wall, showing he'd heard a noise. Nodding, Jalil signaled for his men to take cover and motioned for one man to join him. It was Imad, his father's former personal guard.

They both removed their boots and made their way silently along the path until they found a vertical split in the rock wall. Jalil worked his way up inside the split by pressing his back to one side and his bare feet against the other, and Imad followed. It was slow going and difficult to breathe with their smaller scimitars clenched in their teeth. At one point, Jalil felt his foot slip and pressed back with all his strength, holding his breath. When he regained control, he continued climbing.

Once they reached the top, they climbed out and crouched by the cliff edge until they caught their breath. Hearing nothing but the wind in the pass, Jalil crawled forward until he encountered a trench about four feet deep and four feet wide, running parallel with the cliff face. Easing down inside, he waited for Imad to join then inched forward.

He was thinking the trench seemed unnaturally straight when something caught his eye. Stopping, he could just make out the dark figure of a man not far ahead, sitting slumped over with a rifle by his side, and Jalil could hear the man breathing deep and steady as if asleep.

Summoning his strength, Jalil sprang forward and grabbed him by the throat. The man woke up fighting and thrashing. But Jalil held tight, and Imad grabbed the man's arms, and together they subdued him. He went limp when Jalil struck him on the head with the hilt of his scimitar. Gagging him with his headwrap, they bound his hands and feet, and Imad took the man's rifle. But as hard as they tried to be quiet, Jalil knew they had still made considerable noise. Worried, he waited to see if others hid nearby.

When no one else appeared, Jalil crept to the edge of the cliff, searching for his men on the trail below. He couldn't see them, but he knew they were there, and he tapped twice on the rock face to let them know he was safe and waited until he heard two taps acknowledging his signal. Crawling back to the trench, he dropped inside and turned to look at his captive. It was too dark to see much, and the interrogation would have to wait, but Jalil knew more men had to be involved.

As he knelt and considered his next move, the memory of his father's death surfaced once more. *Is this what happened to my father?* It was just too coincidental—same pass, same message. His mother's instincts had been correct. Then he had a wild thought. *Could this be the same person who murdered my father?* When they had found Akeem, and discovered his medallion and personal dagger were missing, they assumed thieves looking for gold and jewels attacked him. But if it was thieves, why hadn't they taken his sheik's ring too? Surely, they would have seen it. It was large and would have been worth something, just for the gold and gems. And why had they killed Rayham? He was an older stallion but still worth a great deal of money.

None of it made sense, but he put the memories from his mind. *This night is getting stranger and stranger*, he thought with a growing sense of foreboding. But though he might never know the answers to the mystery of his father's murder, he knew one thing. He would not find

Kira or a golden horse in the pass. All he would find was death—if he wasn't careful.

While he was thinking, he had unconsciously been rubbing the medallion under his tunic. It startled him when it flared with heat. Pulling it out, he felt it cooling then, for a second, it appeared to glow, and he bent his head to look at it more closely. That's what saved his life. A shot rang out, and Jalil heard the whine of a bullet pass over his head, and he dropped to the ground. Hearing Imad yell at him to stay down, Jalil glanced over his shoulder to see Imad pointing the invader's rifle toward the north. Another shot rang out as Imad fired up the trench, and Jalil heard a brief scream, then silence.

Both Jalil and Imad remained in place, unmoving, for a few moments. Keeping low to the ground, Jalil checked on their captive only to find he was dead. The man had somehow managed to rise and ended up in the line of fire. Jalil wouldn't be able to question him now. Climbing cautiously out of the trench, he inched over to the edge of the cliff and called softly to his men to move up the pass but warned them to be careful. A killer was on the loose.

Jalil, followed by Imad, made his way northward, ever on the alert for the shooter. He hoped to find him wounded or dead. But they saw no sign of their attacker until they came upon a large boulder blocking their way. Luckily, the stars were bright, and Jalil noticed a wet smear on top of it. Rubbing his finger in the dark liquid, he brought it to his nose and immediately recognized the coppery scent of fresh blood. Smiling grimly, he climbed over the stone and discovered another trench, just as uniform, leading off in a different direction. He followed it as it twisted and turned until he reached a pile of jumbled rocks. He thought he had lost the trail until he found another smear of blood.

Climbing over the pile, Jalil found a natural canyon surrounded by rising cliffs. A horse lay on the ground near the north wall, its throat had been cut. *It must have belonged to the dead man*, he thought. *What a waste.* The shooter was taking no chances that anyone could pursue him. Knowing there had to be a way in and out of the canyon, Jalil searched among the boulders until he found a narrow trail leading northward through the rocks. Sighing with disappointment, he knew whoever had attacked him had escaped, and without men and horses, Jalil couldn't follow. He and Imad returned to the original trench where they had left the dead man and searched him thoroughly but found nothing to help identify his tribe. They left him for the vultures and climbed down the cliff face.

Jalil whistled, and his men came running. They retrieved the horses, and Jalil led them further up the pass just to be sure no one else was around. As he rode, Jalil sorted through his troubled thoughts. Whoever wanted him dead was still on the loose, and it might be the same person who had murdered his father. He needed to make sure his family and tribe were safe, and then he was going to find the man responsible for this attack. But unlike his father, Jalil would not do it alone. He needed help, and he knew who to call. It was time to contact Ehsaan.

CHAPTER 32

Cassie had been looking for Jalil when she had heard the commotion in the main hall. Sneaking closer, she eavesdropped, and her ears perked up when she heard Jalil speaking to Nasira about going to look for Kira. *Damn Kira! Why couldn't she just stay lost?* Seeing she had no opportunity to make up to Jalil for what had happened at the corral the previous night, she headed back to her chamber.

Once she was sitting at her table, sipping a bit of her special wine, she could think more clearly. Cassie remembered hearing Jalil's father had gone looking for a golden horse in the north pass and someone murdered him. Now Jalil was doing the same thing. *What are the chances of that?* The more she thought about it, the more suspicious it seemed. Hashem had never told her how he planned to dispose of Jalil, and she wondered if this was his doing. *Should I say something to Nasira? Should I stop Jalil?* If Cassie was correct, Jalil would find himself in the same situation as his father.

Cassie felt a twinge of remorse at the thought of Jalil's death. If Hashem killed him, she'd never get to sleep with Jalil. But worse, she'd have to complete Hashem's other plan and kill Jabari. And then she'd be right back in bed with Hashem. Being in bed with him had certain rewards, but in the end, she'd be stuck. He was never going to let her go.

Agitated, she paced back and forth while considering her other option. If this was Hashem's plan, then there was no golden horse and no Kira—they were just bait. And if Hashem was unsuccessful, then Jalil would return…but without Kira. If that happened, Cassie could proceed with her own plan. Thinking she still had a chance to come out on top, she assembled a special potion, but by nightfall, Jalil still hadn't returned. Frustrated, Cassie drank some of her sleeping potion just so she could go to sleep.

The next morning, she woke unusually early, with one thought on her mind. *Maybe he's back?* Excited at the prospect, she summoned a servant, only to learn Jalil hadn't returned. Growing restless and determined to find out what was going on, she dressed and made her way to the dining chamber, hoping to join Nasira and the girls for the morning meal. But the room was empty.

When Cassie asked the woman who brought her tea where Nasira was, the woman said the sheikha was not feeling well and didn't want to be disturbed. Remembering the fear in Nasira's voice when she warned Jalil not to go to the pass, Cassie assumed Nasira was still not over losing Akeem. *Well, at least she won't be following me around today*, Cassie thought as she helped herself to a bit of fruit and bread. Afterwards, she spent the rest of the morning in the harem bath, preparing herself in case Jalil returned.

The sun had reached its zenith when she retired to her chamber. After applying crimson dye to her private areas, she debated donning her see-through tunic but wanting it to be pristine when Jalil came home, she opted instead for a robe. Bored and impatient, she looked for something to do and found a bit of embroidery that Nasira had given her to work on. She hated sewing, but it helped to keep her mind off what might have happened in the pass.

It was almost sunset when Cassie heard a distant commotion. Tossing the embroidery aside, she hurried to the front entrance where she could hear men yelling and horses neighing. She watched as Jalil rode into the compound on Mirage, and when he leapt from the saddle, she knew he wasn't hurt. Unsure how much time she had, she turned to run back to her room and almost collided with Nasira.

"Jalil!" Nasira gasped as she ran past Cassie without stopping.

Cassie didn't wait to see their reunion and rushed back to her room to change into her tunic. The corridors were empty as everyone left the house to see Jalil, and she took her goblet, hurried to Jalil's chambers, and slipped inside. The layout of his chambers was almost identical to Qadir's. Stepping into his bedchamber, she pulled the doors half-closed and slipped between the overlapping panels of silk hanging along one wall behind a huge potted plant to hide.

She didn't have long to wait. When she heard noises in the front room, she held her breath. It sounded like a door opening and closing then a chair being moved. The light in the outer room brightened, and a shadow passed by the doorway, and she heard someone walking into Jalil's private bathing chamber. There was some faint rustling then the footsteps returned. Hearing the door open and close again, she waited and listened, but all was quiet. Curious, she tiptoed over to peek into the front room and knew who had made the noise. A platter piled with bread, roasted meat, fresh fruit, and soft cheese sat on the table, along with a few small bowls of various sauces. Next to the platter were two pitchers and an ornate goblet. A servant had brought the sheik his evening meal.

Eyeing the pitchers, she hurried over to see what was in them. One held sweetened tea and the other wine. *Perfect!* She dumped the tea in a nearby potted plant and set that pitcher on a table across the room. Then she added her potion to the wine, shook it gently, then filled his goblet. Seeing the lamps in the bathing chamber had been lit, she surmised Jalil would probably take a bath first. Resigned to having to wait longer, she returned to her hiding place, but not before discarding her robe, wrapping it around her empty goblet, and stuffing it under the bed.

It wasn't long before she heard the door open and close again, but this time with more force. The noise startled her. It sounded like someone was angry, and she hoped it was Jalil. Anger was a strong passion, and men were usually more impulsive when they were angry. She stayed hidden, but when she heard someone walking into the bathing chamber, she couldn't resist. She snuck over and peered around the half-open doors to see Jalil standing just inside the bathing chamber doorway, pulling his clothes off—first the boots, then his top, and finally, his trousers—revealing his wide shoulders, taut buttocks, and long muscled legs. Cassie saw every part of him as he stepped down into his pool and had to cover her mouth. *Oh, my!* Even un-aroused, he was impressive, and it was all she could do not to run over and join him. Excited, she slipped back into her hiding place, shivering with anticipation.

When she heard him return to the front room, she crossed her fingers. Everything depended on him drinking the wine. After what seemed an eternity, she heard the chair as he pushed back from the table then entered the bedchamber. She sighed silently with relief when he blew out the lamp and she heard the bed creaking, followed by a low groan. Her patience was wearing thin, but when she could stand it no longer, she eased from her hiding place. Enough light shone through the doors to the front room that she could see him lying spread-eagle on top of his bed with the coverlet and sheets pushed away. He had one arm flung over his eyes, and she could hear him breathing deeply. He was asleep. *Perfect!*

Tiptoeing to the bed, she looked down at his beautiful body. *Yum.* Suddenly inspired, she quickly removed her sheer silk tunic, ripped it down the front, and tossed it across the foot of the bed. Quivering with excitement, she eased onto the bed and snuggled close to his body.

Unable to resist touching him, she lightly ran her hand over his jaw, feeling the stubble of his unshaven face and tracing his lips with a fingertip. He stirred and moaned, and she held her breath, but he didn't waken, and her lips curled in satisfaction. Growing more confident, she touched his neck, felt his strong pulse, then lightly stroked down his shoulder, over his chest, and paused again. He sighed softly but still didn't waken.

She slid her hand down his rippled abdomen then reached further and boldly stroked him, excited he was responding. It was the perfect time to complete the act, but she hesitated. It wasn't enough that she could finally have him. She wanted him to be aware of who he was making love to, especially after the way he treated her at Qadir's.

Taking a risk, which fueled her passion even more, she took one of his hands and placed it on her breast and ran her wet tongue around his ear. "Jalil, Jalil, it's Kira. I need you, Jalil. Touch me, love me," she crooned, trailing kisses down his neck and chest. Feeling bolder, she took his hand and slid it slowly down her belly until it rested between her legs. She was so aroused, she moaned and arched upward.

Overcome by desire, she couldn't wait any longer. She crawled on top of him, rose to her knees, and spread her legs over his hips. As she took him in hand and prepared to take him, she was startled by a loud growl and froze. His eyes were open, and she knew at once he was not only awake but aware—he knew who she was. She lowered herself anyway, hoping he wouldn't stop her in time, but he was quicker. When he grabbed her by the shoulders, she tried to hold on and scored his neck with four long fingernails before she found herself flying off the bed to land with a painful thump on the floor.

He rose from the bed with a roar and stomped over to where she lay. Seeing him standing over her in his natural glory, she was even more aroused. She grinned evilly when she saw him wince as he touched his neck and stared in shock at the blood on his fingers. She ignored him and ran her hands up his legs, intent on one thing, but he jerked her upright and held her away from his body.

"Just what do you think you are doing, Cassie?" Jalil growled as his eyes flashed and his lips thinned in anger.

Cassie was already thinking. "Jalil, what's wrong?" She pretended to be confused and tried to look hurt.

"What is wrong?! I will tell you what is wrong! You are in my bedroom—UNINVITED!" He shouted the last word close to her face.

"But Jalil, darling, I was just trying to welcome you home," she whined and forced a few tears. "You invited me in, but then you got carried away, and well, you simply took control," she cried, squeezing out more tears and pointing to her torn tunic.

Jalil stared at the tunic then at her, and his eyes narrowed dangerously. "I do not remember letting you in my room," he said. "And I would never tear a woman's clothes off. I would not have to do that," he added with a smirk.

Cassie's eyes narrowed, and her tears vanished. "Well, you did, and that's what I'm going to tell everyone. And that I could even be pregnant with your heir."

Furious, Jalil gripped her shoulders so hard she whimpered.

"Let go, Jalil, you're hurting me. I'll show the bruises to your mother. She'll be the first person to learn of what you did to me," Cassie hissed.

"Just who do you think she will believe, Cassie?" he said then pushed her away.

She stood breathing hard, but when she saw Jalil's eyes running up and down her naked body, she smiled, thinking he might be interested in her after all—until he donned his robe and threw a spare one in her face.

"Put this on. You sicken me," he said. "Oh, and don't forget this." He tossed her the ruined tunic and stormed into the front room without waiting for her response.

Furious, Cassie donned the robe and stuffed her ruined tunic into the pocket before rushing after him. She found him holding the goblet, sniffing suspiciously. Then he dipped one finger in the pitcher and brought it to his lips. She saw the minute he figured it out.

Jalil's eyes widened, and he whirled to glare at her accusingly. "What did you put in my wine?" His voice was deep and threatening.

"I don't know what you're talking about, Jalil," Cassie said nonchalantly, but she flinched when he slammed the goblet down on the table.

"Fine. Play your little game, Cassie, but you should probably pack now. My mother will tell me what is in this goblet, and then I will personally escort you from my kingdom."

Cassie had had enough and finally lost her temper and, with it, any semblance of control. "Hashem will kill you for touching me! You wait and see," she hissed.

Jalil appeared to be unfazed. "Hashem, huh? I thought you ran away from him. Interesting. Perhaps there is more to your escape than we first thought. As for Hashem, I would not be too sure about him. Yes, he may try to kill me, but he will fail," Jalil said then he paused as his face filled with a look of dawning understanding. "Maybe he already has."

It was too much for Cassie. Afraid she may have already said too much, and now sexually frustrated, she let out a long, loud scream. Jalil seemed to sense her ploy at once. He grabbed her by the arm, dragged her to the main door, and pushed her out into the hall.

Cassie was stunned. *He threw me out!* And to add insult to injury, the doors opened again, and her slippers came flying out, forcing her to duck. "You bastard!" she screamed.

Hearing footsteps behind her, she whirled to see a guard running toward her. She wailed loudly when the guard grabbed her but stopped when suddenly the door opened again.

Jalil stood just inside with a surprised look on his face. "What is going on out here?" He looked at the guard with arched eyebrow then at Cassie. "Oh, I see. You two need to take this somewhere else. I asked not to be disturbed." Then he looked directly at the guard. "Please send another guard to my door for the night. And you two should be more careful." The look on the guard's face was priceless, and Cassie could see Jalil was struggling not to laugh before he quickly closed the door.

Cassie wasn't laughing, she was fuming. The guard looked confused, but when she tried to pull loose, he shook his head and half-dragged, half-carried her back to her room. When he closed the door, she could see his boots just under the edge. Evidently, he wasn't going anywhere.

With a scream of rage, Cassie stomped around her room, throwing anything she could get her hands on. Something seemed to break inside her. *Enough is enough!* She was going to do anything she could to get out of here now, including whatever Hashem asked her to do, as long as Jalil suffered. Breathing hard, she was so upset that she knew she wouldn't be able to sleep without help. Searching for her goblet, she almost screamed again when she remembered she had left it in Jalil's chambers.

Locating a small cup beside her bed, she crumbled some of the remaining herbs into it, added some tea from the pitcher on her table, and gulped it all down, grimacing at the bitter aftertaste. Crawling into bed, she waited impatiently for the potion to take effect, sighing with relief when she finally felt the familiar feeling of lightness spreading through her arms and legs. Her eyelids grew heavy, and she slipped into a dreamless sleep, unaware her world was about to change yet again.

CHAPTER 33

It didn't take long for Kira to assemble her meager belongings and begin her journey. As she stood by the tunnel that would take her back to Jalil, she stared out over the valley and enjoyed one long last look at her private paradise.

A stray thought passed through her mind as she absent mindedly rubbed the ancient medallion that hung from her neck. *Should I leave it behind?* Perhaps it should remain here, safe from the outside world, like the herd, the water, and the gold. But when she started lifting the heavy chain from around her neck, it suddenly sparked, and she dropped it hastily. *What was that?* She must have imagined it, and she touched it again, only to experience the same shock. For a second, she felt a trace of fear, but it dissipated, replaced with a feeling of peace, and she sighed with relief. She had been prepared to leave it behind and was happy to know she would have a piece of the valley with her, one she vowed never to give up.

A soft whinny reminded her that Amber was waiting. Together, they wound their way through the old tunnel and soon emerged into the bright light that bathed the rocky foothills. Once they reached the bottom of the steep trail, Kira climbed into the saddle and allowed Amber to take over. Kira remembered the trail from the oasis to the valley but had no memory of how she had gotten to the oasis.

She thought Amber was taking her to the oasis, but Amber surprised her by suddenly veering eastward. As was her wont, Kira spoke out loud, "Amber, where are we going? Is this the way to Jalil's?" She didn't expect a reply, but when Amber nodded her head and nickered softly, Kira relaxed. Undoubtedly, her horse knew exactly where she was going. They maintained a steady pace, and Kira paid attention, making note of several unique landmarks along the way. She might never return to the valley, but she would be sure to share the way with Jalil. Deep in her heart, she knew he would love it as much as she did, and she could trust he wouldn't reveal it to anyone else.

Worried how long it would take to reach Jalil, Kira prayed there would be water along the way. She had brought as much food as she could pack in her simple pannier tied to the back of her saddle, but she only had the one waterskin. Her relief was immense when, after a long day's ride, Amber wove her way between some boulders and carried her to a tiny hidden spring marked only by a few scruffy bushes. It was cool and clear, and they both drank their fill. It was a nice place to camp, but Kira knew water drew many things, predators in particular. So she chose a protected area farther down the trail, and with Amber keeping watch, Kira slept without fear.

The next day passed in similar fashion, but this time they found no spring, and by sunset, Kira was feeling nervous again. She had enough food and water for one more day, but then it would be hard going. As she lay looking up at the night sky, she glanced over at Amber, who once again stood guard. Amber stood like a shimmering statue in the starlight and appeared to be dozing lightly. But periodically, she would lift her head and huff softly—testing the night wind for signs of danger. Amber's ears swiveled once at the distant howls of hyenas, and Kira tensed but settled almost immediately when Amber lowered her head and remained silent. Kira finally dropped off to sleep, knowing that as long as Amber stood by her she would always be safe.

The next morning, they got off to an early start. The stars had faded, and the sun was rising in the eastern sky when Amber suddenly slowed to a stop. Kira recognized the narrow opening of the pass to Jalil's kingdom and saw the guards positioned high in the rocks. She waited for their acknowledgement. Undoubtedly they would recognize Amber but maybe not Kira, so she removed her headwrap, freeing her long golden hair, and waited patiently. When a sliver of sunlight blazed down from over the tops of the cliffs, setting Amber aglow, two shots rang out. One guard waved, and Kira smiled and waved back. She was home.

It was but a brief ride to the main compound, and as she drew closer, she recognized the tall man standing on the steps, fisted hands resting on his hips. Her heart pounded, and her palms grew damp. But by the time she reached the steps, apprehension quickly replaced her joy at being home. She had been so excited when she reached the pass and wanted to gallop to meet him, but the minute she saw him, her heart dropped. Jalil's eyes were unblinking as he stared at her, and she couldn't tell what he was thinking. Kira sat perfectly still, waiting for his permission to dismount.

"Kira." He didn't smile.

"Sheik Jalil." She watched him closely, swallowing hard. He wasn't happy.

"What brings you to my kingdom?" he said without emotion.

His chilly reception took Kira aback. *Maybe I made a mistake. Maybe I shouldn't have come?* Filled with sudden doubt, she still pressed on. "I was hoping to speak to you and the sheikha." She didn't elaborate.

"About?" He wasn't giving an inch.

"Someone once said there might be a place for me in your kingdom. I was wondering if the offer still stood," she said, swallowing her pride.

He remained silent, and Amber pawed impatiently at the ground.

Kira was holding her breath when Nasira came bursting forth from the house. It was clear the sheikha had heard some, if not all, of their terse conversation because she glared at her son before turning a smiling face to Kira.

"Welcome back, Kira. We have missed you. I expect you are tired from your journey. Will you stay with us for a few days?"

Jalil looked at his mother like he wanted to strangle her.

Kira saw his reaction and worried she shouldn't have come back. "Thank you, Sheikha. It is good to see you again. I would like to visit with you, but I fear I have not received permission yet," she said, cutting her eyes to Jalil but keeping her expression neutral.

His face was stony, but his eyes were full of conflict. "Kira, it appears the sheikha decided for me. Please join us. I would have someone see to your horse, but that was never a good idea. If you wish, Sakhr can show you to a place where you can store your equipment."

"Thank you, Sheik Jalil." She dismounted and stood by Amber's head.

Nasira stepped forward. "Kira, after you have Amber settled, please join us in the dining chamber. We were just about to have our morning meal."

"Thank you, Sheikha." Kira nodded and looked back at Jalil one more time. "And thank you, Sheik Jalil." She bowed.

He nodded curtly and walked into the house. Kira watched him until he disappeared, fighting tears. *He must hate me!* It was obvious he didn't want her back. She had made a dreadful mistake and didn't know what to do. She didn't want to go back to the valley, and yet, she didn't want to go back to America either. Nothing was waiting for her there anymore.

Maybe she could stay here until she could find another place to go. Ehsaan and Issa might let her join their tribe, and she knew she could contribute to their community. She enjoy living there and missed Adara and even Gigi. Her head dizzy with confusing thoughts, she headed to the old stable where she used to keep Amber's food and equipment. Sakhr greeted her with a welcoming smile and, once she removed the saddle and halter, helped her store them. After giving Amber a good rubdown and checking her hooves, Kira made sure she had grain and water.

Before she headed back to the main house, she spoke with Sakhr. "May I turn Amber loose in the back pasture later?"

"Certainly, Kira. She is always welcome, as are you. In fact, if she will let me, I will take her there myself after she eats." Sakhr beamed happily.

"Thank you, Sakhr. I am sure she will allow it. She likes you." Kira smiled at his obvious pleasure at hearing that. Grabbing her blanket and bag, she was on her way to the house when she barely escaped being bowled over by a silver-eyed dust devil.

"Kira! Kira! Is it really you?!" Jabari grabbed her by the shoulders.

"Ow... easy Jabari." But she was laughing. "Yes, it is me. Now, let me look at you. Hmm, I believe you have gotten taller—and stronger too!" She bowed.

He blushed. "Kira… a sister does not have to bow to her brother."

When she saw his loving expression, Kira refrained from answering and struggled not to burst into tears. Jabari saved her from embarrassment when he blurted out, "Where is Amber?"

As soon as the words left his mouth, a loud whinny rang out, and Jabari's face lit up when he saw the golden horse peeking out from the stable door. "Amber!" he shouted. The horse trotted forward, and Jabari ran to meet her. Throwing his arms around her neck, he hugged her hard, and Amber whinnied again then lowered her head over his shoulder and pulled him closer.

"She thinks you're stronger too." Kira laughed, her heart warmed by the sight of their reunion.

When Jabari stepped back, he checked the horse all over. "Amber, you look wonderful." When she responded by nodding her head, as if to say, "Of course," Jabari laughed. He gave her a final pat on the neck, and she snorted and trotted back inside to finish her breakfast.

Jabari turned to Kira and grinned, but it faded after a minute, and he looked at her with a serious expression. "Are you going to stay now, Kira?"

Kira glanced toward the stables and the hills beyond. She listened to the morning sounds of the compound, hearing Sakhr in the foaling barn, the herd in the distance, and several women laughing on their way to their looms. Looking back at the young man who had become like a brother to her, she nodded. "Yes, Jabari, I will stay, at least for a while, as long as the sheik allows."

Jabari's grin returned, bigger than ever. "This is wonderful news, Kira! Of course Jalil will allow it. Everyone knows how he feels about you. And besides, this is my home too. You can be my guest!" He stood with his hands on his hips, and she couldn't help but smile. He looked so much like his big brother.

"Well then, will you show me to my room?"

"Yes, but please allow me to help," he said, reaching for her bag.

Kira followed him into the house while he peppered her with questions, wanting to know where she had been and what she had been doing. Not wanting to reveal the secret of the valley, she answered in vague terms, but Jabari appeared to be so thrilled to have her back he barely seemed to notice. Once they reached her room, she excused herself to freshen up, promising to meet him in the dining chamber shortly.

Removing her robe, top, and trousers, she replaced them with a serviceable tunic she found in the cabinet. Kira smoothed her hand over the lovely garment, appreciating the excellence of the weave and simple embellishment. The fact Nasira had never removed her things from the room brought a tear to her eye.

After a quick wash with a face cloth, she combed and re-braided her hair. Then she added a touch of her favorite lotion, still in its ceramic jar on her table, breathing in the light citrusy fragrance while she smoothed it on her face and neck. The rest of her body would have to wait until after the meal when she hoped to spend some quality time in the old harem bath.

Akilah and Lina both jumped up with squeals of welcome when she walked into the dining chamber. Once the hugging was done and the girls had calmed down, Nasira stepped forward to embrace her. "Welcome home, Kira," she murmured in her ear. "We are so glad you came back."

Kira barely held back her tears. "Thank you, Sheikha. I am glad to be home."

Jabari came running in, and as usual, broke up the emotional scene. Everyone settled into their usual places, but when Kira saw the empty chair at the head of the table, she couldn't hide her disappointment. Nasira reached over to pat her on the arm and smiled warmly. "Kira, I do not know where Jalil is, but I am sure he would have joined us if he could. He has been very busy lately. We have had some excitement since you've been gone."

Nasira took a sip of her lemonade and almost choked when Jabari blurted out. "Yes, Kira. Jalil almost got killed!" He was chewing furiously on a piece of bread and reaching for some fruit.

Kira paled, and her eyes widened in horror. "Killed?! What are you talking about? What happened? Was he hurt?!" She rose halfway out of her chair. The girls stopped talking, and Nasira glared at Jabari, who was still chewing away, clearly oblivious to the impact his words had on Kira.

"Kira, he is all right. It was just a small fight. He is fine. I expect he will tell you about it later," Nasira said, but she looked uneasy. Kira got the distinct impression she was holding something back and knew something was up when Nasira suddenly changed the subject. "So, Kira, you should see what Jabari has done with Sarii."

Of course, that did the trick. Jabari got so excited he wanted to take Kira right out to the corral to see Sarii and his colt.

Nasira chuckled. "Jabari, there will be plenty of time for that later. Kira needs to settle in after her long absence."

"Thank you," Kira said and turned to Jabari. "Jabari, I promise to find you later today. I want a full update on Sarii's development, as well as Rizu's."

"Of course!" Jabari was grinning from ear to ear. "Now, may I leave, Mother? I need to make certain my horses are ready." When Nasira nodded, he took off like a whirlwind.

"Does he ever just walk?" Kira asked no one in particular. Everyone laughed, and Kira began feeling at home. It was as if no time had passed. After they finished eating, Nasira walked with her to her room and stayed long enough to ensure she had everything she needed. Kira smiled and assured her she did and declared her intent to head to the bathing chamber.

Nasira rose to leave then paused by the door. "Kira, I need to visit with you after you have bathed. Would you come to my chambers before you visit with Jabari?"

"Certainly." Kira watched Nasira's face, slightly alarmed at her serious expression.

"Please, Kira, call me Nasira. And please forgive Jalil for his rudeness this morning. He had a difficult time while you were away, and much has happened. Come straight to see me as soon as you can. We have much to discuss."

Kira nodded and waited until Nasira had closed the door before putting her things away. She removed the old medallion and carefully tucked it back in her travel bag, which she placed inside the cabinet. As she gathered what she needed to take to the bathing chamber, Nasira's words played in her head. *What has happened? What does she want to talk about?* Kira's sixth sense was sending her signals, and she worried all the way to the harem bath.

When she entered the outer chamber, she smiled to see a familiar face. "Greetings, Dareen."

The old woman looked up, surprised. "Kira? Is that you?" She set her mending aside and tried to rise, but Kira stopped her

"No, Dareen, do not get up. And yes, it is me," Kira said, waving her down.

"Oh, Kira. It is good to see you again. Can I help you with your bath?"

"No, don't worry about me. I know where everything is."

"Well, you call out if you need something. I will be right here," Dareen said and returned to her mending.

Kira wondered briefly what Dareen was doing working in the bathing chambers but was too eager for her bath to give it further thought. Seduced by the scent of jasmine from the warm waters, she laid her clean garments on the closest bench. She didn't notice the motionless figure floating in the pool, but when she turned and removed her robe, she gasped aloud.

Emerald eyes flew open to see blue-green ones. "You!" they both shouted at the same time.

CHAPTER 34

Kira couldn't believe her eyes and fought to control her expression seeing her nemesis floating in her pool. Cassie eyed her warily then leaned back against the side of the pool with a sly grin. Her crimson hair was slicked back from her face, and as Kira watched, she pulled the long, wet ends around one shoulder, letting them trail down the side of her breast.

"Well, well, well, if it isn't Jon's little brat back from the desert again. Where have you been Kira?"

Kira studied her adversary, watching Cassie flaunt her nude body in the water. The old Kira would have looked away in embarrassment at the wanton display, but the new Kira had been through too much, had survived too much, to be intimidated anymore by the likes of Cassandra Miller. The new Kira was very aware of her own body, and she had learned men found her attractive, too. Ignoring Cassie, she slowly removed her tunic and laid it over the bench, pleased to see a hint of jealousy in the older woman's eyes.

Kira's time in the valley had done wonders for her physical appearance. Her hair was a luminous gold with silver highlights, and her skin had taken on a golden hue. Her arms and legs were toned, her belly flat, and her breasts were high and full. She walked with her own natural hip swing to the smaller pool where she soaped her body and hair, taking her time, almost making a sensual show of it. After she rinsed, she moved to the main pool and slid into the water like a silky seal.

Cassie was at the far end, trying to hide her look of hatred. Kira dunked her head then rose, letting her slick, golden mane drape down around her shoulder to lie against her belly. She smiled slowly at Cassie. "I have been on a trip, and now I am back. That is all you need to know."

Cassie's eyes widened at Kira's new confident attitude then slowly narrowed as if in challenge. Shrugging, she said, "Well, it matters little to me. But aren't you going to ask me what I'm doing here?"

Kira moved to the edge of the pool closer to the steps and leaned back to watch Cassie, as if she didn't have a care in the world. But her mind was spinning. The last time she had seen Cassie was at Qadir's, and she couldn't wrap her mind around how the woman could have ended up at Jalil's. Some part of her felt a tinge of compassion. Not even Cassie had deserved to be held captive by Qadir. But another part of her was worried. Kira knew how conniving Cassie was around men, and she was certain Jalil would be her next conquest. Holding tight to her emotions, Kira tried to be nonchalant. "I'm sure I don't want to know."

Cassie ignored her, eager to explain. "Well, Jalil was kind enough to take me in when I escaped from Qadir's. You remember Qadir, don't you?" She smiled evilly, staring pointedly at Kira's faint scars.

Kira had actually forgotten about her scars. But she had a sinking feeling Cassie knew exactly what happened at Qadir's. "Yes, I remember him. He's dead, isn't he?" she said with a smile.

Cassie clenched her teeth then relaxed her face. "Yes, someone murdered him the night you were with him. But I expect you still had a good time—he seemed to be enchanted with you."

Kira closed her eyes and pretended to relax, trying not to think about that night and praying she wouldn't experience another flashback. "Yes, he seemed to like me more than some others." She peeked out the corner of her eye and hid her smile when she saw Cassie bare her teeth in a brief display of jealousy.

Cassie huffed then steeled her features. "Well, Kira, you should have stuck around for the show. Qadir passed out, and Jalil came in and killed him. Slit his throat. It was a messy business—all that blood."

Kira failed to hide her reaction to Cassie's slander. She had heard Qadir was dead, but this was the first time anyone had suggested Jalil had done it. But Kira knew Cassie had to be lying because, in her heart, Kira knew Jalil would never kill a man in that way.

Cassie appeared to revel in Kira's reaction, and a sinister smile snaked across her face. "You remember the blood, don't you, Kira? I think some of it was yours," she hissed.

Kira had enough of Cassie's game. Her eyes darkened to a glacial blue, and she stared hard at Cassie. "Yes, Cassie, I believe it was. But how would you know that?"

Cassie's eyes narrowed, reminding Kira of a desert rattler coiled to strike. "Honey, I saw Jalil kill Qadir. I came to help you when I heard you screaming, but I was too late. You had already escaped, and I caught Jalil in the act. And of course, I saw what had happened to you. Your blood was on Qadir. I made sure Jalil saw it. Now you are no different from me." Cassie chuckled cruelly, clearly reveling in hurting Kira.

Unfortunately for Cassie, she misjudged Kira. She had no way of knowing what Kira had been through and what she had survived. While cut to the quick by Cassie's words, Kira once again brushed them off. She wouldn't let the red-haired viper win this time. Ignoring her, Kira casually climbed out of the pool, padded to the bench, and picked up her towel. Drying her body and wrapping another towel around her head, she slipped into a clean tunic, stepped into her slippers, and donned her robe.

Cassie was still smiling when Kira turned to her and said, "I will never be like you. What happened to me was unfortunate, but it was not of my doing. I was the victim of an evil man. Thankfully, Jalil was the one who made me see that." Kira shook her head sadly. "Oh, Cassie, you could never understand. How could you when you always give yourself to any man who is handy."

It was a near thing. Kira underestimated how crazy the woman had become. Cassie rushed out of the pool with a snarl, but Kira reacted quickly and tossed her wet towel right in Cassie's face, effectively slowing her down.

And that's when Nasira walked into the chamber. She gave Cassie an angry glare and looked like she was ready to come to Kira's aid. But when Cassie detangled herself from the towel, only to fall backward into the pool with a screech and a big splash, Kira began laughing, and Nasira joined in. When Cassie rose, sputtering and cursing, Kira looked at Nasira, shrugged, and walked regally from the room.

Kira waited for Nasira in the hall, and when she saw Nasira's apologetic expression, she put her at ease. "Nasira, please do not worry. Yes, it was a surprise to find Cassie here, but I think I will be all right. Cassie is always going to be Cassie. At least I know what to expect. But I am tired of her cruelty. She said some terrible things, and I think you and I need to talk."

"Yes, we most certainly do. And I do not want you alone with her ever again. I do not trust her, and you will soon hear why. For the time being, I am having you moved to the chambers next to mine. They were formerly Jalil's before he moved to the sheik's quarters. I will go with you now, and we will get some of your things. Will that be all right with you?"

"As long as the sheik does not object."

"The sheik? What happened to calling him Jalil?" Nasira asked.

"I am not sure. I was hoping you could explain," Kira said.

Nasira was quiet for a moment. "I can probably enlighten you, but I need to speak with Jalil first."

Kira nodded. That would do for now.

Kira's new chambers were much larger than her old room. They reminded her of the man she had fallen in love with. The wall hangings were predominately turquoise with white and tan accents. The front room had a small dining table with two chairs and a long side table on one wall. Another area had huge cushions, a low table, and a plush rug. The bedchamber contained a wall cabinet, a chest, another side table, and a full-size bed. *That will take some getting used to,* she thought, as she tested its softness with one hand. After the incident with Cassie, Kira was glad to see the door had a lock on the inside, as well as another chamber with a small, private pool.

Rays of sunshine streamed through the scrollwork that covered the window high on one wall, creating mosaic patterns on the floor. She turned to see Nasira watching her with a smile. "Nasira, this is lovely. Are you sure you want me to stay here? This is the family wing. Shouldn't this be Jabari's room?"

Nasira was quick to put her at ease. "Kira, I want you to stay here until you decide what you want to do. I am sure Jalil will agree. And as for Jabari, well, he spends many nights in his tent. Apparently, Rizu cannot live without him." She chuckled. "Now, let us sit, and I will call for refreshments. We can take our time and answer each other's questions undisturbed."

"I would like that. I'll just finish dressing." Kira ducked into her new bedchamber and took a minute to comb out her hair and hang up her robe. When two servants showed up with everything she had left in her old room, Nasira helped her put it away. Another servant showed up with platters of food and pitchers of drink.

Once they were alone, Nasira spoke first. "Kira, may I ask where you have been all this time? You do not have to tell me, of course, but I am curious."

"There is a place, one that Amber took me to after I found her in the desert. She took me back there the night I ran away." Kira hid her discomfort at having to keep information from Nasira. And after Jalil's unfriendly reception and finding Cassie, she wasn't sure if she should even share her secret valley with Jalil.

"I see. Can you tell me why you ran away?"

"You mean Jalil said nothing?"

"Jalil told me basically what happened, but I wanted to hear your side, if you can talk about it."

As Kira sipped her tea, she wondered if he had shared the intimate details of their night by the pool. She was thinking this would be hard until she saw Nasira's eyes. It was like looking into her mother's. Understanding, sympathy, kindness... it was who Nasira was. Taking a deep breath, she spent the next hour telling Nasira everything about her night with Jalil, the flashback, her feelings before, and her feelings after.

Nasira listened without judgement and asked few questions. When Kira finished, Nasira smiled. "Is that all?"

Kira choked on her tea. "Is that all? I think that is enough, don't you?"

Nasira quickly apologized. "I did not mean to make light of what you have been through, Kira. I would never hurt you intentionally. I just think that you are in love, and you are experiencing what all women in love experience—complete and utter chaos."

Nasira had summed up Kira's situation in four words and Kira was speechless. Instead of feeling embarrassed, she started laughing. Nasira stared at her oddly, and that just made Kira laugh harder. Finally, Nasira joined in, and that was how Jalil found them.

CHAPTER 35

Jalil was coming to see his mother when he heard laughter from his old chambers. *What is going on?* Half fearing he would find Cassie up to no good, he burst into the room then stopped, mouth agape, when he saw Kira and Nasira leaning over the table, laughing so hard tears streamed down their faces. When they looked up and saw him, they laughed harder. Jalil was not seeing the humor in it at all. What were they doing in there?

He closed his mouth with a snap and cast a steely look at Nasira. "Sheikha, can we step outside and have a word?" He held open the door and gestured with one long arm.

Nasira grabbed a cloth and wiped her eyes, still smiling, but Kira looked anywhere but at Jalil. "Certainly, Sheik," Nasira said, rising to join him in the corridor.

Jalil saw Kira try to smother a small laugh and shot her a suspicious glare before turning to follow his mother out into the hall. He was still angry at Kira for having stayed away so long. Slamming the door, he moved a few feet away. "Explain."

"Now, Jalil, she's had a hard day." Nasira raised her hands in a placating gesture.

"You could have fooled me." He frowned. He thought Kira looked amazing but was a little hurt she didn't look like she had suffered as much as he had.

"Jalil, do not be that way. You do not know what she's been through."

Jalil tried not to think about Kira in the bathing chamber, naked in the bathing chamber. Gritting his teeth, he had to ask, "Did Kira say anything about me?"

"Like what, Jalil?" Nasira said.

"I do not know… I was hoping she might have missed me, but I guess she does not care," he said petulantly, feeling out of sorts.

"That is something you will have to discover on your own. But for now, I want Kira next to me, if for no other reason than she sacrificed herself for my son. She's the reason Qadir did not get his hands on Jabari. And Cassie has proven she is untrustworthy, and I believe she will do harm to Kira, if given the chance."

Jalil was thinking about the kidnapping and how Kira had made Amber take Jabari to safety and almost missed what Nasira had said. "Harm? You think Cassie will hurt Kira?"

"Yes, I do. Unfortunately, Kira ran into Cassie in the harem bath before I could warn her. Cassie was not nice."

Now Jalil was worried, but he tried to hide it from his mother. "I see. Well, perhaps you are right. I will talk to Kira soon, but I need to figure out what to do with Cassie first. I want her out of here, and I would appreciate any ideas you might have regarding that."

Nasira nodded. "I, too, wish her gone. I will give it some thought, but until we have a solution, you must be very careful around her, especially while Kira's here."

Jalil shook his head. Life was getting more complicated. "I will. I am putting more guards on Cassie, and I will not get caught alone with her again. You should search her room and remove all her potion making ingredients. She might do someone real harm."

"What are you talking about? What is Cassie doing making potions? This is the first I have heard of it."

Jalil rubbed his forehead impatiently. "Oh, I forgot. I was on my way this morning to tell you what happened last night until Kira arrived."

Nasira's voice rose. "What happened last night, Jalil?"

"Calm down. Nothing happened, but it almost did." He quickly related the details of Cassie's sordid attempt to seduce him. At first, Nasira couldn't speak. Jalil watched the play of emotions on her face—first surprise then disgust. But the disgust in her eyes quickly changed to fury as his story concluded.

She didn't mince her words. "I have heard of women and their attempt to grab power in other kingdoms, but this has never happened in my household before, and I assure you, it never will—not on my watch. We can thank Allah you woke when you did. Please allow me to handle this matter," she said and fixed him with a steely look.

"Certainly. But what will you do?" Jalil said, curious to hear her plan.

"I will have to give it more thought. First, I need to finish with Kira. Then I need to talk to the servants. I am putting an end to Cassie's potion making right now," she said and turned to open the door then stopped. "Jalil, shall I tell Kira about last night, or will you?"

"It is my responsibility, and I will handle it," Jalil said solemnly.

"All right but do it soon. I fear Cassie will use that against you with Kira. Kira is different now, but she is still vulnerable."

"What do you mean...different?"

"You will find out. Now, I must get back. She and I have a few more things to talk about. Will we see you at evening meal?"

Jalil hesitated then said, "Yes, I think you will. And thank you for helping me with this."

"You are my son, Jalil. I will always help you...always." She bowed to him and disappeared into Kira's room.

Jalil smiled and wished he could be present when Nasira had her talk with Cassie. He wasn't sure what she was going to say or do, but he suspected Cassie would regret ever coming to his kingdom.

CHAPTER 36

After about a week, Kira settled back into life at Jalil's. For the first few days, she woke early at sunrise and hurried to the dining chamber, hoping to see Jalil. But he was never there, and that morning was no exception. Disappointed, she grabbed a bite of bread and fruit and headed out for her morning ride.

Amber was waiting at the gate, as usual, and soon they were riding through the pastures, but this time Kira directed Amber towards the cliffs. Kira had been avoiding the pool, afraid it would trigger terrible memories. But seeing it in the light of day, she relaxed and remembered what she had felt with Jalil before the flashback. She had been so consumed with desire that she had totally succumbed to his advances. If she hadn't had the flashback, she knew she wouldn't have been able to stop.

Kira thought her time in the valley had dampened her desire, but it returned in full force whenever Jalil was near. She wanted to feel his lips and his arms around her again, but it was frustrating because she didn't know where the physical attraction was leading or what it meant. And she didn't understand his attitude. He had seemed just as thrilled by their encounter, and yet now, he avoided her and seemed uncomfortable having her in his home. The few meals they had shared had been with his family, and he limited his conversation with her to talking about Amber or the herd.

Kira felt somewhat better when Nasira told her Jalil was avoiding Cassie, too. And he never talked about Cassie, and for that, she was thankful. Nasira explained how the woman had shown up one day seeking sanctuary, claiming she'd escaped from Hashem, but Kira didn't understand why Cassie was still there. Growing tired of having the same conversation with herself, Kira cleared her mind, and said a quick prayer for peace, sending her discontent heavenward.

After an invigorating gallop, Kira returned to the compound, leaving Amber at the gate. As she walked toward the house, she heard shouting from one of the corrals. *What is going on?* Squinting in the glare of the midday sun, she saw Jabari trotting beside a rider on an unfamiliar horse. From the looks of it, it was a woman, and by the way she was bouncing all over the place and screeching, Kira knew at once who it was. Curious, she cut behind one of the stable buildings until she was close enough to see what was happening and could listen in.

"Stop, Jabari. Stop! I'm going to fall off!" Cassie yelled, clutching the front of the saddle.

Jabari brought the horse down to a walk and stopped along the side of the fence opposite where Kira was hiding. "Cassie, you must relax if you are going to become one with the horse," Jabari said.

"I don't want to become like a horse. I just want to ride without falling off!" Cassie lowered her voice. "This horse is no good. I think I need another one."

Kira smothered a chuckle. The mare was old but likely well trained—Jabari would never try to teach someone on a lesser animal.

"Cassie, I am sure if you would relax and not hold on so tight, you would find riding to be much more enjoyable. Let us try this again," Jabari said. He started walking around the corral once more, leading the horse.

Kira wondered why the woman would bother learning to ride. Cassie had made it clear to her how much she hated horses. After a few more turns, Cassie seemed fed up and demanded Jabari stop. But when Cassie slid off the horse, she stumbled and almost fell then snorted loudly and wobbled over to the fence.

"Cassie, you will never learn if you do not practice more," Jabari said.

"Jabari, I'm tired. I've had enough riding today," Cassie whined.

When Cassie winced as she straightened her robe and passed her hand over her bottom, Kira smirked, seeing her obvious discomfort. But her ears perked up when she heard Cassie's next words.

"Besides, you promised I could see Rizu today," Cassie said in a sugary voice.

"All right, Cassie. But first I must take care of this horse. Why don't you meet me at Rizu's corral?"

"Fine," Cassie said and walked carefully toward the stable where Jabari kept his colt.

Curious why Cassie wanted to see Jabari's colt, Kira waited until after Cassie and Jabari had both disappeared before heading toward Rizu's corral. Kira walked quietly around the building until she could again see them and hear what they were up to.

"Jabari, you have done such a wonderful job with your little horse." Cassie stood inside the corral and timidly touched the colt. Jabari held him by the halter and was stroking Rizu's nose.

"Thank you, Cassie, but he is very smart and easy to train," Jabari said with obvious pride.

"Rizu is such an unusual name, Jabari. Does it mean anything?"

"All our names have meaning, Cassie. Rizu means 'mighty.' He is just a colt, but he will be a mighty stallion one day."

"Oh, I'm sure he will. So, what does your name mean?" Cassie said.

Kira was on the alert, seeing Cassie's familiar flirty smile.

"Jabari means 'courageous.' My mother, Samira, gave me that name. She says I was always fearless, but I think she should have named me Fuduli because I am so 'curious.' It has gotten me into trouble a few times." He chuckled.

Cassie chuckled, too. "Oh, I am sure she got it right. You are certainly courageous. And so smart. Just look at what you have done with Sarii. And your magic is amazing."

She's laying it on thick, Kira thought. *But why is she being so nice? She hates children. What is she up to?* Kira's sixth sense kicked in, remembering Cassie never did anything without a reason, usually something that would further her own gain.

"It is only because I practice all the time. And that is what you have to do too, if you want to learn to ride better. We need to keep up with your lessons. I am sure tomorrow will go better."

Cassie grimaced then said sweetly, "You are right, I'm sure. But I want to learn more about Rizu too. What does he eat? What is his favorite treat? I noticed you always have something in your pocket for him."

"Rizu loves many things, but he really loves dates. He will do anything for those." To illustrate his point, Jabari pulled one from his pocket, and Rizu eagerly snatched it from his palm.

"I see." Cassie nodded. "And when will you be able to ride him?"

"Oh, that will not be for a long time—at least two years—and only when he is strong enough to bear a rider. I will have him trained by then, and it should not be very hard to convince him to let me ride. I can't wait because I know he will be fast. Adara and I have a bet about who will be faster, Rizu or her filly, Hiba."

"So you have to talk to him about it?" Cassie wrinkled her brow in confusion.

Kira had to cover her mouth not to laugh aloud at Cassie's question and couldn't wait to hear Jabari's answer.

Jabari was laughing now. "Cassie, you are so funny. I will not have to ask him, not like you are thinking. But I will have to have his permission," he said cryptically. When he started removing the cord he had tied to the halter, Cassie stopped him.

"Jabari, can I try to walk him? I would love to see if he will let me. I promise to be careful. Can you show me how?" As Kira watched, Cassie gave him an innocent look, flashing her beautiful green eyes and smiling sweetly.

Jabari paused for just a moment, but when she continued to give him alluring glances, he caved. "Uh…um…well... all right. I will show you how, but you must be very gentle."

When Kira saw Cassie take his hand in hers, and Jabari's eyes widen, she almost stepped forward but then stopped to think. She needed to decide whether to intervene or continue to watch. Painful as it was, watching felt more important. Cassie wasn't actually doing anything wrong, but Kira knew she was up to something. But exactly what? That was the question Kira needed to answer.

"Oh, I'll be very gentle," Cassie said. Jabari handed her the rope and stepped back. The colt huffed and looked wary, but when Cassie cooed to him and walked forward slowly, he appeared to relax. After a few steps, Cassie stopped and held out her other hand to Jabari. "Maybe if I gave him a treat, he might trust me."

Jabari seemed to hesitate then handed her a sugary date, and Cassie accepted the sticky lump, but her subtle cringe was obvious to Kira. However, Jabari didn't seem to notice. When Cassie gave him a stunning smile, he looked like someone had hit him with a pole.

Cassie offered the treat to the colt and appeared to shudder when the horse's lips touched her hand but quickly hid her reaction and acted excited. "Oh, Jabari, this is so much fun." And when she continued to walk forward, Rizu followed her more willingly.

Perplexed, Kira stood in the shade of the stable. Cassie had never shown any liking for animals of any kind and certainly not horses. Deep in thought, she wasn't aware of anyone behind her until she heard a voice.

"What are you up to, Kira?"

Hearing the low, deep voice that always made her heart pound, she turned around and found herself inches from a very wide chest. Looking up, she stared into Jalil's deep green-gold eyes.

"Jalil." It was all she could say.

He stared down into her blue-green eyes, and if he had planned to say something, it must have slipped his mind because he remained speechless. Time stood still as they gazed into each other's eyes. Jabari was saying goodbye to Cassie, and several tribesmen walked by talking and gesturing to each other, but Jalil and Kira were so engrossed in each other, they saw and heard nothing until a loud bugle from Mirage's corral startled them into awareness.

Jalil's eyes skittered left and right then focused on her again. "Kira, I saw you just standing here and wondered if you were lost or if you needed something."

Kira thought it an odd statement—why would she be lost? But the pinched expression on Jalil's face suggested he also thought it had been a stupid thing to say. Deciding to ease his discomfort, she said, "Oh, well, I was putting Amber away and heard Jabari working with Rizu, and I thought I would watch him. He is really good at training." Now she was saying stupid things.

"Yes, he has a natural talent. But I am curious why he is letting Cassie handle the colt. She has never shown any interest in horses before. I thought she didn't like horses." Jalil said, his attention on Jabari, who was leading Rizu into the pasture to rejoin the herd.

Kira was watching Cassie walking back to the house and had forgotten about Jabari and Rizu, more concerned with what Jalil had just said about Cassie. *How does he know that about her? Just how well does he know her?* She wanted to ask him but hesitated, having told herself she was going to wait for him to broach the subject. After her altercation in the bathing chamber, she knew Cassie was up to no good. *But does Jalil know her well enough to know that, too? Or is he as smitten with her as Jabari seems to be?* Thinking about Cassie having anything to do with Jalil made her angry, and she felt something she had never felt before—jealousy, pure and simple. She wanted to take Cassie, throw her on a horse, and send her packing. *Well, maybe not on a horse. I wouldn't do that to the horse. It would have to be a camel.*

Suddenly she realized she was thinking too hard and forgetting about the man standing just inches away, the man who was even now bending his head down toward her as if he couldn't help it. She couldn't resist tilting her head back and rising toward him, her hands inching upwards as if to rest on his chest. His eyes were on her lips, and she looked at his lips as they drew closer. Almost... almost... and then Jabari called out, breaking the spell.

"Jalil, are we going to practice sword work today?" Jabari was walking toward them, and Jalil let out a low curse and stepped back.

Jalil licked his lips and cleared his throat. "Kira, I was wondering if we could meet sometime to talk about Amber. I have a few questions and thought you might help me." He smiled and cut his eyes toward Jabari then back at her.

Feeling the blood rushing to her face, Kira blinked rapidly. "I guess we could meet sometime. Just let me know when it is convenient, Sheik Jalil." Without another word, she turned to seek refuge in Amber's stable. She could hear Jalil behind her talking to Jabari but didn't pay any attention. In fact, she almost broke into a run, desperate to get control of her emotions.

Kira didn't know how it had happened, only that she had welcomed his advance without hesitation. She was going to have to be careful in public, and even more so in private, when she was around him. After a few deep breaths, she felt her composure return and made her way back to the main house. It was time for the midday meal, and she had promised to meet with Nasira. She was hoping to stay with Jalil's tribe, and she prayed Nasira could help her figure how to make that happen. Immersed in her thoughts once again, she was not paying attention and pulled up hard when Cassie stopped her just inside the front doors.

"Were you spying on me?" Cassie hissed.

"Well, good morning to you too, Cassie. I really do not know what you are talking about. I just got back from my morning ride, and I see you had a morning ride, too." Kira smiled sweetly. "Did you enjoy it? Was it fun?"

Cassie's eyes narrowed. "Oh, yes. I always enjoy a good ride and not just on a horse. Perhaps you know about that now. In fact, you might enjoy a ride on Jalil. He's much better than a horse." A cruel smile crawled across her face.

Kira had to work at hiding her shock at those words. *Cassie and Jalil! No!* Bolstering her courage, she answered as if nothing could interest her any less. "I wouldn't know about that, Cassie, because I only ride my horse. Having not spent as much time as you riding anything else, I guess I'll just have to take your word for it."

"Or you could ask Jalil, but then he might tell you more than you want to know." Cassie smirked meanly and turned to walk away. She spoiled the effect by grimacing and wobbling.

Kira couldn't muster a laugh because she was falling apart inside. *Jalil slept with Cassie? Could it be true?* The very thought made her heart stutter and her stomach roil. Feeling nauseous, she skipped her meal with Nasira and returned to her chambers instead. Once inside, she locked the door and lay on her bed, succumbing to her tears as she tried to get the image of Jalil and Cassie out of her head.

CHAPTER 37

Two weeks later, Jalil hadn't been able to get rid of Cassie. She continued to cause trouble in his family and seemed to take great pleasure in taunting Kira. He had let go of his pride and was trying to get closer to Kira, but Cassie seemed to always be in the way. It was time he cleared the air and shared his feelings with Kira.

He had awoken that morning with only one thing on his mind—Kira. Hoping she might take a ride with him, he went to find her. She was always more comfortable when riding her horse—just like him—and he smiled, thinking how much they were alike. But as he approached the front doors, he heard two shots from the pass. *Who could this be?* Stepping outside, he watched two men, escorted by his guards, ride in and stop at the steps.

One of Jalil's guards dismounted and bowed. "My sheik, these are Sheik Hashem's men. They have a message for you."

One of the messengers held out a red leather pouch. "We will wait for your reply," he said, without the customary honorific or bow.

Jalil's guard scowled at the rude man and took the pouch to Jalil. The messengers were typical of Hashem's tribe—scruffy men on poor horses. Jalil felt sorry for the horses.

"My men will see to your needs." Jalil said curtly then headed back inside and called for a servant. "Please find Fahad and send him to my chambers. And have someone find the sheikha and ask her to join us."

The servant bowed and scurried off.

Jalil waited until Fahad and Nasira joined him before he opened the pouch. At first, he couldn't believe his eyes, but as he read it, his disbelief quickly turned to rage then became something more, something deadly. When he finished, he handed it to Fahad without saying a word. Fahad must have seen how upset he was and gave him a questioning look, but Jalil just shook his head, unable to speak yet.

After Fahad finished, he appeared calm as he passed it to Nasira, but when his advisor glanced at him, Jalil saw the same rage boiling in his eyes.

Nasira read it slowly, but when she finished, she startled both men by slamming it down on the table. "This is preposterous!"

"Oh, it is beyond preposterous, and I will not stand for it," Jalil said, placing his hands flat on the table and leaning forward, his face infused with fury. Fahad appeared to be concentrating, and Jalil waited for him to speak.

"Let me get this straight. Hashem is accusing you of the murder of his half-brother, Qadir, as well as the woman known as First Wife," Fahad said. When Jalil nodded but remained silent, Fahad continued. "It is all a fantasy. We know you are innocent."

"Of course he is innocent," Nasira declared forcefully.

Jalil felt a surge of pride at Fahad's steadfast belief in his innocence.

"But now he is formally claiming blood money?!" Fahad said, his eyes wide with disbelief.

Jalil nodded grimly. "Fahad, we heard that rumor some time back. You knew this was a possibility."

"Yes, I remember, but surely, this is pure fabrication. How can Hashem prove Qadir is his half-brother? And just who is the witness he says he can produce?" Fahad sat back in his chair with a disgusted look on his face.

Nasira had fallen silent, and Jalil wondered what she was thinking. "What is it, Mother?"

"Well, in his complaint, Hashem mentions a murder weapon. What I want to know is exactly what weapon he has, and what makes him think it belongs to you?"

"I wonder if he is referring to the dagger," Jalil said. "When I found Qadir, his throat was cut, and a large dagger was stuck in his chest, but it wasn't mine."

"Well, it looks like we have little time to figure this out. He says he will be here in a week," Nasira said, sounding worried for the first time.

"Well, if he thinks I am going to give him Mirage and my golden mares, he is a fool," Jalil said, feeling his anger return.

"But if you do not, he says he will demand the death of one of your family," Fahad growled.

Furious, Jalil slammed his fist down on the table, shocking both Fahad and his mother. He would never give up Mirage or his golden mares. And he would never let anyone hurt his family, especially based on a bunch of lies.

When Nasira reached across the table and placed her hand on his, he saw the look in her eyes. It was as deadly as his, and he knew she would fight, as they all would, for her family, her tribe, and her sheik. He glanced at Fahad, expecting him to keep a cool head, and his advisor didn't let him down.

Deceptively calm, Fahad held up a blank scroll. "My sheik. Your reply?"

Jalil looked at his mother, and she nodded and left the room. It was her signal that she trusted him explicitly. Whatever he decided, she would support him, and he knew it deep in his soul. A cold, hard smile broke out on his face as his thoughts came together. He took a blank scroll and wrote a short message. Dripping hot wax on the parchment, he sealed it with his ring, slipped it into a turquoise message bag, and handed it to Fahad. "Send this to Ehsaan by your fastest riders."

Fahad raised an eyebrow in question then asked, "What about your reply to Hashem?"

"I have no reply. I will tell his messengers."

Fahad nodded and departed.

Jalil grabbed Hashem's message bag and started toward the stables to speak with the messengers, then stopped when he heard voices just outside in the hall.

"Fahad?" It was Nasira's voice.

"Yes, my sheikha?"

"This business about blood money is ridiculous. But even more ridiculous is Hashem's claim to have a witness. It is pure fabrication," she said.

"I agree, my sheikha. Surely, Hashem cannot think anyone will believe this nonsense."

"I am not sure, Fahad. With all the unrest in the region, some might be swayed. But I would not put it past him to pull some trickery. We must be ready, and we only have a short time to prepare."

"Do not worry, Sheikha. My men will be ready."

"As will I," she said, her tone resolute.

As their footsteps receded, Jalil smiled, his heart full. He had people surrounding him he trusted with his life, and he knew they would do all in their power to help him. *Allah, please let it be enough.*

Jalil's guards stood at attention when Jalil approached the two messengers sitting on the bench in the shade of the stable. The messengers rose, and Jalil handed them Hashem's pouch.

One looked inside. "There is no message. Did it fall out?"

"No. There is no reply. Now leave my kingdom immediately."

The messengers appeared shocked but quickly mounted their horses and made a hasty retreat. As they rode off, Jalil laughed along with his guards when someone said, "I would not want to be in their boots when they get back to Hashem's."

On his way back to his chambers, he ran into Nasira on her way to speak with him. Something was bothering her, and she appeared agitated. "What is wrong, Mother?" he said.

"That woman! She is disrupting my house, and I am tired of it."

"Come, sit with me," he said, stepping into the dining chamber. She followed him inside, and once they sat down, Jalil waited for her to speak.

"Jalil, Cassie is up to something. I just know it," Nasira said as she poured herself a cup of water.

"What has she done now?" Jalil was almost afraid to ask. Cassie was capable of anything, as he knew well.

"She convinced Jabari to take her riding. I do not know what she said to him. Your little brother is having a hard time telling her no. It is difficult for him—he has such a kind heart, and it is easy to take advantage of him. She knows that too."

Jalil studied her face. Her anger and frustration were easy to see. He was also tired of the conniving woman. Despite many warnings, she continued to pick at Kira as well. "Mother, I will speak to Jabari."

Nasira shook her head. "Jalil, would you mind if I spoke with him first? I believe I know how she has manipulated him."

Jalil felt surprised when he saw his mother blushing. *What is she talking about?* He almost asked but decided she probably knew best…as she often did. "I have no problem with that. Just let me know if you need me to talk to him."

"I will, but I expect I can convince him to be more careful. As for Cassie, it is time we take stronger measures. We must restrict her movements completely and step up our plan to send her away. If only I could find someone traveling beyond our kingdom. I do not care where she goes, but go she must, especially now that Hashem will be coming. I get nervous thinking about the two of them together," she said, rubbing her temple. "And I have been wondering how Cassie could have escaped a man such as him… although now that I know her, I can almost believe he wanted to get rid of her as much as we do."

Nasira's words set Jalil's mind in motion. It wouldn't have been strange for Hashem to sell Cassie to slavers. He was a greedy man. It was odd she escaped, though, especially on foot. "Mother, I am the last person who would disregard your premonitions, and I agree we must keep her from any more mischief. If that means she cannot leave her room, so be it."

Nasira smiled. "I hoped you would see it that way. And I want to be the one to tell her."

"Certainly, you are the sheikha. You rule this house."

Nasira bowed her head. "Thank you, my sheik. But before I speak to Cassie, have you any more ideas on how to get her away from here? Maybe you could have your men take her to the coast."

"No, I need all of my men here and ready for him. But that gives me an idea," Jalil said, his eyes gleaming. "What do you think about sending her home with Hashem? He would probably be open to the idea. He sold her once and he can sell her again."

"Jalil, that is a wonderful idea! Akeem would be proud," she said, patting his hand.

"Well, then that is decided. You can inform our guest of her imminent departure, and I will speak with Saad. We will need more provisions for our future guests."

Nasira rose to leave but paused at the door. "Jalil, shouldn't we tell Kira that Hashem is coming?"

Jalil thought about it for a second. It would be difficult for Kira to see the man who was responsible for kidnapping her and delivering her to Qadir. He hated the idea that it might trigger another flashback, but it was risk he had to take. It would be best if Kira knew. "Maybe you are right, Mother. Would you talk to her?"

"Certainly. It might be easier hearing it from me right now," Nasira said and disappeared toward the guest wing.

Jalil thanked Allah his mother was helping him take care of Cassie and now Kira. He had enough to worry about with his latest enemy planning to destroy his family.

CHAPTER 38

By the time Nasira reached Cassie's chamber, she had worked up a full head of steam. Though she felt like kicking the door in, she restrained herself. It would only upset the guard. She knocked instead. When Cassie didn't answer, she knocked again.

"Who is it?" Cassie's voice was loud and revealed her irritation at being disturbed.

"Cassie, it is Nasira. I need to speak to you." She waited, tapping her foot impatiently. Then she heard the door being unlocked, and it opened just enough for Cassie to peer out.

"What do you want?" she said haughtily.

Nasira had no time for Cassie's insolence. "Cassie, I will make this short. For some time now, you have been making advances to Jalil. He does not return your feelings, and I am here to advise you to stop."

Cassie stared at Nasira with unconcealed contempt. "Don't be too sure of that, Nasira," she said, refusing to call her sheikha. "He wants me, and it will only be a matter of time before you see that."

Nasira leaned forward and shot her a glare that would have made a desert lion back down. "Let me be very clear, Cassie. You will stay away from *both* of my sons and Kira too. If you do not, you will not live long enough to regret it," Nasira said, feeling a cold satisfaction when she saw Cassie's face drain of color.

But Cassie hadn't finished yet. "And just what will you do if I don't?" She sputtered, her white-knuckled hands gripping the table.

"Have you ever seen what a scimitar can do in the hands of someone who knows how to use it?" Nasira said like a true desert born.

When Cassie opened her mouth to speak, Nasira cut her off.

"Do not say a word. From now on, you will remain in your room. Your meals will be delivered, and you may only leave to bathe and then only with a guard. There will be no more riding and no more playing with Rizu. Do. You. Understand?" Nasira said coldly, each word distinct and dripping with ice.

Cassie's face rivaled her hair. It turned a bright shade of crimson, and Nasira could see how furious she was.

"And just what am I supposed to do? Do you intend to keep me here forever?" Cassie snapped.

"Allah forbid! As a matter of fact, you will leave us soon," Nasira said.

"Thank God," Cassie spat. "I am sick of you all. I can't wait to leave this country."

"Believe me, Cassie, the feeling is mutual.

"But how will I get to the coast?"

"I do not know. That will be up to Hashem."

Cassie was stunned. "What do you mean?"

"Oh, I forgot. Hashem will pay us a very brief visit soon, and you will leave with him. Whether he takes you to the coast remains to be seen." With those final words, Nasira stepped back into the corridor and slammed the door behind her.

She paused and waited. The guard looked puzzled and was about to speak, but Nasira shook her head and held a finger to her lips, signaling silence. He jumped at the loud screeching that echoed from behind the door. His eyes widened, and Nasira chuckled when they heard several items hitting the wall, one after the other. Her unwelcome guest would likely damage the guest room, but it was a small price to pay for the satisfaction she was feeling, and she returned to her own chambers with a lighter step.

She was resting, thinking about Hashem's message with its threats and accusations, when she heard a knock on her door and a voice call out.

"Mother, may I come in?" It was Jabari.

"Of course, my son." She opened the door and saw him looking very serious. "Jabari, come in. What is wrong?"

"Oh, nothing really, I just need to talk to you," he said as he sat down at her table.

She poured him some lemonade and waited to hear what he had to say.

"Thank you. I was just wondering about Jalil and Kira. I do not understand them sometimes. It is obvious he likes her, and she likes him, but they do not seem to get along."

"Oh, Jabari, love can be very complicated." Nasira nodded wisely.

"You mean they love each other?"

"I believe so, but you must not talk about this. They have not really decided yet."

"You mean they love each other, but they do not know that they love each other? Now I am really confused." He sipped his lemonade, looking bewildered.

"As I said… it is complicated."

"Well, I wish they would decide. I love Kira, and I want her to stay with us always. And Amber too. Why is it so hard for them to admit they love each other?"

"Well, Jabari, exactly how much do you know about men and women… and love?" Nasira was curious.

"I am not sure about all of this. I had a conversation once with my father, Saad. He explained some things to me." Jabari blushed. "I think I understand enough about all that, but I just do not see why it is so complicated."

"One day you will, my son. But let me ask you a question. Why are you still helping Cassie?" she asked but grew alarmed when she saw him blush.

"I know Jalil said I needed to be careful around her, but she really is nice to me, and she only wanted me to teach her how to ride and how to handle horses. It is hard to say no to her." He looked down at his cup as if it had suddenly become very interesting.

"Is that all she wanted?" she asked gently.

"Really, yes, that is all." He looked up at her with a guilty expression. "Did I do wrong, Mother?"

"No, my son, but I think if you are old enough to understand what happens between men and women, then you will understand what I am about to say. Cassie appears to be interested in Jalil, but he is not interested in her. And she has also hurt Kira before. It is complicated, and you must trust me on this. Just know she will no longer be taking riding lessons from you. And she will be leaving us very soon, but until she does, she is to remain in her room under guard."

"Has she done something wrong?" he asked, his youthful face full of worry.

"Not yet." She hated lying but if she told him all that had happened, it would just raise more questions. "Jabari, listen. It is important you do this for me and for Jalil. You are a young man now, and I trust you will do the right thing."

He beamed at her praise. "Thank you, Mother. I will be careful. I promise." He jumped up and hugged her before dashing from the room.

Nasira couldn't help but tear up at his words. He was becoming a man that his father would have been so proud of. And thanks to Jalil, he would be a credit to his family and his tribe. *Some girl will be very lucky someday*, she thought. Satisfied with her day so far, she knew she still had one task to perform. She needed to tell Kira about Hashem, but the safety of her family was weighing on her mind, so she went to look for her daughters instead. Kira wasn't going anywhere, and she would catch up with her later in the evening.

CHAPTER 39

Kira sat in her room, working on a basket and wondering if Jalil was as attracted to her as she was to him. She'd tried, unsuccessfully, to ignore the effect he had on her and was thinking about the one subject she'd never wasted time on before—sex—and it was all Jalil's fault.

It wasn't like she'd never thought about. She used to dream of a husband and children but had given it up and chased her father's dream. Did she still want to follow in her father's footsteps? Was that really what she enjoyed doing? As she concentrated on her random thoughts, images from the valley filled her mind, and she felt an urge to return and solve the mysteries of the cavern, the tunnels, and the herd of golden horses.

She set her work aside and walked to the large cabinet and pulled out her travel bag. Dumping its contents onto the bed, she sorted through the tangible reminders of her father—the worn money belt, his tattered shirt, and the tiny compass. Unwrapping the old robe, she pulled out the ancient medallion and, gripping it tightly, she closed her eyes. As it warmed her hand, her mind filled with an image of Ndee standing proud, his coat shimmering in the blazing desert sun. She missed him. And she missed the valley. But she now realized if she returned there, she would miss someone else more. Jalil.

Images of their night at the pool washed over her and through her. This time, all she remembered was Jalil. Qadir was gone. Qadir was dead. She tingled with the memories of Jalil's touch and his kiss. Then she remembered Cassie's words and felt chills down her spine. *Cassie with Jalil. How could that be?* Cassie said she'd been with him, that she had "ridden" him. *Only Cassie would say something that crude*, she thought with distaste.

Except it wasn't the thought of being with Jalil in that way that Kira found disgusting. Being with Jalil was something she'd been thinking about more and more. It was hearing Cassie say it and knowing how Cassie meant it. Cassie always talked about sex but never mentioned love. She must not have ever experienced anything like what Kira was feeling, and somehow, even though she didn't want to, Kira felt sorry for her.

In that moment, Kira decided she wouldn't let Cassie ruin her life anymore. It was time to fight fire with fire. Filled with new resolve, she returned to her basketwork, but when she realized she was working it too aggressively she set it aside before she ruined it. She needed to calm down and decided a soak in her own bathing pool would help.

After shedding her clothes, she eased into the water and rested her head on the side. She had almost succeeded in stilling her mind when she heard a knock on the door. She climbed out of the pool and thinking it was probably Nasira or a servant, she grabbed a simple robe and opened the door. It was the last person she expected. Tongue-tied, she stared at Jalil, waiting for him to speak.

Jalil seemed to be having the same problem, though. He stood unmoving, except for his eyes. She saw them travel downward and when his jaw dropped, she glanced down and blushed. Her silk robe was clinging to her wet body, outlining her breasts and the tops of her thighs. Her eyes flew up to meet his, and when his eyes darkened, she recognized the look he had given her the night at the cliffs. And just like that night, he moved quickly, taking her in his arms and kicking the door shut behind him.

Unable to resist, she went willingly into his embrace, pressing herself against his firm body, and lifting her lips to his. He lowered his head and kissed her deeply, almost roughly, then gently, probing her mouth, his tongue dancing with hers.

Awash with pleasure, she felt a hot coil of desire spiraling up from within. She didn't know what was happening but pushed harder, her hips moving almost involuntarily. He suddenly reached down and lifted her up and began moving slowly while holding her hard against him. She moved faster, searching for something, needing something, and wrapped one leg round him. He held her with one large hand and reached down with the other to lift her leg higher.

Kira closed her eyes, and when he bent her back over one arm and pressed his lips to her breast, she moaned softly, feeling pulses of fire race through her body. "Jalil, oh Jalil, please... please… " She didn't know what she wanted, but he responded as if he knew what she needed. He lifted her and pulled her fully against him, covering her mouth with a long kiss. She spiraled higher and higher, only to come crashing down when he suddenly stopped, holding her so tightly, she couldn't move.

He was breathing harshly, and she could feel the stubble of his jaw pressed against her cheek. And she was breathing just as hard. "Jalil...?" Needing to see him, she tilted her head back and found his warm green-gold eyes gazing into hers with a new emotion. There was no confusion, no lust, just love.

Jalil blushed and appeared to be struggling with what he wanted to say. Finally, he spoke. "Kira, I…I am sorry. I lost control," he said with a look of astonishment. "That has not happened since I was a very young man." He relaxed but didn't release her.

"Jalil, I don't know what to say. What was that, I mean…?" Kira was still reeling from her strong desires, but when she felt his arms tremble, she wondered if he had felt something similar. Dazed, she couldn't stop looking at his lips, and he startled her when he suddenly pulled her close and kissed her. This time, slowly, gently, and without passion. Just love, she thought, and she moaned softly when he stopped again, gently lowered her until her feet touched the ground, then pulled her damp robe back in place, but didn't release her.

"Kira. Kira, we need to stop. You realize my mother's chambers are just next door."

Kira blinked and looked around, and her face, still flooded with the evidence of her passion, turned even redder. When she realized what she had done, she filled with shame. *I'm no better than Cassie. What must he think?* "Oh, Jalil… I mean Sheik Jalil. I'm so sorry. I don't know what came over me. Please, please accept my apology."

She tried to pull away, but he stepped closer and tilted her chin up with his finger. "Kira, *ya hayati*, there is nothing to apologize for. You are an innocent. This was all my fault. I will not say it will not happen again, because if my dreams come true, it will. But it cannot happen again like this."

Struck dumb, she reeled from his having called her "ya hayati." *My life.* It was a serious endearment and was overwhelming. *What does he mean it cannot happen like this again?* She looked at him, trying to understand. "What are you saying, Jalil?" In a million years, she would never have expected to hear what he said next.

He fixed her with a determined gaze. "Kira Fontaine, I am saying I want you, always. I need you always. Will you be my wife?"

And that's when she fainted.

CHAPTER 40

Kira felt something cool and wet on her face. At first, she thought she was back in the valley, floating in the lake. Smiling, she sighed, stretched her arms outward, and spread her legs, floating, until she heard two noises, noises she wouldn't have heard in the valley. A deep groan, followed by the slam of a door. Her eyes flew open, and she discovered she was on her bed, still wearing her damp robe. Rubbing her forehead, she suddenly remembered. *Jalil!* Jalil had done something to her, something wonderful, and her body felt warm again just thinking about him.

Rising slowly, she made her way to the mirror. She saw a very different Kira looking back at her. Tousled hair waved about her as if it were alive, and her lips were dark red, slightly swollen from his kisses. She rubbed her hand down her neck, tracing the red marks from his passionate bites that extended down to the tops of her breasts. *Oh my.* She was afraid to open her robe, afraid of what else she might see, then remembered he hadn't touched her there. He just held her tight against his hard body, and it had felt wonderful.

The eyes in the mirror widened when she realized she had experienced the passion Cassie always alluded to—and Kira had loved it. No, that wasn't entirely correct. She loved what she felt with Jalil. *Love.* She loved him and knew that without a doubt. And she desired him, too. And he desired her. But wait, he didn't just desire her. He called her his life. *Ya hayati.* He said he wanted her and needed her. He asked her to be his wife! *Oh my God. What did I say?* She couldn't remember. *That must have been when I fainted!* Her brow furrowed when she recalled his groan and the slam of the door. *Why did he run away? Did he regret his words? Did he really mean them? He never said he loved me. What am I going to do now?*

Looking in the mirror, she saw a woman who had given in without restraint. She could still smell him... a combination of leather and sandalwood, and closing her eyes, she imagined him standing in front of her, his wide chest warm and hard. *Oh, it was happening again!* She needed to cool down, and she didn't need to go to the evening meal smelling of his cologne.

After a long soak in the pool and a short nap, she donned a white tunic with a pale blue robe and made her way to the dining chamber. She had intended to act as if nothing unusual had happened to her that day but just before she entered the room, Jalil appeared, and her resolve fled.

She saw him studying her, running his eyes up and down her outfit. Then his green-gold eyes focused on her neck and narrowed slightly. "Kira, uh, um, you might need to adjust your robe," he said softly and pointed to his own neck, about where the marks of his earlier passion were showing on Kira's.

Kira's hand flew to her neck, and she felt the blood rushing to her face. Horrified Nasira, or the girls, would see the evidence of her wanton behavior, she was about leave when those powerful hands, the ones she was so familiar with now, reached out to stop her. She was afraid to look up at him, but when she did, she could see him looking at her with loving concern.

"It is not obvious, Kira. I think if you just pull your robe up a little higher, no one will notice." Jalil's deep voice sent warm spirals through her body.

Filled with gratitude for his kind remark, she allowed him to adjust her robe higher on one side.

"There," he said. "Now, shall we?" He gestured toward the door, and she took his arm, and he escorted her inside to the chair right next to his.

When Nasira entered the room, she smiled. "Good evening, Kira," she said as she took her seat on the other side of Jalil.

"Good evening, Sheikha," Kira said returning her smile.

Akilah and Lina bounced into the room, chattering as young girls do, caught up in their own little world, and Nasira admonished them lightly. "Girls, quiet down and take a seat."

Jalil poured tea for Kira and his mother while his sisters continued to chatter quietly. Kira exchanged pleasantries with Nasira, but thoughts of Hashem's upcoming visit were weighing heavily on her mind. She couldn't help but think how badly Cassie could make her look in front of her new family. What would they think of her once they heard Cassie's lies? Glancing at Jalil, she noticed him watching her with a worried expression and she looked away. But not before she saw him exchange a look with Nasira who shook her head and cut her eyes to her daughters. Kira sensed Nasira had things to say but couldn't say them in front of the girls.

And she was right when Nasira turned to her and said, "Kira, I would like to talk to you later, after the girls go to bed. May I stop by your room for a visit?"

"Certainly, Sheikha," Kira said, feeling nervous, wondering if Jalil's mother had heard her passionate encounter with her son outside her room earlier. She was relieved when Nasira smiled because she needed to talk to another woman and found herself drawn more and more to Nasira instead of Samira. She would always love Samira, but Kira felt like it was time to step back from Saad's family. They had started a new life, and it was time Kira did the same.

Kira returned her attention to her meal and watched Jalil while she ate. He had turned his attention to his little sisters, encouraging them to share their thoughts and latest adventures. It always amused Kira to hear what was on their minds—they saw the world so differently. They carried on for some time, and Kira laughed along with Jalil when they tried to convince their mother they needed a sand cat like Adara's.

After the girls finished eating and left, Kira found she needed a break and excused herself. It had been a tumultuous day, and if she was going to talk to Nasira later, she wanted to freshen up.

While she waited, Kira let her doubts get the better of her and started to tear up. Even though he proposed, she knew she couldn't be his wife—not after Qadir. Feeling miserable, she was reminding herself again of her unsuitability for Jalil when she heard a knock at her door.

"Kira, may I come in?"

"Yes, Nasira. One moment." Kira hurriedly wiped her eyes, sniffing once, and steeled her face, hoping to hide her recent breakdown. But when she opened the door, she could see her attempt to hide her condition from Nasira was for naught. One look at Kira, and Nasira closed the door and, without saying a word, opened her arms. Kira burst into fresh tears and rushed into her comforting embrace. When Kira regained some semblance of control, Nasira led her over to sit at the table.

"Now, tell me Kira…is it Cassie or Jalil?"

"Both," Kira cried and immediately launched into the tale of what had happened earlier in her chambers, but she left out some details, including Jalil's proposal.

With a mother's touch, Nasira smoothed the silver-gold hair from Kira's tear-streaked face. "Kira, are you really ashamed of what happened between you and Jalil?"

Kira bowed her head and tried to summon her earlier shame, but it seemed to have vanished. "No, I'm not."

"Well then, I do not see a problem," Nasira said.

Kira's head whipped up in surprise. "You don't think I was too forward?"

"Do you?" Nasira asked.

"I don't know. I've never had such strong feeling for a man before." Kira blushed and looked down.

Nasira lifting her chin with a soft hand. "But he didn't touch you anywhere else, did he?"

Kira knew what she was referring to. "Oh, no, not like that! But that's not why I'm so upset." She fiddled with her unfinished basket, nervously plucking at the loose ends.

Nasira's brow furrowed. "Then why are you so upset?"

Kira looked over at her, and it suddenly hit her she was speaking to the sheikha of the tribe and Jalil's mother. Intimidated, she mumbled her reply.

"What was that, Kira?"

Kira blurted out, "He proposed."

It took a second, but then Nasira clapped her hands in joy. "He did?! Well, it is about time. I thought it would never happen!"

Kira was confused. "You're not upset? But I am not a suitable candidate, you know, after what Qadir..."

Nasira didn't let her finish and pulled her into a hug. "Silly, silly girl. That means nothing if there is love. You love him, do you not?" she asked with a hopeful tone.

"Yes, oh yes, Nasira. I love him so much! I don't even know when it happened, but I am afraid he doesn't love me." There. She had said it. It was her worst fear.

"But you said he proposed and asked you to be his wife?" Nasira sounded frustrated.

"Yes, he called me 'ya hayati' and said he needed me and wanted me."

"Well, that is wonderful! So, what is wrong?" Nasira sat back, looking relieved but still confused.

"He never said he loved me!" Kira cried out, her voice filled with a deep sadness.

Nasira reached over and patted her hand. "Oh, Kira, he does love you. In our country, what Jalil said was, in fact, the same as saying those very words. That is one of the ways we say it."

Kira's heart filled with hope, but she burst into tears again, worried she might have driven him away. "Oh, I didn't realize, and...oh my, I didn't answer him. I fainted! He must think I don't care or that I'm afraid of him, like last time." She dropped her head and sobbed in her hands.

Nasira continued to pat her on the hand and made soothing noises. "Kira, look at me. This is fixable. It is all right. Come now, no more tears. I will take care of this."

Kira looked up at Jalil's mother. "Do you think you can?"

"Oh, yes. All is not lost, Kira. I am positive Jalil will want to talk to you first thing in the morning."

"Oh, I hope so. And I will do my best to apologize to him and hear what he has to say." She sniffed, feeling better until she noticed Nasira frowning slightly. "What is it, Nasira?"

"Kira, I need to tell you something, but I don't want to upset you."

"Nasira, you can tell me anything," Kira said earnestly but felt a strange foreboding and steeled herself. Whatever was on Nasira's mind was not good.

"All right. There is no easy way for me to tell you this, but you must know so you can be ready. Hashem is coming to our kingdom. He will most likely be here in another week."

Kira's heart stuttered, and feeling a little faint, she grasped the edge of the table for support. "What?!"

"I am sorry, but it is unavoidable. Hashem has made certain claims against Jalil."

"Claims? What claims?" Kira's initial fear at the thought of seeing one of her kidnappers was rapidly replaced with anger at the thought of that man threatening Jalil.

Nasira must have seen the fury brewing in Kira's eyes. "Kira, calm down and I will explain."

Kira took a deep breath, and tried to remain calm as Nasira told her about the message, the "blood money," and Hashem's threats. When Nasira was done, Kira didn't know what to say. The concept of blood money was barbaric to her. She thought she knew so much about the culture of the people she'd grown to love. Her father's copilot had called them barbarians, and she had agreed. But that was before the crash, before Saad's family had found her, and before Jalil had rescued her. So many people had risked their lives for her, a total stranger. But were they barbarians? No, she couldn't accept that—she wouldn't accept that. Maybe their laws were harsh, but so was their world. And their justice was as swift as the horses they loved, and their faith was as strong as Kira's.

The fact that Hashem accused Jalil of murdering Qadir was ridiculous and didn't surprise her. Cassie had already made the same claim. Kira also wasn't surprised to hear Nasira express her steadfast faith in her son and in his innocence because Kira felt the same way. Kira would pray to God that justice would be served. Filled with a new peace, she relaxed and was still deep in thought until she felt someone patting her hand.

"Kira? Are you all right?" Nasira was staring at her with a quizzical expression.

Smiling, Kira glanced at Nasira. "Yes, I am just fine."

But Nasira didn't look convinced. "You are not worried about Hashem?"

Kira thought about it for a second longer, but oddly her fear of Hashem was gone. "No, Nasira. But I am worried about Cassie."

Nasira smiled for the first time. "Well, do not worry anymore. She is leaving with Hashem. It is already arranged."

"Really?" Her heart soared hearing her wish come true. Soon, she and Jalil would be free of the meddlesome Cassie. It would be wonderful not to see or hear from her ever again.

"I knew you would be as pleased to hear that as I was."

"Oh, yes. That is good news." But her sigh of relief turned into a deep yawn.

Nasira chuckled and patted her gently on the hand. "Come, you are tired. Do not work on any projects. Go to bed and get some sleep. We can talk more about this tomorrow." Nasira rose to leave.

"Yes, ma'am," Kira said without thinking then took her hand one last time. "Nasira, you have been a good friend. I can never thank you enough."

"Nonsense," Nasira said and gave her a quick hug. Then, with a wave of her hand, she departed.

Kira closed the door behind her, making sure she locked it. Jalil might think Cassie wasn't a threat anymore, but Kira didn't trust her, and she wouldn't rest easy until Cassie had left the kingdom. Until Cassie was gone, Kira knew she'd have to keep her guard up.

Following Nasira's advice, she changed into a soft sleeping tunic, slipped under the covers, and tried to clear her mind. She thought briefly of Hashem, but knowing in her heart he was lying, she dismissed his outrageous claims. But she couldn't stop wondering if what Cassie had said about sleeping with Jalil was true. She had almost asked Nasira earlier if she knew anything about it but had been too embarrassed. *Maybe I should ask Jalil about it,* she thought. He deserved an opportunity to explain, and if they were going to have any kind of relationship in the future, they would have to be totally honest with each other. Remembering how Cassie always lied and twisted the truth, Kira felt better. Undoubtedly, Jalil could explain.

Saying a brief prayer, she allowed herself to think only positive thoughts about her future. *Jalil loves me!* Just the thought of that was enough to warm her whole body. Smiling, she curled up and drifted off to sleep, serenaded by the sighing wind through the scrollwork and soothed by the ever-present scent of sun-soaked sand.

CHAPTER 41

While Kira was blissfully sleeping, Cassie was executing her plan. She wasn't sure how much time she had, but if the rumors of Hashem's pending arrival were true, she didn't have as much time as she hoped. And now that she'd been told she'd be leaving with Hashem, she needed to do whatever was necessary to stay in Hashem's good graces. That meant she had to take care of Jabari. And after the scene at the evening meal, she was happy for the opportunity to have her revenge on Jalil and his stuck-up mother. If Kira also got hurt, all the better, she thought.

With her round-the-clock guard, the window was the only way she could sneak out. Disguising herself with clothes she stole from Jabari's tent before Kira's return, she made her way to the corral where Jabari kept the old mare he used to teach her to ride. She chuckled silently remembering how she had complained when he made her ride without a saddle, insisting it was the best way to learn to balance and become one with the horse. *One with the horse. Who says that? Utter nonsense.* But in the end, it was exactly what she had needed to learn. She led the horse into the back pasture and, finding a convenient rock, mounted and cantered toward the river. The worn path was easy to see in the starlight, and the mare knew the way.

Once Cassie located the herd, she whistled for Rizu like Jabari did. When she heard the approaching hoofbeats, she dismounted and waited for him to approach. He was difficult to see in the near dark, but he whinnied in greeting, obviously remembering who she was. She calmed him with a treat then secured him with a small halter and rope she'd stolen from the foaling barn. When she saw the moon peering over the horizon, she knew she needed to hurry and climbed back onto the mare and followed the stream north, leading the colt behind her.

It was purely by accident that she had discovered the hidden trail in the cliffs. When she was still contemplating her orders from Hashem to "dispose" of Jabari, and had access to the old mare, she explored the cliffs near the pool. Hoping to find a place where she could hide Jabari's body, she had stumbled upon a trench behind a pile of enormous boulders. Trying not to think of the stories she'd heard about desert lions and hyenas, she'd swallowed her fear and followed the steep twisting path until she came to what looked like a dead end. Maybe at one time it had continued, but it was now blocked by a landslide.

It was when she had turned to head back down the trail that she saw the opening of the cave. It hadn't been visible on the way up because a large rectangular stone block hid the entrance. Afraid she might surprise a lion in its den, she hadn't ventured very far inside, but it appeared to be tall enough and wide enough for her purposes. And it was so well hidden, it seemed perfect for her needs, and she had come back on another morning's ride to stash the items she thought would be helpful if she executed Hashem's orders. It seemed oddly uniform in construction, and she even found a rusted iron ring embedded on one wall but had not given it further thought. It was full of stony debris and was obviously not in use.

She mentally patted herself on the back when she found the stones she had placed to mark the hidden trail on her last visit, and leaving her mare tied nearby, she led Rizu up the narrow path. The colt was nervous, but she kept urging and praising him, all the while petting him and slipping him treats. She finally lured him inside the cave. After she tied him up, she located the bag she'd left just inside the cave and changed into a clean robe and tunic. Leaving the bag containing the dirty robe and boy's clothes in the cave, she left a pile of dates for the colt and hurried back down the trail.

When Cassie exited the trail and saw the eastern sky streaked with bands of peach and gold, heralding the coming of the sun, she knew she had timed it perfectly. Untying the mare, she mounted and rode slowly back towards the stream. She was tired but so full of adrenaline, staying awake wouldn't be difficult. She only had one more thing to do.

As the sun crested the hills, she heard a familiar whistle. Jabari was looking for Rizu. She rode toward the sound, pretending to be out for her morning ride. Seeing Jabari astride Sarii, she called out to him. "Good morning, Jabari. Isn't it a lovely morning?"

"Cassie? Is that you? What are you doing here? Are you supposed to be out of your room?" He sounded both surprised and worried.

When Cassie saw him looking around with a strained expression, she knew he was looking for her guard. "Oh, I wanted an early morning ride. It's so nice and cool, and I spoke with the sheikha, and she was kind enough to allow me to get some exercise. My guard said he would wait for me inside the stable. He even offered to help me with a saddle, but I told him I needed to practice riding bareback if I want to become 'one with my horse.'" She smiled sweetly with an innocent air.

"I see," he said, but he still looked skeptical. "Well, I also like to come out in the early morning. It's the best time to see the herd." He waved his hand at the horses all around. "But I am looking for Rizu. Have you seen him?"

"Rizu? You know, I think I saw him earlier up by the pool near the cliffs."

"Really? That is a long way for him to go by himself." He looked one last time toward the herd as if he couldn't believe Rizu was not there.

"I bet he's still there. Why don't I help you look for him? It won't take as long." She smiled her sweetest smile.

"Well, I guess that would be all right," he agreed, somewhat reluctantly, but followed willingly behind her.

When they reached the cliffs, Jabari whistled again but had no response. He frowned. "This is not good, Cassie. He always comes running when I whistle. He knows I will have treats for him."

She pretended to be concerned. "You are right, Jabari. Maybe he wandered farther away. Let's go down this way and look. There are lots of places he could be hiding. Let's leave our horses here and walk. That way, we won't miss his tracks, and if he comes back while we're gone, he will probably stay with Sarii."

He nodded in agreement, and they tied the horses near to the pool and continued on foot. Jabari kept whistling but still received no response.

When she reached the boulders by the hidden trail, Cassie pretended to hear something. "Did you hear that?"

He looked around. "No. What did you hear?"

"It sounded like hoofbeats. Maybe...somewhere over here." She walked around the boulder and called out in false excitement. "Jabari, Jabari, come quick. I may have found him." When Jabari ran to her side, she pointed up the path. "Maybe he went this way."

Jabari bent to study the ground. "Something passed here recently. You could be right!" he said excitedly.

"Well, come on. We have to find him." She moved up the steep trail and led him past the entrance to the cave, hoping the colt would remain silent. When they reached the dead end, Jabari stared at the tumbled rocks blocking their path and shook his head in obvious disappointment.

"I guess he did not come this way after all."

"I'm sorry, Jabari. Come on, let's go back down and search some more," Cassie said. When he turned away, she grabbed a rock from the pile, and before he could take another step, she struck. He fell forward with a cry and lay still.

Looking down at his body, Cassie felt a small twinge of regret. *Such an attractive young man. A shame, really.* But her regret quickly vanished at the thought of her success, and an evil smile twisted across her face. Hashem had told her to make sure Jabari was dead, but Cassie couldn't bring herself to cut his throat as instructed. For all she knew, he was already dead or dying. All she needed to do now was make sure he didn't return to the house anytime soon. She had to be sure he wouldn't get away if he survived and that no one would hear his calls.

Tossing the bloody rock away, she hurried to the cave, intending to release the colt, but the cave was empty. She stared at the broken halter and rope lying on the ground. Rizu was gone. *Where did he go?* He was probably somewhere in the pasture now, but it didn't matter. It was only Jabari she was supposed to get rid of. With that in mind, she tied his hands behind his back, bound his feet, and stuffed a rag in his mouth. Even though she was afraid of the darkness, she dragged his body deep into the cave.

She scurried back down the trail and released Sarii, who immediately cantered off to join the herd. When she drew closer to the stables, Cassie released the old mare then circled around the pasture to approach the house from the rear. She walked slowly, hoping that if anyone saw her, she would be mistaken for a servant or a weaver. Once again, luck was on her side, and when she was safely back inside her room, she stuffed her dirty robe under the bed, rinsed the blood and dirt from her hands, and tossed the dirty water out the window. Exhausted and too tired to eat, she donned a sleeping tunic. It wouldn't take them long to miss the boy, but if they came to her door, they would find her in bed. She was still smiling when she drifted off to sleep, thinking about how much she was going to enjoy seeing them all suffer.

CHAPTER 42

Hashem settled into his saddle and contemplated his day so far. He had been on the trail for four days and would be at Jalil's sometime the next day. Jalil hadn't replied to his message, but frankly, he hadn't expected him to. His messengers said they saw a couple of Jalil's men ride out before they left, but they didn't know where they went. They didn't see Cassie or the boy. But that was over a week ago, so he didn't know whether she had been successful with either Jalil's seduction or Jabari's death.

His arm was healing, but it was still sore, reminding him of his failure in the north pass. After he shot the man Jalil had captured that night, Jalil, or one of Jalil's men, had winged him with a lucky shot. When he got to the canyon where he'd left the horses, he found one missing. Realizing his other man had already fled, he disposed of the dead man's horse, eliminating possible pursuit, then mounted his own, whipping it furiously through the narrow trail leading to the north route.

He'd found his missing man at one of the small springs on the way back to his kingdom. That man would never talk now—he was food for the vultures and hyenas. It was yet another botched attempt to get rid of Jalil, but this time he couldn't blame it on Nadim. By the time he'd arrived home, his anger had grown to the point that he'd lost control. One harem girl was still recovering.

If only he'd been able to kill Jalil, he wouldn't have to be here today. His original plan was to eliminate Jalil and his heir and destabilize the region enough to cause tribal wars, but all he could think about now was just killing Jalil. It had become an obsession. Unfortunately, he didn't have another plan to kill him yet, but at least he'd be able to inflict a great deal of pain and suffering on him and his family. The "blood money" angle would be a hard blow to Jalil. Taking Mirage and his golden mares would ruin Jalil's breeding program for the foreseeable future. The mares were worth their weight in gold and Mirage would also bring a very good price on the market. But knowing what the stallion meant to Jalil had Hashem considering something rather drastic…and painful. It would be a shame if someone changed Mirage from a stallion to a gelding.

As for Kira, Hashem intended to take her for his own use. He didn't want to kill her. She was just another way to make Jalil suffer. Eventually, he would sell her but not until he had his fun. *Oh, yes. Everyone is going to pay.*

Excited at the thought of inflicting pain, he found it harder to concentrate on the task at hand. Frustrated, and needing to think of something else, he reviewed his current plan step-by-step in his head. He would have to be extremely careful when he presented his falsified facts and was counting on Cassie to play her part. She wouldn't fail him because he knew the only thing she really wanted was to get out of the country, and he used that as the lure. Afterwards, he had no intention of setting her free, at least not until he no longer desired her, or she became too much trouble. She was also worth a tidy sum.

He hated that Cassie had a hold on him and wondered what it was about her he found so stimulating. She was certainly beautiful, and her body was magnificent, but he could have any woman now. *Is it because she is a foreigner? Are other foreign women as exciting?* Well, he knew where he could get more foreign women. He had heard of an opportunity in one of the port cities, one involving foreign women, that might prove lucrative and personally enjoyable too. But it required money, and he could only get that by proving Jalil's guilt.

Hashem felt his pocket to make sure he had Akeem's dagger—the one he had removed from Qadir's chest—the one Qadir had stolen and used to slit Akeem's throat. Stroking the handle, feeling the patterns of inlaid stones, he tried to imagine everyone's reaction when he revealed the murder weapon and told the story of how Jalil had murdered Qadir and First Wife. There was no doubt the dagger belonged to Jalil, and Cassie had agreed to back up his story by saying she saw Jalil cut Qadir's throat and plunge the dagger into his chest. She would also make sure they knew Kira had been in on the plan from the very beginning and helped Jalil poison Qadir's mother, First Wife.

Hashem considered telling everyone that First Wife was his mother. No one remembered his real mother, and he had trouble remembering her too. When he was very young, First Wife sold him and his mother to slavers. They sold her later, and he never saw her again. He spent his youth working as a servant, performing the lowliest chores. But he'd never forgotten where he came from, and when he was old enough, he ran away and joined Qadir's tribe. Working his way to the top, he earned Qadir's trust by his willingness to do any deed asked of him.

When Hashem discovered First Wife had killed his real father, who was also Qadir's real father, and was the one responsible for selling his mother to the slavers, he secretly plotted against her. He helped her with her schemes and learned her secrets, hoping one day to take his revenge against her. It was ironic that someone had done the job for him, and he wished he knew who to thank.

Hashem saw the long shadows forming and felt a growing excitement. He was one day away from destroying Jalil. He would take the horses and Kira, and if Jalil resisted, he would destroy him. Hashem's ally, Sheik Amit, and his men were camped near Jalil's pass, ready to assist as needed. Together, they outnumbered Jalil's men two to one. He rather hoped it would escalate into a battle because he would enjoy killing Jalil and his mother and adding his little sisters to his harem or selling them on the market. Soon he would have enough wealth to move to the coast where he could establish himself as a powerful and wealthy man. Then he could make plans for contacting the foreigners.

While he was contemplating his bright future, his scouts interrupted him with news of a safe place to stop for the evening. Pleased to see they were on schedule, Hashem gave the order to make camp. He looked forward to food and rest. The next day would be busy, and he would need to be ready.

CHAPTER 43

Kira awoke the next morning surprised to see her room already aglow with morning light. It was unusual for her to sleep past sunrise. She lay still for a moment then stretched and sighed with pleasure. Feeling refreshed and better than she had in a long time, she thought it was probably because of her talk with Nasira the previous night about Jalil. Suddenly, she sat straight up. *Jalil!* She had almost forgotten her plan to talk to him today, and excited, she jumped out of bed and hurried through her early morning routine. She debated whether to stay in her room, in case he sought her out, but she couldn't wait. If she hurried, she might catch him finishing his morning meal with the family.

But when she arrived in the dining chamber, it was empty with no evidence of a meal having been served. Confused, she determined to go the stables to see if he had gone riding, but as she neared the main hall, she heard raised voices. Stopping in the doorway, she saw Nasira and Samira sitting side by side, holding hands with their heads bowed. Fahad was staring down at a large piece of parchment spread out on the table. Sakhr stood nearby with his hand on Saad's shoulder, and the sight of Saad's face filled her with fear. He looked distraught and helpless.

Jalil stood with his back to her, but when Kira stepped into the room, he whirled around, and she froze seeing the fury on his face.

"I…I'm sorry, I didn't mean to interrupt," she said, taking a few steps back, prepared to flee until she saw Jalil's face soften.

"No, Kira, do not go! You are not interrupting, and I need you here," he said, waving her closer.

She didn't hesitate and went right to him. "Sheik Jalil, what is wrong? What is going on?" The look in his eyes filled her with warmth, and she had the strangest feeling she was supposed to be with him, but her heart stopped at his next words.

"Kira, we cannot find Jabari."

For a second, she wasn't sure what he said. "What do you mean, you cannot find him?"

Nasira interrupted. "Kira, we haven't seen Jabari since last night. You know as well as we do, he is usually the first one at the morning meal and that is after he has checked on his horses. Sakhr did not see him at the stables, and we searched his tent and his room. Have you seen him?"

Kira knew Jabari was a free spirit, and she was thinking he was probably just off on one of his adventures. "I wish I could say yes, but no," Kira said. Seeing everyone looking at her as if she knew, she tried to think about where he could be. "Maybe he's just gone to the pool or to check on the herd."

Sakhr shook his head. "No. He is not there. We found Sarii running loose, but there was no sign of Jabari…or Rizu."

"You don't think something happened to him? Surely, he is safe in your kingdom," Kira said to Jalil.

"Kira, I did not tell you, but before you returned, I was ambushed in the north pass."

Kira inhaled sharply, unable to hide her emotions. "Oh, no. Were you hurt? Are you all right?" She was so focused on Jalil, she missed the knowing look on Samira's face and the smile on Nasira's.

Jalil looked strangely pleased. "I am fine, Kira. Really. But not long after that, I received a threat from Hashem. I fear he may have something to do with this."

"Yes, Nasira told me about that," Kira said.

Up until that point, Samira had remained silent, but Kira could see her staring intently at Jalil. He must have noticed and gestured for her to speak. "Samira? Do you have something to say?"

"My sheik, I think something has happened to Jabari," she said, pressing her hand against her heart. "We need to find him soon." No one asked why she knew—she spoke with a mother's certainty.

Familiar with Samira's ability to sense things about Jabari, Kira couldn't discount the possibility she was right. But thinking of Hashem brought another malicious creature to mind. "Has anyone talked to Cassie yet?"

Everyone in the room seemed to freeze. Then Nasira abruptly stood, and Kira saw her hands gripping the edge of the table. "What are you saying, Kira?"

"Again, I know nothing about this, but you know how I feel about her. Maybe Cassie knows something?" Kira looked at Nasira then at Jalil.

"I will talk to her now," Jalil said, his voice hardening.

Nasira immediately spoke up. "Jalil, let me handle Cassie. You need to organize the search parties."

He hesitated, then nodded, but added a word of caution. "You should not go alone."

"You are right," Nasira said and turned to Kira. "Will you go with me?"

Kira didn't hesitate. The days of her being afraid and humiliated by Cassie were gone. She wouldn't allow her to hurt the only family she had now.

When they reached Cassie's door, the guard looked at Nasira questioningly, but she waved him aside and knocked loudly.

The door opened a crack, and Cassie peered out. "What do you want?" she said petulantly.

Kira frowned at Cassie's lack of respect for the sheikha but admired Nasira's control. Except for her narrowed eyes and the tic in her jaw, it was hard to read Nasira's expression—until she spoke. Her voice was chilling. "Cassie, have you seen Jabari this morning?"

"Jabari? How could I have seen Jabari this morning? I haven't seen him since you made me a prisoner." She assumed an innocent expression, but it was spoiled by her sneer. It was clear she was enjoying herself at Nasira's expense.

Kira wondered if Cassie saw Nasira tense and clench her fists and figured she had when Cassie's voice became surgery sweet.

"What's wrong? Has something happened to Jabari?"

Kira had a sinking feeling that Cassie was playing with them when she saw Cassie's eyes. They had that familiar triumphant shine that usually signaled she was happy about something, something bad for someone else. Kira was about to speak when suddenly Cassie fixed her with a glare.

"Maybe you should ask Kira where the boy is? She seems to be very close to *both* of your sons." Cassie smirked openly, but if she thought she could embarrass Kira, she was wrong.

Kira's tolerance for Cassie vanished like water in the desert sun. She wanted to reach out and grab Cassie by the throat. But Nasira must have noticed because she took charge, and Kira got a look at a real sheikha in action.

"Cassie, you should be the first to know that Jalil has asked Kira to be his wife and sheikha. I know how much you want them both to be happy. Oh, and as for Jabari, if you know anything about him, you had better tell me." Nasira's voice was as hard as the mountains bordering her kingdom.

Kira struggled not to laugh as Cassie's normally pale complexion turned the color of her crimson hair.

Cassie seemed to collect herself. "I don't know anything about him, and obviously, I won't be seeing him again. So, I think we're done here," Cassie said in a dismissive tone with clenched teeth and a fixed smile. She started to close the door until Nasira slammed her palm against it, holding it in position.

Nasira's final words thrilled Kira. "If I were you, Cassie, I would start packing today. You have outworn your welcome, and it is time for you to go home. You can be sure that I will see to that shortly." She turned without waiting for a response and stalked away.

Kira paused and added her own warning. "Cassie, I have tried many times to feel sympathy for you and help you, but you've always tried to hurt me. And that's all right, I can take it. But as God is my witness, if you hurt Jabari, I will make sure you never hurt anyone again." The guard at the door smiled at Kira and nodded. Cassie slammed the door in her face, but not before Kira had seen the fear in her eyes and what looked like guilt. Kira felt a sense of apprehension and hurried after Nasira.

The sun had reached its zenith, signaling the time for the midday meal, but Kira wasn't hungry, and evidently, neither was Nasira. While Nasira went to check on her daughters, Kira made her way to the stables. When she had first learned Jabari was missing, she had thought they were all overreacting. Jabari had only been missing since early morning. But the more she thought about it, the more worried she became. Jabari was like a little clock. He kept to his schedule, just like his big brother. She could almost tell the time of day by either of them. For him to miss one meal was unusual, but two was unheard of.

Seeing the men collecting near one of the corrals, she hastened to see what was going on. Jalil was assembling search teams and was busy calling out commands. Seeing him and hearing his deep voice made her weak in the knees, a new feeling for her, and she steadied herself by holding on to the fence. The desire that flooded her body when he was near had her flummoxed. *Does he feel something like that too?* She had her answer when he looked over at her and stopped in the middle of a conversation with Fahad. He smiled and actually took a step in her direction then he caught himself. They shared a look before he turned back to his men. She blushed. *Yes, he feels the same way.*

Not wanting to distract Jalil, she made her way to the back pasture, and Amber came running before she even reached the gate. *How does she always know when I need her?* Kira waited for her to stop then leaned in and touched her forehead to Amber's. Praying for her to understand, she whispered, "I need your help, Amber. Something has happened to Jabari. I don't know what to do, but we have to find him... soon."

When Kira stepped back, Amber shook her head and whinnied, gazing at her as if she understood, and Kira felt a sudden surge of hope. Amber had always found her when she needed help. And Amber had taken Jabari to safety when Kira got kidnapped. Perhaps Amber could find Jabari. Kira wanted to begin the search, but if she was going to ride Amber, she needed to put on trousers. Asking Amber to wait, she ran back toward the house.

As Kira neared the front steps, she heard Jalil call from behind and turned to see him hurrying in her direction. She waited for him to approach, and the closer he got, the more she felt that wonderful feeling again. He looked stern, but as he drew near, his frown turned into a smile. When he was close enough that she could reach out and touch him, he stopped. For a second, neither spoke.

Then Jalil's smile faded. "Kira, I think you had better stay inside until we know more about what is going on. I do not want anything to happen to you," he said, his eyes reflecting how much he cared.

"But Jalil, I can help. Amber and I are going to look for Jabari," she said.

His smile returned, and he touched her cheek and whispered, "I love when you call me Jalil." She blushed, flustered, unable to speak. He hesitated, leaning closer, then seemed to collect himself. "Will you at least wait a little while? I need to give my men a chance to run the far perimeters and check the north pass. They should be back before the evening meal, and we could take a ride together then... if you want." He wasn't aware of the longing he projected with his words.

The only thing Kira heard were the words "ride together." Her blush deepened and she looked down for a second. When she answered, it was with the same unconscious longing in her voice. "Yes, Jalil. I will wait for you." They shared another intimate look until he suddenly broke away and headed back to the stables. She smiled as she climbed the steps but gasped in surprise when she found Cassie waiting behind the door like a coiled cobra.

"What are you doing out of your room? Where is your guard?" Kira searched the hallway with alarm.

"Oh, he's around here somewhere," Cassie said nonchalantly. "I just came to see if you found Jabari yet, but I guess you're too busy flirting with Jalil to worry about the boy."

Kira blushed but didn't take the bait. She needed to find out what Cassie was really up to. "Cassie, what do you want from me? I'm rather busy at the moment."

"I don't want anything from you, Kira, and I certainly don't want Jalil. He wasn't very good anyway, although I did get *some* pleasure out of him. I didn't mean to hurt his neck, though. But passion will do that sometimes," she said, looking like the cat that ate the canary.

Once again, Kira wanted to reach out and grab her by the neck. In the past, it had been difficult to maintain her control around Cassie, but now that Kira had released her inner warrior, she found it easier to fight back. "Well, I am sorry it was not enjoyable for you, Cassie. Jalil has no problem satisfying me." She smiled and turned to leave, but Cassie grabbed her by the arm.

"You're such a little slut now, Kira, giving it away for free—first to Qadir and now to Jalil. You're spoiled goods," she spat viciously.

Feeling a surge of fury, Kira hauled back and slapped Cassie as hard as she could.

Cassie yelped and stumbled backwards. "How dare you, you little half-breed!" she screeched.

Kira took a step forward and saw a momentary flash of fear in Cassie's eyes then tensed when Cassie's eyes hardened. The woman looked ready to strike.

Before they could get into it, Fahad appeared in the doorway, startling them both. Kira wasn't sure how much he'd heard or seen until she saw him smile and wink. He looked like he was trying not to laugh, but when he spoke, his voice was serious. "Kira, is everything all right? Can I be of assistance?"

Kira could see his eyes locked on Cassie even though he was speaking to her, and it felt good to have Fahad's respect and support. "Thank you, Fahad, but I am fine." Kira said calmly.

"What about me? I'm the one who got slapped!" Cassie whined, but when Fahad fixed her with a steely gaze, she physically took a step back. She must have seen the threat in his eyes, and with a huff, she turned to walk away.

But before Cassie had taken two steps, something made Kira grab her by the arm and pull her to a stop. "Cassie, I asked you once already. Do you know anything about Jabari?"

Cassie struggled to control her expression. "No, Kira, I told you already. I haven't seen the boy today. Now, let go of my arm." She glared at Kira with a murderous look.

Kira hesitated, but she had seen something different in the hateful woman's eyes. It looked almost like triumph. She dropped Cassie's arm but answered in a voice laced with steel. "I hope you are telling the truth, Cassie. If I find out any different, you will answer to Jalil and Nasira. But that will be the least of your worries. You will also answer to me!" Kira flung the words at her then headed toward the family wing.

As she walked away, Kira smiled with grim satisfaction when she heard Fahad add, "Cassie, if you had anything to do with Jabari's disappearance, I will be the one you need to worry about." Cassie didn't say a word, but Kira heard her gasp. Then Fahad informed Cassie it was time she returned to her chambers and that he would personally escort her.

Kira was relieved Fahad was putting Cassie back in her room. She didn't like having her loose while everyone was outside searching for Jabari. *The sooner they get rid of Cassie, the better*, she thought then put Cassie from her mind. She had more important things to worry about, like finding Jabari.

CHAPTER 44

Jalil had finished organizing the search parties and, having nothing else to do but wait, looked in on his mother. She seemed to be fine, but he knew inside she was reliving the horror of Jabari's kidnapping over a dozen years ago. He couldn't imagine the depth of a mother's fear. She must be terrified.

As he approached her door, his pace quickened when he heard someone crying. He was about to knock, thinking he could help, but stopped. She was speaking to someone, and he listened in.

"I know I am being silly. I just cannot stop thinking about it. It is like it is happening all over again," Nasira cried. Jalil heard someone speaking softly and had to strain to make out the words.

"Nasira, Jabari is not a helpless baby anymore. He is a smart and resourceful young man. You must have faith—he will find his way back to you." Jalil now recognized Kira's voice.

"I know you are right, Kira. But what are the chances of him disappearing the same time our enemy is on his way," Nasira said, sniffing loudly. "And now Jalil has to worry about Hashem, too. It is not right."

"I agree with the sheikha." Jalil now heard Samira talking. "There is more going on here than we think. But I also agree with Kira. Jabari has always been a survivor, and I believe he is a special child, destined for greatness. He will come back to us. He has a destiny to fulfill, and it does not end here." Samira spoke with great certainty.

"You are both right, my friends. Thank you for helping me to see reason," Nasira said, sounding more like the mother and sheikha that Jalil knew. His heart swelled with love for her and Kira too, especially when he heard Kira's next words.

"Come, my sheikha. We need to be strong for Jalil. He will need our help before this is all over," Kira said.

"You are right again, Kira."

Thrilled to hear Kira's concern for him, Jalil knew it boded well for their future. Believing Nasira was in good hands, he quietly walked away with a lighter step, thinking he would spend some time grooming Mirage, a task that he found calming. He was almost at the front door when he heard the shots. There were two, but a little more time passed between them than was usual. Standing on the front steps, he waited to see who had made his guards hesitate. Jalil had a sneaking suspicion he wouldn't like these visitors, and he was right.

Jalil watched Hashem ride into the compound, leading a contingent of twenty men. Dressed in black, from his boots to his turban, Hashem looked exactly like Qadir and even carried the dead sheik's whip tied to his waist. He also carried a full complement of weapons—javelin, scimitar, long sword, flintlock pistol, and a rifle—as did his men.

Only a few of Jalil's guards were in attendance, as the majority were out searching for Jabari, but Jalil wouldn't reveal that. One should never show weakness when confronted by a predator. Instead, Jalil acted as if it was just another day. Forcing himself to relax, he waited for Hashem to approach the steps. He heard Nasira and Kira speaking in low voices behind him just inside the door. Jalil smiled when Fahad stepped out to stand beside him. His advisor wore his scimitar, and his hand rested on the hilt.

When Hashem stopped in front of the steps, Jalil could see him staring past him and knew he was eyeing Kira. Jalil refused to be baited and didn't follow the direction of his gaze but when Hashem's eyes lit with obvious lust, Jalil struggled to hide his anger while he waited for the man to speak.

Finally, Hashem turned an insolent stare at Jalil. "Greetings, Sheik Jalil."

"Hashem." Jalil merely nodded, not bothering to use a title. It pleased him to see Hashem's eyes narrow at the insult.

"I have come to collect 'blood money' for your murder of my brother, Qadir."

"And just why would I offer you restitution for what is obviously a lie?"

"A lie? No, Jalil, it is no lie. I have the proof, and I have the witness." He sneered triumphantly.

Jalil already had a plan. "Hashem, if you want to present your case, you are welcome to try. My men will take care of your men and horses, and you can join me in the main hall. I am sure we can clear up this confusion." He turned away then paused. "Oh, and Hashem, it appears I have something that belongs to you." Jalill smiled inwardly when Hashem looked at him askance. "I believe I have your sheikha. And just for the record, she will be returning with you. I have no need of her." With that said, Jalil turned and walked away, not waiting to see if Hashem would follow. He chuckled to himself when he heard the man's boots on his steps almost before he had made it through the door.

Jalil knew Sakhr would take charge of moving Hashem's men to a suitable camp site as Fahad escorted Hashem to the main hall. It was as they had planned. He watched with satisfaction as Kira and Nasira fled down the corridor. Their destination was the screen room behind a wall in the main hall. It hid them from view while allowing them to listen in.

When Jalil heard his mother crying earlier, he had been worried she would succumb to depression again, as she had after the kidnapping of her baby and again after Akeem's death. But he had mistaken crying as a weakness, when in fact, it had just the opposite effect on these women. He wouldn't make that mistake again. Jalil was learning more every day about the incredible power of women, and Kira was now his greatest teacher. He felt amazed that even after all she had been through, Kira had become his fiercest supporter. Oh, she was still the Kira he knew and loved, and he could make her blush and stammer with just a look, or a touch of his hand. But hearing her stand up to Cassie and Hashem, she had become a warrior, willing to fight for Jalil, his family, and his tribe.

Jalil took a seat in his carved chair upon a dais, forcing Hashem to sit in a smaller chair below him. Sitting in front of his enemy, the man who wanted to destroy everything he loved, Jalil felt a new strength fill his heart and soul. Glancing over at the carved screen covering one wall, he knew Kira and his mother were watching him, ready to follow his every command without question. It was a heady feeling. He also knew they were counting on him to protect them and their tribe—he wouldn't let them down.

After almost an hour, Jalil was aware Hashem had finished outlining his case and was waiting for his response. Jalil looked over at Fahad and saw his trusted advisor looking at him with total and complete confidence, just like he had with Akeem. It was a humbling experience, and Jalil nodded, hoping Fahad could see Jalil's acknowledgment and thanks for his support. Fahad smiled, and Jalil saw he understood. Taking a deep breath, Jalil now needed to stall. A little more time was necessary for his own plans to be a success.

When Hashem fidgeted and fingered his whip, while impatiently tapping his foot, Jalil could tell his plan was working. He wanted to keep Hashem on edge, knowing the man might make mistakes if emotion clouded his judgement. Treating Hashem dismissively in front of his men when he arrived had been just the beginning.

Peppering him with questions, he made Hashem repeat everything all over again without acknowledging the "blood money" claim or asking Hashem to produce the witness or the murder weapon. Though he enjoyed seeing Hashem's face darken with rage, Jalil knew he needed to proceed with caution. Hashem continued to toy with his whip, but his other hand was now resting on the flintlock hanging from his side. Jalil sensed it was time to move on.

Jalil stood abruptly, startling Hashem, who scrambled to his feet, his hand gripping his flintlock. Fahad rose also with his hand on his flintlock, and Hashem's eyes darted back and forth between them. Tension permeated the room. Jalil thought he heard a noise from the screened chamber and knew Hashem heard it too. The man cocked his head, and his lips curled in a scowl. Jalil hid his smile, quite certain Hashem didn't like being humiliated in front of women.

Ready now to implement the next step in his plan, Jalil said, "Well, Hashem, you have presented a very interesting theory today. There is much to discuss, but it will take some time to look at all the evidence and determine the truth behind your claim. As you know, the accused has a right to provide a witness and evidence on his own behalf. I am sure we can resolve this matter tomorrow. And it is getting rather late, and I expect your men are both tired and hungry. Allow me to provide you with food and shelter, as is custom." Jalil saw Hashem's anger growing—the man's face flushed an ominous red and beaded with sweat—and he actually looked ill.

Hashem sputtered, but before he could answer, twenty of Jalil's warriors filed into the room with the announcement they needed to meet with their sheik on a very important tribal matter. Jalil asked them to wait for a moment so he could finish his business with Hashem. He turned back to the angry sheik. "Hashem, food is being prepared for you and your men. Unfortunately, my guest wing is full, but Fahad will escort you to a private house we have designated for your use. Your men will find tents and bedding provided for them, along with a meal served in the courtyard." He glanced down at some scrolls on the table but then looked back up as if surprised to see Hashem still standing there. "I can meet with you tomorrow after morning meal. I am sure we can conclude our business then." And with those final words, he turned to speak to his men.

Out of the corner of his eye, he saw Hashem shaking with anger and looking odd. The man was breathing heavily, sweating profusely, and quite pale. Jalil thought he looked sick then dismissed the idea, thinking it was probably just Hashem's reaction to being outsmarted. When

Fahad walked over and gestured towards the door, Hashem stomped out of the hall. Jalil sighed with relief. He trusted Fahad to take Hashem to the small stone house he'd set up for his use. It was near the edge of the compound, well away from the main house, and close to the temporary tents provided for Hashem's men. It was best to keep his enemies together in one spot—easier to manage, easier to kill.

Jalil was tired from his encounter with Hashem, but knew he'd have little time to rest that day. Taking advantage of a break, he returned to his chambers to freshen up before the next meeting. There was much to discuss and more to do. Sighing as he strode down the corridor, he picked up his pace. If he was quick, he might even have time to take a treat to Mirage.

CHAPTER 45

Jalil had just enough time to freshen up before Fahad appeared at his door, accompanied by Nasira, Kira, Sakhr, and Saad. They all took a seat at his table and waited for him to speak.

"Where is Samira?" Jalil asked.

"She is not feeling well, Sheik. She is worried about Jabari even though she will not admit it," Saad said. "Should I go get her?"

"No, Saad. She needs her rest." Jalil was well aware of Samira's advancing pregnancy. He turned to Fahad. "Did you have any problems?" He was referring to Hashem.

"No, Sheik," Fahad said. "But I must report, he does not look well."

"What do you mean?" Nasira said.

"He was having difficulty breathing, or so it seemed to me. It was like he had been in the deep desert for too long."

Jalil noticed a thoughtful expression on Nasira's face but didn't have time to waste worrying about Hashem's health. He chuckled when Saad offered to help.

"I would gladly escort him there, my sheik. Just say the word," Saad said, with a hopeful expression.

"I wish I could give that order, Saad, but we need him here if we are to finish this business. And I want everyone to stay clear of him from now on. I would not put it past him to hurt anyone now, especially you, Sheikha. And you, Kira." Both women nodded in agreement.

Jalil leaned back and studied the faces sitting around the table. Everyone had the same expectant expression. They were waiting for their orders. Smiling in satisfaction, he laid out his plan of action. "Before we get started, I need to know if Cassie is in her room with a guard on her door and one outside her window."

"Her window?" Nasira asked with a puzzled look.

Fahad was quick to explain. "Yes, Sheikha. We believe Cassie has been using her window to sneak out. That will not happen again. I also had a servant go into her chamber to verify she was there. We do not have to worry about her for now."

"Thank you, Fahad. We can continue then. As you are all aware, Hashem has made his claim for 'blood money' and is going to provide a witness that saw me kill Qadir with a weapon that supposedly belongs to me. I hope you all know I did not kill Qadir." He paused, but no one said a word and a few nodded. "So, we have established I did not do the deed. However, I did see Qadir's body with a large dagger in his chest and his throat cut."

Everyone seemed unaffected, but he saw Kira glance down for a minute. He kept an eye on her while he described his actions that night. "I want you all to be aware of everything I witnessed. When I entered Qadir's bedchamber, Cassie showed up almost immediately. I think she was hiding in the room. She said she had been coming to help Kira and..." Jalil stopped immediately when he saw Kira drop her head and grip the arms of her chair. He waited until she raised her head and looked at him before continuing. "Kira, if you would rather not hear any more of this for now, you may leave and come back later." Her face was inscrutable, so he smiled gently, praying she could sense his love, and was relieved to see her face lighten.

"No, my sheik, I will be fine. It is important for everyone to know all the facts if we are going to defeat Hashem." Her gaze was fierce, and Jalil saw everyone smiling at her with compassion.

But Jalil's smile was the biggest. He loved his warrior woman. He bowed to her then continued with his story. "Well, as I was saying, Cassie told me she heard screams and thought she could help Kira, but when she had arrived, she said she found Qadir dead and Kira gone. She then suggested Kira killed Qadir, but based on what I saw, and knowing Kira like I do, I know she did not kill him." Jalil wouldn't go into the other things Cassie had said about Qadir and Kira's night together. He would spare Kira that. When he noticed Kira was smiling, he felt more comfortable and continued with his summary of the facts. "And that's when I found my father's medallion."

Jalil heard several gasps as he pulled the medallion out of his tunic, letting it fall on his chest. He hadn't shown it to anyone except his mother and Kira. Saad's eyes widened in recognition, but Fahad appeared shocked, as did Sakhr. Jalil's heart hurt seeing the sadness in both Kira's and his mother's eyes.

It was Saad who broke the silence. "But that is Kira's medallion. She said it belonged to her father."

"And it did, for a while. But Saad, this medallion disappeared the day my father died. When Cassie saw it, she said it belonged to Kira's father, but I did not know then that Cassie knew Kira and had survived the very plane crash that killed Kira's father and stranded them here in our country," Jalil said. Then seeing the questioning faces surrounding him, he remembered some of them didn't know the whole story. "But that is a story Kira can share with each of you when she is ready. Cassie told me Kira's father had purchased the medallion in the marketplace in Cairo, and Kira later confirmed it." Jalil saw Kira nod, but Fahad still looked puzzled. "No, Fahad, I do not understand either, but I believe the medallion was meant to end up in Cairo, and it was meant to be found by Kira's father. Which also means it was meant to be saved from the plane crash by Kira and stolen from her by Qadir. And then I found it…on the floor, of all places." He shook his head at the memory. "I think there is a greater power at work here."

Nasira suddenly spoke. "Kismet," she muttered.

Jalil stared at her. "It may very well have been fate, Sheikha. But Kira believes her God had a hand in it," he said and saw the effect of his words on Kira. Her smile shone like the sun. "I just thank Allah I found it, because I know He has returned it to me for a reason. I will learn how the medallion came to be in Cairo, and I will solve the mystery of my father's death. But not today."

He paused for a sip of water then finished his account of that night at Qadir's. "I did, in fact, leave Cassie at Qadir's, but I had my reasons. When I left the compound, I met up with Sheik Ehsaan, and that is when Jabari turned up. He found Kira and Fatima escaping." Jalil gestured to Kira so she could add her account of that night.

"Yes, Fatima saved me," Kira said. "I remember First Wife gave me something to drink then took me to Qadir. I believe she drugged me because I don't remember much after that. I must have passed out because the next thing I remember is waking up in the harem pool. Fatima revived me, and we snuck out through a secret door. We were running away when we ran into Jabari. He had brought Amber, and he also found a horse to carry Fatima. I don't remember much after that." She stopped to take a drink from her cup, and Jalil saw her hands trembling, and his heart went out to her. Nasira placed a comforting hand on her shoulder.

Jalil picked up the story again. "We rode back through Qadir's hidden pass—the same pass Hashem used to kidnap Kira—then went straight to Sheik Ehsaan's. We owe a great deal to Sheik Ehsaan and his family." Everyone nodded in agreement. "We will find out what really happened at Qadir's soon enough, but right now we need to make sure we are ready for tomorrow, and we also need to find Jabari." Seeing he had everyone's attention, Jalil turned to his herdmaster. "Sakhr, have you been able to move the herd to a safe location? Do you need any additional guards?"

"The herd is safe, and I have plenty of guards," Sakhr said.

"And is Mirage safe?" Jalil leaned forward.

"Yes, I moved him to his stall inside the back of the house, along with the younger foals."

"Thank you, Sakhr. And Saad, how are the provisions?" He listened as Saad gave a report on their stock of munitions and food then turned to his mother.

"Sheikha, what about my sisters and the house servants?"

"I moved the girls to my chambers with two guards. The servants are on alert, but I have released many to stay with their own families. I hope that is all right with you."

"Certainly. We will manage. Is there any news about Jabari?"

Nasira had taken over responsibility for the search parties, freeing up Jalil to deal with Hashem. "No, Sheik. I am rotating some of the search parties, but I suggest we keep them to a minimum. I am trusting in Allah that Jabari is all right." Nasira was putting on her best face, but Jalil could hear the waver in her voice.

Fahad made a suggestion. "Sheik, I would advise we pull more men back to the main compound except for a contingent to be kept at the north pass and the main pass, at least for the next day and night. I do not want to give up on Jabari, but we have many more that need protection right now." He seemed nervous when he said the last part.

Jalil was quick to put him at ease. "Fahad, you were my father's right hand, and now you are mine. I trust your judgment in this matter. Do what you think is necessary, and keep me informed."

"Thank you, my sheik." Fahad nodded, his face reflecting his pride in hearing those words.

Jalil saw Kira looking at him and could tell she was wrestling with something. "Kira, do you have a question?"

"Yes, Sheik. I was going to ask if I could take Amber and search for Jabari and Rizu. I know it is dangerous for me to be out of the compound, but that is a risk I am willing to take, and I feel Amber can help. She is attuned to Jabari and Rizu, and I am sure that together we might find at least one of them. I will, of course, take an escort if Fahad can spare the men, and I will dress accordingly. I will not put myself or the men in any danger."

Jalil hated putting her at risk, especially now he had accepted his feelings for her, but what she said had merit. Amber was an amazing horse and had proven to have an uncanny ability to track. When he looked at his mother and saw her nod, he sighed, resigned to the only answer he could give. "I think you should try."

Kira smiled fiercely. "Thank you, my sheik. I will coordinate with Nasira and Fahad."

"Does anyone else have questions?" Jalil looked around the table. "No? Good. Then before we go, I have two more things. First, I would like for us to meet in my chambers tomorrow after morning meal, before our meeting with Hashem, to go over our final plan. Then second, I need to share something with you. The day I received Hashem's message, I also sent a few of my own. I want you all to know we are not alone in this fight against Hashem. We have allies, but that is all I can say for now. Just know that we will not let Hashem hurt our tribe. Tomorrow will be a very busy day, so for now, I think we should all go enjoy our evening meal. If anyone needs me, let me know at once, day or night." As he rose, he glanced at Saad. "Saad, you and Samira are welcome to dine with us," he said warmly.

Nasira agreed. "Yes, Saad. I would prefer if you both stayed in a guest room tonight."

Jalil chuckled, remembering how he had told Hashem there was no available space in their guest wing.

Saad nodded. "Thank you, Sheikha. Samira would feel safer in your house. I will fetch her now."

Everyone left the room, but Jalil saw Nasira lingering and walked to her side. She didn't say a word, just reached out and hugged him tight. She hugged him like a mother hugs her son, and they shared a long moment, but she was the one to let go first. Kissing him lightly on the cheek, she walked away, leaving him feeling better and somehow stronger.

After he returned to his chambers and washed away the grime of the day, Jalil met his mother and sisters in the dining chamber, and Saad and Samira joined them. Conversation was subdued as everyone was feeling the strain of the recent events. He spoke to his sisters to make sure they understood what was going on and to see if they had questions or problems. They assured him they were fine, but both were anxious about Jabari. Samira assured them Jabari had always taken care of himself and that they had nothing to worry about. Then she launched into tales of Jabari from the days on the trading routes and soon had the girls laughing at his exploits. Jalil was grateful she kept them distracted.

But at the mention of Jabari's name, he felt guilty for having forgotten his little brother for a moment. Jabari might be in danger or, Allah forbid, hurt. Jalil wouldn't even consider that. He couldn't. Then he realized Kira had yet to appear. *Where is she?*

Nasira must have noticed his worried expression. "What is on you mind, Jalil?"

"I was wondering where Kira is. She is late."

"She has gone to search for Jabari."

"Already?" Alarmed at this news and afraid she was putting herself in danger as sunset was not far off, he rose but stopped when his mother laid a hand on his arm.

"Calm down. Fahad sent an escort with her, and remember, she is on Amber, the same horse that saved her in the desert, the same horse that saved her from the lion, the same horse that took her to Jabari's family. If anyone can find Jabari, it will be that horse. I know that in my heart."

Relieved, he slumped back in his chair. She was right, and he knew it, but he felt powerless.

Nasira tugged lightly on his arm, and he focused on her again. She was not smiling. "I want to tell you something. I think my earlier suspicions of Cassie being involved in Jabari's disappearance are true," she said, keeping her voice low, obviously not wanting his sisters to hear.

He sat up. "What?! What makes you say that?" He struggled to keep his voice under control.

"I am not sure, but while she was in the bath this afternoon, the servant cleaned her room and found some clothes stuffed under her bed. They were dirty and slightly damp. And after what Fahad said about her window, I think she snuck out recently. It concerns me because of how much time she has been spending with Jabari and her sudden interest in riding. It just does not seem like Cassie," Nasira said with narrowed eyes.

Jalil sat back again as he considered her words. Cassie disliked animals of any kind, and riding, and everyone knew it. The more he thought about it, the more he agreed. "I think you may be right. Hashem arriving today…Jabari missing… and Cassie sneaking around? It is all too suspicious by far," he said. "I think it is time I take a ride on Mirage."

Nasira nodded her approval. "Be careful, my son."

He kissed her on the forehead and left the room. Kira might not like him checking up on her, but he wasn't worried about her reaction. She was too important to him now. Eager to see her, he quickened his pace, and soon he was racing through the pastures on Mirage.

CHAPTER 46

The first thing Jabari felt was the cold, hard stone under his cheek. He was shivering, and his head hurt terribly. *Why can't I see anything? Why is it so dark?* He tried to open his eyes, but his eyelids were stuck. He tried again and was able to open one. *So dark. So cold. What is going on? Where am I?* He tried to rub his eyes, but he couldn't move his hands. As his awareness sharpened, he realized why—his wrists were bound behind his back. *What!?* He was lying on his side, and he struggled to get up, but he couldn't move his legs. They were also bound. For a moment, he panicked but ceased struggling when a sharp pain ripped through his head, and he felt like throwing up.

Lying still, Jabari took stock of his body. As far as he could tell, he was uninjured except for the horrific pain on the side of his head. When he was able to open his other eye, he still couldn't see anything. He tried concentrating but it only made his head hurt worse, and his nausea increased. Aware of a growing thirst, he suddenly realized something was in his mouth. *A gag!*

He almost lost control again, but a few deep breaths helped to steady him. He knew he could get through this because he'd done it before. Then he remembered. *Rizu! Cassie! What happened to Cassie? Is she tied up too? Is she hurt?* Holding his breath, he listened, but if she was nearby, he couldn't hear her. Inhaling deeply, he searched for clues as to his whereabouts. The ground was hard under his back, and he smelled something familiar. The air was cool and heavy with the scent of water. It was the damp smell of a cave.

Caves were common in the mountains and provided welcoming shelter from the relentless sun. Unfortunately, humans were not the only ones that used them. They were also very popular with predators such as desert lions and hyenas. That thought panicked him again, and he struggled to stand but couldn't. *Think... think... what did Kira do in the pass to get free? Oh, yes, I remember! She got her arms around her legs. Can I do that?* He tried, but it was very difficult. *Why is this so hard? If only I had a knife!* Then he remembered his gift from Nasira.

Jabari twisted his arms around to one side until he could reach his trouser pocket. Bending his legs and bringing his knees to his chest forced the pocket to open further. He pulled and tugged on the material at his hip until he felt the smooth surface of his new dagger. It was not as fancy as the one he had given Adara, but Nasira said he should have a man's dagger and had given this one to him when she discovered he was her son. *Thank Allah!* It wasn't hard to pull it free of its sheath, and holding it just right, he cut through the rope that bound his wrists.

Jerking the gag from his mouth, he sat up slowly, his head throbbing, and untied his legs. He secured the knife in his pocket and tried to stand but was too dizzy. When he tenderly probed the side of his head, his fingers came back wet and sticky. He couldn't see them, but he recognized the coppery scent of blood. *Someone attacked me! But why did they not kill me?* It was a mystery he would have to solve later. Right now, he needed to get out of the cave.

Unable to walk and unsure of which direction to go, he crawled along the wall. It seemed to take forever in the dark, but feeling a fresh breeze gave him hope. Inching his way down a steep slope, he winced at the hard pebbles that cut his hands and knees. When the wall suddenly fell away, he paused, panting, with his head hanging. Gulping air, he slowly raised his head, puzzled to hear a roaring sound. It was not very loud and was coming from straight ahead. Feeling his way, he drew closer to the noise until he encountered a gap in the stone floor. The sound was directly beneath him, and he reached out and felt a cold spray on his hand. *Water!* Desperate, he reached down inside the hole, groaning in defeat when he couldn't touch the water.

Fighting tears of despair and anger, he rolled over on his back with a curse. *What is wrong with my eyes?* Frightened at the thought he was blind, he lay still and prayed. *Allah, please help me. Please give me strength.* Swallowing hard against the ever-present nausea, he gasped when he heard a distant whinny. *Rizu?* Rolling back onto his hands and knees, he yelled, "Rizu! Rizu!" His voice echoed loudly, and he held his breath and clenched his eyes tight, waiting for the echoes to die. His heart almost stopped when he heard another whinny.

His eyes flew open, and he gasped again. *I can see!* It was very dim, but he perceived a brighter light to his left, and without fear, he crawled toward it, ignoring the pain in his head, hands, and knees. All he could think about was the light. It wasn't long before he had to close his eyes again, this time against the brightness before him as the light stabbed into his head.

Whimpering in pain, but more determined than ever, he kept going until he could feel the desert sun enveloping him in welcome warmth, and he fell forward with a groan. Lying on his stomach with his arms outstretched, he lay still, panting, his eyes tightly closed. When something pulled at his shirt, he bit his lip to keep from crying out. But then he heard a welcome sound—a familiar snort and huff, followed by a high-pitched whinny. Squinting against the glare, he opened his eyes to see not one Rizu, but two, snuffling his shoulder. His double vision was disconcerting, but he ignored the implication of what it meant as he cried out in joy, "Rizu!" Startled, Rizu threw his head up, but when Jabari reached up with his arms, his colt lowered his head to receive a loving hug. Jabari was glad there was no one to see his tears.

After thoroughly soaking Rizu's cheek, he released his colt and forced himself to sit up. He risked a look around, wincing at the light, and swallowed down the subsequent nausea when he saw a scene out of his dreams. Everything appeared doubled, but Jabari thought he was in paradise. Before him was a valley of unbelievable beauty, bordered by ruddy cliffs and lined with gently rolling hills of pale green. And right in the middle, a silver thread that could only be one thing—water.

Shivering with shock and feeling disconnected from reality, he looked behind him and saw the dark opening from which he had crawled. *Where am I?* As much as he wanted to explore the beautiful, if surreal, panorama spread before his eyes, all he could think about was how to get home. Wherever this was, it wasn't home, and it felt more and more like it was a dream. And when a great golden stallion cantered up, Jabari knew for sure it was. Exhausted, he lay back down and succumbed to darkness.

Jabari wasn't sure how long he'd been unconscious, but when he came to, he found himself very close to a very real golden stallion. The noble beast stood nearby and seemed to study him. As Jabari stared into the stallion's liquid brown eyes, he felt like he knew him somehow, and strangely, he was unafraid.

Rizu appeared unconcerned and nudged Jabari's shoulder insistently. A sudden stab of pain in his head reminded Jabari of his injury, and he raised his hand to probe it gently. But when he saw the bright red color of the blood on his fingers, he felt a fission of fear. The wound bled sluggishly, and it wasn't stopping. He needed to get help right away.

Groaning, he struggled to rise and finally made it to his feet. He stood with his legs splayed and his arms outstretched, but he still saw double, and his nausea was unabated. He took one step and felt himself on the verge of falling. Crying out, he closed his eyes, knowing it was going to hurt, but just as he started falling forward, he felt something next to his arm. He reached out instinctively and grabbed a handful of silky mane. It was the stallion.

Jabari leaned against the golden shoulder and buried his other hand in the mane, holding tight. His legs shook, and he could hear the deep rhythmic beat of the stallion's heart and could feel the slow rise and fall of the stallion's chest. It steadied him, and he felt his strength returning, but his dizziness was increasing. The horse must have sensed his discomfort and eased them both closer to a boulder that was the perfect height for mounting. Jabari looked into the stallion's eyes, and once again, he felt as if the horse spoke to him. Without any doubt or hesitation, Jabari used the last of his strength to pull himself up on the rock then swung a leg over the horse's back. Once he was in place, he slumped forward, overcome once again. He was barely aware when the stallion walked toward the dark opening, leaving Rizu behind.

When Jabari came to, he was sitting on the cold, hard ground not far from the rock pile that Cassie and he had discovered on the hidden trail. He tried to make sense of the visions in his head but could only remember looking for Rizu with Cassie. Feeling the pain in his head, he winced when he touched the wound on the side of head. But he was failing fast. At some level, he knew something was very wrong, but delirious from lack of water and loss of blood, all he could think about was getting home to Jalil and his family and finding Rizu.

Praying for strength, he began the arduous journey back down the trail. Loose rocks and debris cut his hands and knees as he crawled, but he never gave up. He had to get home. He had to find Rizu. That was his last thought when he passed out near the bottom of the hidden trail.

CHAPTER 47

While Jalil and his family were having their evening meal, Kira slipped out to search for Jabari. She met Amber by the pasture gate, and her horse followed her to the stables. Though Kira preferred riding bareback, she needed her saddle to carry supplies. She tied a blanket to the saddle along with a waterskin and a bag containing bandages, rope, her knife, and a pouch of dates.

As she left the building, Fahad rode up with two armed guards. No words were exchanged—none were needed. When she climbed into the saddle and threw on a dark robe, Fahad nodded, and the two guards followed her into the back pasture. She stopped for a minute and leaned down over Amber's neck. "Amber, we need to find Jabari and Rizu. Please, Amber, we need your help." If she surprised the men by talking to her horse, they didn't show it. Like her, they often talked to theirs.

Amber nodded her head, neighed loudly, and leaped forward, heading toward the creek. Seeing the other two horses trying to keep up, Kira realized if she wasn't careful, her horse would soon leave them behind. "Amber, slow down, this isn't a race," she called out then sat back a little in the saddle, signaling her to a slow canter. Soon the three of them were passing through the low hills and nearing the pool by the cliffs.

Finally, Amber slowed to a fast walk without prompting. Her ears swiveled forward as she concentrated on the trail ahead. Kira mentally crossed her fingers and prayed silently. *God, please help us find Jabari. Please let him be all right.* The sun was sinking slowly, and the riders drew their robes tight against the cooling air. Kira gave Amber complete control.

As darkness descended, they followed the stream almost to the pool. Kira looked around and realized this was normally the herd's favorite spot. When she saw Amber's ears swivel, she grew excited. *Maybe Amber is tracking Rizu!* But when she heard approaching hoofbeats, Kira stopped, thrilled to hear the familiar bugle. It was Mirage and Jalil.

"Kira, I am glad I caught you. I wanted to see if I could help with the search."

He's asking my permission? Kira was pleased and humbled. "Certainly, my sheik. Amber was checking out this area. I think she knows Rizu has been here recently." *Well, that sounded a little strange.* She was glad he couldn't see her blush. She always talked about Amber as if she were human.

"Yes, that makes sense," Jalil said.

Kira smiled, happy that he agreed. "I am waiting for her to signal where she wants to go next."

As if she understood Kira, Amber began walking toward the cliffs. Mirage fell in beside her and the guards trailed behind. When they reached the pool, Amber stopped and stood still, as if listening. Kira was trying not to look at the pool, but she could see Jalil staring at it. When he turned his head and looked at her, Kira saw the reflection of the rising moon in his eyes and felt a spark of heat inside. She blushed and was thankful it was too dark for the guards to see her reaction. Amber must have sensed it because she suddenly snorted sharply and pushed past Mirage and headed eastward along the cliff face. Mirage huffed loudly, and Kira smiled, hearing Jalil chuckling behind her.

Amber led the way, walking fast but stopping intermittently to sniff the air. After a few more minutes, she walked up to a pile of towering boulders and came to a halt. Everyone waited to see what she would do, but she didn't move, except for her ears, which swiveled back and forth. This time, Mirage seemed to listen as well. Excited and anxious, but refusing to hurry her horse, Kira waited. The guards settled into their saddles, and the quiet of the night enveloped them, broken only by the whistle of the wind weaving through the rocks.

After a few minutes, Jalil opened his mouth, about to speak, when they all heard a low groan. Jalil was out of the saddle in a flash, dashing toward the sound. Kira heard more groans, jumped down, and raced after him.

Jalil suddenly disappeared behind the large boulders and shouted, "I found him! I found him!"

Kira flew around the rocks and almost tripped over Jalil, who was on his knees by the limp body of his little brother. "Jabari!" she cried. She could see the dark wound on his head. The boy moaned, but Jalil was not moving and seemed frozen in place. Kira immediately took charge. She ran back to the guards, calling out commands, "Quick, one of you, go to the house. Hurry! Find the sheikha and tell her we found Jabari. He is alive but injured. Hurry!" One guard wheeled about and took off at a full gallop. She yelled to the other, "Help the sheik."

When she turned to run back to Jabari, she saw Jalil approaching, carrying Jabari in his arms. Kira and the guard held Jabari while Jalil mounted Mirage. Once he was in place, they handed the boy up to him. Kira jumped back on Amber and sidled close to Mirage. She knew instinctively Jalil wanted to gallop home at full speed and get his little brother to Nasira and to safety, but she had to stop him. "Jalil, I know you want to get him home quickly, but Jabari has a head wound. I don't know how bad it is. We cannot go as fast as you would like, and you need to be very careful."

Kira could see the panic in his face but sighed with relief when he nodded and said, "You are right." He did not hide his tears as he directed Mirage back to the compound.

Kira need not have worried. Mirage knew what to do. He walked fast but avoided twists and turns and kept his gait smooth. Amber kept pace, and the guard followed behind, keeping a lookout for any trouble. To Kira, and she was sure to Jalil as well, it seemed to take forever to get home. She watched as Jalil stared down at his brother's face and heard him praying to Allah for help. His tears fell, and he never looked up, obviously relying on Mirage and Kira to get them home.

Kira prayed like she never had before. *Please God, let him live.* Trusting the horses to find a smooth path, she kept her eyes on Jalil. She could see the trail of tears on his cheeks in the starlight and could feel her own falling. Wiping her face with her robe, she sat up straighter. She needed to be strong, ready for whatever came next. Jabari was no longer making any noises and lay limply in Jalil's arms. Kira feared the worst.

Soon they found themselves surrounded by other riders, and when they got to the house, Nasira was ready. She directed them to carry Jabari to her own chambers then ordered everyone out except Jalil and Kira. Covered with dried blood, Jabari lay unconscious, and Kira prayed as she watched Nasira cleaning his wound.

"He has a nasty gash and a great deal of swelling. I will have to watch for infection, but I believe it is the location of the wound that is causing him to remain unconscious. It is very close to his temple. Any closer and it would have killed him instantly," Nasira said as she gently spread a thick paste around the injury.

Kira felt Jalil take her hand and, reveling in the warmth and comfort of his touch, she turned to look up at him and lost herself in his eyes. For a second, the world stood still, and it was just the two of them, until broken by a low moan. Jabari was trying to speak, and Nasira placed a firm hand on his chest when he tried to rise. "Rizu! Rizu!" he called out hoarsely before slumping back in the bed and losing consciousness once more. Kira was alarmed, but Nasira did not seem as worried.

"My poor boy," Nasira whispered, but she was smiling. "This is a good sign. I was praying he would wake, even if just for a moment. I truly believe he is going to be all right."

Kira felt Jalil squeeze her hand when they heard Nasira's encouraging words, and they shared a look of hope and joy. They stared into each other's eyes again until Nasira cleared her throat. When they turned to her, she motioned them closer. "Jalil and Kira, thank you for bringing Jabari home. He will need to be watched tonight, and I will take care of that, but don't worry, he will recover. Now both of you should get some rest. Tomorrow is almost here, and you both need to be ready."

Kira placed a light kiss on Jabari's forehead and stepped back. Jalil looked down at his brother and placed his hand on Jabari's chest. His hand rose and fell with Jabari's steady breathing, and he smiled and looked at his mother. "Thank you." Then he turned to Kira, took her by the hand, and led her from the room.

When they stood before her door, he looked into her eyes, and Kira waited for him to speak.

"Thank you, Kira, for finding Jabari. I owe you so much."

"Jalil, it wasn't me. It was Amber. You need to thank her." Kira said earnestly.

Jalil said nothing and took her in his arms, not to kiss her, but just to hold her. They stayed that way for a long time, just listening to each other's heartbeats. When he leaned back and looked at her, she did the one thing she had been wanting to do for some time. She reached up and pulled the edge of his tunic down, exposing the faint red marks of Cassie's fingernails on the side of his neck. He must have realized what she was looking at because his eyes widened in alarm. He opened his mouth to speak, but Kira pressed her soft fingertip against his lips.

"Jalil, Cassie is a liar. She has always been a liar. She cannot hurt me anymore, and I will not let her hurt you again." With no accusation in her eyes, no demand for an explanation, she smiled at him. When he tried to speak again, she shook her head, reached up, and pulled his head down to hers. She kissed him long and deep and sweet. He groaned and pulled her into his arms and kissed her with all the love in his heart.

Kira felt his passion, and she felt her own, but this time, she was in control. It was not the time for passion, so she gently pulled herself away. "Jalil, you don't need to say a word. I know what Cassie was trying to do, but she will not keep me from you ever again." With that parting remark, Kira backed into her room and started closing the door, but before it was completely closed, she peeked out at him with a playful smile. "Jalil, maybe we can do that again... after tomorrow." Jalil looked dazed and started leaning forward, and she laughed softly. "Tomorrow, Jalil. Good night." And she closed the door.

Kira looked down and saw the tips of his boots under the door. She waited, curious what he would do, but after a few minutes, they disappeared, and she listened to his slow steps as he walked away. Hugging herself, she was full of joy and was afraid she wouldn't be able to sleep, but after a quick wash and a sip or two of tea, she slipped under the covers and smiled as she drifted off. Her last thought was that she couldn't wait for tomorrow to be over.

CHAPTER 48

Early the next morning, Jabari failed to wake, and Nasira grew concerned. He hadn't awakened since that one moment when he called for Rizu. She was tired, having been up all night, but at least Samira had been there to help. Together, they had watched Jabari throughout the long night, praying for his recovery. Since neither of them could sleep, Nasira shared her idea of how she planned to help Jalil. It was a brilliant plan, and the timing would be critical, but with Samira's help, Nasira felt sure she could pull it off.

Sighing, Nasira dampened another clean cloth and draped it over Jabari's fevered brow. Looking down at her son, she smiled sadly. He was so special, and she couldn't imagine losing him again. She took his hand and lifted it to her cheek. Closing her eyes, she prayed silently, tuning out the sound of Samira who was busy grinding herbs into two large ceramic bowls. After a moment, she heard Samira mumbling to herself.

"Samira?"

Samira glanced up from her work. "Hmm? What?"

"You said something," Nasira said.

"Oh, I was wondering if you were going to tell Jalil what we are planning to do," she said.

Nasira cocked her head and smiled. "Well, I have always found it is easier to ask forgiveness than to ask permission."

Samira chuckled. "Perhaps you are right," she said and glanced down at one of the large bowls that was almost filled to the brim with finely ground herbs. "Do you think we have enough?"

"I hope so because it is all I could spare. I had to leave some for Jabari," Nasira said and rose to her feet, rolling her shoulders and stretching to ease the ache in her back. She glanced up at the window. The sun was rising, and time was short. "I need to get to the kitchen. Hashem's men will assemble in the courtyard soon for the morning meal. I hope they are very hungry," Nasira said with steely satisfaction. "And thirsty."

"But wait! What about Hashem's food?" Samira looked up with concern.

"Oh, I took care of that already. I believe someone has already taken it to his house," Nasira said.

Samira nodded. "Excellent. Then I will take this to the kitchen," she said, picking up the bowl. "You stay with our son."

Nasira held the door for her. "Thank you, Samira. But be careful, and Allah be with you."

Samira grinned and departed.

Nasira was wiping up the mess they had made on the table when she heard a soft moan. Whirling, she rushed to the bed. When she saw Jabari looking at her, his eyes clear, she burst into tears. He groaned and tried to rise, but she laid a firm hand on his chest. "No, Jabari! You cannot get up yet. You have been hurt."

Jabari lay back and raised his hand to touch the thick bandage around his head. Wincing, he felt it gently all around. "What happened?"

"You do not remember?" Nasira sat and pulled her chair closer to the bed.

Jabari looked over at her then closed his eyes briefly, his brow furrowed. "I remember we were looking for Rizu, and we went up the trail, and then I rode a golden stallion..." He stopped and moaned.

We? Golden stallion? His words alarmed Nasira, but before she could think more about that, he tried to rise again. She rose from her chair to restrain him. "Easy, my son. Do not think about it right now. You have a terrible cut on your head. Everything will be clear when you are feeling better. There is no rush." Nasira slipped a hand behind his shoulders, helping him to sit up. Once he was stable, she reached over to pour him a cup of tea laced with a light dose of herbs that would help with his pain. "Now, try to drink some of this."

He choked at first then took another sip. Suddenly, he grabbed the cup and started gulping the liquid. She pulled it back gently but firmly and cautioned him to slow down.

"Please, Mother, I am so thirsty."

"I know, I know, and you can have some more in a minute. Let us see if you can keep this down first."

Jabari smiled shakily, and she eased him back against the cushions. When a servant knocked on the door and peeked in, Nasira asked her to find Samira right away. Tucking his blanket around him, she removed his bandage, relieved to see the bleeding had stopped with no additional swelling. She would wait for Samira before putting on a fresh bandage. Jabari was resting more comfortably, thanks to her potion, and was soon sleeping peacefully.

Samira returned a few moments later. "Is he all right?"

"Oh, better than that. He woke up, and he spoke to me! And he had a dose of our tea." Nasira moved away from the bed so Samira could see for herself.

"Thank Allah," Samira whispered fervently as she leaned over to look closely at his head. "His wound looks better."

"I was just about to put on a new bandage," Nasira said as she liberally dabbed thick ointment on the gash. With Samira's help, she wrapped his head with a clean bandage, and just as she finished, he awakened and smiled up at them.

Nasira sat down next to the bed and held his hand while Samira stood behind her. "How are you feeling, Jabari?"

"Well, I have been better," Jabari quipped and tried to laugh, only to end up moaning.

Nasira laughed then burst into tears. She felt Samira squeeze her shoulder.

Once again, Jabari reached out to Nasira, eyes wide. "Mother, please do not cry." He looked up at Samira questioningly. "Why is everyone crying? Am I not going to be all right?"

Nasira wiped her eyes and ended up laughing.

Samira was sniffling behind her. "Our son does not seem to understand women."

"You are right," Nasira said. "Jabari, we are women, and crying is what we do when we are sad, or mad, or just very, very happy."

"Well, I am going to guess you are both very happy," he joked weakly then groaned again.

Both women shushed him, telling him he must be quiet and remain still. Samira collected the soiled bandages and cloths along with the basin of dirty water. "I will be right back," she said.

She turned to leave, but before she did, Nasira asked, "Is everything in place?" Samira nodded and left. Nasira watched her go, grateful to share her son with such a courageous woman.

"What was that all about, Mother?" Jabari asked with his eyes closed. "Is what in place?"

"It is nothing you need to worry about right now. You need to rest. We can talk about it later."

"But how did I get here? And where is Cassie? Is she all right?"

"Cassie?" Startled, Nasira felt an icy finger of fear trail down her spine.

"Yes. Is she hurt? Did you find Rizu? Did you see the golden stallion?" His eyes were still closed, and he was clearly agitated.

Alarmed, but needing to keep Jabari calm, Nasira lied. "She is fine, and Rizu is fine."

"But... but..." His voice trailed off as he faded and slipped back into a light sleep.

"Rest, my son, rest. Hush now." She wiped his face with a cooling cloth, but her mind was in turmoil. She heard the door open when

Samira returned with clean bandages and a basin of fresh water, and Nasira rose to help her.

"How is he, Sheikha?" Samira asked as she set everything down before moving closer to the bed.

"He is better, and he should sleep for a while. But he mentioned something strange earlier and again just now. Something about a golden stallion."

Samira chuckled lightly. "I would not be too concerned about that. Almost from the moment he could speak, he has talked about golden horses. He always dreamed about them and insisted that one day he would ride a golden stallion."

Nasira sighed. "Maybe it was just the fever talking. And I, too, have discovered his obsession with golden horses." She rinsed the cloth and laid it on his forehead. "But we have another problem. He mentioned Cassie." She looked up at Samira, her eyes hard.

Samira's eyes narrowed, and she returned the stern look. "Do you think she had something to do with this?"

"Oh, yes, I believe she had a great deal to do with this. I suspected as much earlier and said something to Jalil, but now I am even more certain. And today, I am going to find out exactly what she has done. I think more is going on than Hashem's 'blood money.'" Nasira could feel her anger simmering, and she nursed it, feeding it, until it flamed higher, filling her with righteous heat. She was close to losing control but held tight, saving it for the right moment.

When someone knocked on the door, interrupting their conversation, Nasira rose to answer it. It was a guard with a message for her.

"It is time," Nasira said cryptically as she rose and went to a cabinet on the far wall. She opened the doors, pulled out a wide leather belt, and buckled it around her waist. When she attached a curved metal scabbard, she saw Samira watching her silently, her eyes wide. But when Nasira slid the scimitar out halfway and tested the blade, she noticed Samira's eyes widen farther, but still she said nothing. Nasira slid the blade back into its sheath with an audible click. *Yes, this will do.*

Then she pulled out a leather bag and laid it on the table beside the bed. Reaching inside, she withdrew an ornate flintlock pistol and held it out to Samira. "Do you know how to use this?"

"Yes." Samira's former look of surprise was gone. She took it without hesitation.

"Good." Next, Nasira pulled out a long knife and set it on the table. "This is for you, too. Do not hesitate to use it." She watched as Samira lifted the knife and tested its weight.

"It is well balanced," Samira said, nodding. Then she looked up at Nasira. "Where will you be?"

Nasira pulled on a heavy robe, one whose folds effectively concealed her weapon. "I will be in the main hall. Remember, stay in this room and keep the door locked. Do not open it unless you hear me, Jalil, Kira, Fahad, or Saad."

"Yes, Sheikha... but please... be careful."

Nasira smiled grimly. "You too."

"I will. I am scared, but if you can fight, so can I... to protect my son, our son. I might not be the daughter of a sheik, but I am desert born, and I know how to protect my own." Samira's eyes blazed with the sincerity of her words.

Nasira nodded. "Of that, I have no doubt," she said and stepped from the room. When she heard Samira lock the door behind her, she exchanged a smile with the two guards posted outside and hurried down the corridor.

Knowing her son was safe with Samira, Nasira stopped by to make sure the meeting hall was ready. When she peered out into the courtyard, Hashem's men were already consuming the sumptuous dishes prepared for them. They appeared to be enjoying their meal. Most dishes had a little extra salt which would make the men a little thirstier, but she was sure it would still be tastier fare than they had on the trail. She would have laughed if she could have heard their thoughts. Most of them were wishing they could live here—the food in Hashem's compound was never this good. Nasira made sure plenty of sweetened tea was available... and only sweetened tea. Watching them drinking brought a smile of satisfaction to her face.

She didn't bother to go to the guest wing to check on Cassie, knowing she'd be seeing her later. But before she went to Jalil's quarters for the final meeting, she checked on her daughters. She had moved them in with Kira when she put Jabari in her own chambers. Two heavily armed guards stood at the door. Her daughters were in good spirits and told her Kira was on her way to Jalil's chambers. Nasira gave each girl a hug before hurrying out the door. It was time to put an end to Hashem's madness, and she couldn't wait to hear how Jalil planned to do it.

CHAPTER 49

Jalil stood at the head of the table as he waited impatiently for the last person to arrive.

"I apologize for being late," Nasira said as she rushed into the room and took her seat next to Fahad. Jalil heard a metallic clank and noticed his advisor smiling, but Nasira merely straightened her robe and stared at him calmly.

"It is not a problem, Sheikha. And how is our patient?" Jalil didn't use Jabari's name. He had sent word to everyone in the tribe to keep Jabari's return a secret.

"All is well," she said.

"That is good to hear," he said then addressed the group. "Now that we are all here, I want to tell you what is going to happen today. After we take our places in the meeting hall, I will send an escort for Hashem. He may bring a few of his men." He looked at his mother. "Nasira, I would like for you and Kira to be in the room with us today. Your chairs will be behind me." Nasira and Kira exchanged pleased looks.

Jalil turned to his advisor. "Fahad, I want you on my left." Though Jalil could handle a sword with either hand, he preferred using his right for his long sword and didn't want Fahad in his way should it become necessary to fight. Jalil didn't expect that to happen, but with Hashem, anything was possible. He apparently was as crazy as Qadir. When

Fahad nodded with a look of understanding, Jalil glanced at his herdmaster.

"Sakhr, I want you to stay with the herd. I will keep Mirage in the house, and I want Amber inside as well." Sakhr nodded, but Jalil looked at Kira for her approval, pleased when she nodded as well.

Jalil paused, overwhelmed for moment, when he saw the looks of respect on the surrounding faces. He felt a surge of pride and knew in his heart they'd follow his every command. Clearing his throat, he continued. "And now I can share the rest of my plan." But before he could continue, Nasira interrupted him.

"Yes, Sheikha?"

"My sheik, I must ask your forgiveness. I have done something that might have a bearing on your plans today," she said with a half-smile, half-grimace. His eyes narrowed, and he noticed everyone staring at her with curious expressions, except for Fahad. His advisor looked intrigued. Jalil returned his attention to Nasira and gestured for her to continue.

"Well, I was overseeing the preparations of the tea for Hashem's men this morning, and it is possible some of my special herbs fell into the kettles. I am not sure, but I think it was some of my pain medicine." She looked contrite, but her eyes sparked with amusement.

He frowned then realized exactly what she was talking about. His brow smoothed, and his eyes widened. "Sheikha, am I to understand you have done something to Hashem's men?" He struggled not to laugh.

"Well, um, yes, my sheik. It will not hurt them, but I think they may not be as responsive today as Hashem needs them to be." She rolled her eyes and smiled.

Jalil couldn't help himself and started laughing, and everyone in the room joined in. After he had composed himself, he noticed her smile had vanished. It was obvious she wanted to speak. "Is there something else you need to share?"

"I heard something this morning from our patient that implicates our redheaded guest in recent events," Nasira said with a hard voice.

Based on the reaction of everyone in the room, Jalil knew it would not go well for Cassie. "Please, go on," he said.

"I have not approached her because of what is going on today. And I will not pursue any further information gathering without your approval." Nasira's hand strayed to her hip, and Jalil wondered what she was hiding.

But when he saw Fahad smiling at her, as if he understood, Jalil suddenly had a fleeting childhood memory of seeing Nasira sparring with his father. When he asked her why she was fighting like a man, she'd told him that his father wanted her to know how to protect herself and her family if needed. His mother was carrying her sword and was obviously ready to wield it.

Knowing he'd never underestimate a woman again, Jalil's eyes reflected his admiration when he said, "Sheikha, you are as brave as you are resourceful." She colored slightly, and Jalil noticed the others looking at her with pride and love, all except Kira. Kira was staring at him and when he looked into her eyes, the room disappeared until all he could see were pools of cool blue green. Entranced, he felt his heart racing, until someone coughed and broke the spell, and he saw his mother shaking her head. Cutting his eyes back to Kira, he saw she was looking everywhere but at him. He half expected to feel embarrassed but discovered he felt nothing but love for her. And he didn't care who knew it now.

Taking a deep breath, he collected himself and smiled. "Well, it seems I have a warrior in my tribe that I had not counted on participating in today's activity. Thank you, Sheikha, for sharing that information. As for the first part, your efforts will help our cause. As for the second, I think it will also prove to do the same. Now, if that is all?" He looked at her with one eyebrow raised then added, "That is all, is it not?"

Laughter again filled the room, and Nasira smiled and nodded.

"Excellent," Jalil said. "Now I will share my news. Some special guests will arrive shortly through the north pass but will remain in the screened gallery until they are called for. Saad will be in charge of those guests."

Jalil glanced at Saad, amazed to see the effect of his words on Saad. Gone was the fat, jolly trader. This man was ready to do battle. He smiled inwardly and continued. "A large number of others have arrived, but they are not on the guest list. They are hiding on the trail, not too far from our main pass. They are armed and wear the colors of Hashem and Amit. But there is no need to be alarmed. Our allies have surrounded them with a like number of men, and it is unlikely these uninvited guests will make it to our pass. Just be alert and stay focused."

Seeing Nasira's and Kira's stunned expressions, Jalil quickly said, "I am sorry to have not told you both earlier. It is not that I did not trust you, but I wasn't sure it had gone according to plan until earlier this morning. I did not want to give false hope."

"Sheik, we understand," Nasira said, and Kira nodded in agreement. "It was just a shock. That could have been our undoing."

"My thoughts exactly. But we have everything in hand," he said, then looked once more around the room. "Remember, no matter what Hashem says today, or what he has planned to do, he will fail. I only ask two other things of each of you. First, be careful. You are all very important to me, and I do not want to see anyone hurt. And secondly, whatever happens, Hashem is mine." His voice brooked no argument.

But Nasira had one thing to add, and her voice was as hard as Jalil's. "I also have something to ask. Whatever happens, Cassie is mine."

Jalil knew it would be futile to argue with her and merely nodded, but he exchanged a look with Fahad, who nodded imperceptivity. Nasira would have a shadow. "Well, I believe we have finished here. I will see you all in the meeting hall." He watched as they filed from the room but gestured for Kira to stay. "Kira, a word, please?" She approached him with a questioning look, but when he held out his arms, she didn't hesitate and stepped into his embrace. Pulling her closer, he lightly rubbed her back. "Are you going to be all right with what is coming? You know Hashem will call on Cassie to testify. She is undoubtedly the witness he claims. But she will say things you do not wish for everyone to hear." He leaned back to look into her amazing eyes, expecting to see fear, but she appeared calm.

"Jalil, there is nothing she, or anyone, can say that can hurt me anymore. But I fear she could damage your reputation with what she will reveal about me today," she said with honest concern.

"Kira, there is nothing she or anyone can say today about you that will embarrass me or my family. You are an honored member of our tribe, and we will support you as you have supported us," he said and hugged her again. When Kira laid her head on his chest, Jalil's arms tightened, and it was as if he had found a missing part of himself. Again, time seemed to slow, and he reveled in the moment, wishing it would never end.

But suddenly she pulled back. "Jalil, it is almost time, and I need a few minutes to get ready," she said, stepping further away.

Jalil blinked, trying to focus, then muttered sheepishly, "Unfortunately, you are right, Kira." She was already gone, but he heard her chuckle as she fled down the corridor. Kira was right, he thought. Time was short, and he still needed to change. Filled with new determination, he hurried to get ready. It was time to take care of Hashem once and for all.

CHAPTER 50

As Hashem approached Jalil's house, he scowled, remembering how Jalil had treated him the previous day. After meeting with Jalil, he'd been so angry he had trouble breathing and collapsed in the guest house, unable to eat or drink. Jalil's servants had brought him refreshments at sunrise, but though he felt somewhat better, he was too nervous to eat.

Accompanied by four of his guards, he marched up the steps, but when he reached the front doors, Jalil's men surrounded him. They forced Hashem and his guards to surrender their firearms, and Hashem's anger returned in full force. He felt somewhat mollified that they were allowed to keep their swords and scimitars.

The meeting hall was empty when he entered. A guard escorted him to a group of chairs facing a dais. He sat in one of two, separated by a small table, and his guards sat behind him. As he took stock of his surroundings, he stroked his whip with one hand and rested his other on the hilt of his scimitar. Four empty chairs sat upon the dais, with more lined up on either side of it. He thought he heard a noise behind him and glanced over his shoulder at the screened wall. Probably Jalil's women, he thought with a sneer. Women had no part in tribal business. Jalil was a fool.

When a servant entered and placed a tray with a pitcher of sweetened tea and a goblet on the table next to his chair, Hashem filled the goblet and sipped it slowly. He continued to stroke the coiled leather of his whip and waited. But the longer he waited, the angrier he got. He was about to confront the guards by the door when Jalil's advisor led Cassie into the hall. As she approached, Hashem couldn't help his reaction. Her robe hugged her lush curves and covered a tunic that was too sheer to be decent. Her sultry smile showcased her dyed lips, while bands of black and gold highlighted her emerald green eyes. She always knew how to make an entrance, he thought with a cruel smile. He had missed his plaything.

When he saw her look at him with a hopeful expression, he refused to respond and kept his look neutral. He would not play any games with her today. He was here for one purpose, and if she didn't help him with that, he would make sure she regretted it.

As soon as Fahad left the room, Hashem reached across the little table, grabbed her arm, and squeezed tightly. She gasped in pain, and he felt a surge of pleasure. "Listen to me, witch. I am about to destroy Jalil and his family. I will take his golden mares and his women. He cannot refute my claim as long as you play your part." He watched her eyes widen, but when she tried to speak, he cut her off. "I will not have you ruin this for me, Cassie! You will tell them everything we discussed."

When he saw Cassie's eyes flashing, he released her arm. He realized she was not afraid of him. Perhaps he needed to be careful. She was the key to his plan. Luckly she didn't lash out. Instead, she leaned closer until her lips were inches from his. "Don't you want to know about the boy?"

Hashem studied her for a second then cut his eyes around the empty room. They were far enough from Jalil's guards and the screened room that no one should be able to hear them. Seeing her gloating expression, he knew she had good news, and he had to know. "What about him?" he whispered.

"He's dead. I got rid of him and his little horse. It was easy," she whispered loudly then launched into the story.

But as excited as he was to hear of her success, he had to stop her because her voice was growing louder the longer she talked. He grabbed her arm again and shook her. "Shut your mouth, Cassie. This room has ears."

She jerked her arm free and glared at him. Hashem thought she was about to say something again, and he was ready to silence her until he saw her looking over his shoulder. She gasped softly, her eyes widened, and her lips parted slightly. Hashem heard footsteps and turned to see Jalil, dressed entirely in white, stride into the room, looking every inch of a warrior. Gold and turquoise cords secured his headwrap. A gold leather bandolier crisscrossed his chest, and a matching wide belt with a long sword and a scimitar encircled his waist. He could see the ornate handles of a knife and a dagger sheathed in the bandolier itself.

Hashem schooled his features and tried to appear bored, but when he saw what was hanging from Jalil's neck, he gripped the arms of his chair to keep from rising, and his anger began spiraling. *Akeem's medallion!* He was so focused on the great gold disk, he barely noticed when Fahad, armed with swords, stepped up onto the dais to stand on Jalil's left.

Seeing the women following Fahad raised Hashem's anger to greater heights. *Women had no place here!* Nasira entered first, her dark hair, with caramel highlights, twisted intricately around her head. The bodice of her golden tunic was encrusted with yellow diamonds and turquoise stones. Her outer robe was pale gold with blue bands and a sheer golden scarf draped over her head and around her shoulder. As she walked, a curved silver scabbard swung from her hip. Shocked to see her armed, Hashem began feeling a stirring of unease.

She ignored Hashem, and he watched in disbelief as Jalil held out his hand to assist her to a chair behind him. He expected her to sit, but she remained standing, her eyes fixed upon Cassie. Hashem refused to acknowledge her and casually sipped from his goblet as if unconcerned. Cassie, on the other hand, fidgeted uncomfortably beside him.

But when Kira walked in, showing no emotion, he slammed his goblet down hard. He could almost forgive Jalil letting the sheikha attend the meeting, but to allow a foreigner, a common harem girl, to sit in was almost more than he could stand. He tried to ignore her, but he couldn't look away. She was beautiful in a solid white silk tunic, the bodice lightly sprinkled with gems of white and gold, and her robe was turquoise, banded in white. Her silvery golden locks, barely covered by a white scarf, drew his eye, as did the large jeweled dagger hanging from her golden belt. When she reached the dais, Jalil walked down to meet her, took her hand, and led her to the chair next to his mother. Kira also remained standing with her eyes fixed on Cassie. Hashem noticed Cassie looking everywhere but at the Kira.

Finally, Jalil sat down, and the women behind him followed suit. Fahad remained standing, and Hashem saw he held the scroll that represented his claims against Jalil. The man calmly unrolled it and began reading it aloud. As Hashem listened, he smiled and grew more excited. He was about to destroy this tribe. When Fahad finished, he handed the scroll to Jalil, and Hashem stood up, prepared to present his evidence, when suddenly Jalil stood up, as did the women.

Hashem listened in disbelief when Fahad made a formal announcement. "Sheik Jalil, Sheik Hashem, the required witnesses to the hearing of this claim have arrived. Please welcome Sheik Ehsaan, Sheik Malek, and Sheik Sayyid." Three older men entered wearing their formal tribal attire, and Jalil bowed to them as his guards showed them to their chairs. Two of their own men, heavily armed, accompanied each sheik.

Hashem saw Cassie's mouth open, and it was all he could do to keep his shut. He knew technically Jalil could have up to three sheiks witness the proceedings, but he didn't think Jalil was familiar with the ancient law or had the time to invite them. Hashem was still standing and could do nothing but wait for the sheiks to sit. He had no problem disrespecting Jalil but knew it was not wise to do the same to three ruling sheiks. He waited for them to get settled then took his seat.

After the servants brought refreshments for the sheiks, Fahad turned to Hashem with a dismissive look. "You may continue."

Hashem glared at the other sheiks, all allies of Akeem, and now Jalil. Now he understood who it was he had heard earlier in the gallery. *Well, all the better. I am going to show these sheiks how I deal with my enemies, and I will destroy Jalil and his tribe.*

CHAPTER 51

Kira sat on the edge of her chair and watched the drama unfolding around her. It was obvious Hashem thought he had the advantage with his stupid claim, at least until the three sheiks had arrived. He didn't look so cocky now, but he did look murderous, and Kira's sixth sense was screaming at her. He was planning something. She was sure of it.

The more she saw of him, the more he resembled Qadir, from his soulless stare and cruel smile to his coal black outfit and coiled leather whip. And he even spoke like him. Kira was heartily tired of his long tirade as he reiterated the entire raid on Qadir's, and it was almost a relief when he finally introduced Cassie as his witness.

When Cassie rose, she stood in front of Jalil but kept her gaze fixed on Hashem. Jalil looked slightly bored, and the visiting sheiks seemed more interested in watching Hashem then Cassie. Kira hid her smile when she saw a flash of disappointment on Hashem's face when no one looked worried. But he quickly covered it with a cruel smile as he cut his eyes in her direction. Kira ignored him, taking pleasure in seeing his smile vanish, then steeled herself as he began asking Cassie questions.

"Cassie, do you know the foreign woman named Kira?"

Kira's eyes widened. She hadn't expected him to start his presentation with her.

"Yes, my sheik," Cassie said, her eyes cutting to Kira then back to Hashem. "Kira and I entered this country together. Our plane crashed, and she abandoned me in the desert. Qadir rescued me. I don't know what happened to her."

Kira struggled to control herself upon hearing Cassie's blatant lie. She unconsciously laid a hand on her dagger and took a deep breath.

"And is the woman you know as Kira in this room?"

"Yes, my sheik." Cassie pointed at Kira with a smirk on her face. "That's her."

"So after Kira left you to die in the desert, when did you next see her?" Hashem was strolling slowly back and forth, tapping his chin with one finger, and Kira almost laughed aloud at his self-important manner.

"It was after she attacked Qadir at the Tri-Annual race. I saw her in the harem bath. She was very angry. I tried to talk to her, but she ignored me. Then Qadir's mother, First Wife, took her away." Cassie said, casting a pitying look at Kira, but Kira saw her crocodile smile lurking.

"And what happened next?" Hashem stopped and crossed his arms, assuming a serious pose.

"Some time had passed then I heard her calling for help. It was awful," Cassie said dramatically.

"So what did you do?"

"I snuck out of the harem."

"But how is that possible? Were you not locked in? Were there not guards?"

"I knew where First Wife kept a hidden key, but there were no guards. I could hear shouting and gunshots outside, and I knew I had to help Kira."

Kira could not believe the extent of Cassie's lies and came close to losing control until Nasira coughed lightly, as if clearing her throat. When she glanced at Nasira and saw the warning in her eyes, she breathed deeply and forced herself to relax.

Hashem apparently didn't notice. He focused on Cassie. "What happened next, Cassie?" he asked. Kira saw him cut his eyes to Jalil and could hear a growing excitement in his voice.

"I made it almost to Qadir's quarters, but that's when I found First Wife. Someone had kicked her door open, and she was dead. Looked like poison to me. There was nothing I could do, so I ran to Qadir's chambers. His door was open, and I heard voices in the bedchamber, so I looked inside."

"And what did you see?"

"Jalil and Kira were standing next to Qadir's bed. Qadir looked like he was asleep. Before I could say anything, I saw Jalil cut Qadir's throat and stab him in the chest with a dagger." Cassie grimaced as if sickened by the memory then flashed a quick, cruel smile at Jalil.

Nasira gasped, and Jalil reached for his sword, but he withdrew his hand when Fahad cleared his throat. Ehsaan made a noise but covered it with a cough. Kira gripped the arms of her chair and could almost feel the wood giving way but stared unblinking at Cassie, who had the good sense to look away.

Hashem appeared unperturbed at their reaction. "So, Cassie, you saw Jalil kill my brother, Sheik Qadir."

"Yes, my sheik." Cassie dropped her head in pretended sorrow.

Hashem walked back and forth, as if pondering all the evidence, then stopped and reached into his pocket. With a hateful look at Jalil, he pulled out a gold sheath, removed the dagger, and held it up for all to see. "Cassie, have you ever seen this dagger before?"

Cassie acted shocked. Her eyes widened, and her hand flew to her mouth. She gasped dramatically. "That is the dagger I saw Jalil use to kill Qadir. I would recognize it anywhere."

Her performance was over the top, Kira thought. *How can anyone believe this?* But then she saw Jalil's reaction when he looked at the dagger. He sat as if frozen. But when both Nasira and Fahad stood, he suddenly rose, stepped down from the dais, and moved closer to Hashem. "Where did you get my father's dagger?" His words were as sharp as his sword.

"Your father's dagger? Well, thank you, Jalil, for confirming who the murder weapon belongs to. It was you who killed my brother, and it is you who will pay for the crime." Hashem stepped closer to Jalil with his hand on his sword hilt, his mouth twisted in a snarl.

Kira held her breath, fearing the worst, but was relieved when Fahad and Ehsaan both stepped between them. Ehsaan held out his hand. "Let me see that dagger." Hashem reluctantly handed it to him, and Ehsaan appeared to study it closely. "Yes, this is Akeem's dagger." He shook his head sadly.

Hashem let out a triumphant cry, and Kira's heart dropped, but then Ehsaan held up his hand. "You did not let me finish. This is Akeem's dagger, but it was never Jalil's."

At those words, Hashem growled. "That does not matter. This is the dagger used to kill Qadir. This dagger belongs to Jalil's family. Of that, there can be no doubt now." Hashem smiled, acting as if he was back in control.

To Kira it seemed the evidence was irrefutable, but she was wrong. Two people had yet to speak. She saw Nasira step down from the dais and approach Ehsaan, who bowed and surrendered the dagger to her.

She stared down at it, and Kira could see tears forming in her eyes, but when Nasira looked up at Hashem, her eyes were dry. "That dagger does indeed belong to my family. It belonged to Jalil's father and his father before him," she said. "But it disappeared the day of Akeem's murder. The question is where has it been all this time, and how did Qadir get it?" Nasira stared hard at Hashem, and he averted his eyes and stared at the other two sheiks. They sat with their heads together, whispering, and Kira could see they were considering Nasira's words.

No one was paying any attention to Hashem, and Kira noticed his hands fisted and his face growing red. Once again, she realized how like Qadir he was, and she wondered if he was losing control. His next words confirmed her suspicions. "You are obviously making this up, woman. You have no say in this," he spat with no respect, ignoring the collective gasp at his insult to the sheikha.

Kira was already moving. Calling Nasira a liar was unforgivable, and Jalil, Fahad, and Ehsaan joined her. They immediately surround Hashem.

Jalil leaned forward. "Be very careful, Hashem. You do not call the sheikha of this tribe a liar and live to tell about it."

The two men looked like they were about to start something that could only end in bloodshed, but Kira's eyes were drawn to the dagger. It was very familiar, and suddenly she could hear Qadir's cruel taunts in her mind.

"Wait!" she shouted. Everyone took a step back at the vehemence of her voice. She pointed at the dagger in Nasira's hand and looked straight at Hashem. "That's the dagger Qadir had when he tied me up in his room before Jalil got there. He showed it to me when he was trying to decide whether to cut me or beat me first."

Nasira gasped, and Kira saw Jalil pale. He took a step toward her but stopped when she held up her hand. She turned toward Ehsaan and the other sheiks.

"If you need to see the evidence of that night, I will show you, if it will prove to you that man and that woman are the only liars in this room." She blushed and pointed to Hashem and Cassie and couldn't help trembling, but she stood resolute.

Hashem's eyes widened then narrowed, and Kira could tell he was trying to come up with a response when the door burst open, surprising everyone, as Fatima, her face full of fury, marched up to Cassie. "Cassie is lying. Hashem is lying. I know this dagger. Qadir often wore it when he would come to the harem bath."

Hashem glared at Fatima, but she didn't back down. "Qadir selected that woman many times," she said, pointing at Cassie. "She was his favorite. But she was also sleeping with Hashem. She told Qadir she was carrying his child, but Qadir could not have children."

Ehsaan's eyes widened at this news, and he looked at Cassie. "Is this true?"

Cassie's face flooded with color as everyone stared at her with contempt. "I don't know what this woman is talking about," Cassie said then immediately sat down and refused to say another word.

But Fatima had more to say. "I was the one who found Kira. She was tied to Qadir's bed. She had been whipped and was unconscious. I cut her loose and dragged her away from that monster. But when I found her in his room, Sheik Qadir was still alive. He was on his bed, and he was also unconscious. He was not dead! That dagger you are talking about was on the table beside his bed. And that is the truth." She was breathing hard and holding her hand against her stomach.

Kira knew Fatima was in the same condition as Samira and was worried about her baby, but before she could help, Nasira reached out. "Fatima, you need to sit down." She led her to a chair near the visiting sheiks.

Hashem's face was redder than Cassie's hair. "You would take the word of a harem girl over a sheik?" he shouted.

Jalil gave Hashem a chilling look. "And yet *you* are asking us to take the word of a harem girl," he pointed to Cassie, "over the word of a sheik." He pointed to himself.

Hashem began stammering. "She is not a harem girl. She is a foreigner."

Suddenly, Ehsaan turned to Cassie with a calculating expression. "Cassie, tell us again how you got to Qadir's."

"Like I already told you, Hashem found me in the desert."

"I thought you said Qadir found you?"

"Well, no, Hashem found me."

"Ahh. But Hashem worked for Sheik Qadir, so you belong to Qadir. And when Qadir was murdered, Hashem became the sheik. So, now you belong to Hashem?"

"Yes...I mean, no! I do not belong to anyone." Cassie's temper was showing.

"So, how did you end up at Jalil's?" Ehsaan looked puzzled.

She looked up, confusion etched on her face. "I... I escaped."

"You escaped from Hashem? But I thought he made you his sheikha."

"Yes," Cassie said with a defiant expression.

"Yes, you escaped, or yes, you are his sheikha?" Ehsaan said with a sly expression.

"Uh, um, well, I escaped. Hashem just told everyone I was his sheikha."

Kira noticed Nasira looking at Cassie with a puzzled expression and remembered hearing from Nasira how Hashem supposedly sold Cassie to slavers, but she escaped from them. Kira thought Nasira would say something, but Nasira just smiled and remained silent.

"So, you escaped. Hmm. And how did you get here?" Ehsaan rubbed his chin as if perplexed.

"I rode a horse," she spat.

"You rode a horse…all the way from Hashem's? You rode for four days?"

Kira was catching on to Ehsaan's game. Cassie fidgeted and appeared flustered.

"I don't know, I mean, no or… yes, yes, I rode all the way here."

"So, you rode four days to escape from Hashem, to get help from a murderer?"

Kira stifled a laugh. Cassie's eyes grew enormous, and she began sweating. "Well, I… I needed to get help. I am trying to get home to my country," she whined petulantly.

"And you thought Sheik Jalil, the man you saw murder your former sheik, the same man you planned to testify against, would help you? Is that right?"

Cassie turned to Hashem with a pleading look, but he scowled and turned away. Kira knew he had made a mistake when she saw Cassie snap.

"You have no idea what I've been through since I came to this God-forsaken country. I've been raped and beaten and lied to. I've had my freedom taken away and all because of some man. Well, I've had enough. I've done nothing wrong, and I want to leave here," Cassie half shouted, her eyes full of fire.

Ehsaan paused, seeming to consider her response. "All in good time, Cassie. But first I have a few more questions. Now, Cassie, you say you have done nothing wrong, is that right?"

"That's right," she huffed.

"I see. Well then, Cassie, what can you tell me about Jabari?"

Kira noticed Nasira sitting forward in her chair and Ehsaan exchanging a look with Jalil, who gestured to Fahad. Fahad moved closer to the sheikha.

"Jabari? What do you mean?" A bead of sweat trickling down Cassie's face.

"You know, Jabari, brother of Sheik Jalil, son of Akeem, son of Nasira?"

Hashem stole a glance around the room and reacted to the heated stares of the other sheiks by taking another step further away from Cassie.

Cassie gulped. "I don't know anything about him."

"Did you know he was missing?"

"How would I know that?"

"Have you not been taking daily riding lessons from him? Oh, and yes, learning how to handle his colt which, strangely enough, has also gone missing?"

Kira's eyes narrowed as she realized exactly what Ehsaan was saying. She waited, dreading what she might hear next.

Cassie glanced at Hashem, but he refused to make eye contact with her. "He has been helping me, yes, but I don't know where he is."

"I see. So, when you told Hashem you had completed your task, that you kidnapped the boy and his colt, and killed the boy, you were not talking about Jabari and his colt, both of whom are missing?"

Cassie turned to Hashem again and pulled on his sleeve. "Hashem?" she whispered pleadingly.

Hashem jerked his arm away. "I do not know what anyone is talking about. I know nothing about this Jabari or his horse," he said with contempt.

Everyone was looking at Cassie, but Kira noticed Hashem staring at the door with a look of relief, and she turned to see one of Qadir's allies walk into the room.

"Sheik Amit," Jalil said, "have you come to witness Hashem's claim? I was not expecting you, but you are welcome."

Kira looked at Jalil and wondered for a second if he had lost his mind. From the look on Nasira's face, she must have been thinking the same thing. But Kira knew she could trust Jalil. *What is he up to?*

Nodding to the other sheiks, Amit moved to stand in front of Jalil, who had stepped back up on the dais. "Thank you, Sheik Jalil. I heard the rumors regarding the death of Sheik Qadir and my supposed involvement. I have done some investigating on my own. It is true I have long been an ally of Sheik Qadir's, but things have changed in our region. This has led me to consider other possibilities."

Pausing, Amit looked at the other sheiks. "I realize there are also some who think I had something to do with the attempt on Sheik Jalil's life during the race. Yes, I proposed the course change that redirected the racers through the pass where he was ambushed. But I only did that because my ally, Sheik Qadir, requested it. He assured me his horse, Shar, would easily beat Mirage because Shar could handle the high pass and Mirage could not. I did not realize what Sheik Qadir had planned." When he finished, everyone in the room began talking at once, and Hashem's eyes darted from one person to the next.

Jalil quickly called for order. "Everyone, please be quiet and let Sheik Amit speak."

Kira saw Hashem edging toward the door and was about to signal Jalil, but he had noticed too and stopped Hashem with a sharp, accusatory look.

Amit nodded and continued. "As I was saying, Sheik Qadir had planned to kill Sheik Jalil and win the race, and of course take Mirage and some of Sheik Jalil's golden mares. Thank Allah for sparing Jalil and Mirage." Amit's smile didn't reach his eyes.

"Wait a minute, Sheik Amit," Jalil said. "If you knew nothing about the plan to kill me, then how did you find out about it?"

All eyes were on Amit now, but Kira kept hers on Hashem, and she saw Fahad watching him closely, too. Hashem was sweating profusely, and his eyes were shifting left and right, reminding her of a wild horse about to break and run.

Amit ignored Hashem and answered Jalil. "Because I also have a witness." He gestured toward a scruffy tribesman standing in the doorway. "Nadim, why don't you join us and share what you know about this."

Hashem's eyes widened, and all the color drained from his face. Kira thought he looked as if he'd seen a ghost.

Nadim sauntered forward, clearly enjoying being the center of attention. He stopped in front of Hashem. "Hello, Hashem. You remember me, don't you? Or did you forget me already? Perhaps after you left me to die during the race?"

Hashem's face turned a horrible shade of crimson, and he sounded like he was having trouble breathing. "You?! How did you get here? You were dead," he growled.

"Evidently not. And once I found help and recovered, I was lucky enough to find service with Sheik Amit." He turned and bowed to Amit.

Hashem was shaking with fury. "This man is a liar! He was working for Sheik Qadir. Whatever he did, he acted alone."

Nadim showed his outrage. "Alone?! You were the one who shot that golden horse in the desert. You were the one who shot Jalil during the race."

Kira rose to her feet, looked at Hashem, and gasped aloud. "You're the one who shot Amber?!" She pulled her dagger and took a step forward but stopped when she saw Jalil raise his hand and step down from the dais.

"Shut up, Nadim," Hashem warned and reached for his sword.

Jalil rushed forward and grabbed his arm. "Let the man finish, Hashem."

Nadim darted behind Jalil. "Yes, Hashem, and perhaps they would like to hear what you did to the baby."

It took a second for Kira to realize what he was talking about until Nasira rushed toward Hashem with a growl of rage, her sword in hand. Fahad leaped forward and grabbed her just in time. "My apologies, Sheikha." She struggled briefly, then stilled while breathing heavily.

Hashem stumbled backwards, brandishing his sword. "You are mad. I had nothing to do with that baby. It was Qadir's doing." Hashem didn't realize he had just admitted knowing about the kidnapping.

But Nadim wasn't quite done. "Yes, Hashem, it was Qadir's plan, but you did the deed. And I am sure Sheik Jalil will also want to hear about what you did to Rayham. You know, the day you stole Akeem's medallion, and Qadir stole Akeem's dagger and murdered him."

Complete chaos ensued. Kira stood shocked, finally hearing the whole horrible story. The visiting sheiks huddled against the far wall, deep in conversation. Fahad was holding Nasira, who was eyeing Cassie. Cassie sat frozen in her chair, her face bloodless and her eyes fixed on the door. Jalil stood looking undecided, as if struggling to process what he had just heard. When she looked for Hashem, she saw he was gone, and she noticed Amit creeping out of the hall, his face full of fear. Alarmed, she turned back to see Jalil run over to speak to Ehsaan and the other sheiks.

"I am going after Hashem. If any of you have an objection to what I am about to do, tell me now," Jalil said. The sheiks looked at each other, their faces grim, and shook their heads..

Ehsaan reached out and placed his hand on Jalil's shoulder. "Go, Sheik Jalil. Justice must be served."

Jalil nodded and bowed to the sheiks before turning to run back to his mother. "Sheikha, Hashem will pay for what he did to our family." Then he looked at Kira, unbuckled his scimitar, and held it out. "Here, take this. Just in case."

"But you might need it," Kira said, worried about his safety.

"No, *ya hayati*. All I need is my long sword."

Hearing his endearment, her heart swelled with love. She took the scimitar then glanced at the door. "You'd better hurry. He might get away." She winked and pushed him lightly toward the door. "Go."

Jalil said nothing, but he gave her a look filled with promise and ran after Hashem.

CHAPTER 52

Hashem wasn't the only one to take advantage of the chaos. When Cassie came to her senses, she fled to her chamber. It was obvious Nasira and Kira would not let her get away with what she had done to Jabari. She had seen the look in Kira's eyes, but it was the look in Nasira's that had her shivering in fear. Nasira would show her no mercy. It was time to go.

Grabbing some clothes and a head wrap, she rolled them in a blanket. Haphazardly stuffing bread and fruit into the bag Nasira had given her for her mending work, she stopped long enough to fill an old waterskin, spilling half of it on the floor in her haste.

Donning her one heavy robe, she hurried to the window, relieved to see the guard was gone. He must have responded to the commotion at the front of the house, she thought as she threw her bag and blanket over the sill then dropped down beside them. Looking across the compound, she saw a row of tents and ran toward them, hoping to find anyone who would help her get out of Jalil's kingdom. When she got closer, she slowed down, horrified at the sight of all the men lying on the ground. *Oh my God, they must be dead! Can this day get any worse?*

When Cassie saw a horse, fully saddled, standing in front of a tent, she didn't think twice. Tying her bag and blanket to the saddle, she grabbed the reins and hauled herself up onto its back. Jerking its head around, she began kicking, but the horse didn't move until she yelled and slapped it on the rump. Holding on for dear life, she pulled it in the direction of the main pass. She was still wearing the sheer silk tunic under her robe, and it bunched up around her thighs, providing no protection against the rough saddle. Gritting her teeth against the pain, she urged the horse faster.

When she saw Amit riding toward her with a dozen of his men, she waved him down. Seeing the look of lust on Amit's face, Cassie pulled up close to his horse and smiled her sultry smile. "Please, oh please, Sheik Amit. I need your help. I am trying to get away from that horrible Hashem. Will you help me?"

She watched him leer as his eyes traveled down her body. He immediately signaled to one of his men and pointed at Cassie. "Take her. We have to hurry."

In a matter of minutes, Cassie found herself, without her horse and bags, sitting in front of a smelly tribesman who looked familiar. She was further startled when she recognized who it was. *Nadim!*

"Well, hello, Cassie," he whispered loudly against her ear.

Cassie tried to turn her head so she could get a better look at him but was prevented when he jerked her back against him.

"Let me go," she cried out loudly.

"Oh, I think not. I expect Amit will have plans for you," he said in a low voice. "And if you do not behave, you will meet the same fate as Qadir." He laughed harshly.

"What would you know about that?" But Cassie was already having second thoughts.

"Have you not figured it out yet? If Hashem and Jalil didn't kill him, who else could have done it?"

"You! You killed Qadir! But how did you get in? I was there and I didn't see you. And there were guards outside."

"They were not paying attention, as usual. And really, it was easy. Zahra was only too glad to help sneak me inside the house."

"Well, you had better find a way to get me out of this, or I'm going to tell…" She wasn't able to finish as Nadim cut her off.

"Who? Who will you tell? Amit? He knew all about it. He paid me to do it. But I would have done it anyway. Qadir! Pah! He deserved to die like Akeem. Always putting me down, just like Hashem. Nadim do this…Nadim do that. Always the dirty jobs, and for what? Hashem took the credit and money. I was tired of both of them before Hashem shot me. But now, no one tells Nadim what to do except Nadim. As for you, you had better keep your mouth shut"

After everything that had happened that day, Cassie was at the end of her rope. She tried to protest further, wishing he would move his sword away from her bottom, but he ignored her. It was all she could do to just hold on when the entire group took off at a gallop. Her former relief at having escaped vanished. She had escaped from Hashem at last, but perhaps she had made a mistake. Closing her eyes, she held on, with only one thought on her mind. She was never coming back here again.

***

When Cassie darted from the room, Kira sprinted down the corridor to where Mirage and Amber were being kept and threw open the door leading to the outside. The startled guard stood in her way until he saw who it was. She flung open Mirage's stall door, clipped a rope to his halter and tied the loose end around his neck. Standing back, she yelled at the horse, "Go! Find Jalil!" She pressed back against the wall when he streaked by, leaping outside and heading toward the tents at a fast gallop. She then opened Amber's stall and stood to one side, allowing her horse to step out. Kira was still in her silk robes, but she couldn't wait. She took her dagger and split her tunic high enough to allow her to pull herself up and onto Amber's bare back to sit astride. As she rode through the doorway to the yard, she snatched the rifle from the startled guard's hands. He stood, stunned, and watched her ride off.

***

It was a good thing Cassie was not in her room when Nasira burst in through the door. "Cassie! Where are you?" Nasira spun about, brandishing her scimitar, ready to carve Cassie from head to toe. She stopped and lowered her sword when she saw the open shutters, and her fury morphed from boiling hot lava to glacial ice. Cursing, she ran back to the front of the house.

She arrived just in time to see Mirage race by. Shading her eyes, she saw Jalil near the tents, and Mirage was headed straight towards him. Hearing a sudden shout, she turned to see Kira on Amber, a rifle slung over her shoulder, her white robes shining in the sun. Smiling grimly, she watched her galloping after Mirage.

Satisfied Kira was going to help Jalil, Nasira ran back to the main hall. Two of the visiting sheiks were leaving when she arrived. She apologized for the confusion, but they waved and kept going, appearing eager to get in on the action. Ehsaan stayed behind. He was helping Fatima, but Nasira stepped in. "Ehsaan, I will take her with me. We will be in my chambers with Jabari."

"Thank you, Nasira. I must go. I need to be ready to assist Jalil." He nodded and left.

***

Jalil stared at Hashem's men lying on the ground and smiled. They were no threat, thanks to the handiwork of his mother, and he ran to the guest house. The door was open, and Hashem's horse was gone. He was too late. He looked toward the main pass, but all he could see were his own men. No rider in black. *Think, think! Where would Hashem go?* Then the cold realization of Hashem's plan fell into place. *The north pass!* That's where he would head. Frustrated, Jalil needed Mirage, and knew he was going to have to run back to the house to get him. He was going to lose precious time, time that could allow Hashem to escape. Turning to run back, he shouted with joy when he saw his silver stallion running toward him with all speed. He waited until the horse slowed, and when Mirage came alongside, Jalil grabbed his mane and leaped onto his back. Mirage was wearing a halter, and someone had clipped on a short rope, one that could serve as reins if needed. Somehow, Jalil knew Kira had done this for him. His heart swelled as he raced to the north pass, eager to take care of Hashem once and for all.

CHAPTER 53

When Hashem saw his men lying on the ground, he didn't wait to see what was wrong with them. All he could think about was getting away from Jalil. If he could just make it to his kingdom, he could empty Qadir's treasury and escape to the coast. He knew he could never recover from this if he stayed.

For a fleeting moment, he thought of Cassie with her long, crimson hair, soft as silk, and her full, pale breasts, and her remarkable skill in bed. He would miss her, but there had to be more "Cassies" in the world. He would just have to find one.

Grabbing a waterskin and a rifle from one of his men's tents, he made a beeline for his horse tied beside the guest house. Jumping into the saddle, he galloped off toward the north pass, hoping Jalil had moved most of his men closer to the compound. Hashem had left some of his men outside the main pass, ready to ride in to assist in the takeover, but when he saw the other sheiks in the meeting, he assumed his men had been detained, or worse. He whipped his horse harder, knowing that once he made the north pass, he could get away from Jalil.

But just before he entered the pass, he heard a distant shout and turned to see a far off flash of silver. *Jalil!* With no time to waste, he whipped his horse non-stop, but by the time they were high in the pass, his horse stumbled and came to stop. It was blowing hard and could barely walk. Hashem didn't know anything about horse breeding, but his herdmaster, or rather Qadir's herdmaster, had given him this horse saying it was from a superior bloodline and was a strong runner. As far as Hashem was concerned, it was no better than a camel. What Hashem didn't realize was that the horse hadn't been fed or watered that morning, so it wasn't at its best. And never trained to race and unused to a whip, it had been pushed to the limits of its endurance

Hashem tried beating it harder but only succeeded in frightening the animal. The horse started bucking, forcing him to slide out of the saddle. He was so angry he almost shot it then reconsidered. A gunshot would only alert any potential pursuers and give away his position. Disgusted, he grabbed his waterskin and abandoned the horse on the trail.

Without a horse, staying on the trail was not an option, but Hashem was familiar with the hidden trails surrounding Jalil's pass. He had spent years mapping them for Qadir, who had always wanted to steal Jalil's mares. Hashem had also used the trails to escape with Akeem's baby and to ambush Akeem, and more recently, Jalil. But this would be the first time he had to climb to the top of the wall from inside the pass.

He knew if he could find the right vantage point, he could kill Jalil. *How fitting*, he thought. He had helped kill Akeem not far from this same spot. Hopefully, he wouldn't have to kill Mirage. He needed a horse to get back to his kingdom before any of his men did, or worse, Amit. He realized now what Amit was planning. That man wanted to overthrow him and take control of Qadir's kingdom.

Scowling at the thought of Amit's duplicity, Hashem scurried farther up the trail, scanning the west wall for telltale breaks. He spied a vertical split lined with jutting stones and was soon standing on top of the wall. Dropping into the same trench he had used to ambush Jalil before, he found a spot to hide and crouched down to wait, ready to do it again.

***

Jalil was in a hurry to catch up to Hashem but as he approached the north pass, he signaled for Mirage to slow. He had not forgotten being ambushed in this same place and after witnessing the debacle of that day's trial, he knew it was Hashem who attacked him. But Hashem was a coward, and Jalil knew in his heart Hashem was going to try something—something dishonorable. Remaining on constant alert, he let his horse take the lead.

Mirage's ability to move without making noise never failed to amaze Jalil, and he often wondered about his stallion's true origins. Then he remembered how close to the north pass he'd been the day he found him wounded. Mirage had to have come from somewhere in the mountains or beyond on the north route. A sudden memory popped into his head of the hidden canyon he'd discovered while chasing the wounded man when he was ambushed. Maybe he would need to do some exploring once he had dealt with Hashem. That thought brought Kira and Amber to mind. It would be much more enjoyable to have them join him on such an excursion. But when Mirage stopped and huffed a warning, Jalil forgot all about the hidden canyon. Mirage knew they were in danger, and Jalil needed to pay attention.

Mirage was on full alert, and Jalil paid attention to his stallion's ears and body. Riding bareback made it easier to sense his horse's reactions. As he tried to concentrate on the trail ahead, Jalil couldn't help wondering what was happening back at his house. But realizing he couldn't afford distractions, he cleared his head, knowing he could trust his mother, Fahad, Kira, and especially Ehsaan to handle anything that might arise. *Thank Allah for Ehsaan.*

Suddenly, Jalil felt Mirage's shoulders stiffen and saw the horse's ears swivel then point forward. Mirage slowed and stopped, huffing softly. Suspicious, Jalil eased him closer to a jagged outcropping on the west cliff wall, hoping for more cover. He looked up, scanning the tops of the cliff, afraid of seeing Hashem standing over them, but there was nothing to be seen.

Mirage snorted softly and huffed again, and Jalil heard hoofbeats—very slow hoofbeats—from around the next bend. In his haste to follow Hashem, Jalil had no rifle, only his long sword, having given his scimitar to Kira. But he wasn't worried. He also had his father's dagger neatly stored in his bandolier. It would be enough.

Leaving Mirage under the shelter provided by the outcropping, he slid off and crept up the trail, crossing to the opposite wall. As the hoofbeats drew near, he pulled his long sword and flattened himself against the rocks but was surprised when a riderless horse approached from around the bend. It walked with its head drooping, and Jalil saw it was favoring one of its hind legs. He sheathed his sword and waited until the horse was almost beside him before stepping out into the trail.

The horse stopped, breathing harshly, but whickered softly and remained calm when Jalil patted its neck. Removing the saddle, he held the reins as he checked it over. Standing by the horse on the side by its wounded leg, he leaned his shoulder gently against its rump. The horse responded by shifting its weight and allowing Jalil to lift its hoof.

Jalil had already pulled out the smaller dagger hidden in the embellishment of his bandolier, and he gently dug out a rock he found wedged inside the hoof. The horse would still limp, and the bruising would take time to heal, but at least it wouldn't get worse. He set the hoof down, and the horse snorted and took a tentative step then looked back at him. Jalil had to chuckle seeing the relief in its eyes. Stripping off the bridle, he urged the horse back toward his pastures. The horse didn't hesitate and limped down the trail.

Now that Jalil had found the horse, he knew Hashem was on foot, and he no longer needed Mirage. He returned to Mirage's side and gently stroked his silky neck. When his hand passed over the old scar from Hashem's bullet, he remembered Hashem's treachery during the past Tri-Annual race. Jalil and Mirage had both been shot that day. Jalil had a score to settle with Hashem for that but would not risk Mirage a second time. "Mirage, I need you safe." He removed the rope but left the halter. "Now, go. Wait for me by the pool." Then he reached back and lightly slapped him on the rump. Mirage took off down the trail. Jalil watched until he disappeared around the bend. He hoped his horse would follow his command. He would never forgive himself if something happened to Mirage.

Jalil had not forgotten Hashem had used the west wall for his last ambush, so he kept tight to the base as he crept up the trail. Studying the trail floor, he looked for some sign of where Hashem had abandoned the horse. Close to the top of the pass, he saw multiple hoofprints and, just past, a boot print on the edge of the trail. He stopped and crouched down while he considered how best to proceed.

Although Jalil had no rifle, he was betting Hashem had grabbed one before heading to the north pass. But Jalil wasn't worried. He wanted to settle this with his sword. Feeling the hilt of his father's sword jutting from the ornate scabbard, Jalil smiled. How fitting it would be to kill Hashem with Akeem's blade.

As he watched the long shadows building in the pass, he knew sunset was not far away. *Should I wait until it is darker?* He felt torn. The longer he waited, the further Hashem could travel, but remembering the look on Hashem's face, he was betting Hashem would try to kill him first. The man was out of control and had exhibited a wildness of temperament, exactly like Qadir. If they were indeed brothers, Hashem could be prone to the same mental instabilities. Jalil wondered if maybe he could use that against Hashem. Glancing back at the shadows, he knew he needed to find him while he still had light and crept northward, scanning the ground often.

It was easier than he thought to find where Hashem had left the trail. He took a chance and stepped into the opening of the vertical cleft and looked up, half expecting to see Hashem's rifle pointed down at him. But he saw nothing and heard nothing. With a quick prayer to Allah, he began climbing.

When he reached the top, he stopped and held his breath. Still hearing nothing, he erred on the side of caution and raised one hand, only to jerk it back when a gunshot rang out and a bullet whistled by. It ricocheted off the opposite cliff face, and he knew Hashem was shooting from the same trench he had used before. It reiterated what he already knew—it had been Hashem who tried to kill him that day when he had gone to find the golden horse.

Breathing deeply, Jalil clung tightly to the rocks, thinking about Hashem's treachery. He had felt relief when he found Qadir's dead body the night he went to rescue Kira. He thought then all his troubles were over, although he'd felt cheated because he was not the one to deal the final blow. But it wasn't just Qadir who plotted to kill his family, it was also Hashem. At least now he would have his chance at retribution. The thought of that helped to steady him, filling him with an icy calm, a sense of being invincible, a feeling he was on the right path. *Kismet.* His mother was right, as always. Smiling grimly, he took another deep breath and waited for the cover of darkness.

***

Hashem peered over the edge of the trench in which he was kneeling. He was about thirty yards from the cleft in the rock where Jalil was hiding. The light grew dimmer as he waited for a glimpse of his enemy, and he began having doubts. Everything had gone wrong, almost from the moment he had ridden into Jalil's kingdom, and he couldn't comprehend how it had happened. He had spent years scheming and plotting, sacrificing his whole life to get to this point—and he had failed, all because of Jalil.

Since the first time Hashem became involved with Jalil, everything he tried to do to Jalil had failed. He had successfully kidnapped the baby, but somehow it had survived. Killing Akeem had been successful, but Jalil only grew stronger. And both attempts at taking Jalil's life, the race and weeks ago in this same spot, had been for naught. With Qadir gone, along with the meddlesome First Wife, Hashem should be enjoying his reward as sheik of a powerful kingdom. Instead, he was stuck in the middle of nowhere, without food, water, or a horse, and his greatest enemy was trying to kill him. *Why am I even here anymore?* Thanks to Jalil, it was all gone now, and he could never go back. All he could do was try to survive. *Is it worth my life to try to kill Jalil now?*

Hashem leaned back against the cold stones and realized he was tired, tired of fighting, tired of being angry, and tired of looking over his shoulder. Maybe he should just forget the whole thing. But then the other voice in his head, the one that never shut up, reminded him of how he felt in Jalil's hall today, how the other sheiks had looked at him with contempt, and how Jalil's women stared at him like he was nothing. A myriad of images assailed his mind as the memories of past injustices he had suffered paraded through his head.

The madness that was part of who he was began asserting itself, and an insidious curl of rage filled his being, its fiery tentacles spreading through his gut, down his legs, and into his arms. He gripped his rifle tighter. He was going to get out of here, but first he would watch Jalil's blood drain from his body when he sliced his throat.

As the darkness above reached down and melded with the shadows surrounding him, Hashem heard a noise echo in the pass, like a stone bouncing on the trail. *Jalil!* He rose cautiously but froze when he heard another noise—the deadly sound of a well-honed blade sliding from its sheath—followed by a voice, just as deadly.

"Hashem, I know you are there. It is time for you and me to finish this."

Hashem's heart stopped. In the dark grip of his madness, it was a voice from the past that he heard. *Akeem! He has come for revenge!* At some level, he recognized the voice and knew it was Jalil, but for a moment it sounded like Akeem. And the fact Hashem was near the same place where he helped murder Akeem didn't help. The hair rose on his neck, and sweat dripped down his back. He tried to swallow but his mouth was dry. "Jalil, you should go back to your family. You will not survive this fight. I helped kill your father, and I will kill you. There is no Mirage to help you this time." When he heard Jalil laughing at him, his rage exploded, and something snapped inside.

***

After the events of the day, Jalil now knew Hashem was just like Qadir in every way. If he could push him a little too far, Hashem would lose control. "Oh, Hashem, I would tell you to go home to your family... oh, that's right, you do not have any. That is too bad. You could go home to your kingdom... oh, that's right, you will not have one after today. I will make sure of that. I guess the only thing left for you to do is fight me. And it is you who will not survive." Jalil tensed, hoping Hashem would react like he thought he would, and Hashem did.

Crouching near the edge of the cliff, Jalil saw a dark form framed by stars leap from the trench, screaming in fury, and fire wildly at him. Jalil heard the bullet whine as it passed close to his head, but he was already on the move. He charged. Hashem panicked, dropped his rifle, and drew his sword, and they came together with a clash. The fight was furious! Thrust and parry, stab, and retreat. Jalil was finding Hashem to be a better swordsman than he thought, and the man's madness made him bold. Jalil was hard pressed to escape his blows, especially on the uneven surface of the cliff top.

Wanting to stay away from the edge of the cliff, Jalil jumped into the trench. Hashem followed suit, and they continued fighting, moving southward. The ring of their swords, interspersed with yells of pain when they felt the sting of each other's blades, echoed nosily in the pass. But Jalil found his second wind and felt a new energy as he fought. He couldn't see Hashem's face clearly and heard the older man's labored breathing, but Hashem didn't slow down, and the fight raged on.

Listening to Hashem snarl and growl like an animal, Jalil realized Hashem was out of his mind. The man fought with almost superhuman strength, and Jalil grew concerned as Hashem forced him farther and farther down the trench. When they reached a dead end, Jalil found himself with his back against the rocks, struggling to fend off a flurry of blows. His opponent was striking wildly from every angle with tremendous force, surprising Jalil with the intensity of his attack. But Jalil would not give up. He had to win this fight. Searching deep within, he had a sudden vision of his father's face and found his hidden strength. He leaped forward, no longer on the defensive.

As he forced Hashem back up the trench, Jalil could sense him weakening. They were both bleeding profusely from many cuts, and Jalil knew Hashem had to be feeling the pain. The man was having trouble fending off his blows, but unfortunately, Jalil's foot slipped on a stray rock, and he cried out in agony as Hashem's blade sliced deep into his thigh. Falling to one knee, he was able to steady himself and surprised Hashem by slicing him across the ribs, feeling his sword grating on bone.

Hashem screamed in pain and staggered backward but didn't fall. Jalil couldn't stand and held his sword at the ready. He wouldn't give up.

Hashem began to laugh. "I hope you said goodbye to your horse, Jalil. I am going to kill him like I killed Rayham. And I am going to cut your throat, just like Qadir did to Akeem. Then I'm going to kill your mother and take your sisters. I will destroy everyone in your family except Kira. I have plans for her." He sneered as he advanced.

Suddenly, Jalil gasped as he felt a burning sensation on his chest. Looking down, he saw his father's medallion had slipped through his shirt and was in full view. It glowed with an unearthly light, and he stared at it for a second then tore his eyes from the sight. He couldn't afford to be distracted. But when he looked up, he could see the whites of Hashem's eyes. The man seemed mesmerized by the medallion—his sneer had vanished, and his sword tip was wavering.

Jalil knew in that moment he was being given a chance. And he took it. Summoning his remaining strength, he lunged upward, knocked Hashem's blade aside, and buried his sword in Hashem's heart. Then Jalil grabbed him by the shoulder and pulled him closer, pushing his blade completely through Hashem's body until he stood inches from his face.

Hashem glanced down at the hilt of Jalil's sword sticking out of his chest then looked up, and even in the dim light, Jalil could see his eyes fill with shock and surprise.

Jalil smiled grimly. "Goodbye, Hashem."

As Hashem's body slumped to the ground, Jalil pulled his sword free but fell backwards when his leg gave out. Catching himself on the side of the trench, he slid downward until he ended up sitting with his back against the wall, breathing heavily. It was over. He closed his eyes, and he saw a vision of his father's smiling face and could see the pride in his eyes. He had avenged his father's death. Jalil could finally rest and look to his own future.

Listening to the wind whistle through the rocks, he began feeling faint and grew cold. He wiped his sword on the remains of his robe and sheathed it. Feeling along his body, he discovered a multitude of painful cuts, but when he touched his thigh, he groaned. His trousers were soaked with blood. It was a serious wound. Removing the cord from his waist, he tied it around the top of his thigh, pulling it tight. Gasping aloud, he almost passed out from the pain but knew he had to stay awake if he was going to get home.

Climbing out of the trench, he dragged himself to the split in the cliff he had climbed up earlier and collapsed at the edge, shivering in despair. When he heard the stallion's bugle, his heart filled with hope.

"Mirage! Mirage!" he yelled. Then he heard the voice that would forever ring in his heart.

"Jalil! Jalil! Where are you?" He knew then, as he had known since the first time she'd said his name, she would save him. *Kira!* Looking down into the cleft, he saw she was almost at the top. When she looked up, he gazed into her eyes, her amazing eyes. They were full of stars.

"Kira," he sighed, and darkness descended.

CHAPTER 54

"Kismet," Nasira whispered as she watched Jabari eating a bowl of warm soup.

"What did you say, Mother?"

"Nothing, my son, nothing." She was thinking about everything that had happened since the kidnapping of her baby. It had all started with a gold dagger, and it had ended with a gold dagger. *But has it ended?* She was worried. Jalil and Kira were out there somewhere, and it was growing dark.

Hiding her worry from Jabari, she walked to the table to fetch a cup of lemonade. She considered trying to get him to drink some warm tea with her special herbs, but Jabari had told her he knew what she was up to and said he preferred a little pain over the potion. After hearing about Hashem's men, he had been leery of drinking anything Nasira or Samira tried to give him. She chuckled to herself. *He is a smart boy, well, a smart man.* She gave him the cup, exchanging it for the empty bowl.

"Mother, I can't stop thinking about Rizu. Do you think he's all right? I really need to go search for him." He wiped his mouth and took a sip of his lemonade.

"Do not worry about Rizu. We have men out looking for him. They will tell us when they find him, and they will find him," she said, returning to the chair by his bed.

"I pray to Allah it will be so. But I am also confused," he said and yawned deeply.

"I will try to help you if I can, but this is the last question. You need to rest."

"I was wondering about Cassie," he said, his expression serious. "Did she take me up that trail on purpose? Was she the one who hit me?"

Nasira had been waiting for him to ask about Cassie. She had given him a brief summary of the trial, but she hadn't been sure if he had understood his own part in Hashem's evil plan. "Jabari, what do you think?"

He looked down at the cuts on his hands and the rope marks on his wrists and frowned. "I think Cassie used me to steal Rizu then left me on that trail. But I do not understand why." He looked lost.

Nasira wanted to spare him further pain, but he needed to know the truth. "Jabari, it may be hard for you to hear this, but Hashem wanted you eliminated because you are Jalil's only heir. And we know Cassie was working with him all along."

"I am sorry I caused so much trouble. I should have known better." He was still staring at his hands.

"Jabari, look at me." She waited until he raised his head. "You have done nothing wrong. You tried to help someone, and they took advantage of you. It could have happened to anyone. I should have done something sooner about Cassie, but she had me fooled, too."

Jabari seemed to relax, but he still looked worried. "Do you think she hurt Rizu?" he said with a hitch in his voice.

Nasira knew how much he loved his colt, and seeing his pain almost broke her heart. "Jabari, listen to me. Cassie may have meant to kill you, but you survived. I believe, as does Samira, that you are destined for greater things, and I also believe Rizu is part of your destiny. So no, I do not believe she hurt Rizu. Her plan failed, as did Hashem's, and we have Allah to thank for that. And Jalil and Kira and Ehsaan. So many people care about us, and we owe them everything." She smoothed the hair from his brow and felt his forehead, checking for fever.

"I will remember that always, my sheikha." He nodded with a small smile.

She knew he was being sincere but smiled at his use of her title. "Thank you, Jabari the Magnificent," she answered in kind.

"You are welcome. But I was wondering—"

She cut him off. "I already told you. No more questions."

"But, please, one more?" he said as she tucked the blanket around him.

"What is it you must know now?"

"Is it true you ran down the hall brandishing a scimitar?" he said wide-eyed.

"Me? With a scimitar? Oh, Jabari, you must have a fever," she said, trying not to laugh.

He studied her seriously, but his eyes were drooping. "Jalil is right. I should never underestimate a woman," he muttered as he fell asleep.

She relaxed hearing Jabari's breathing deepen, pleased he was sleeping peacefully.

Samira showed up at sunrise with Nasira's senior healer, Maryam, by her side, and motioned frantically for Nasira to come out into the corridor.

Nasira hurried to her side. "Samira, what is it? What is wrong?"

"My sheikha, they have found Jalil! We need you in his quarters immediately."

Nasira's heart stuttered, and her face paled. "Is he…is he…" She couldn't finish.

"He is alive, but he is injured and has lost a great deal of blood. You must hurry. Maryam will stay with Jabari."

Nasira didn't hesitate and ran to the sheik's wing, leaving the pregnant Samira trailing behind her. She found Jalil on his bed, unconscious, surrounded by Kira, Fahad, and Sakhr. The men had cut away his tunic and trousers and covered him partially with a sheet. One leg lay exposed, and Nasira's eyes were drawn to the bloody thigh. Kira had wrapped bandages around the cuts on his arms, tying them tight enough to stop any bleeding, but seemed hesitant to touch his thigh.

When Kira looked at her with indecision, Nasira understood and gently pulled her away. "Kira, go sit in the front room. I will handle this wound." Kira nodded tearfully and, after a long, lingering look at Jalil, hurried from the room.

Nasira swallowed hard and prayed. *Allah, be merciful.* She wiped away the gore, revealing a long, deep gash. It bled sluggishly and she sighed with relief that the major vein wasn't cut. *Allah be praised!* It was a serious wound and would require a lot of attention to prevent infection. She would need to drain and repack it several times over the next few days. Then it would have to be stitched, inside and out. It would take time to hea,l but heal it would. She would see to that. For now, she wrapped it then placed rolled blankets on either side to prevent him from moving his leg.

When Samira showed up, Nasira put her in charge of organizing the servants to bring hot water, clean bandages, and as much suture material as they could find. While Nasira flushed the gash and packed it with herbs, she had Samira fix some of her pain draught. Jalil hadn't awakened, and she needed him to drink the potion. She tried calling his name and stroking his face, but when he didn't stir, she was afraid he might have lost too much blood. *What can I do? What will make him wake up?* Then it came to her. "Kira, I need you," she called aloud.

Kira rushed into the room but kept her eyes averted from Jalil's mostly naked body. Nasira could see her blushing. "It's all right, Kira. We covered him enough. But I need him to wake up and drink some medicine for pain and healing."

"What can I do?" Kira said, wringing her hands.

Nasira could see evidence of her tears. "Talk to him. Try to get him to wake up. He will listen to you." She pulled Kira to the side of the bed, and Fahad brought a chair over so Kira could sit close to Jalil. Nasira sent everyone from the room, then handed a cup to Kira. "Try to get him to drink this," she said to Kira and stepped just outside the room where she could watch and listen, ready to assist if Kira needed her.

Kira was looking down at Jalil. She laid her hand on his brow, and she traced his dark eyebrows with a fingertip. She lightly ran her finger down his straight nose and gently across his lips. "Jalil... Jalil. Wake up, Jalil. It's Kira. I need you." She half-whispered, moving her hand to cup his firm jaw.

Jalil stirred, and hearing him groan in pain, Nasira almost rushed back to his side but forced herself to wait and see what Kira would do next.

Kira took one of his hands and wrapped hers around it. "Jalil, please wake up. It's Kira." She let out a little squeak when his eyes flew open, and he squeezed her hand tightly.

He stared at her and whispered hoarsely, "Cassie?"

Nasira gasped. *Cassie?* She held her breath when she saw Kira start to pull away but exhaled with relief when Jalil suddenly smiled. "Kira," he breathed.

Kira nodded. "Yes, Jalil, I'm here." She leaned down and brushed his lips with hers.

Jalil moaned again, but Nasira didn't think it sounded like he was in pain. His eyes closed, and he sighed loudly, "Kira, ya hayati."

Kira's blush deepened. "Jalil, I need you to drink something for me. Can you do that?"

When Jalil attempted to rise, Kira called for Fahad. He rushed in and lifted Jalil's shoulders high enough for Kira to hold the cup to his lips.

Jalil's eyes fluttered open, and he frowned. "Kira, ya hayati, do not cry."

With tears in her eyes, Kira laughed lightly. "It is all right, Jalil. I am just happy to see you. Now, you need to drink something. Please try for me."

Jalil never took his eyes off Kira, and though he choked at first, he persevered until he finished most of it. When Jalil shook his head and groaned, Fahad eased him back then left the room. Kira leaned over, kissed Jalil gently and rose, but when he grabbed her hand, she sat back down. She stayed beside him until he fell asleep.

Nasira was pleased to see them finally connecting and smiled as she stepped back into the room. Once she determined Jalil was feeling no pain, she checked his other wounds and took time to show Kira how to stitch some of the deeper cuts. Jalil slept on, oblivious to their work, allowing them to finish without causing him any more discomfort. Once they were done, Nasira put Maryam in charge, sent Kira to get some rest, and went to check on her children. It would be a long night, and she would not rest until she knew Jalil had survived the hours ahead.

When next Jalil woke, it was late the next afternoon. Nasira heard his groans and rushed to his side. "Jalil, don't move!" She pressed lightly on his shoulders when he tried to rise.

"Where am I?" he said groggily, glancing around his room.

"You are in your bed," she said, grimacing when he cried out in pain.

"My leg! It hurts!"

"Hush, Jalil. At least you still have a leg. Now, please try to calm down," she said brusquely, determined not to coddle him too much.

"But…what..," he stuttered, then suddenly, his eyes widened. "Hashem!"

"Is dead. He will no longer bother our family, thanks to you," Nasira said as she wiped his face with a damp cloth.

He seemed to digest this then suddenly grabbed her arm. "Kira?"

"Is fine. She would not leave your side until I forced her to go get some rest."

Sighing, he closed his eyes. "Thank Allah." But then his eyes flew open. "But what about Cass—"

Nasira cut him off. "Cassie is gone. Now, you need to drink your medicine," she said, holding up a large cup.

Seeing him eyeing the cup suspiciously, she used her best "I am your mother" voice. "I will not answer any more questions until you do." When he suddenly scowled and looked so much like he had when he was a little boy, she struggled not to laugh.

"You think this is funny?"

"Absolutely not, my sheik," she said firmly, turning away to hide her smile.

He pouted, but in the end, he drained the cup then settled back on his pillow. "Now, tell me what is going on."

Nasira described what happened when he left the meeting hall while she fussed with his blankets and checked his stitches. She dragged out her story to give her potion time to work.

"How is Jabari?" he said drowsily.

"Jabari is fine. Mirage is fine. Amber is fine. And, as you have already been told, Kira is fine. Now, that is enough questions for today. We can talk about this tomorrow."

"I get it. Everyone is fine…except me," he mumbled as he dropped off to sleep.

Nasira smoothed the damp hair from his brow. "Good night, my sheik," she said and sighed tiredly. She was exhausted, but before she could rest, she needed to check his leg. With Maryam's help, she removed the bandages and applied more ointment. Making sure it was still draining well, she re-wrapped it. Leaving Maryam in charge, Nasira sent for Fahad. He arrived within minutes and declared he would guard his sheik the rest of the day and through the night and would send for her if Jalil needed her. Satisfied Jalil was in good hands, she went to check on her daughters. Nasira would stay with them until she could move Jabari from her own chambers back to his.

But on her way, she had one more stop to make. Kira answered on the first knock. She was wearing a sleeping tunic, and her long golden hair was in wild disarray. It was obvious she had been asleep.

"How is he?" Kira said breathlessly.

"He is fine. He woke up, but I made him drink more tea, and now he is sleeping."

"Thank God," Kira said. "May I see him?"

"Perhaps later. Right now, he must rest. But I would like to talk to you for a minute if that is all right?"

"Oh, yes, Sheikha. I am so sorry. Please come in," Kira said, apparently embarrassed for having made Nasira stand in the hall.

"Thank you, Kira. And from now on, please call me Nasira," she said and settled in a chair by the table.

"Yes, Nasira. Can I get you something to drink… or…"

"No, thank you. Now, come and sit. I need to tell you something," Nasira said and waited for Kira to take a seat before continuing. "Kira, I want to thank you for bringing Jalil home to us."

Kira's eyes widened. "But it wasn't me. It was Mirage and the men. If they hadn't shown up when they did, I don't know what I would have done. I could never have gotten him down from that cliff."

"Oh, I am sure there is more to the story, but all that can wait. When Jalil is stronger, we will all sit down together to hear the whole tale."

"I look forward to that, but how is Jabari?"

"He is much better. At first, I was very concerned. He was talking nonsense when he first woke, but that is not unusual with head wounds. Still, it was alarming," Nasira said.

"What kind of nonsense?"

"Oh, something about a trail and Rizu and a golden stallion," Nasira said.

"Golden stallion?" Kira sounded alarmed.

Nasira looked over at her. Kira's eyes were wide with an unreadable expression, and she was pressing a hand to her chest.

"Yes. He said he rode a golden stallion. Oh, Kira, you know he has always talked about golden horses. Samira said he did it his whole life. Why does that upset you?"

"Oh, no, I'm not upset," Kira stuttered then continued more calmly, "I just know how dangerous head wounds are."

Kira was acting strangely, but Nasira figured she was just worried about Jabari. "Kira, why don't you check on Jabari? I know he would love to see you. I am going to take a nap. Perhaps we could meet for the evening meal then we can check on Jalil."

"Yes, I would like that," Kira said but stopped her by the door. "Will you be serving tea at the evening meal?"

Nasira thought it a strange question until she saw Kira smiling mischievously. Shaking her head, she chuckled as she made her way next door. Within minutes, she was soundly sleeping—her worries forgotten, and her world restored.

CHAPTER 55

Kira woke suddenly, breathing hard. She blinked slowly and glanced up at her window, the scrollwork barely visible. Shivering in the pre-dawn cool, she stumbled out of bed, lurched over to the table, and sat down with a huff. She rubbed her temple with one hand and reached for the water pitcher. Filling a goblet, she gulped noisily. When she felt her heartbeat slow, she sighed. A dream. It was only a dream. *Wasn't it?* Faint images flitted through her mind, and she closed her eyes again, concentrating, trying to recapture what she had seen.

She had been in the valley, swimming in the lake, and when she rose from the waters, she saw the herd spread across the hills. She saw the ruins, but they changed, wavering like a mirage, and became buildings of bleached stucco. It was beautiful. Leaving the water, she walked toward the structures but stopped when she heard a distant shout. Turning, she looked toward the cliffs and gasped at the sight of a horse with a rider galloping toward her. At first, all she could see was the dazzling white of the rider's robes and the shimmering gold of the horse's coat. When they were almost upon her, she recognized the rider. His silver eyes were shining, and he smiled and waved. Jabari! The stallion bugled, and she recognized him at once. Ndee! They flew past, and she called to him to stop, but they didn't slow.

Hearing a sharp whinny behind her, she spun around and watched a blood-red colt dash by. Rizu?! Running after him, she stumbled and fell to her knees. Looking up, she was in the cavern. And it was full of light, and she heard the rushing water from the holes in the cavern floor. Rising into the air, she floated closer and closer to the eastern tunnel, and the engraving on the entrance began glowing in bands of turquoise, gold, and white. Her ears filled with a stallion's bugle. It seemed to come from everywhere and nowhere, and the last thing she saw was Ndee and Jabari disappearing into the tunnel.

It had seemed so real. She poured herself another cup of water and gulped it down. Wiping her mouth, she took a few deep breaths and cleared her thoughts, but the image of Rizu running behind Ndee in the valley flashed through her mind. Suddenly, she knew what she had to do.

Throwing on her riding clothes, she grabbed a robe and headwrap and turned to go but stopped and ran back to grab the old medallion. She had taken to wearing it more—she actually felt complete with it around her neck. She briefly considered checking on Jalil, but she'd stayed in his room for hours after the evening meal the previous night, just watching him sleep. The urge to see Jabari was stronger.

When he didn't answer his door, she peeked inside, thinking he might be asleep, but the room was empty. He must be with Sarii, she thought. Hurrying outside, she spied him standing by the fence, talking to his mare.

"Jabari," she called out.

Jabari turned when she approached. "Kira! What are you doing out so early?"

"I was going to ask you the same question. Aren't you supposed to be in bed?" she chided.

"Mother has pronounced me almost healed. She said I could go outside. But not for long periods. I do not see what all the fuss is about. I feel fine," he said.

"It must be hard not being able to ride every day, but you'll be back in the saddle before you know it," Kira said encouragingly. "Just do what the sheikha says. She knows best."

"Yes, she does…and she often reminds me of that." He chuckled ruefully. Then he must have seen her trousers peeking out from beneath her robe because he asked, "Are you going riding?"

"Yes. I think Amber needs a little exercise this morning. A good gallop will do her good. She is getting lazy, I think."

"Oh, I wish I could go with you," he said. "I miss Rizu. I need to find him, Kira. What if Cassie did something to him?" His eyes were full of pain for his beloved colt.

"Jabari, she didn't hurt Rizu. She was only after you. I am sure he just ran off. But I'll tell you what. I am going to take a long ride along the cliffs and maybe, just maybe, Amber can find him."

"Oh, Kira, if anyone can, Amber can," he said fervently. "Do you remember where you found me?"

"Yes, and I will start there," she said, reaching out to pat Sarii. "You really have done a wonderful job with Sarii."

"She has exceeded my expectations, considering she belonged to Qadir's tribe. But she is not Rizu, and she is not gold."

His words reminded her of his dream. "Jabari, your mother told me you dreamed you rode a golden stallion?"

Jabari absently stroked Sarii's cheek and stared off at the cliffs with a pensive expression. "Kira, you know I have always dreamed of riding a golden stallion. Ever since I was very small. But this time, well, this time, it was different."

"Why?"

"Well, I dreamed I was crawling in the dark, and there was a cave and water. I heard roaring water," Jabari said and clenched his eyes tight. "And then I was in a beautiful valley. I remember seeing a stream and hills—it was amazing. And Rizu was there. He found me."

Kira steeled herself to listen and not react. His story was all too familiar. Her hand strayed to the medallion under her shirt, and she shivered in the hot sun. "What happened next?"

"The golden stallion came, Kira. He helped me, and he let me ride him. He carried me through the darkness and brought me home." Jabari turned, and his eyes darkened to stormy gray. "No one believes me, but it does not matter. I know he is real." He turned back to look out across the hills. "He is out there," he whispered, "and I will ride him again someday."

Kira was reeling. Jabari had just described the valley, the cavern, and Ndee. *How is this possible?* When she felt the ancient medallion against her chest flare with a burst of heat, she jerked, filled with a sudden urgency. "Jabari, I believe you. Don't ask me why, but I do," she said sincerely.

He surprised her by pulling her into a quick hug. "Thank you, Kira," he whispered in her ear. Then he released her just as quickly and turned away, but not before she saw him blush.

Knowing he was struggling with his emotions, she left before she started to tear up. "I'll be back, Jabari. I will find your Rizu." But before she took one step, Jabari looked over her shoulder, and his eyes widened. She turned to see Amber galloping toward them.

Jabari laughed. "It looks like someone is ready to run."

Bewildered, Kira shook her head. Amber slid to a stop in front of her and furiously pawed the ground. "I guess I'd better hurry," Kira said and climbed up on Amber's back. Waving at Jabari, she held on as Amber took off for the pasture, barely slowing to jump the gate.

After hearing Jabari's dream, Kira wondered if there was a connection between the hidden trail where Cassie had ambushed Jabari and Rizu's disappearance. Amber must have read her mind—she was already galloping in that direction—and didn't stop until they neared the familiar boulders. Kira slipped from her back and signaled for Amber to wait, but her horse ignored her and pushed past to disappear behind the rocks.

Hurrying to catch up, Kira followed Amber up the narrow path. She had a feeling that Amber had been on this path before because the horse moved quickly, as if she knew the way. Once the ground leveled off, Amber abruptly stopped. Kira peered around her and saw a rock pile blocking their way ahead. *Landslide. Is it recent?* Disappointed, she considered turning back until Amber whinnied loudly and pawed the ground. Curious, Kira watched as Amber calmly walked over to a tall rectangular block of stone on the west side of the trail and disappeared behind it. Kira stood frozen, shocked at the implications. *Oh, my God!* Hearing a loud whinny echoing from within the cliff, she came to her senses and dashed around the stone. She hesitated when she saw the dark tunnel but threw caution to the wind and plunged inside.

It was fortunate she had slowed. The tunnel was steep, and she almost pitched forward on the slippery slope leading downward. Hearing Amber ahead, she crept forward cautiously, but suddenly, she felt her medallion growing hot. Alarmed, she glanced down and saw a brief glow from under her shirt, but it quickly vanished along with the burning sensation. Shaking her head and blaming her overactive imagination, she continued down the slope for some time until she thought she could see a dim light ahead. With one hand on the wall, she eased closer to what appeared to be an exit, but when she stepped out of the tunnel, she fell to her knees. It was all she could do to breathe. It was *the* cavern and in that moment, something clicked in her head, and she understood then—she understood everything.

Kira wasn't sure how long she kneeled there in the dim light that fell from the cracks far above her. It was quiet except for the rushing of the river underneath the stone floor. She finally rose to her feet and walked through the main tunnel she knew led from the cavern into the valley until she could see the bright glare of the desert sun calling to her at the far end. Now she picked up her pace and began running. When she burst forth into the light, she couldn't help but cry out. The valley! It had been here all along.

Flinging her arms outward, she spun in circles, laughing in joy, but stopped when she heard a familiar bugle. Turning, she watched in awe as two shining horses raced towards her. Ndee and Amber slid to a stop, tossing their heads and stamping their hooves. Grinning hugely, Kira walked quickly towards them, pleased when Ndee allowed her to stroke his arched neck. "Hello, old friend," she crooned. He bent his head and nickered softly. "I missed you too," she said, daring to give him a hug. He tolerated it for a second before stepping back with a huff. She chuckled at the look in his eye. He wasn't really mad.

Kira had a sudden thought. "Amber, I've noticed you disappear occasionally. Is this where you go?" Kira had often wondered what Amber did all day after their morning ride. She was never around the stables. "I wish I had known sooner." Then she had another thought. "Why did you want to come here today?" As if Amber could read her mind, the horse neighed loudly, once, then twice, and Kira heard a high-pitched whinny, and her heart soared when she saw the blood-red colt running toward her.

"Rizu!" she yelled. Rizu tossed his head high, neighed again, and cantered to her side. She threw her arms around his neck, and he snorted and huffed but didn't pull away. "Oh, Rizu, I am so glad to see you. Jabari is worried sick. You must come home at once," Kira said then quickly inspected him and noted a few minor scrapes on his knees and one mark on his hip. It was clearly the nip of a horse, and she looked at Ndee accusingly, but he wouldn't meet her gaze. Chuckling, Kira shook her head, and once she determined Rizu was without injury, she stepped back and said, "How am I going to get you home?"

Rizu was busy sniffing at her pockets, and Kira watched as Amber moved behind the colt and nudged him gently but firmly. He snorted and took a step forward, and Kira smiled, immediately understanding what Amber was doing. Kira noted Ndee watching them, but he didn't interfere. He nodded once and cantered back toward the lake. She knew she would see him again. Amber continued to herd Rizu toward the tunnel, and Kira followed. Soon they were making their way up the steep, slippery slope of the little tunnel that led toward home.

As she struggled to keep up, Kira's mind was spinning with everything she had learned that morning. She wanted desperately to share her findings, and only one person came to mind—the one person who needed to know, who deserved to know. Kira had discovered Jalil's legacy and couldn't wait to tell him. But first, there was a boy waiting for his colt.

CHAPTER 56

Nasira stood on the steps and waved goodbye to Ehsaan and his men and thanked Allah for good friends and strong allies. She appreciated he had waited to leave until Jalil was past danger and would never forget how he had helped to defeat their common enemy.

Across the compound, she saw Saad directing the removal of the temporary tents, and couldn't help chuckling, remembering how Fahad had rousted Hashem's men the previous day, not too gently, and sent them on their way, even though most of them were still groggy from her tea. Everyone was still laughing about that, and Ehsaan had asked her to send the recipe to Issa.

Glancing toward the stables Nasira saw Jabari standing by the fence talking to Sarii. She'd asked Sakhr to keep an eye on him and remind him when it was time to rest. Jabari was healing nicely, but she was concerned about his growing depression over the loss of Rizu and was half afraid he would try to search for him. She would prefer he stay inside a few more days but knew she was fighting a losing battle.

Jalil was Nasira's greater worry. Though he was out of immediate danger, she was uneasy about the deep slash in his thigh. It required constant attention. As it was already time to check it again for drainage, she made her way to his quarters.

When she entered, she nodded at Maryam, who sat at the table grinding herbs for more potions. Jalil was still sleeping, and she felt his forehead, pleased there was no fever. While she checked his leg and replaced the bandage, he moaned, but didn't waken. After disposing of the dirty bandages, she mixed a fresh batch of medicine, adding a lighter dose of the sleeping herb. Leaving instructions for Maryam to coax him into drinking more water if he woke, she went to fetch some meat broth from the cook.

On the way to the kitchen, she stopped by her chambers, relieved to find Jabari had returned from the stable and was taking a nap. Evidently, he had paid attention when she described the side effects from head wounds. Satisfied, she went next door to check on Kira, but she was gone. *Probably out riding,* she thought, and figured she would catch up with her later.

When she returned to Jalil's quarters, he was awake and hungry. As she spoon-fed him the rich, meaty broth, she caught him smiling at her with an amused expression.

"What is so funny, Jalil?" Nasira asked as she wiped a bit of broth from his chin and set the empty bowl aside.

"I feel like a child again." He chuckled.

"Jalil, you are the biggest child I have ever seen." She teased and felt his forehead.

"By the way, how is your other child?"

"Jabari is doing well, but I am having trouble keeping him inside. He has been to see Sarii already. As usual, he is more concerned about a horse than himself."

"Hmm, that sounds familiar," Jalil said with a grin.

"Yes. But Jalil, I still have trouble thinking about what Cassie did. If she had hit Jabari any harder, he would not have survived." Nasira shook her head, feeling a rush of anger. "She should thank Allah I didn't catch up with her," she said fiercely.

"I know you told me something about what happened after I left, but I remember only a little after chasing down Hashem. Did anyone see where Cassie went?" He eyed her closely.

Nasira wished she had a different answer. "After she ran out of the main hall, I went to her room, but she had fled. One man thinks he saw her on a horse headed for the main pass, but in all the confusion, no one was paying attention to her. I do not know where she thinks she can go. Without an escort, she will likely come to a bad end, but frankly, I do not care. She is gone, and I hope we never see her again," Nasira said with a growl.

"I have no doubt Cassie has seen a side of you she will never want to see again. She will never return here." He smiled and patted her hand.

Nasira relaxed. "Humph. If she ever comes back here, it will be the last thing she ever does. But enough about her. I am worried about Jabari. He is insisting he needs to search for Rizu."

"I had forgotten about Rizu." He frowned and settled deeper into his cushions, grimacing when he shifted his leg. "I hope this thing gets better soon. I need to help Jabari find his colt."

"But Jalil, after what Cassie did to Jabari, I fear for Rizu. What did she do with him? Where could he have gone?"

"I do not know, but I cannot conceive something bad has happened to him."

"I pray you are right, Jalil. It would devastate Jabari. I think he feels like it is his fault since he is the one that taught Cassie how to handle Rizu in the first place."

"Poor Jabari. All he was doing was being Jabari. He is always helpful, and I am proud of him and could not wish for a better brother."

"He feels the same way about you. I just hope you are right about Rizu," Nasira said as she stood. "Now, I am going to look for Kira. Is there anything I can do for you?"

"Well, now that you ask, I was going to talk to you about Kira. I want to try again with her and do it right this time, but I would rather wait until I can get out of this bed. When do you think I will be well enough to move around?"

"You cannot rush your healing. This is a very serious wound, and I still have to stitch it, which I cannot do yet. I think we might know more in about a week. I am sorry, Jalil. But I also do not think you should wait too long to talk to her." She knew what he wanted to talk to Kira about. "It might help if you ask her to sit with you daily. I know she wants to. It will give you both time to talk and get to know each other better."

He smiled slowly. "I think that is a good idea, Mother. Would you let her know I would like her to spend time with me? Tell her it might help me heal faster."

"Oh, there is no doubt she could help you. I will send her to see you. Now, you need to rest some more. And this time, I left you two goblets. If you have pain, drink the tea, otherwise drink the lemonade. Both will help."

"All right. Could you send Fahad to see me too? I want to talk to him about Rizu."

"I will, but you must promise to keep it short." She gave him a stern look.

"I promise, but I suspect you will say the same to Fahad." He gave her a mock glare, and she laughed all the way out the door.

Nasira joined her daughters for the midday meal. They were in good spirits now that both their brothers were out of danger. Of course, Lina wanted to join in the search for Rizu, but Akilah said she was happy to leave it to Fahad. When they pestered Nasira for details of the last few days, she shared an abbreviated version of the trial and Jalil's battle with Hashem. The tale of Hashem's men and the now infamous tea had them laughing out loud. Pleased to see her girls unaffected by the drama, she sent them off to their chambers with the promise they could visit Jalil and Jabari later in the day.

Making her rounds, she again stopped by Kira's room, only to be disappointed. Where had she gone? Trying not to worry, she went next door and found Jabari finishing a bowl of stew at the table. "And how is my other patient doing?"

"I am tired of staying inside, Mother. I want to go look for Rizu."

"Jabari, we have had this discussion. You cannot ride yet. It is too risky."

"Riding is not risky." He scowled.

"Falling is." She fixed him with a no-nonsense look.

Jabari laughed. "I never fall off." He glanced up at her, but when she didn't laugh, he changed tactics. "Well, I will not ride then. I will walk," he said stubbornly.

"Oh, Jabari," Nasira said sitting down next to him. "I know you miss Rizu, but I cannot let you go looking for him just yet."

"Well, at least Kira is trying."

"Kira?"

"I spoke with her as the sun was rising. She and Amber have gone looking for Rizu," he said as he finished his stew.

Nasira sat back and considered his words. That explained why Kira had been gone all day.

Seeing Jabari's empty goblet, she refilled it with tea but was curious when he stared at it as if hesitant to drink. She wondered why until she noticed his skeptical expression, and it suddenly dawned on her.

"Jabari, it is just tea," she said, chuckling. It appeared the story of Hashem's men would not be forgotten soon.

When he gave her a sheepish grin then took a sip, she studied her youngest son and noted his good color and clear eyes. He was doing better than expected, and inspired, she reached over to tap him on the arm. "Jabari, I think you need to take a walk. It would do you good to get more fresh air and exercise." She rose and extended her arm.

Jabari's face split with a huge grin, and together they walked sedately toward the front door. Just as they reached the bottom of the steps, they came to an abrupt stop when they noticed several tribesmen, including Sakhr and Fahad, approach, along with Kira and Amber. They all looked at Jabari and smiled. Nasira was thinking they were probably wanting to ask about setting up search parties for Rizu until she heard a little whinny.

Jabari inhaled sharply, took a tentative step, and put his hand to his chest. Kira and Amber stepped aside to reveal Jabari's colt. "Rizu!" he cried out and ran forward. Luckily, he didn't have to go far because Rizu leaped forward and ran into his arms. Rizu was as happy to see Jabari as Jabari was to see him.

Nasira didn't try to stop her tears. Everyone was laughing. Amber was snorting, and Kira was crying. When Jabari looked at Nasira, his eyes just as wet as hers, it was a moment she would never forget. She knew there would be other horses and other moments if Allah allowed, but this one was special and would stand out in her memory. Filled with joy, she felt a surge of love for Kira, who stood with one arm around Amber's neck, tears running unashamedly down her face. *Thank you, Allah, for Kira.* Nasira bowed to her and when she straightened, Kira bowed back. They both smiled, and Nasira's heart filled with hope. The future was looking bright for Jalil.

CHAPTER 57

The next month proved extremely frustrating for Kira. She loved sitting beside Jalil's bed, listening as he shared his life with her, and she with him, but as the weeks passed, he was all she could think about. He would often touch her when he talked, holding her hand or caressing her cheek. Sometimes he would take a strand of her hair and just stroke it. When she helped him to walk and he put his arm around her shoulders, she would feel that now familiar surge of desire, and her heart would race. He must have noticed because he often gave her a special look, one she found harder and harder to resist. Afraid she would give in again, like that day in her room, she began limiting her time with him. He seemed unconcerned, which bothered her more than she cared to admit.

Then one day, she avoided him completely and spent the day visiting Samira and riding Amber. She told herself that he must be tired of her always hanging around, mooning over him. And now that he had almost recovered, he needed to spend more time with tribal affairs. Also, during their last conversation, he had questioned her again about Amber, speculating on her origins. Kira was still hesitant to tell him of the valley. It just didn't feel like the right time. And then she remembered he had also asked her if she was still interested in going home.

Jalil had put her on the spot. She couldn't tell him about her vision and that she knew her grandmother had died. He'd probably think she was crazy. And even if he believed her, it would only bring up questions about where she had gone that day she'd run away. Luckily, Nasira had interrupted them and saved Kira from having to answer. But Kira had seen the look in his eyes before she left and knew she would have to tell him something sooner or later.

It was late in the afternoon before she returned to the house. She thought of stopping by his quarters, telling herself she'd only stay for a moment, but just thinking about him was enough to set her heart racing. Not trusting herself, she hurried to her chambers, hoping a cool dip in her pool would help. She was about to remove her tunic when she heard a knock on the door. She opened it and saw Nasira looking pleased.

"Kira, may I talk to you for a minute?"

"Certainly. Come in. Are you thirsty? Can I get you something to drink?"

"Oh, no, thank you. I want to invite you to join the family for the evening meal. We are having a small celebration for Jalil and Jabari."

"Oh, that would be nice. I know Jalil will enjoy getting out of his room, too." She smiled with pleasure. It appeared she would get to spend some time with him that day, after all.

"Yes, I am sure he will," Nasira said enigmatically. "I will send someone to let you know when we are ready." She turned then added, "Oh, and you should wear that new tunic Fatima sent you.

"That is a wonderful idea. And thank you for including me."

"We love having you in our family, Kira. We would never want to leave you out. Now, get ready, and I will see you soon."

Excited at the prospect of seeing Jalil, she shrugged off her clothes, took a long bath, and bound her hair into an intricate braid. She donned the new tunic, a finely woven cotton in pale blue and embroidered with white and gold geometric designs. When a servant arrived to tell her the family was gathering, Kira checked her face one last time and hurried down the hall.

Afraid she'd be late, she rushed into the room, but it was empty except for Jalil. He sat in his usual place, wearing simple, unadorned white, and looking every inch a sheik. He abruptly rose, and she couldn't help but stare at the gold medallion on his chest. A flood of memories raced through her mind, and she saw her father's face and her mother's smile. But when he cleared his throat, he broke the spell. She looked up and saw the admiration in his green-gold eyes and felt her face grow hot. Aware of his admiring scrutiny, she started toward her usual chair, but he shook his head and gestured for her to sit next to him.

"Kira, I am so glad you could join us." He poured her some tea and some for himself, as if nothing unusual was happening. "And I must say, you look lovely tonight."

"Thank you, Jalil, but where is everyone else?" She took a small sip, avoiding his eyes. It was always trouble when she looked into his eyes, especially when he was close enough to touch.

"I asked everyone to wait until I sent for them. I wanted a private moment with you." He pushed his plate to one side and surprised her by taking one of her hands in his. He gently massaged her palm with his thumb, causing her to blush harder.

She was having difficulty forming a rational thought. *What did he say?* But he seemed not to notice and forged ahead.

"Do you know why I wanted to speak to you alone?" He looked very serious, and she suddenly felt very nervous.

"No, Jalil. I have no idea." She swallowed, waiting to hear what he was going to say.

"Kira Fontaine, I asked you this before, but I did not do it correctly, or like I should have, and therefore, you did not understand. Kira, ya hayati, I have loved you almost from the first day we met, and I do not wish to live my life without you. I love you, Kira Fontaine. Will you be my wife, my sheikha, and the mother of my children?"

Kira froze, staring at him in disbelief. Had she heard him correctly? *Did he say...?* He must have seen her confusion because he quickly pulled her into his arms. He kissed her forehead, he kissed her on each cheek, and then his lips found hers, and he kissed her with all his love.

Then he leaned her back against his arm and kissed her harder until she could hardly breathe, but she didn't want him to stop. Time slowed, and it seemed like an eternity before he finally pulled back. When he did, she gazed into his eyes and put every bit of love she had for him into her words. "Yes, Jalil, yes!" Then she kissed him back.

When they came up for air, Jalil hugged her close, and Kira heard footsteps and laughter, and suddenly they were surrounded by his family. The girls squealed in delight, and Jabari pounded Jalil on the back, but Nasira looked relieved.

Kira found herself back in her chair, completely dazed. From time to time, she looked over at Jalil to see him looking at her, and her heart would pound. When he had asked her before, it hadn't felt real. And after everything that had happened since, and when he didn't mention it again, Kira had completely dismissed the earlier proposal. But it was real. It was real and wonderful! It was like a dream come true, and the rest of the evening passed in a blur.

Before she knew it, Jalil was kissing her at her door, pledging his love again, and promising they would meet the next day to plan their joining ceremony. As she listened to his receding footsteps, she leaned back against her door, still having difficulty processing what had just happened. *I'm getting married!* Sighing, she changed into a sleeping tunic and snuggled into her bed, hugging her pillow tightly. She dreamed again of the valley, but this time it was not Jabari riding Ndee—it was Jalil.

It was very early the next morning when Kira heard a knock at her door. She had just finished getting dressed for a morning ride and was wearing her trousers and shirt. Throwing on a robe, she opened her door to find Jalil dressed in a white tunic, his tan trousers tucked into tall black boots. She sighed inwardly at the sight.

"Good morning, Kira. Would you and Amber like to join me and Mirage for a ride," he said with a grin.

She couldn't say no, but after her dream last night, she had something else in mind. "I would like that, but could we talk for a minute first?"

"Of course. I need to talk to you as well. About our ceremony," he said but hesitated.

She knew he was waiting for an invitation. "Please come in," she said and gestured to a chair by her table. Once they settled, she continued. "I was wondering what was involved. Will it be like Amal and Fatima's?"

"It can be anything you want, Kira," he said and winked. "As long as it is soon."

"Jalil, you are the sheik of this tribe. We need to do this as it should be done, according to tribal tradition. So, you tell me what is expected."

He smiled and leaned over to kiss her forehead. "I knew it would be this way with you. You are going to be a great sheikha."

"I don't know, Jalil. How does Nasira feel about that?"

"She does not have a problem, especially as it will be you. Besides, it is our way. And she already told me she is looking forward to less responsibility. She wants to concentrate on her garment making business."

Kira chewed her lip, thinking about the responsibilities of being a sheikha. She couldn't hide her worry from Jalil.

"Kira, I have never met anyone more capable of being a sheikha than you. Our people love and respect you. That is half the battle. Do not worry. You will be wonderful, and you will have me and Nasira to guide you."

She reddened at his praise and nodded. "I hope you are right, Jalil. I will try very hard to make you proud."

"Of that, I have no doubt, ya hayati. Now, let us plan our joining because I am ready to be your husband."

Kira had never known a man so kind, so thoughtful. At that moment, she knew in her heart his love for her was real, and she would never doubt it. She reached up and laid her hand against his jaw and smiled. "And I am ready to be your wife." Then she kissed him lightly on the lips, but when she felt his arms reach around her, she remembered the effect they had on each other and pulled back.

He sighed in obvious frustration and bent his head to touch his forehead to hers. "You are right. I will try to control myself."

"Jalil, it is just as hard for me too," she said, bringing a smile to his face. Trusting her instincts, she knew it was now time to reveal her greatest secret. "Jalil, I need to tell you something, something very important, something I have been wanting to share with you for a long time," she said seriously.

He sat back in his chair and reached for her hand. "You can tell me anything, Kira," he said, squeezing it gently.

Summoning her courage, Kira took a deep breath and rose to retrieve her travel bag from the cabinet. Jalil leaned forward, clearly curious. Reaching inside, she pulled out her ancient medallion and chain and placed them on the table. When he failed to speak, she realized he was in shock.

He stared fixedly at the golden disk, and he reached out as if he was going to touch it then quickly withdrew his hand. For a second she saw doubt in his eyes, then he laid his hand on his chest, and she could see him clutching his own medallion. He blinked and sighed in obvious relief. When he looked at her again, she couldn't read his expression, and as she watched, he removed his own medallion and placed it next to hers. For an instant, both medallions seemed to shine brighter.

"They are the same!" he whispered in awe and looked at her in wonder.

"Yes, Jalil. Almost exactly the same."

Jalil tentatively reached out and touched hers. He inhaled sharply.

"What is it?" Kira leaned forward, trying to understand what had startled him.

"It…it…I cannot explain it, Kira. But it almost felt alive or…" His voice trailed off as he continued to study it. After another moment, he asked, "Where did you get it?"

Kira straightened. "Well, that's a long story. I was going to tell you, but I think it would be easier if I just showed you." She rose and placed her medallion around her neck.

Jalil's head jerked up in surprise. "Showed me?"

She held out his medallion and rose. "Put this on and come with me."

CHAPTER 58

Jalil's confusion increased exponentially the closer they rode to the place where they had found Jabari. "Where are we going, Kira?" he asked when she finally stopped and dismounted.

"I really can't explain, Jalil. Do you trust me?" Kira stood beside Amber, staring up at him intently.

He immediately slid off Mirage and walked toward her, drawn into the depths of her blue-green eyes, but when she held up her hand, he stopped and grinned at her ruefully. "Of course I trust you," he said.

"Good," she said and stepped aside as Amber moved forward and disappeared between the large boulders that had hidden Jabari from sight. He reached for his reins, but Mirage refused to budge.

"No, Jalil. Mirage must stay here."

He was about to argue until he felt Mirage backing up. Mirage was acting strangely, but Jalil had learned that one didn't argue with Mirage. He released the reins, and Mirage stopped not far away, his attention focused on the distant herd. Jalil glanced back at Kira, and she gestured for him to follow. When he saw the hidden trail, he was stunned. He hadn't seen it the night they found Jabari by the boulders. "I did not know this was here," he said. "How did you find it? Where does it go?"

"I'll explain soon," she said cryptically and started climbing the steep trail.

He caught her glancing back at him occasionally, and his heart warmed when he realized she was worried about him. Soon he was huffing from the strain, but finally the ground leveled, and the trail widened. After a few more steps and another turn, he almost ran into Kira. She appeared to be studying a pile of rocks dead ahead. Amber stood to one side as if waiting.

"I hope we will not have to climb over that," he said, rubbing his aching leg.

"No, no," she said and turned to face him. "That is undoubtedly the result of an earthquake or possible water intrusion into the fault lines of the cliff face."

Jalil had forgotten what he had learned about her life before she came to his land. She was an amazing woman, and he realized his life was going to be very different with her as his wife. "So, why are we here?"

"Turn around," she said, her eyes flashing with excitement as she pointed to the side of the cliff.

When he saw a tall rectangular block of sandstone, he wasn't sure what he was supposed to see. Perplexed, seeing Amber walk forward and around the stone, he was even more so when Kira followed her horse. Not wanting to be left behind, he scrambled after her and gasped when he saw the dark opening. *A cave?* Amber and Kira were nowhere in sight, but he heard her calling him, her voice echoing from within. "Come on, Jalil, but be careful and watch your head."

Keeping close to the wall and trailing one hand on the rough ceiling, he moved forward cautiously. It seemed he had been walking for some time when the path dropped steeply, and he proceeded more slowly. But he grew alarmed when he could no longer hear Amber or Kira. Suddenly, he felt his medallion growing hot, and when he glanced down, he was astonished to see it glowing through his tunic. *What is going on?* Engrossed, he wasn't paying attention to the trail, and when it came to an abrupt end, he stumbled forward with a cry, landing on his hands and knees. Cursing his weaker leg, he struggled to his feet and gasped in wonder. The light was dim, but he could tell he was in a cavern of some sort and could smell the damp stone.

Jalil felt Kira take his hand, and together they stood quietly while he caught his breath. He couldn't see her clearly, but when she tugged on his hand, he followed blindly, trusting her completely. Hearing a rushing noise near his feet, he stumbled, but she steadied him. "Is that water?" He gasped and tried to edge closer to see where it was coming from.

"Yes, but that's not the only thing I want to show you," she said, pulling him away.

"There is more?"

"You'll see," she said mysteriously. And they walked on.

What Jalil experienced next was life changing. The moment he stepped into the sunlight and saw the valley spread before him, something clicked in his mind. He laid his hand upon his medallion, and an old memory surfaced—his father astride a mighty chestnut stallion, one he rode when Jalil was a young boy. Jalil was riding his first stallion, and his father had stopped to gaze out over their pastures towards the cliffs by the pool. The sun was bright, the hills were green, and he could smell the sharp scent of sand.

The medallion lay against Akeem's chest and winked in the sun. His father had looked at him and said the strangest thing. Jalil could hear his deep voice even now. "Jalil, my son. There are things I would tell you, things you need to know, but you are not ready."

"What things, Father?" Jalil didn't understand.

"One day, I will tell you what you need to know. Our greatest secret, Jalil. And then you will understand." Then he held up the medallion. "And this medallion will be yours, and you will be sheik. Just remember, the medallion is the key. You must always keep it safe. It is your legacy."

As Jalil stood now, staring out over the hidden valley, marveling at the green hills and the silver stream in the distance, he felt like he understood. Feeling Kira's eyes upon him, he turned to see her watching him closely. "Is this where you ran away to?"

She smiled. "Yes. Amber brought me here after the plane crash and after the night I had my flashback. And it is where I found this." She pointed at the medallion that lay on her chest.

Jalil shook his head and looked back across the valley. "Now I know what my father was trying to tell me long ago. This was his greatest secret."

"Oh, Jalil, I think not."

Surprised, he looked at her, bewildered by her huge grin. She gave an ear-splitting whistle, and he jerked when he heard a stallion's bugle. It rang out loud and clear, and he whirled around. A growing thunder heralded the approach of what Jalil had sworn was only a myth. A golden stallion galloped toward them, his mane and tail streaming behind, looking like a piece of the sun. The magnificent beast slid to a stop in front of him, huffing and blowing. Kira strode forward to meet him.

"Kira…careful," he cautioned, shocked when she reached up and stroked the mighty stallion's neck.

"It is all right, Jalil. This is Ndee." Then she spoke to the horse, "Ndee, this is Sheik Jalil."

To Jalil's everlasting delight, Ndee walked forward and lowered his head to sniff Jalil's head and shoulders. With a soft knicker, he nudged Jalil's chest and nibbled at the medallion. Jalil slowly raised a hand and laid it on Ndee's cheek. He looked into the dark brown eyes and saw both intelligence and recognition. Stroking Ndee's iridescent coat, Jalil trailed his hand down the muscled neck, admiring his deep chest and strong shoulders. Ndee was, without a doubt, the finest stallion Jalil had ever seen. And he understood why Mirage wouldn't follow Amber. But when he thought of Mirage, he looked at Kira, and she seemed to read his mind.

"Yes, this is where Amber came from and I expect Mirage too," she said and slipped her arm around his waist.

He looked down at her amazing face and kissed her tenderly. "I do not know what to say."

"Well, that is good, because there is more."

"More?!" Jalil shook his head in disbelief. "How can there be more?"

"You'll see."

And he did.

By the time he stepped from behind the boulders back into his own kingdom, Jalil's mind was spinning, and he struggled to make sense of everything Kira had shown him that day. The ruins, the lake, the gold mine. But more important than all of that was the magnificent golden stallion, Ndee, and his herd of iridescent horses.

When he asked her what she thought the medallions signified, she was very clear. The medallions were obviously a map of the secret valley. She believed the turquoise stones represented oases and the yellow diamonds were the golden horses. It even showed the location of his own kingdom's water source. The more he studied it, the more he agreed with her. It must have been an invaluable tool, but why were there two? And why did his father have one? And why was one buried in the valley? Somehow Jalil knew the two medallions were meant to be together, just like he and Kira, but the answer would remain a mystery, for now.

Kira had tried to explain her theories of the other tunnels. It was clear the one leading back to his kingdom was marked with his tribal colors. But whose tribes were represented on the other tunnels? And exactly why was one of them abandoned. It was mind-boggling, and they both agreed they would return sometime to explore, but right now, they had to get home. The hour was late, and Mirage was waiting.

As he rode back to the stables with Kira by his side, he saw his own lands with new eyes. Everything looked different. He was overwhelmed, and Kira must have sensed his mood for she remained silent, and when they reached the corral, she helped him store their gear.

Once they released Mirage and Amber, Jalil escorted Kira to her chambers. When he asked her if she wished to be present when he told his mother about the valley, she declined. He wasn't surprised. What she said made him love her even more. She assured him it was his family's legacy and was pleased to know it would not be just the secret of the sheik. It was too important.

Excited, he gave her a quick kiss and a warm hug, and he left her to freshen up. It was almost time for the evening meal, but he needed to speak with his mother first. He couldn't wait to share what he had learned, knowing the valley would change their lives forever.

CHAPTER 59

A few weeks later, Nasira stood with Jalil and Kira on the steps, waiting for their guests to arrive. She was still reeling from what Jalil had shared with her about the secret valley. She always knew there was something special about Akeem's medallion, but he had never told her the story behind it. *I wonder why?* Maybe he had planned to tell her when he told Jalil? But he never got that chance. She shivered. If it hadn't been for Kira and Amber, the valley could have been lost forever. *Kismet.* She would never know now why he hadn't shared such information, but it explained why he had left without help that day. Maybe he thought Ndee had escaped the valley, but without Akeem to fill in the blanks, though, they could only theorize.

They now understood the significance of the odd marks on the map Akeem had used the day of his murder. Evidently, Akeem had been investigating and mapping one of the tunnels Kira told her about. She said one led to a box canyon, and Jalil thought it might be the one Hashem had used to escape during his botched attempt to kill Jalil the first time. Nasira shook her head. *Oh, if only Akeem had lived. He could have explained everything. Why didn't he? And why are there two medallions?* Those thoughts swirled around in her head until she finally shut her mind down, vowing she would never wallow in the past again. Her tribe would have a new sheikha shortly. And now they had the valley, and Jalil would join with the love of his life. The future was bright indeed.

Nasira turned her attention back to the present. She was just as excited as Kira and Jabari to see Sheik Ehsaan ride in on Mukhtar, followed by Issa, Adara, and Fatima on their camels, along with Amal on his new stallion. Adara and Jabari immediately took off for the stables, and Nasira, with Kira's help, led Issa and Fatima to their guest rooms. The women had much to do before the joining ceremony and soon became immersed in their plans.

The day of the ceremony was a flurry of activity. The tables were prepared in the courtyard, the fire basins were ready to be lit, and the musicians were assembling. Nasira was decorating Jalil's bedchamber for his joining night when he walked in. She saw him eyeing the trays full of special refreshments. "Jalil, those are for you and Kira—in case you get hungry. There should be enough for tonight and tomorrow."

She had decorated his bathing chamber too, adding new robes and towels, and a few extra oil lamps. She also added an assortment of lotions and conditioners she knew Kira favored. He smiled as he looked around, but she saw him eyeing the bed. Nasira had draped a shimmering golden coverlet over a set of brilliant white silk sheets with the silhouettes of running horses embroidered in delicate gold and silver threads along the edges. When touched by the light, the horses seemed to come alive.

Luxurious pillows in shades of turquoise and gold lined the headboard. She watched him smooth his hand along the sheet. When he looked up at her with a questioning expression, she knew what he was thinking. White sheets were for a virgin's joining night. They were to show the proof of a sheik's wife's purity.

Nasira came around the bed and took his hand. "Jalil, Kira deserves these sheets, even though she will not know their significance. She only knows you believe in her and that you love her, no matter what. She is a virgin in your eyes, and in all the ways that really matter." When Jalil pulled her into a tight hug, she sniffed and patted his broad back, before hurrying off to get ready.

Issa and Fatima joined her to dress in her chambers. Nasira was helping Issa with her hair when she noticed Fatima standing with a thoughtful expression, one hand rubbing her belly.

"Fatima? Are you all right?" Nasira said.

Fatima glanced up. "Oh, yes. I was just thinking."

"About the baby?" Issa chimed in.

"I am always thinking about the baby." Fatima grinned. "But no, I was thinking about Kira," she said, and her grin faded.

Nasira stopped and gave Fatima their full attention.

"I never dreamed I would have been able to escape a monster like Qadir and find a man like Amal who would love and cherish me above all others," Fatima said as her eyes grew damp. "This child would not be but for Kira. I rescued Kira, but really, she rescued me."

Nasira felt her own tears threaten and shook her head. "Fatima, you are going to ruin my makeup." She sniffed loudly and chuckled.

"I am sorry, Sheikha." Fatima grinned ruefully.

"Come on, you two. We do not want to be late," Issa said, and the three friends rushed to finish.

They were about to leave the room when Fatima called out, "Wait! I forgot Kira's veil."

A minute later, Nasira heard Fatima gasp loudly and turned to see her standing with eyes wide in shock, one hand gripping a small package wrapped in turquoise silk and tied with a golden ribbon. In her other hand was a tattered tunic of sky blue silk.

Nasira rushed over and took her by the shoulders. "Fatima, what is wrong? Are you all right?" She tried to steer the woman toward a chair, thinking it might be something to do with her pregnancy, but Fatima wouldn't move. Issa came over and together they coaxed Fatima to sit down. Issa took the small package from her hand, but Fatima wouldn't let them take the blue tunic.

Fatima moaned. "Oh, no! No! Kira should not see this!"

Nasira gently pried it from Fatima's fingers, and Issa took Fatima's hands to keep her from grabbing it back.

"No, Sheikha, you must not!" Fatima wailed.

Nasira stared at the distraught woman, concerned she might be ill. "Fatima, what is wrong?" She could see Fatima's eyes fixed on Issa who was holding the tunic up to the light.

Issa peered at it closely then looked at both of them. "Fatima, is this something you were going to wear? I do not think you could repair it. Someone has torn it and ruined it with dye."

Fatima gave Issa a wild look and stared hard at the tunic. Nasira took it and lifted it up where she could study the stains. "Issa is right. You cannot fix this. The dye is permanent."

Aghast, Fatima looked at Nasira. "Dye? Did you say dye?"

"Yes, it comes from a berry used to make this purplish color. Issa and I use it regularly," Nasira said, and Issa nodded.

"But it was red!" Fatima wailed.

"When it is first applied, it is indeed red, but once it sets up, it turns purple," Nasira said, still not understanding why Fatima was so upset. "Fatima, was this supposed to be a gift for Kira? Is that why you are upset?"

Fatima shook her head, and her face filled with color. "Sheikha, when Kira was kidnapped, that is the tunic Kira was wearing the night she was with Qadir. She was lying on it when I found her. I just couldn't leave it there for everyone to see what he did to her." She blushed harder. "It was the evidence of her loss. I stuck it in my robe at the time and forgot about it until we reached Sheik Ehsaan's. Then I hid it in my pack and forgot about it."

Nasira looked at Issa who was staring at the tunic. Issa's eyes widened, and she looked back at her. It took a minute, but then they both smiled. Nasira started chuckling, and soon all three women were laughing.

When Samira stopped by to see if they were ready to go to the courtyard, they were bent double with laughter. "What is wrong with all of you?" Samira's brow furrowed. "We are going to be late. I do not know what is so funny, but Kira is ready, and we need to go." She stood with her hands on her hips, tapping her foot.

When they saw her expression, they laughed harder. It took a few minutes before they could compose themselves, but once they calmed down, they became very solemn. Nasira explained to Samira what they had learned.

Samira's impatient expression became one of astonishment and relief. But then she looked at Nasira with concern. "Kira does not know?"

Nasira shook her head.

"She must be told," Samira spoke with finality. "But who will tell her?"

Nasira stared long and hard at the torn tunic and decided. "Right now, my son loves a woman so much he does not care if she is not a virgin, and for a sheik that is unheard of." Nasira looked at each of the women in the room. "I will tell Kira. She should know what to expect, and I will let her decide whether to tell Jalil. He loves her, regardless. She loves him even more because of that." Nasira took the tunic, rolled it up, and wrapped it in a towel. "Go. I will bring Kira, and we will meet you all at the entrance to the courtyard." The other women departed, and Nasira hurried to Kira's room, clutching the evidence of what she could not know was the last effort of First Wife's scheming.

CHAPTER 60

Kira stood at the entrance to the courtyard and closed her eyes, absorbing the sounds she never wanted to forget—the lively beat and exotic melody from the musicians and the chatter and laughter from the assembled tribesmen and their families. When she opened them, she saw the courtyard, full of tables laden with fragrant spicy food and drink and, at the far end, a long table draped in gold for the sheik, his family, and their guests. Huge fire basins on stone pillars lined both sides, the flames dancing and flickering in the fading light. The setting sun cast streamers of purple, pink, and gold across the sky. The scene before her wavered and shimmered like a mirage in the desert. It was exotic and foreign, and she felt like she was in a dream. *Is this really happening?* She reached out to a nearby pillar to steady herself.

"Are you all right, Kira?" Nasira whispered from close by.

Feeling a hand on her arm, Kira saw the concern on Nasira's face and knew she was thinking about their conversation before they lined up to enter the courtyard. Poor Fatima blamed herself for the confusion, as if it was her fault for misleading Kira about what happened with Qadir, what Kira now knew had not happened.

Kira had always thought First Wife had drugged her that night out of kindness, like she said, but she wondered now if it had been for another reason. Maybe she believed Kira, as a foreigner, wasn't worthy to bear Qadir's heir. But if Cassie was to be believed, Qadir was unable to have children. That didn't make sense, unless First Wife knew differently. That might explain why Qadir was also drugged—to make sure he couldn't follow through.

But what was even stranger to Kira was why First Wife made it look like he had done the deed. Why the subterfuge? Then it hit her. First Wife was as mean and sadistic as her son. While she didn't want some half-breed child as a grandchild, she certainly wished to cause Kira shame and heartbreak by making the her believe she was a ruined woman.

In the end, however, drugging her son had led to his demise. It made him easier to kill. Whatever the old crone's reasons, Kira didn't care anymore. It was done and she resolved to never think about it again.

When Kira asked Nasira if she had told Jalil, Nasira said no. She was adamant it wouldn't matter and said it was up to Kira whether to tell him. Kira had smiled at the thought of how surprised he would be. But her smile faded when she thought of what she would face later.

Nasira had noticed her fear and assured her all would be well. She made some suggestions that still had Kira blushing. At first, she couldn't even imagine the things that Nasira told her, but she was determined to make the night memorable for Jalil. The fact he thought she was not a virgin but still declared his love for her and wanted her for his wife and sheikha was proof of his feelings for her.

She steadied herself and nodded, letting Nasira know she was fine. Nasira signaled the musicians, and they began playing a slow, soft melody with flutes. Kira watched Adara and Issa walk down the center of the courtyard. Issa wore her finest ceremonial tunic and new robe reflecting the emerald green of Ehsaan's tribe. Adara was adorable, dressed just like her mother. Ehsaan stood in front of the head table, waiting for his sheikha and his daughter. He greeted them with a proud grin and led them to their seats, where they remained standing.

Jabari walked out from the side to stand in front of the table. Gone was the simple trader's son. In his place was the son of a sheik, resplendent in gold and turquoise silk ceremonial robes with a turquoise head wrap. At the flash of his smile, Kira saw what Samira had always seen. He was touched by greatness.

She watched Akilah and Lina make their way forward together. They wore matching robes of pale turquoise, and a sprinkling of tiny seed pearls and turquoise stones embellished the bodice of their tunics. Kira could see them laughing when Jabari stepped forward to meet them, taking each one by the hand. Together, the three of them found their places at the table and stood waiting.

The courtyard fell silent when Nasira, dressed entirely in golden silk, began her walk. Her tunic sparkled with yellow diamonds, and she wore Akeem's dagger on a gold leather belt. No man stood to meet her, and Kira's heart ached for her, wishing Akeem could have been with her to witness the joining of their son. She couldn't imagine what Nasira was thinking at that moment. But before Nasira reached the table, Jalil came striding in from the side, and Kira gasped at the sight.

His white silk robe woven with silver threads billowed around his tall black boots as he walked, and he seemed to glow in the firelight. An elaborate white turban banded with silver and gold covered his head. And his only adornments were his father's medallion suspended from his neck and the sheik's ring on his right hand. Kira saw Nasira's shocked look of surprise turn to one of love and pride when he held out his hand and led her to her place of honor. Then he almost ran to the front of the table, and several chuckles echoed at his haste. He stood with his hands at his side and waited for Kira.

With a deep breath, Kira began walking toward the man waiting for her. The last light of the setting sun edged the far mountains in gold. The torches burned brighter, and when her robes caught the light, she too began to glow and shimmer. She wore all white like Jalil except for the edges of her robe. Slender golden threads were woven in a solid band at the bottom which thinned as it rose to become the ethereal shapes of running horses. The horses appeared and disappeared in the flickering light as they circled her hem. A whisper of translucent golden silk draped from her head, falling around her shoulders and floating down her back. It wavered around her shining golden hair like a dream half-seen.

A gossamer panel of sheer white silk was suspended from a delicate headdress of gold that encircled her head like a crown and covered Kira's face. Fatima had used all her love and skill to embroider and embellish the veil. Issa had contributed the tiny white seed pearls and golden gems that adorned the edges. The gold embroidery created an intricate pattern, leaving a sheer panel for Kira's eyes. She had no difficulty seeing the tall figure in shining white waiting for her like a glowing beacon. When she took Jalil's hand, she sighed, relieved to find he was real, flesh and blood, and not a mirage.

***

Mesmerized by the glowing white and gold figure approaching him. Jalil was afraid she wasn't real. She shimmered in the torchlight like a vision created by the heat of the desert. *Is it really her?* When he felt her warm hand, he gripped it tightly as he looked into her luminous blue-green eyes blazing through the silk. *Kira.* He continued to gaze into her eyes until he realized the music had stopped and he heard a discreet cough. He grinned sheepishly at his mother when she gestured toward the crowd.

Jalil glanced around the courtyard at the assembled guests, his tribe, and his family, but when his eyes returned to Kira, she was looking only at him. He reached out and took her other hand in his, cleared his throat, and began. "Kira Fontaine, today I wish to tell the whole world of my love for you. Because of you, I have my father back." He touched his medallion. "Because of you, I have my brother back." He gestured to Jabari. "You are brave, strong, and honest. I know in my heart you are worthy of being the mother of my children and the sheikha of my tribe. Today, I ask you, Kira Fontaine, to join your life with mine." He raised her hands and kissed each one. Then he pulled a ring from his robe, a ring he'd had made especially for her. It was silver and inlaid with alternating yellow diamonds, white diamonds, and turquoise stones. He kissed it and placed it on her finger.

Kira gripped his hands tightly, and he could see the love in her eyes. "Jalil, I have lived my whole life waiting for this moment. I just did not realize it until now. Everything that I was, everything that I am, and everything I will be, is yours. From this day forward, I will be your wife, I will bear your children, and I will die for our tribe. I will love and honor you all the days of my life." Kira reached into her robe and removed a ring of silver, inlaid with turquoise, or sacred "sky stone" according to her Zuni culture, and mother-of-pearl. Jalil knew it was her father's ring. She kissed it and placed it on his finger. He reached up and unhooked Kira's veil from the gold headdress, revealing her beautiful face, flushed with excitement and love. Folding the delicate veil, he tucked it into his robe. Then he did something that shocked her and his family. Reaching into his other pocket, he pulled out the ancient medallion, the one Kira had found in the valley. Kira had given it to Jalil saying it belonged to him and his tribe. But he placed it around her neck. "This medallion is part of our legacy, but it belongs to you now," he said. "From this day forward, the sheikha of this tribe will always wear it." Jalil then took her hands in his, turned to face the crowd, and his deep voice rang out, "Welcome your new sheikha."

Everyone began clapping and cheering. He could see Nasira over Kira's shoulder, tears slipping down her cheeks. His sisters were grinning, Issa was sniffing, and it looked like Ehsaan was surreptitiously wiping his eyes. Jabari rolled his eyes. But Jalil's eyes returned to Kira who was laughing with joy. When he slid his arm around her waist, she looked up at him and he down at her, and their love for each other shone from their eyes. He led her around the table to her place of honor on his right side. Nasira leaned around, and Jalil saw her wink at Kira. Kira started laughing again, and soon, everyone was eating and drinking, enjoying the feast.

As the music played on, Jabari the Magnificent, accompanied by Adara, his lovely assistant, performed feats of magic. His grand finale was to produce two white doves, which he presented to his sheik and sheikha.

As Jalil sat and watched his family, smiling and laughing, his heart was full. He glanced toward the entrance, and for just a second, he saw the tall form of his father as he had looked the day he had ridden to his death. He heard a gasp, and glancing at his mother, noticed she was staring at the entrance too. Her eyes were wide, and a tear slipped down her cheek. As he watched, her lips curled in a tremulous smile, and she raised her hand. When he looked back at the entrance, his father lifted one hand and smiled. Jalil raised his hand to wave as his father faded and disappeared up into the starry sky.

Glancing at his mother, he saw her drop her hand, and he reached over and squeezed it gently, thinking she might need comforting. But when she looked at him, her eyes told a different story. The lingering sadness that always seemed to be just under the surface was gone. She looked almost happy. She nodded at him, acknowledging they had shared something special. He wanted to speak with her about what they had both seen, but it could wait until another time. Sighing, he was going to speak to Kira until he saw Nasira staring at Fahad who sat at the end of a table closest to the family.

Fahad was staring down into his goblet of tea with a wary expression, tilting it back and forth as if looking for something. Fahad must have felt Nasira's eyes on him because, suddenly, he stopped and looked over at her. Nasira cocked her head and narrowed her eyes. He smiled sheepishly and shrugged then raised his goblet as if in salute and drained it in one gulp. She chuckled and nodded, and Fahad nodded back. Jalil laughed, glad to see her good mood restored.

When Jalil turned to Kira, she nodded in understanding. It was time for them to bid their guests farewell. They exchanged hugs with family and friends then hurried from the courtyard. Once they were clear of the columns and out of the torchlight, Jalil swept Kira up into his arms. "Kira, ya hayati." He kissed her softly. "Are you ready?"

"Yes, my sheik."

He grinned and, carrying her gently, headed for his quarters, almost at a run.

"But Jalil, your leg!"

"Does not hurt." He was focusing on navigating the corridors and in such a hurry, he barely saw her grin.

Kira held on and grinned. Two guards stood in front of his chambers, and as Jalil approached, one quickly opened the door and stepped back. The guards left the corridor without a word. Jalil carried her inside and kicked the door shut behind him. He passed through the front room and into his bedchamber but stopped at the foot of the bed.

"Jalil?" she whispered.

"Hmm?" He looked down at her. He wasn't sure how to proceed.

"You can put me down now."

He set her gently on her feet, keeping his hands on her waist.

She laid her hands on his chest. "Jalil, what is wrong?"

"Kira." Jalil trailed a finger down the side of her cheek. Seeing her smile and her eyes wide, showing no fear, he lifted the golden headdress from her head and set it on the table. He removed the gold filigree combs buried in her hair, allowing the waves to tumble down. Sighing, he stroked the silken mass with one hand, cupped her chin with the other, and tilted her head back. He kissed her lightly, feathering his lips back and forth, nibbling and teasing hers with his.

His heart pounding, Jalil moaned softly against her lips when she pressed closer and pulled back to glance down at her face, wanting to remember this moment forever. Her eyes were closed, and he gazed in wonder at her long golden-brown eyelashes resting on her smooth cheeks frosted with a sprinkling of gold dust. Her lips parted, and when she opened her eyes, he watched them darken with desire. He felt the gentle pull on his tunic as she tried to lift herself closer again. Coming to his senses, he gently took her by the hand and led her to a bench in the bathing chamber.

It was obvious Kira had no clue what to do, and Jalil had an idea to make it easier for her. He removed his high turban and laid it on the bench. She was watching him silently, her eyes glowing, and the blush on her cheeks deepened when he removed his robe and placed it next to the turban. Sitting, he pulled off his boots then stood to face her, but when he stepped closer, he saw her eyes widen and thought he detected fear. "Ya hayati... Kira, are you afraid? Should I stop?" He waited anxiously for her response, praying she wouldn't have a flashback.

***

Kira was afraid, but not of having a flashback. She had prayed long and hard to get rid of the memory of her night with Qadir. What she feared was the unknown. Nasira had assured her it would be all right, but now that it was about to happen, she wondered if she could go through with it. She swallowed nervously.

Then suddenly she was filled with a new feeling. Seeing Jalil's handsome face filled with concern, she could see he was as nervous as she was. This man, this wonderful, thrilling, smart man was only worried about her. It was his joining night, and as the ruling sheik of his kingdom, he would be in his rights to take her anytime he wanted, in any manner he wished. And yet, he waited on her command. He waited for her to decide.

Her fears and doubts melted away, and she was filled with love and passion. She knew this man would never hurt her and would always cherish her as she would cherish him. Her grandmother's words echoed in her mind. *"Follow your path, Kira. Be brave and strong. I know you will be all right."* Her path had led her to Jalil, and she would be brave. Stepping closer, she took his hand, held it against her cheek, and leaning into it, pressed a kiss on his palm. His lips parted, and his breathing increased, and she reveled in the knowledge that she, Kira Fontaine, could make this man come alive with passion.

Feeling a growing sense of her own power, she placed his hands on her belt and waited. She saw him pause and look into her eyes, looking for her assent, and when she nodded and smiled, she saw a new fire in Jalil's eyes as the gold flecks buried in the deep green seemed to expand. Within minutes his clothes were gone, as were hers. Before she could react, he pulled her flush to his body and kissed her with all his love and desire. She was consumed, and her body burst into flames. While his tongue dueled with hers, she ran her hands down the hard planes of his back to clutch at his hips. He groaned loudly, and her moans were barely muffled by his kisses.

Wanting to get even closer, Kira rose on her toes and lifted one shapely leg higher and higher. She felt the rough ridges of Jalil's scars from Hashem's blade, but she knew he could feel the deep furrows on her thigh from the lion, and she knew he didn't care.

When he suddenly pulled back, she gasped. "Don't stop…please."

"Are you sure, ya hayati? It might hurt."

"Jalil, you could never hurt me. If you would just do what you were doing a few seconds ago, I think I might be able to bear it." She blushed and smiled wickedly but squealed in surprise when he lifted her in his arms and placed her gently on the bed. Then he started all over until she was as aroused as he was. When she felt him testing her, she tensed, thinking this was the moment, but he surprised her by stopping again. Seeing the shock on his face, she realized he must have detected she was still a virgin. The fact that he was able to stop, willing to stop, just made her want him more.

Seeing him going from shocked to confused, she stoked his cheek gently. "Jalil, I just found out today. I did not tell you because I was not sure myself, until just now. Apparently, the evidence Fatima and Cassie saw was false. I will tell you all about it later, but right now, I need you, and I don't know what to do. Please, Jalil, make me your wife in every way."

Jalil didn't hesitate to do just that, and there was pain, but he took his time until she was consumed with ecstasy, and he too experienced his greatest pleasure.

Time stood still for the lovers, and they spent the long night exploring each other and climbing to new heights together. Eventually, they slept, wrapped around each other, oblivious to the cooling wind that caressed their bodies and carried the sounds of their contentment up into the night sky.

***

Mirage was restless and paced back and forth in his corral as he gazed out across the moonlit hills. Suddenly, he heard thundering hoofbeats approaching and watched Amber gallop up to his corral, her coat shimmering in the light of the stable torch. She slowed to a halt by the fence, and he bowed his neck and huffed a greeting. This time she didn't ignore him but moved gracefully forward to touch noses with him. She huffed again, and he snorted. She whinnied sharply and turned, as if to gallop off, but stopped not far away. When she whinnied again, he couldn't help himself. He dashed to the far end of his corral, pivoted, and galloped toward the fence. In one mighty jump, he cleared it, his coat flashing silver, his mighty hooves pounding as he ran toward her. She threw up her head and took off running, and Mirage raced after her. She was incredibly fast, but in the end, he was faster, and they raced off together, silver and gold, to vanish into the far hills.

***

The cool, silvery moon sailed across the infinite sea of stars, seeking its bed below the far horizon, clearing the sky for the hot golden sun that would inevitably rise to bathe the desert in beams of gold. Celestial creatures, they would forever remain the constants in the world of the desert born.

EPILOGUE

Kira awoke to a quiet, dark room. She heard Jalil's breathing behind her and felt his long, warm body curled against her, one arm draped down her side, his hand resting on her growing belly. It was her second child, and she didn't have long. Sharif, her firstborn, lay in his own bed with a guard at his door. Their son had chestnut brown hair with golden highlights, that curled around his light brown face. He had her coloring, but she hoped he would be as tall and strong as his father.

Restless, and feeling her baby kick, she rose, leaving Jalil asleep in their bed. He had joined her earlier in the bathing pool and spent a great deal of time reminding her how much he loved her. She sighed, remembering the pleasure when he made love to her, gently and skillfully. Searching for her robe, she saw a flicker of light on the wall next to the bed and smiled. The two medallions, Jalil's and the ancient one, hung suspended from one hook. They rested together and often sparked in the night. A mystery still—one of several. Perhaps, someday, she, or someone like her, would solve them, she thought.

She located her robe but ignored her slippers and padded barefoot down the corridor to the front of the house. The one guard posted bowed when she appeared and moved to a discreet distance. The guards were familiar with her ways and allowed her some privacy.

Kira stood in the doorway and gazed in wonder at the multitude of brilliant stars flung like diamonds in random swirls of light across a blanket of midnight blue. The full moon was on its way toward heaven. It reminded her of the night she'd joined her husband, her wise, handsome, smart husband, fearless in all things, except perhaps with his son. When Sharif was born, Jalil seemed overwhelmed when he first held him, but he'd settled into fatherhood and, as he did in all things, took charge. He worked diligently to show his son love and affection, teaching and playing with him.

She remembered when he explained how he was content to manage the herd and kingdom and make love to his beautiful wife. He had considered racing Mirage one more time but said whenever he thought about losing him, he couldn't bring himself to commit. Maybe one day he would have another champion, one he knew would win without a doubt and once again take part in the Tri-Annual Race.

Maybe he already had that champion, she thought, hearing the high whinny of Amber's first-born in his corral by the foaling barn. She and Jalil had both been with Amber when the foal was born, and they cried tears of joy to see the perfect little colt. When they cleaned him up, they were stunned to see his shimmering coat of gold. A golden stallion.

Jalil was still trying to figure out what it was about Amber that she could produce a golden colt. Would all Amber's foals be gold? Would she have another male? Kira didn't care. She was just pleased to see the colt was healthy and that Amber had an easy birth. She and Jalil had decided that Mirage must be the father—he was the only stallion Amber would allow close to her. Based on when the colt was born, Sakhr suggested Amber and Mirage must have come to an agreement close to the night of Kira and Jalil's joining ceremony. That was the cause for much laughter in the stables.

Kira's thoughts wandered to Jabari. She had been worried he'd be upset when her Sharif was born. Her son would be the next sheik. But Jabari said he wasn't upset because he had other plans and didn't want to be a sheik. He had grown up so much, she thought. She would be sad when he left. He would be leaving soon, off to the American University in Cairo, and there was even talk he might go to England for further studies.

The whole family was excited for him, but Kira knew it would be very difficult to see his empty chair at the table, and she would miss seeing him dash about on Rizu. The two of them were inseparable, and Kira imagined Rizu would miss him as much as she would. Sarii was much older, and Jabari had turned her out to enjoy the herd life. She seemed content, and Akilah and Lina both enjoyed riding her.

Jabari still spent time with Saad and Samira, but after the birth of their baby boy, Saad spent most of his time teaching his new son, and Jabari gracefully bowed out. Samira had added a baby girl to their family, too. Jabari embraced his new adoptive siblings and never acted jealous.

As Kira had taken on the duties of sheikha, she was relieved to see Nasira take more interest in her weaving industry. The influx of foreigners created a booming market for silk garments, and Nasira and Issa continued to expand their business. This involved more travel between the two tribes, and Jabari was often called upon to escort his mother to Ehsaan's kingdom. He was always happy to comply. It seemed he had taken more than a friendly interest in Adara.

However, Kira worried about Adara. Always hardheaded, Adara had taken her role as heir to new heights. She was a fearless rider, an excellent shot, good with a sword, and also a tough negotiator, all strong traits for the heir of a sheik. But being a woman was still a problem for Adara—though her tribe accepted her, most of the other tribes didn't recognize her like they would a man. It was a source of constant irritation for Adara, and she could speak volumes about the subject, so Kira tried not to bring it up ... ever. Kira knew Adara would have a tough time if she was planning on being the sheik someday.

Once in a rare while, Kira thought of Cassie and those days of trouble with Qadir and Hashem. After that infamous day when Jalil had killed Hashem, Cassie had disappeared. The region had quieted considerably without the constant agitation Qadir and Hashem had tried to cultivate. Sheik Amit had taken over Qadir's old holdings, and spies reported he enlarging his tribe again and that Cassie was still in his "care." Kira didn't feel sorry for her anymore, though. Cassie had chosen her path a long time ago.

Germany and the Allies were still in the midst of a war, but buried in the mountains, Jalil's tribe felt little of that drama. Rumors were flying, though, of foreigners flooding their country in search of resources. Kira had learned the hard way the lengths men would go to for wealth and power. Jalil's kingdom had many of the things the foreigners were searching for—ancient treasures, amazing horses, gold, and the newest one, bitumen Remembering the oily pits in the hidden valley, she prayed her family could keep its secrets hidden.

As she stood, bathed in the light of the moon, her eyes were drawn south toward the encircling mountains. Breathing deeply, she savored the desert scents carried by the evening breeze and let go of her worries for that night. Kira glanced up at the stars and smiled as one flared brightly and raced across the sky, falling towards the horizon. *Another warrior reborn*, she thought. *But for whom?* A brief memory of her grandmother's words whispered through her mind, and her thoughts turned to her warrior, Jalil.

Before Jalil, Kira had been alone—alone like she had been when her mother had died, alone like she had been when her father had buried himself in his work, and alone like she had been when she buried him in the sand. But she had bravely walked the path God had laid out for her, a path that led to Jalil and a new life, in the very desert that had almost taken hers.

Her deep thoughts were interrupted when she heard a sound behind her, and she sighed when she felt strong arms surround her. Jalil had awakened and had come in search of her, as was his wont. She felt his lips graze her ear.

"Come, ya hayati," Jalil whispered softly and tugged gently on her hand.

Without hesitation, she accompanied him inside. Kira bid a silent and final farewell to her past and vowed to boldly follow her path to her future, knowing she would never be alone again.

ACKNOWLEDGMENTS

My journey to tell Kira's story began over forty years ago, but I was never able to finish it until now. Because life got in the way. Like many things we want to do, things that need doing take precedence. School, work, marriage, children, care taking…the list can be endless. When I was finally able to spend the time necessary to tell this story, I discovered I needed help.

Both of my sisters stuck by me from the beginning (that would be my birth, actually). Thank you, Linda and Trish, for hanging in there, cheering me on, picking me up, and yes, cracking the whip when necessary. I've said it before and I'll say it always, y'all are amazing teachers and wonderful readers, but the best sisters. Your continuing faith in me is a blessing.

I owe a great deal to another sister, one who didn't swim in my genetic pool but is a sister, nonetheless. Thank you, Sari Celeste Ramirez, for your personal commitment to Desert Born. You were there when Kira climbed from the wreckage and when Jalil's blade found its mark. You helped make book one, "Desert Brave," a success, and because of you, "Desert Bold" will be as well. I am looking forward to your insight on all of my future stories.

A special shoutout to Erica Yvonnet, my media queen, friend, and fellow conspirator. Thanks for my fantastic website, gincoleman.com, and for keeping me in touch with the rest of the world though Facebook, email, and Instagram.

And I want to give a special shout out to Sheila Murray, the newest member of "Gin's All In" beta readers. Girl, you've got a sharp eye and a real feel for my stories. Thanks for your help with Desert Bold. It's better for having been read by you. Of course, having your husband, Sonny, as Larry's fishing buddy is a plus.

I am also beholden to my publishing team at Black Rose Writing: Reagan for taking another chance on me, Dave for another beautiful cover, and Justin for getting my books where they need to be (when they need to be).

I am blessed to work with a great bunch of authors who are always willing to share their wisdom and experience as well as provide inspiration.

I saved the best for last. Thank you, Readers! Your kind words and supportive feedback add fuel to my writing fire. I hope you found something in this story to inspire you or entertain you or help you escape into another world, if only for a few hours. You are the reason I write!

So, now you know what happened to Kira and Jalil as well as all of the desert born. But I'm not done yet. For those of you who love this story so far, you'll be excited to know I'm already working on the next one. I mean, who doesn't want to see Adara grown up and getting in trouble again, on a grander scale?

Until then, find something fun or inspiring to read. There are so many wonderful stories being told. Check out the talented authors at Blackrosewriting.com. Memoirs, Mysteries, Thrillers, Horror, Fantasies, Adventures…you name it, they write it.

Keep calm and read on.

Gin

I'd love to hear from y'all. Feel free to contact me at gincoleman.com.

ABOUT THE AUTHOR

Gin Coleman was born in the United States but calls no state home. A story-telling tumbleweed, she currently parks her trusty computer in Mississippi. When she's not writing, she spends an inordinate amount of time and money feeding the birds and any wild creature that ventures into her yard. A lifelong lover of most non-human lifeforms, she grew up in the Ozarks, was raised by wolves, and her favorite car is a truck. It was said that the night she was born, her family reported a green light at the window and a crop circle in the back yard. The proud mother of the Desert Born Series, Gin will soon give birth to the Lost and Found in the Lone Star State Series.

GIN COLEMAN
Desert Brave
DESERT BORN | BOOK ONE

NOTE FROM GIN COLEMAN

Word-of-mouth is crucial for any author to succeed. If you enjoyed *Desert Bold*, please leave a review online—anywhere you are able. Even if it's just a sentence or two. It would make all the difference and would be very much appreciated.

Thanks!
Gin Coleman

We hope you enjoyed reading this title from:

BLACK ROSE writing™

www.blackrosewriting.com

Subscribe to our mailing list – *The Rosevine* – and receive **FREE** books, daily
deals, and stay current with news about upcoming
releases and our hottest authors.
Scan the QR code below to sign up.

Already a subscriber? Please accept a sincere thank you for being a fan of
Black Rose Writing authors.

View other Black Rose Writing titles at
www.blackrosewriting.com/books and use promo code
PRINT to receive a **20% discount** when purchasing.